DATE DUE

#4

PETER AND THE SWORD OF MERCY

PETER AND THE SWORD OF MERCY

By **DAVE BARRY**
and **RIDLEY PEARSON**

Illustrations by GREG CALL

Disney • Hyperion Books
New York

ACKNOWLEDGMENTS

First, we thank all the readers—especially the young readers—who kept asking us to write another Starcatchers book. We really hadn't planned to, but you talked us into it, and we're very happy you did. It was great fun to bring the familiar characters back, and to introduce them to some new ones.

We appreciate all the great people at Disney • Hyperion Books, especially our wise and ever supportive editor, Wendy Lefkon, and our unflappable publicist, Jennifer Levine. We promise them that at future book-signing events, we will try to make sure that there are no snakes.

We salute the amazing, brilliant, ever enthusiastic archaeologist Patrick Hunt of Stanford University for digging around the world of swords and museums for us. That there's a character in this book named Patrick Hunt is, of course, purely coincidental. We also thank Sam Thomas of the London Underground Customer Service Center for helping us with historical research for scenes set in the Underground. Any inaccuracies in those scenes, or any others, are completely our fault.

We thank Judi Smith for her diligent research and ruthless proof-reading.

And hats off to our wives, Michelle Kaufman and Marcelle Pearson, for letting us do this instead of getting real jobs.

TABLE OF CONTENTS

The Sword

The Palatine Chapel, Aachen, Germany, A.D. 811

CHARLEMAGNE, CONQUEROR OF EUROPE, knelt before the stone altar. He was seventy, but with his reddish beard and full head of hair, he looked much younger. His lanky frame still held much of the strength that had made him a feared warrior.

Although usually surrounded by his knights, he chose to pray alone. He prayed for the peace to continue. And, as always, he prayed for forgiveness for his son, now forty, but still a boy in his father's eyes—a foolish boy. He had killed the son of Ogier the Dane, who had been one of Charlemagne's most trusted knights. Charlemagne regretted that any man should lose a son, but especially a man who had served him so well.

Charlemagne bowed his head, his lips moving as he recited the Scripture.

He sensed something behind him. Instantly, with an instinct honed in battle, he ducked his head and hurled himself sideways. A sword cleaved the air where his neck had been and struck an iron candle stand, slicing it cleanly in two as though it were a stick of kindling.

As Charlemagne scrambled to his feet, the burning candles fell onto the linen altar cloth, setting it ablaze. In the glare of the flames, Charlemagne recognized his attacker: it was Ogier the Dane, and the sword he held, known as Curtana, had been a gift from Charlemagne himself. Its blade—some said it had been forged from magical metal—had a distinctive notch six inches from the tip, a notch created forty years earlier, when Charlemagne and the Dane had been young men, and the best of friends. . . .

Charlemagne did not want this fight. If he could have stopped it with an apology, he would have done so. But the look in his former friend's eyes told him that words would be useless. Ogier wanted blood. Blood for blood.

Charlemagne drew his sword, known as Joyeuse. Both men grunted as they swung their weapons, the blades glinting in the firelight, the clash of metal echoing off the chapel's stone walls.

The two old knights, breathing heavily, circled each other warily in the swirling smoke, each looking for an opening. Ogier swung his sword, just missing Charlemagne's jaw but slicing off a piece of the king's beard.

Ogier swung again and Charlemagne jumped back, holding out Joyeuse to block the strike. The swords clanged together. Charlemagne stumbled backward, tripping on a prayer rug that had bunched beneath his feet. He fell to the stone floor, sprawled on his back, helpless. Ogier began to raise his sword, preparing to strike the fallen king. As he did, Charlemagne saw a brilliant light. He thought at first it was firelight reflecting from Ogier's blade, but in the next instant, the light, dancing in the swirling smoke, seemed to form itself into . . . Could it be?

An angel.

Charlemagne stared, transfixed, at the face smiling at him, shimmering through the smoke with unearthly beauty. Charlemagne smiled back at the angel; if this was death, he welcomed it. Ogier, disconcerted by the man's smile, paused. Then, with a grunt, he swung Curtana down toward the head of his former king. As he did, Charlemagne reached toward the angel, using the right hand in which he still held Joyeuse.

The two blades met. Charlemagne lost his grip. Joyeuse tumbled to the stone floor. The king was now unarmed; Ogier's next blow would surely be fatal. Holding Curtana in both hands, the Dane raised it for a stabbing, downward thrust. And then he stopped, staring at its blade.

Curtana had lost its tip, broken off at the notch that Charlemagne had put into the blade all those years before.

The sword was blunt now, useless for stabbing. The tip, a piece six inches long, lay on the floor by Charlemagne's shoulder.

Ogier, panting, stared at his sword—the sword that had served him faithfully for decades, in fight after fight. Then he looked at Charlemagne.

"It is not your day to die," he said. "Curtana does not want to kill you."

He laid the sword on the stone floor at Charlemagne's feet.

"It was your sword at the start," he said. "Now it is yours again."

Charlemagne looked at the sword, then back at his old friend.

"You must go," he said. "Before my knights pursue you. Go, and live in peace."

Ogier nodded. "And you," he said.

Charlemagne looked down at the sword's broken tip. He picked it up, seeing light reflected in its smooth surface. He looked up, hoping to see the angel again, but saw only smoke drifting in the glow of the fire.

The angel was gone. So was Ogier.

Only Curtana remained.

ᏟHE ᏋYES

Osborne House, Isle of Wight, England, January 22, 1901

QUEEN VICTORIA LAY DYING.

At eighty-one years old, she had reigned over the vast British empire for sixty-three years and seven months, longer than any other British monarch. She had assumed the throne as a teenager, in an age of sailing ships and horse-drawn carriages; she was leaving a world that knew telephones, electric lights, and motorcars.

The queen lay on a large four-posted bed, her eyes closed, her face peaceful. Close by stood her physician, Sir James Reid, and the white-haired Bishop of Winchester, who murmured a prayer. Gathered around were members of the royal family, including the queen's son, Crown Prince Albert Edward; upon her death, he would become king. The only sounds in the room, aside from the archbishop's soft voice, were the ticking of a clock and the whispers of some of the smaller children, too young to feel the sorrow of the moment.

Almost everyone stood near the queen's bed. The lone exception was a tall, extraordinarily thin man, standing alone in a gloomy corner of the room. The man's gaze appeared to be focused on the crown prince. There was no way to know for certain, because the man wore eyeglasses with wire rims and lenses tinted a dark shade, almost black. He always wore these glasses, even at night. This was one of a number of strange things about him.

People avoided the tall man.

The archbishop finished his prayer. Sir James stepped forward and bent over his patient. The room went utterly silent now, save for the ticking of the clock.

At exactly 6:30 in the evening, Sir James stood and solemnly raised his hand. The onlookers immediately understood the meaning of this gesture.

Queen Victoria was dead.

Some gasped; some moaned; others simply bowed their heads. The archbishop began the benediction.

———◆———

From inside the cluster of mourners, one of the younger children, a girl of five, peered around her mother's dress at the tall man in the corner. She had been keeping an eye on him. Like most children who found themselves in his presence, she felt afraid of him, though if pressed she could not have said why.

As the little girl watched, the tall man beckoned toward the open doorway. A second man entered: short, bald, and stocky. The girl could tell by the hesitant way in which the shorter man approached that he, too, was wary of the tall man.

The man with the dark glasses leaned over and said something quietly to the short man, who then nodded and quickly left the room. Still bending over, the tall man turned toward the mourners, and as he did, his dark eyeglasses slid about an inch down the bridge of his long, thin nose. Immediately, he pushed them back up.

But for a half-second, the little girl caught a glimpse of what lay behind the tinted lenses.

She let out a scream.

Her mother, embarrassed, quickly swept up her daughter and carried her, still screaming, from the room. The rest of the mourners assumed that the child had been overcome by grief.

Later, when the girl had calmed down, she told her mother what she had seen. The mother dismissed it. A trick of the light, she said; an overactive imagination. No, insisted the girl. It was true. She had seen it! Finally the mother, embarrassed by her daughter's outburst, ordered the girl to speak of it no more.

And so the girl spoke of it no more. But she could not rid herself of the memory of the tall man's eyes. It came back to her over and over. It would come back to her for years, in her nightmares.

CHAPTER 1

$\mathcal{D}$ISAPPEARANCE

London, 1902

JAMES SMITH, SURROUNDED BY A THRONG of home-bound commuters, climbed the steep stairs leading out of the South Kensington Underground station. Reaching the top, he felt the chill of the night air and pulled his overcoat tighter around him. He got his bearings and started toward Harrington Road. As he passed a newsstand, his eyes fell on a blaring black headline in one of the evening papers:

FOURTH DISAPPEARANCE
LINKED TO UNDERGROUND

James stopped and examined the illustration accompanying the story. It was a drawing of a middle-aged businessman in suit and tie, a man who looked like many in the crowd flowing past James now. James already knew the details of the story. Two nights earlier, the man had stayed late at his job at a bank on Surrey Street. He left the bank at 8:30 and was last seen by a coworker descending the steps to the Temple Underground station. The banker's usual route home was to ride the train to Westminster, where he would leave the Underground and board one of the new motorized omnibuses for the rest of his journey.

But he never reached his home. As far as the police could determine, he never emerged from the Underground. He was the fourth passenger to vanish this way in the past two weeks.

All four of the missing had been on the District Line—the same line James had just ridden. And while Londoners were generally a stoic lot, James had sensed an unusual level of tension in his fellow passengers—wary glances, an uneasiness as the train rocked its way through the dark tunnel, a general eagerness to get back up to the street.

James was not a fearful person. By the time he was twelve years old, he had survived ordeals more deadly and frightening than most people, of any age, could ever imagine. In his current job he was routinely exposed to London's dark and violent underworld. He remained calm in the face of danger; he was viewed by his coworkers as an exceptionally level-headed man.

But even James had felt something in the tunnel. He

wouldn't call it fear, exactly. But there had been a feeling at the back of his neck as the train rumbled along a particularly dark stretch of track, and a jerk of his head when he thought he'd seen, out of the corner of his eye, something through the window: a quick and fluid movement; a shifting shadow.

It was nothing, he'd told himself. A trick of the light. But the image had stayed in his mind—the flicker of shadow. It awakened memories he did not welcome, memories that had slept for more than twenty years—memories of other shadows, in another place. . . .

James shook his head as if to fling these thoughts away. He had urgent business to attend to. This was no time to wallow in unpleasant memories, or in the mysterious Underground disappearances. Whatever unfortunate fate had befallen the banker and the other three, it could not possibly have anything to do with the purpose of James's trip to South Kensington tonight.

He turned away from the newsstand, pulled his coat around him tighter still, and set off along Harrington Road.

CHAPTER 2

THE SKELETON

Liège, Belgium, 1902

FOUR FIGURES SWEPT ACROSS the cobblestone plaza like wraiths, wrapped in heavy wool cloaks with pointed hoods that obscured their faces. A cold mist hung in the air, along with bitter smoke from coal fires. Of the hundred or so people crisscrossing the plaza, not one was smiling this foul day.

The figures—a man in the lead, followed by a woman, then two much larger men—approached St. Paul's Cathedral, said to be modeled after Notre Dame. Its spires rose into the endless gray. Life-sized ornate carvings of saints, Popes, and revered patrons, stained by centuries of neglect, occupied recesses in the massive wall, judging all who entered.

The lead figure went to the cathedral's massive door and

raised his right arm, reaching toward the wrought-iron ring. The cloth of his robe slid down, revealing something barely recognizable as a hand—a mass of scar tissue, shaped like the gnarled root of a long-dead tree.

The woman reached out, restraining the leader's arm.

"Not here," she said.

The leader jerked his arm away.

"Do not touch me!" he spat, his heavily accented voice a dry rasp.

"But . . ."

"No!" said the leader. "You must *never touch me!*"

"I'm sorry," said the woman. "But we don't go in here."

"Is this not the cathedral?"

"The old cathedral was torn down a century before this one was built. It is the museum we want, around back. That's where we'll find the curator."

"And he will know where it is?" rasped the leader.

"He knows as much as anyone."

The leader turned toward the woman. She fought the impulse to look away from his face, which was as hideously scarred as his hand, the shiny purplish skin drawn tight to the skull, hairless except for a few random tufts. A lone yellow eye glared from a deep socket; where the other eye would have been was only a hole. There was no nose; the mouth was a lipless cavern that could not fully close and thus revealed jagged teeth in a permanent mirthless grin.

He was called the Skeleton. It was said he had once been handsome.

"Take me to him," he rasped.

The woman led the three around the cathedral. The museum entrance was a modest door at the back, with a sign displaying its hours. At the moment it was closed.

"I was afraid of this," said the woman. "We're quite late in the day."

The Skeleton's clawlike hand reappeared. He grasped the brass door-knocker and rapped it hard once, twice, thrice.

The door creaked as it opened. An elderly woman looked out, her eyes peering into the Skeleton's hood. Seeing his face, she screamed and tried to close the door. But one of the large men had anticipated this; his hand was already on the door, pushing it open. The woman, still screaming, backed away.

The four figures, led by the Skeleton, moved quickly inside and closed the door. The elderly woman, seeing that her screams were useless, retreated into the cluttered museum.

From a back room, a frail voice called out to her, speaking in the Walloon dialect used in this part of Belgium. The curator appeared. He looked as old as time itself—hair as white as salt, and skin so wrinkled that he seemed to be wearing someone else's body. His eyes, though, were an alert and piercing blue. The man glanced at his colleague, then studied all four hooded intruders. He showed no sign of fear.

"May I help you?" he said in accented English. "We've just closed for the night."

The Skeleton turned to his companion.

"Tell him," he rasped.

The female intruder stepped forward and pulled off her hood. She shook her hair, which fell past her shoulders in a glossy red cascade. Her jade green eyes sparkled in the candlelight.

"My name," she said, "is Scarlet Johns. My employer"—she bowed toward the Skeleton—"has come a great distance in search of something. I believe you know where it is."

"And what might that be?" said the old man.

"The tip of Curtana."

The old man blinked, which was apparently as close as he came to showing surprise.

"And why do you think I might know where it is?" he said. "I am just a curator."

Johns smiled. "You are a direct descendant of Gerard of Groesbeeck," she said.

The old man blinked again. "I am impressed," he said.

"You've spent a lifetime searching for the tip," Johns continued. "As did your father before you."

"And his before him," said the old man. "And so on, back a thousand years to the day the sword was broken. In all that time, nobody has found the tip of Curtana. What makes you think *I* would know where it is?"

"If anyone does," said Johns, "it is you."

The curator studied her. His eyes flicked over the other three figures, lingering for a moment on the Skeleton, then back to Johns.

"And if I did know something," he said, "why would I tell you?"

The Skeleton stepped forward. "Because I want you to," he said.

For a moment the room was silent. Then the curator, his ice blue eyes on the Skeleton, said, "I don't care who you are. I will not betray my ancestors. Do what you want; you will get nothing from me."

Because of the severe damage to his face, the Skeleton was not physically capable of showing pleasure. But he was pleased with the curator's answer.

"You are a brave man," he said. With a swift motion he pulled back his hood, revealing his grotesque skull. The old woman whimpered. The curator struggled not to flinch as the Skeleton moved closer.

"But in my experience," said the Skeleton, "bravery is no match for properly applied pain." He leaned close, his lone yellow eye burning in his monstrous face. "And nobody," he rasped, "has more experience with pain than I do."

CHAPTER 3

*T*HE *V*ISITOR

*T*HE DOORBELL RANG, and Mrs. George Darling sighed. She had just sat down for her first relaxing moment after a long and busy day. She put down the newspaper—another awful story about somebody disappearing in the Underground—and rose from her chair.

"Who is it?" shouted a high-pitched voice from upstairs, followed by a clatter of descending footsteps, followed by the appearance of her two sons, John and Michael.

"Who is it?" repeated Michael, who was three and, as always, was holding his stuffed bear.

"How would she know?" said John, who was seven and therefore knew a great deal more than Michael about everything. "She hasn't opened the door yet, you ninny."

"Mum!" cried Michael. "John called me a—"

"I *heard* what he called you," said Mrs. Darling, glaring at John as she reached the front door, "and I will discuss it with him later. But right now you will both behave." She opened the door, and her frown turned instantly to a smile at the sight of the tall figure standing there.

"James!" she said. "What a wonderful surprise! Do come in!"

"Are you sure?" James said. "I know it's late, but . . ."

"Nonsense!" she said, taking his arm and pulling him into the foyer. "John, Michael," she said. "This is Mr. Smith."

Michael eyed James warily. "Who are you?" he said.

"Michael Darling, that is a rude question," said Mrs. Darling. "Mr. Smith is a very dear friend to your father and me. And we are delighted to see him at *any* hour, especially after . . . James, how long *has* it been?"

"Years, I'm afraid, Molly," said James.

"Molly?" said John. He giggled.

She turned to her son. "It's the name I went by when I was a girl."

James blushed. "I'm sorry!" he said. "I didn't realize . . ."

"There's no need to apologize," said Molly. "It's just that George considers Molly a childish nickname. These days he prefers to call me by my given name, Mary. But that would sound odd coming from you. Please, call me Molly."

"Molly!" said John, giggling again.

"Are you a barrister?" asked Michael. "Our father is a barrister. He wears a wig. But he's not a lady."

"Michael!" said Molly.

"Well, *are* you a barrister?" repeated Michael.

"No," said James, with a glance toward Molly. "I work for Scotland Yard." He saluted the boys. "Inspector Smith, at your service."

"An inspector from Scotland Yard!" said John, delighted. He peered up at James through his round eyeglasses. "Are you looking for a murderer?" he said.

James grinned. "Not at the moment, no. But I am on a top secret assignment."

"Really!" said John.

"Yes. I'm looking for children who skip their baths."

"Oh," said John, disappointed.

"I've had my bath!" said Michael. "Yesterday, I think."

James was about to say something more when a third child descended the stairs—a girl of eleven, with long brown hair and a face that might be called delicate, except for the boldness in her startlingly green eyes.

"My goodness," said James. "Is that . . ."

"Yes," said Molly. "That's Wendy. I imagine she was just a baby when you saw her last. Wendy, this is Mr. Smith."

"How do you do?" said Wendy, offering a curtsy.

"Please forgive my staring," said James. "But you look so much like your mother when I first met her."

"What was she like?" said Wendy, with a disarmingly frank look that James had seen many times on her mother's face. "Was she an obedient child?"

21

"*Obedient?*" said James, barely stifling a laugh.

"Wendy!" said Molly. "Mr. Smith did not come here to discuss my childhood behavior. Now, you three go upstairs. Wendy, please put your brothers to bed, and then yourself. I'll be up to tuck everyone in after Mr. Smith and I have talked."

Reluctantly, the children obeyed. James, watching them climb the stairs, said, "They're fine children, Molly. I can see you in Wendy, and George in the boys."

"And mischief in all three," sighed Molly.

"And how *is* George?" said James.

"He's doing well," said Molly. "Very busy with his career. He's at some sort of dreadful law banquet tonight, as he often is." She paused. "But you didn't come to ask about George, did you, James?"

"No," admitted James, giving Molly a somber look. "Something's come up."

"I'll make tea," said Molly.

A few minutes later they were in the sitting room, cups in hand. James took a sip, swallowed, and began.

"Are you familiar with Baron von Schatten?"

Molly frowned. "The German? Yes. George and I saw him briefly at an embassy dinner. Odd man. Wearing darkened glasses, indoors? And at night?"

"The glasses are far from the only odd thing about him," said James.

"What do you mean?"

"Molly, this is a man who, only a few years ago, had no connection whatsoever with the royal family. He appeared as if from nowhere, and somehow managed to ingratiate himself with Prince Albert Edward. The prince's staff and advisers were wary of von Schatten, of course, but the prince seemed oddly tolerant of him. Almost deferential."

James took another sip of tea.

"Then, one by one," he continued, "those same staff and advisers suffered misfortunes—illnesses, injuries, even two deaths. All of these incidents appeared to be either natural or purely accidental. But each one removed another barrier between von Schatten and the prince, so that when the prince became king, von Schatten was his most trusted—in fact his only—adviser. It is now almost impossible for anyone else, including his family, to get close to him. For all intents and purposes, von Schatten is, next to the king, the most powerful man in England."

"I had no idea," said Molly.

"Very few people do," said James.

"How do *you* know all this?" said Molly.

"Six months ago," said James, "I was given an unusual assignment: to take a menial position on the palace staff, without revealing my identity as an inspector. My instructions were to find out as much as I could about von Schatten and his relationship to the king."

"Spying on the *king?*" said Molly.

"I questioned it myself," said James. "But Chief Superintendent Blake told me that the orders came from the highest levels of government. They're worried about von Schatten's influence, Molly. *Very* worried. And they have good reason to be."

"What do you mean?"

James, leaning forward, lowered his voice. "Molly," he said, "do you know what von Schatten's profession was, before he came to England?"

Molly shook her head.

"He was an archaeologist," said James. "Quite a well-known one, in fact. But his career ended suddenly ten years ago, when he had a serious accident. It's the reason he must always wear those dark glasses. Or so he says."

"What sort of accident?"

"Von Schatten is vague about the details," said James. "But it happened at an archaeological site in the North African desert. Von Schatten was exploring the ruins of a temple—a temple that had stood for thousands of years, only to collapse twenty-three years ago in a mysterious explosion."

Molly went pale. "Rundoon," she whispered.

"Yes," said James. "Rundoon. Von Schatten was exploring the Jackal."

"But it was destroyed!" said Molly. "The rocket . . ."

24

"The temple was severely damaged, yes," said James. "Obliterated, in fact, aboveground. But there was a crater, and at the bottom of that crater a hole, a sort of cave in the sand. Von Schatten went down there. He went alone—the guides would not go within a mile of that cursed place. He was gone for several days. When he finally came out, he claimed to have fallen and hit his head and lost consciousness for a time. He had no visible injuries. But he was . . . changed."

"How so?" said Molly.

"For one thing, he could no longer stand sunlight. That can happen temporarily, of course, after days in total darkness. But the affliction stayed with von Schatten. He is never seen outside, and his eyes are always hidden behind those impenetrably dark glasses. But there was more: his personality had changed. Before, he had been outgoing; now he was reserved, sullen—an utterly different person. His family, his colleagues, said it was as if"—James lowered his voice—"as if someone else were inhabiting his body."

For a moment, the two just stared at each other. Then Molly shook her head.

"It can't be," she said, her own voice a whisper. "After all this time . . . It just *can't* be."

"I wish you were right," said James. "But after what I learned at the palace . . ."

He leaned forward, his eyes boring into Molly's.

"Molly," he said. "I think it's *him*."

"And that," said Wendy, "is why the moon changes its shape."

"Because an *elephant is eating it?*" scoffed John. "That's *silly!*"

"I'm sorry, but that's your bedtime story," said Wendy, rising from the rocking chair at the end of the boys' beds.

"That's the worst bedtime story *ever*," said John.

"Well, it's the one you get tonight," said Wendy. It was true; she usually told a much longer story. But tonight she was more interested in what was going on downstairs.

"How does the moon come back?" said Michael.

"I don't know, said Wendy impatiently. "Perhaps the elephant spits it back out."

"But then it wouldn't be round!" said John. "There would be just pieces of moon, covered with elephant spit."

"Good night," said Wendy, going to the bedroom door.

"But what does the elephant *stand* on?" said Michael.

"I said good *night*," said Wendy, closing the door behind her, leaving the two boys to complain to each other about the declining quality of bedtime stories.

Wendy walked to her own bedroom, paused, then continued down the hallway to the top of the stairs. She listened for a moment, then descended on quiet bare feet to the staircase landing. Now she could hear her mother and Mr. Smith talking. She couldn't make out the words, but her mother's tone was clear: she was upset about something.

Wendy frowned. Her mother was not easily upset. What was this mysterious Mr. Smith telling her? What had brought him here at this hour?

On tiptoe, Wendy started down the stairs.

⇒◆⇐

Molly was shaking her head. "I thought this was over," she said.

"We all did," said James.

"After Rundoon," said Molly, "when years and years passed, and there were no more starstuff falls . . . Father was convinced—*all* the Starcatchers were—that the Others had finally been defeated, along with that awful creature . . ." She stopped, not wanting to say the name.

"Ombra," said James.

Molly flinched, remembering the dark, shifting shape that caused her and her family so much torment and terror. "Yes," she whispered. "Ombra."

"But what if he survived?" said James.

"No," said Molly. "He was on the rocket. It was destroyed in the explosion."

"Yes. But remember that Peter escaped that rocket. And so did his shadow. Perhaps Ombra did, too, somehow."

"And you think he now controls von Schatten? That he has taken his shadow?"

"No," said James. "That's the curious thing. Von Schatten casts a shadow."

"But wasn't that how Ombra controlled people? By taking their shadows?"

"It was," said James. "He did it to me, once." James shuddered at the memory. "But this is something different. I think something happened to Ombra in the explosion, something that weakened him, left him unable to function on his own. I think he stayed down there, deep in the hole in the sand, in the dark, waiting. And when von Schatten came along, Ombra somehow . . . *inhabited* him, and now controls him."

"But how can you know that?"

"I watched him in the palace, Molly. I got close to him only once; he keeps the palace staff at a distance, dealing with them through his assistant, an unpleasant man named Simon Revile. But I was able to observe von Schatten from a distance a number of times. He is always close to the king, and makes physical contact with him often."

"He *touches* the king?"

"It's very subtle—an elbow brushing an elbow, a hand resting for a moment on a shoulder. But once you know to look for it, you see it often. And each time, the king responds. Again, it's subtle—a flutter of the eyelids, a slight twitch of the head. But it's there, Molly; it's definitely there.

I think this contact is how Ombra, through von Schatten, is controlling the king."

Molly shook her head. "I'm sorry, James," she said. "But this is simply too far-fetched. Perhaps something did happen to von Schatten in Rundoon. Perhaps he has a strange relationship with the king. But to say that he's being *inhabited* by that creature . . . how can you possibly know that?"

James leaned toward Molly, and when he spoke, his tone was urgent.

"I told you that on one occasion I managed to get close. I won't go into the details of how I did it, save to say I'm fairly skilled at picking locks. And late one night, through some luck and some lying, I managed to get to the hallway outside the king's bedchamber. The door was open and the hallway was dim; if I stood in the right place, I was able, without being seen myself, to observe the king, von Schatten, and Revile, and to overhear some of their conversation. Von Schatten did most of the talking, and he seemed to be talking to Revile—almost as if the king weren't there."

"Talking about what?"

"The king's coronation," said James. "Von Schatten was very concerned about the date. He stressed several times that they needed to have something ready for the coronation. Then he talked about something else, and I didn't follow most of it, but it had something to do with Belgium, and the missing piece."

"The missing piece of what?"

"I don't know—only that von Schatten wants it found soon. He was speaking softly, and I was missing some of the words, so I decided to try to move a little closer. And that was when it happened."

"What happened?"

"He *felt* me, Molly."

"What?"

"He felt my presence. And . . . and I felt his. It was Ombra."

"But how can you be certain?"

"Molly, Ombra took my shadow once; he controlled me. I shall never, as long as I live, forget that horrible feeling, the cold filling my body, and this . . . this unspeakable *evil* filling my mind. This was the same sensation, Molly. And the worst of it was that as I sensed him, he sensed *me*. He knew exactly who I was. I'm sure of it. He stopped talking immediately and walked quickly toward the doorway."

"What did you do?"

"I ran. I admit it, Molly: I was terrified. I ran down the hallway and kept running until I was out of the palace. I felt such a coward. But I couldn't help myself. . . . It was as if I were a boy again, a frightened little boy."

"I don't blame you at all," said Molly, remembering her own experiences fleeing from the dark shape. "But what did you do then?"

"I went back to the Yard, first thing the next day," said James. "My intention was to report to my superiors." He smiled ruefully. "That did not go at all well."

"What happened?"

"Molly, think about it. They're police officers; they live in the world of crime and criminals. Of fact, and evidence. They know nothing about starstuff, or the Starcatchers, or the Others, or Ombra. When I tried to suggest to them that von Schatten was no ordinary man, that he was influenced by something evil, something inhuman, they looked at me as if I were a madman, or a child telling ghost stories. They don't believe me, Molly. They would never believe me. I'm facing disciplinary action simply for having brought this up."

"Oh dear," said Molly. "How awful."

James waved his hand. "My career at Scotland Yard doesn't matter. This is far more important than that. Whatever von Schatten—or Ombra—intends to do, he must be stopped, Molly. And only the Starcatchers can stop him."

"James, the few Starcatchers who are left are old and feeble."

"But your father . . ."

"My father is very ill, James. He is in no condition, mentally or physically, to cope with something like this."

"But there must be *somebody*," said James.

Molly shook her head. "When the starstuff falls stopped,

the group you knew as the Starcatchers gradually ceased to exist. Essentially there *are* no Starcatchers anymore, James."

James studied her for a moment, then softly said, "There's you, Molly."

Molly shook her head. "I'm not a Starcatcher anymore, James. I'm a mother of three and the wife of a prominent barrister who does not approve of talk of starstuff and evil creatures and the like. Childhood fantasies, he calls them."

"But they were *real*, Molly. Surely George knows that. He was *there*, at Stonehenge, in Rundoon. . . ."

"Yes," said Molly. "He was there. But he is determined that we put that part of our lives behind us."

"We can't, Molly. It has come back. We must confront it."

Again, Molly shook her head.

"I don't think so, James," she said. "I know you believe you felt something in the palace, but what if you were mistaken? I can't just give up the life I've been leading all these years to chase after something you might have imagined."

"I didn't imagine it, Molly."

Molly looked down. "I'm sorry, James," she said. "I can't."

James stared at her for a moment, then said, "I can't believe that Molly Aster would say such a thing."

Molly looked up and met James's gaze. "I'm not Molly Aster anymore," she said. "I'm Mrs. George Darling."

James looked at her for a few moments, then nodded.

"All right," he said. "Then I'll ask a favor of you."

"Of course."

"Just think about what I've told you tonight. Perhaps something will occur to you—someone else I could go to, someone who might be able to help."

"But I don't—"

"Please, Molly. I've nobody else to turn to. The coronation date is approaching. And I fear that von Schatten, now that he knows who I am, will use his position against me. Just give it one day of thought, Molly."

"All right," said Molly reluctantly. "I promise I'll think about it."

"Thank you," said James, rising. "I'll come back tomorrow evening for your answer, if that would be all right."

"All right," said Molly, remembering that her husband had yet another social function the next evening. As she walked James to the door, she said, "Do you need a taxicab?"

"No," said James, "I'll take the Underground."

"Do be careful, then," she said. "Those awful disappearances . . ."

"Oh, I'll be fine," said James.

He turned and gave her hand a squeeze. "It's good to see you again, Molly."

"And you, James. Do you ever see the others? Prentiss? Thomas? Ted?"

"We get together from time to time," said James.

"They're all doing quite well. Ted, if you can believe it, is a fellow at Cambridge. Dr. Theodore Pratt."

"Good for Ted," she said. "Give them all my best."

"I will," said James. He hesitated, then said, "Do you ever think about . . . Peter?"

Molly blushed. "Sometimes," she said. "And you?"

"Quite often," he said. "I find myself wondering if I'll ever see him again."

"I don't know," said Molly slowly, "if that would be such a good thing, after all these years."

James looked at her for a moment, then said, "Well, good night, then, Molly. I'll see you tomorrow."

"Yes," said Molly. "Tomorrow."

James opened the door and stepped out into the fog-darkened London night; in a moment he was gone. Molly closed the door and stood looking at it, her mind swirling with troubled thoughts. She jumped at the sound of a foot-step behind her.

"Wendy!" she said, turning to see her daughter at the base of the stairs. "What are you doing down here? Why aren't you in bed?"

Wendy responded with questions of her own.

"Mother," she said, "what is a Starcatcher?" She stepped forward, her green-eyed gaze fixed on her mother's face.

"And who is Peter?"

CHAPTER 4

The Rescue

THREE MEN SPRAWLED in a small white boat, adrift under a glaring sun. Only one of the three, a huge black man, was awake, his eyes scanning the vast empty sea. The other two were slumped over, dozing, the noon heat raising blisters on their already red backs. A fourth man was in the water behind the boat, clinging to the transom, seeking relief from the heat in the tepid tropical water.

The boat bore the name *Inganno*. Its sail, sewn of red-and-white-striped canvas, was meant to both move the boat and be visible to distant rescuers. But now it hung in tatters from a broken mast, useless. There were no oars; the boat bobbed in the gentle swells, carried by the current.

Suddenly the huge man, whose name was Cheeky O'Neal, sat up and pointed.

"What's that?" he said.

One of the dozing men, whose name was Frederick

DeWulf, raised himself up and squinted through a salt-crusted right eye. "Don't see nothing," he said.

"There!" said O'Neal, pointing toward a dark speck on the horizon. "That's land!"

"Are we there yet?" said the other dozing man, Rufus Kelly, waking up from his nap.

"Paddle!" shouted O'Neal. DeWulf and Kelly leaned over the sides and started paddling with their bare hands. O'Neal turned to the man in the water, whose name was Angus McPherson, and said, "And you: kick!"

Propelled by the men, the boat began advancing, very slowly, toward the island. O'Neal's gaze was riveted on the distant speck. Then he saw something else—something moving. He shaded his eyes for a better look.

"There's something flying toward us," he said softly.

"A bird?" said DeWulf, peering into the bright sky ahead. All four men were looking now, and one by one they saw it, a dark shape swooping across the water toward them at astonishing speed, growing larger and larger. . . .

"That's no bird," said Kelly. "That's . . ."

"That's a *boy*," said O'Neal. "A flying boy!"

McPherson quickly hauled himself into the boat for a better look. The four men stared as the boy zoomed toward them. As he drew near, they saw a second flying shape—a tiny, brilliant ball of light, as if a piece of the sun had broken loose. The glowing orb darted and zipped about

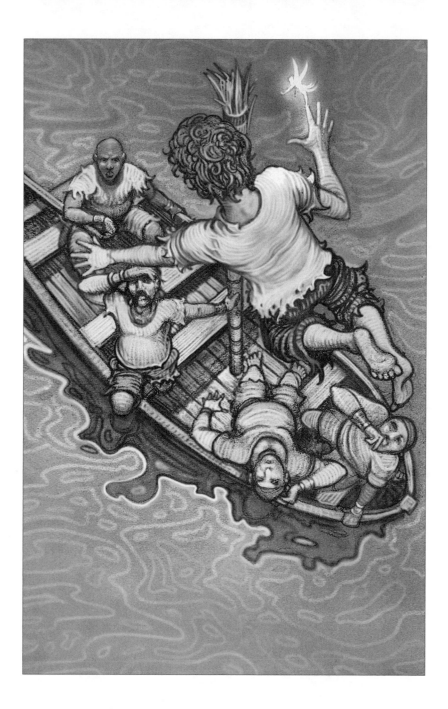

the boat, and the startled men heard the sound of bells.

The boy swooped to an easy midair stop, hovering a few feet above the men's heads. He looked to be twelve or thirteen years old; he had red hair, and freckles still visible in his deeply tanned face. He was studying the men in the boat but listening to the sounds coming from the shimmering, darting orb, which had perched on his shoulder, and which the men could now see was what looked like a tiny winged woman.

"No they're not, Tink," the boy said. "They've just been at sea for a while."

More bells, and then the boy said, "I can't just leave them out here." Speaking to the men, the boy said, "My name is Peter. Who are you?"

The men in the boat looked to O'Neal, who said, "We're crewmen from the freighter *Inganno*. She sank three weeks and two days ago. Terrible storm. We lost our oars, and our mast broke, as you see. We're in a bad way . . . Peter."

More bells, ominous in tone. Peter looked at the tiny flying woman, then shook his head.

"They need help, Tink," he said. This was not what Tink wanted to hear. She flashed red and flew off.

"We're trying to get to that island," said O'Neal, pointing. "Is that *your* island?"

"I live there," said Peter. "With the Mollusks."

"The Mollusks?"

"You'll meet them."

"Then you'll help us get there?"

Peter, hovering, studied them a moment, then said, "I will. You'll get food and water. But the Mollusks won't let you stay."

"Fair enough," said O'Neal. "Men, paddle for the island."

Peter smiled and said, "You don't need to paddle."

"What do you mean?" said O'Neal.

"My friends can help you."

"What friends?" asked O'Neal, his eyes searching the sky.

"These friends," said Peter, gesturing toward the water.

The men looked down and saw, poking out of the water all around the boat, the heads of a dozen lovely long-haired women, looking at them with interest. Then, moving as one, the heads ducked under, and long green tails flicked the surface.

"Mermaids," whispered DeWulf.

"Aye," agreed McPherson.

"These are interesting waters," said Kelly.

"The mermaids will swim your boat to the island," said Peter. "But don't try to touch them. They don't like to be touched, and you wouldn't enjoy their bite."

"Put your hands inside the boat," said O'Neal, but the others, eyeing the mermaids warily, had already done so. The mermaids gathered at the stern of the boat and put their hands on it. Moments later, propelled by a dozen powerful tails, the boat was skimming toward the island, faster than it had ever moved by sail. Peter flew ahead, following Tink, an angry red dot out in front.

Cheeky O'Neal, with a glance back at the mermaids, lowered his voice, so that only the other three men could hear him. "Mermaids," he said. "And a flying boy."

The other three nodded, their eyes on the distant speck of land, which was growing steadily larger.

———

The island was breathtakingly beautiful, its jungle green volcanic mountainsides rising steeply into the vivid blue sky. As the mermaids expertly navigated the lifeboat through an opening in a coral reef, the four men looked across a placid lagoon to a vertical rock cliff with a foaming waterfall plunging hundreds of feet onto a jumble of boulders below. To the left of the cliff stretched a curved beach, easily a mile long, its bright white sand leading up to a line of tall palms guarding the entrance to the jungle.

Peter had flown ahead to tell the Mollusks about the men in the lifeboat. Now he stood on the beach with a dozen bronze-skinned warriors, all holding spears, all watching the approaching boat.

"Look friendly, men," said Cheeky O'Neal.

As the boat reached the island, some of the warriors waded into the lagoon and hauled it up onto the beach. The mermaids, with a flash of tails, disappeared. The four men climbed out of the boat; O'Neal was almost a foot taller than the other three. The four stood on the sand, watching the Mollusks, waiting.

An older warrior stepped forward. He was tall and broad-chested, and although there were age lines at the corners of his deep-set dark eyes, his hair was glistening black, and he had the look of a man who could still hunt, or fight. Speaking to O'Neal, he said, in flawless British-accented English, "I am Fighting Prawn, chief of the Mollusks. Who are you?"

"My name is O'Neal. This is DeWulf, Kelly, and McPherson." The men nodded as their names were spoken.

"Peter tells me your ship sank," said Fighting Prawn.

"That's right," said O'Neal. "We . . ."

"How long ago?" said Fighting Prawn.

"Three weeks and two days."

Fighting Prawn studied the four men for a moment, his eyes lingering on the red, sunburned flesh of DeWulf, Kelly, and McPherson. Then he nodded and said, "You must be thirsty and hungry." He said something in an odd-sounding language to his men, then told O'Neal, "These men will take you to our village. You will be given food and drink. When you are fed and rested, we will see about repairing your boat and giving you supplies so that you can be on your way."

"With all respect, chief," said O'Neal, "we're a long way from anywhere. I don't know if that little boat can . . ."

Fighting Prawn raised his hand, silencing O'Neal.

"You will not stay here," he said.

O'Neal bowed slightly. "As you say, chief," he said, glancing at his three companions.

Surrounded by warriors, the four men started up the beach. Peter turned to follow, but Fighting Prawn caught him by the arm. The two had become close friends, having known each other for more than twenty years, although neither had aged in that time.

"Peter," said Fighting Prawn. "When you found these men, did you see any sign of fresh water in the boat?"

"Not that I recall," Peter said. "Why?"

"Fish bones? Seaweed?"

Peter shook his head. "Why?"

"They claim to have been in the boat for more than three weeks. What did they eat and drink? Why are their lips not cracked, their bellies not swollen? And why is their skin so red, instead of brown, like yours?"

"So you think . . ."

"These men have not been in that boat more than three *days*. Certainly not three weeks."

"But why would they lie?" said Peter.

Fighting Prawn's eyes traveled up the beach, to the men in the company of his warriors.

"I don't know," he said. "But I want to watch them closely."

His gaze returned to Peter's.

"Something is not right."

CHAPTER 5

REVILE'S REPORT

AT THE END OF AN ENDLESS HALLWAY on the third floor of Buckingham Palace was a room the servants knew better than to enter. The room was impressive—high ceiling, marble floors, gold-leaf furniture—but none of these features were visible now, for the room was also quite dark. Black velvet curtains covered the tall windows completely; the only light in the room came from a single flickering candle.

Simon Revile stood close to the candle, drawing what comfort he could from it. Revile was a short, stocky man with a remarkably toadlike face, his unnaturally wide mouth underscoring a flattened nose that separated his huge eyes, a bit too far apart.

Adding to the effect were Revile's cauliflower ears, attached flat to his head like a pair of large dried apricots.

Revile knew he was unpleasant to look at. This did not trouble him. In fact, he enjoyed causing discomfort in others. He enjoyed even more causing fear, and pain. Especially pain.

At the moment, however, it was Revile who was uncomfortable, as he always was in this dark and drafty room—the lair of Baron von Schatten. Upon being summoned, Revile had, as always, let himself in, closed the door, then walked toward the candle. Now he stood by the tiny flame, his eyes darting about, trying to locate von Schatten. Revile knew he was lurking somewhere in the darkness.

"Have you something to report?"

Revile jumped at the voice, which sounded as though it came from the bottom of a deep well. Revile half-turned toward the sound, not wanting to look directly at the tall form of von Schatten, who stood only a few feet away, though he had made no sound approaching.

"Yes," said Revile. "A coded dispatch from Belgium."

"The Skeleton," said von Schatten.

"Yes," said Revile. "It seems he won the cooperation of a museum curator. The Skeleton is on his way to Aachen, on the German border."

Revile, despite his discomfort, smiled, imagining what the Skeleton had done to the curator. Revile took great pleasure in the thought of other people's pain.

"And the tip?" said von Schatten.

"He did not say. But I assume its recovery is imminent."

"It had better be," said von Schatten.

Out of the corner of his eye, Revile saw von Schatten shift position. He did this often. On those rare occasions when he stood still, his upper body moved in an odd manner, almost as if it were flickering, like the flame of the candle in front of Revile.

"The coronation date has been fixed for the twenty-sixth of June," said von Schatten. "By then we must have the tip."

"Yes, Baron."

"And by then we must also reach the vault. What progress can you report on that effort?"

"It proceeds slowly, Baron. The rock—"

"It must go faster."

"Yes, but the diggers are working to the point of exhaustion."

"*Then work them harder,*" hissed von Schatten. Revile flinched, feeling von Schatten's breath on his neck.

The breath was cold.

"Yes, Baron," said Revile, inching forward, toward the security of the candle flame. Von Schatten would get only so close to the flickering light.

"If necessary, you will enlist more diggers," said von Schatten.

"We're doing that, Baron. In fact we . . . *enlisted* one last night. The one you recognized here at the palace."

"Good," said von Schatten. "I shall visit him soon. Meanwhile, you will push the diggers harder. We must reach the vault before the coronation."

"Yes, Baron," said Revile, feeling, despite his fear, a spasm of pleasure at the thought of the pain he would inflict on the diggers.

"And you will remind our friend in Belgium of the urgency of his mission. The vault is useless to us without the tip."

"Yes, Baron. I'll send the dispatch immediately." Revile, eager to escape, turned toward the door to go, only to find his path blocked by von Schatten, whose dark eyeglasses reflected the flickering candle flame.

"Do not disappoint me, Simon," said von Schatten. "You would *not want* to disappoint me." Von Schatten's right hand reached out and touched Revile's arm, and for an instant Revile felt the awful cold filling him. . . .

The tip and the vault by coronation day. It was von Schatten's voice, but it came from inside Revile's mind.

And then the hand pulled away, and the cold was gone. Revile almost cried out in relief.

"I won't disappoint you, Baron," he said, stumbling toward the door.

Yanking open the door, he stepped into the hallway and quickly closed the door behind him. Gasping for breath, he half walked, half ran away from von Schatten's room, the unwelcome voice echoing in his mind.

The tip and the vault by coronation day.

CHAPTER 6

MOLLY GOES LOOKING

$\mathcal{F}$OR THREE DAYS, Molly waited for James to return to her home, as he'd promised. In truth, she wasn't looking forward to it. She intended to tell him that there was nothing more to discuss. Her ailing father, Lord Aster, could not possibly help James pursue his suspicions, and she was far too busy with her duties as wife and mother.

The more she'd thought about everything he'd told her, the more she'd convinced herself that James had to be mistaken about von Schatten. Whatever James had felt in the palace—or thought he'd felt—there had to be some rational explanation for it. She suspected it was just a case of nerves—that James, feeling the pressure of his difficult palace assignment, had felt a cold draft and overreacted.

She would never voice her beliefs to James, of course. She was too fond of him to hurt his feelings. No, she would simply tell him that she could not become involved. She did not want anything to disrupt her safe and tidy life. She definitely did not want her husband to know that James had come around talking of ghosts from the past. George would be furious if he knew his wife had even agreed to see James a second time.

George would be even more furious if he knew that young Wendy was now pestering her mother with questions about James and the Starcatchers. Molly had sternly refused to answer these questions. She'd forbidden Wendy to say anything more about James's visit, or to speak to anyone about it, especially her father. But Wendy was a stubborn child and deeply curious; Molly worried that, given the chance, she would try to learn more.

So in Molly's mind it was settled: when James returned, she would firmly, but politely, turn him away.

When he failed to arrive the night after his initial visit, Molly sent a letter to his office by the morning post. She hoped for an answer by the evening post, but none came. There was none the next day either, nor the next.

With each passing hour, Molly's anxiety increased. James had seemed deeply upset, and had gone to the trouble of seeking her out. He was not the kind of person to simply drop the matter. If he'd changed plans, or decided he did not need her, he would have at least written to her. Why hadn't he? Could it possibly be that he was, after all, in real danger?

On the fourth day, she could stand it no longer. With

George at work, Molly left the children with their nanny, announcing that she was meeting a friend for lunch. Instead, she went to Scotland Yard, taking the Underground from South Kensington to Westminster. This meant she rode the District Line, which was where the mysterious disappearances had been taking place. But she felt safe making the trip at midday, when the tunnels and platforms were fairly busy.

Scotland Yard proved more of a challenge than Molly expected. She was a well-spoken lady from a good family, and she could be quite forceful when she wanted to be. Even so, it took her several hours to talk her way into the office of Chief Superintendent Blake, whom James had identified as his superior.

Blake, a distinguished-looking man with thinning gray hair and piercing blue eyes, rose reluctantly from a cluttered desk. His greeting was polite enough, but his tone left no doubt that he was irritated by her intrusion.

"And how may I help you, Mrs. Darling?" he said.

"I am concerned about one of your inspectors," she said. "James Smith."

She saw Blake react. It was subtle—a flicker of the eyes—and he recovered quickly. But it was there; Molly was sure of it.

"And what is the nature of your concern?" said Blake.

Molly had given considerable thought to what she would say. She didn't want to reveal that James had told her about his spying mission in the palace, and she certainly didn't want to say anything about Ombra or the Starcatchers. So she told Blake only that James was an old friend, that he had visited her home three nights earlier to discuss "an important matter." He had promised to return the following night, and had failed to do so. She had posted several letters, and these had gone unanswered.

Blake listened, nodding. When she finished, he said, "I appreciate your concern, Mrs. Darling. But there is no cause for worry. Inspector Smith is fine. In fact, he is on holiday."

"But . . . are you sure? He said nothing to me about going on holiday. And he promised to return to my—"

"Yes, it *was* a bit sudden," said Blake. "But overdue. Inspector Smith has been working very hard of late, and we . . . that is, *I* thought it would do him good to get away for a month or two."

"A *month or two?* This is very odd, Chief Superintendent," said Molly. "I'm certain he intended to visit me. For him to just leave . . ."

"Perhaps he changed his mind," said Blake evenly, his eyes fixed on hers.

Molly returned his gaze, saying nothing, thinking, *Something is wrong.*

"Perhaps," Blake continued, speaking slowly, "I could be more helpful to you if you were to tell me about this 'important matter' raised by Inspector Smith."

Molly shook her head. "I'm afraid it's . . . personal," she said.

"I see," said Blake. He gestured at the clutter of papers on his desk and said, "Then if you'll excuse me . . ."

"Of course," said Molly, moving to the door. "Thank you for your time."

"Not at all," said Blake, making no effort to sound sincere. As Molly reached the door, he said, "One last thing, Mrs. Darling."

Molly stopped, turned. "Yes?"

"In this line of work," said Blake, "we deal constantly with unfortunate people whose lives have been . . . disrupted."

Molly frowned, wondering what Blake was getting at.

"I have found," continued Blake, "that often people bring these disruptions upon themselves."

"What are you suggesting?" said Molly.

"I'm suggesting," said Blake, "that it's best not to go looking for trouble. Because if you do, sooner or later, you will find it."

Molly blinked. "Are you *threatening* me, Chief Superintendent?" she said.

Blake waved a hand dismissively. "Of course not," he said. "I'm simply making an observation. I'm only thinking of your own well-being, Mrs. Darling. Yours, and your family's."

Molly met his gaze, held it for a moment. "Yes, I'm sure you are," she said. Without another word, she left the office, feeling Blake's eyes on her until she closed the door.

The visit had taken longer than she expected; night had fallen by the time Molly left Scotland Yard headquarters. She hurried to the Westminster tube stop, praying she would get home before George. She descended the steep stairway, paid her fare, and made her way to the District Line platform, joining the scattered dozens of passengers waiting for the next train to rumble out of the dark tunnel.

She felt uneasy—in part because of Blake's thinly veiled threat, and his obvious lie about James. *What was he hiding? Where was James?*

But something else was bothering Molly: a feeling she was being watched. She glanced around the platform, seeing random groups of office workers and laborers, people on their way home at the end of a workday. Nothing out of the ordinary. And yet there was something else, something she could *feel*, a sense of menace in the thick air around her. Molly shivered.

Don't be a ninny, she told herself. *You're imagining things.*

Still, she felt it.

Molly glanced to her left. At the end of the platform, close to the tunnel mouth, stood a bobby wearing the traditional police uniform with its distinctive domed helmet. Molly walked toward him, stopping twenty feet away, ashamed of herself for her fearfulness, yet feeling safer nearer the bobby and farther from the other passengers. She waited there, alone, for a few minutes. Then she heard the low sound of a train coming from the blackness of the tunnel at the far end of the platform. It grew steadily louder, and the train hurtled into view, seemingly going far too fast before shuddering to a stop with an earsplitting screech of brakes. The front car was almost empty. A few feet away, the car's gateman was sliding open its mesh gate. She started toward it.

"Madam!" shouted a deep voice behind her.

Molly turned. It was the bobby. He was coming toward her, a big man with a lush mustache.

"Hold up, please, madam!" he said, still approaching.

"But . . ." said Molly, gesturing toward the train. Down the platform, she saw a few people who'd gotten off and were heading for the stairs. The waiting passengers had all boarded, except for Molly.

"Get on, madam, if you're getting on," said the gateman.

Molly started toward the door.

"Wait!" shouted the bobby, his voice deep and commanding. Molly hesitated.

"Suit yourself, madam," said the gateman, as he began sliding the mesh gate closed.

The bobby had reached Molly now. He reached out and grabbed her coat sleeve with a massive hand. Molly's eyes met his and she knew—she *knew*—that she could not let him hold her there. She drew back her right foot and kicked him hard on the shin. As he bent over in pain, she yanked her arm free with all her strength, ripping her sleeve but freeing herself. She ran to the car, reaching the door just as the gateman was about to latch it closed. She pounded on the gate.

"Let me in!" she said. "Please!"

The gateman looked up from the latch; he had not seen the struggle between Molly and the bobby.

"Make up your mind," he muttered, reluctantly sliding the gate open. Molly lunged inside, gasping, her heart pounding. She looked back fearfully, but the gateman had already closed the gate; the bobby had not boarded the train. Molly looked out the window and almost screamed when she saw him on the platform only a few feet away, staring at her.

The brakes hissed. The train started moving. The bobby's eyes stayed on Molly as the car slid past. And then he was gone from sight, and the train, gaining speed, rumbled into the dark tunnel ahead.

(T)ROUBLING (Q)UESTIONS

CHEEKY O'NEAL AND HIS MEN recovered quickly from their ordeal at sea. They wolfed down the food brought to them by the Mollusks—salted wild pig meat, root vegetables, breadfruit, and hearts of palm. They were less enthusiastic about other Mollusk delicacies, such as lizard kebab and boiled centipedes. But they ate well enough, and washed the food down with water from the island's springs. In three days they appeared completely healthy.

Fighting Prawn remained deeply suspicious of the sailors. He was convinced that they were lying about being shipwrecked, and he was determined to get them off the island. In the meantime, he reluctantly allowed them to roam about, although he had his warriors keep an eye on them.

On their fourth morning on the island, the sailors left the village and wandered along the path leading to the driftwood hut occupied by Peter and his mates, the Lost Boys—Slightly, Curly, Tootles, Nibs, and the twins. The hut was a ramshackle affair, held together with vines; parts of it were always falling down. When the sailors arrived, the boys, under the direction of Peter, were trying to repair a large section that had collapsed. At the moment, there was a good deal more arguing going on than repair as the boys tried to secure some poles with lengths of vine, which were forming an increasingly massive snarl.

The sailors watched for a few minutes, amused. Finally O'Neal said, "What kind of knot is that?"

The Lost Boys all looked at Peter, who looked at the snarl, then O'Neal.

"That's a monkeyshank," he said.

O'Neal smiled. "Never heard of that one," he said.

"It's a local knot," said Peter.

"I see," said O'Neal. "I know a better knot. Want me to show you?"

"No," said Peter.

"Yes!" chorused the Lost Boys.

"Sounds like you're outvoted," said O'Neal, elbowing Peter aside and grabbing the vine in a massive hand. "Come on, men, grab those poles."

The other three sailors—DeWulf, Kelly, and McPherson, stepped forward. In a few minutes the sailors had lashed the poles together expertly and had repaired the fallen section of the hut. When they were finished, O'Neal said, "Looks like your roof could use some work as well."

"The roof is fine," said Peter.

"Except when it rains," said Tootles. Everyone laughed except Peter.

"Let's have a look," said O'Neal.

For the next two hours, while Peter sulked in a nearby tree, the sailors worked on the hut—re-thatching the roof, reinforcing walls—all the while bantering with the Lost Boys, who were deeply impressed by the sailors' skill. As the blazing sun rose high and the heat became intense, the men stopped to rest, sitting in the shade of the hut, entertaining the boys with stories of life at sea.

After DeWulf had told a particularly exciting tale, Slightly said, "I'd like to go on a ship sometime."

Instantly, O'Neal sat up. "But you must have been on a ship," he said to Slightly. "You came to this island on a ship, didn't you?"

"Yes," said Slightly, "but that was . . ." He stopped, cut off by a nudge from Nibs.

"That was what?" said O'Neal.

"That was . . . that was a long time ago," said Slightly.

O'Neal frowned, as if confused. "Well, it couldn't have been *too* long ago, now could it?" he said. "You're all just young boys. How could it have been so very long ago?" He looked around at the boys. They avoided his eyes.

"It's a mystery, is it, then?" said O'Neal. "There seem to be a lot of mysteries on this island. Boys who say they got here long ago and yet are still young boys. Another boy who can fly. Mermaids in the lagoon. And nobody here seems to be sick. Why, we ourselves came ashore just a few days ago, all sunburned and ailing, and look at us now." O'Neal gestured toward the other three sailors, their once red and sun-blistered skin now glowing with healthy tans.

"Yes, it's a mysterious island," O'Neal continued. "It's almost as if"—he looked around the circle of boys—"as if there was something *magical* here. Maybe it's in the water." He laughed as if he'd made a joke, although there was no laughter in his expression. "But that's silly, isn't it?" he said. "How could there be magic in the water?" He looked around at the boys, waiting.

"Well," said Tootles, "there's . . . OW!"

Peter, lightning fast, had swooped down from the tree and landed with a hard bump against Tootles, knocking him sideways. Peter ignored him, his eyes on O'Neal.

"There's nothing in the water," he said. He looked around at the Lost Boys. "We're going swimming now."

"But I want to hear some more sailing stories!" said Slightly. The other boys, comfortable in the shade, grumbled as well.

"I said, *we're going swimming now*," said Peter, glaring at them.

Reluctantly they rose and, still grumbling, started down the path toward the lagoon. Peter, herding them, was the last in line. As they disappeared into the jungle, he glanced back at the sailors. They had not moved. O'Neal was watching Peter. His face was impassive, but there was something in his dark, glittering eyes—something that amused him, and terrified Peter.

Peter looked quickly away, knowing that O'Neal had seen his fear. He hurried forward, into the safe embrace of the jungle.

———

Late that afternoon, Peter found his way to the Mollusk village and went straight to the hut of Fighting Prawn. He found the chief asleep in a hammock and gently shook him. A single eye popped open, giving Peter an inquisitive look.

"Could I have a minute, sir?"

Without a word, Fighting Prawn pulled himself out of the hammock. A moment later he and Peter were standing in the shade of a palm tree on the beach, a warm breeze on their faces.

Peter told Fighting Prawn about Cheeky O'Neal's conversation with the Lost Boys. When he got to O'Neal's question about the island water, Fighting Prawn's face grew somber. "This is bad," he said. "I *knew* there was something about those men."

"He might be guessing," said Peter. "How could he know about the water?"

"I don't know how much he knows," said Fighting Prawn. "But if he finds out . . ." The chief sighed. "I was afraid this would happen some day. We've been blessed on this island, Peter. We were given a gift. Now it seems there's a price to pay. If these men discover our secret, they will never leave us alone." He looked at Peter. "I must get them off the island. Soon, before they learn anything more."

Peter felt relieved that Fighting Prawn wanted only to make the sailors leave. There was a time when the Mollusk chief would not have hesitated to kill the intruders.

"But how will you get them off?" Peter asked.

Fighting Prawn stared out to sea. "I had planned to wait for a ship to pass, and put them on it. But so few ships come near this island . . . it could take months, or even years. We need a ship *now*."

Peter thought for a moment, then said, "There's the ship in the pirate lagoon." He was referring to the ship that had flown from Rundoon to the island years earlier, carrying Peter, Starcatchers, the Lost Boys, Captain Hook—and a hull filled with starstuff, which had kept it aloft.

The chief frowned. "That ship's been sitting on the bottom for decades," he said.

Peter nodded. "Yes, but aside from the hole in the hull where the starstuff fell out, it seems to be in decent condition. What if it could be raised and repaired? O'Neal and his men are quite handy; they repaired our hut quick as you please. With the help of your men, they might be able to do the same to the pirate ship."

Fighting Prawn pondered that, then said, "How do you think Hook would feel about your idea?"

"I should think he'd be happy," said Peter. "He's always saying he wants to get off the island. With the ship repaired, he could sail away, a captain again."

"So," said Fighting Prawn. "We would rid ourselves of our troublesome guests, *and* our unhappy neighbors."

"Yes," said Peter.

Fighting Prawn nodded, a smile spreading slowly over his sun-baked face.

CHAPTER 8

Wendy Learns the Secret

"Not another word of this nonsense! I forbid it!"

George Darling rose from his chair and stood over Molly, his face a deep, angry scarlet. Molly studied her husband, wondering how this could be the same George Darling who once took command of a flying ship in a raging battle over a distant desert. He looked much the same—a bit heavier, with a touch of gray in his hair, but still quite handsome. Yet he sounded so stuffy, so . . . *old*.

"You *forbid* it?" she said.

"Yes, I . . ." George hesitated, seeing the defiance in Molly's glittering green eyes. "Well, I . . . I mean . . . Dash it, Mary! How could you go to the *police*? Do you have any idea what would happen if word of your little escapade got to my firm?"

"*Escapade?*" hissed Molly. "It was not an *escapade* when the constable tried to grab me."

"You have no reason to believe he meant you harm," said George. "He was probably just trying to assist you."

"He was not trying to 'assist' me."

"How do you know that?"

"I just *know*."

"You just *know*," mocked George. "The same way you just *know* that James has discovered that the prince—the *prince*—has fallen under the spell of a . . . ghost."

Molly glanced toward the stairs, concerned that the children would overhear. "It's not a ghost," she said. "You know very well what it is."

"I know no such thing," he replied. "I know only that James felt a chill in Buckingham Palace, and now my wife is jeopardizing my career by traipsing off to Scotland Yard and—"

"Your *career?*" interrupted Molly. "Is your *career* more important than James's safety? Than mine? Is it more important than the future of England?"

"There is no evidence that either England, or James, is in any danger," George said, using his barrister-arguing-before-a-judge voice, which Molly found quite irritating. "You said yourself that James's superior explained how he'd gone on holiday. We have no reason to disbelieve him. Sounds to me as though James was under quite a bit of strain, imagining this preposterous tale about von Schatten. A bit of holiday makes perfect sense."

"But what if it's *not* preposterous?" said Molly. "What if it's true?"

George leaned over, gripped Molly's arms, looked into her eyes, his face somber. "Listen to me, Mary," he said. "If it becomes known that you're making these allegations about the king, it could do far more than ruin my career. It could get you charged with treason. Do you understand that? *Treason.*"

"Let go of me," Molly said softly.

George released his grip. "All right," he said. "But there shall be no more talk of this. *Any* of this. I forbid it. I have worked too hard. I won't have you jeopardizing our family name, everything I've achieved, all because of James's deluded ravings about evil forces taking over England."

Molly stared at him for a few seconds, then said, "You once fought against those same forces, George. James fought at your side. Peter . . . Can you forget so easily?"

George shook his head. "It was long ago," he said. "And far away."

Without another word, he turned and walked from the room.

Molly watched him go, feeling more alone than she could remember ever having felt.

It took her a day to decide what to do.

First, she would go see her father, Leonard Aster, the head of the Starcatchers. Given his poor health, Molly hated to involve him, but she felt she had no choice.

Her second decision was more difficult. She wanted somebody to know what she was planning to do and, in case something happened to her, why she felt it so important that something be done. It was now obvious that she couldn't tell George. He'd only try to stop her.

That left but one person. . . .

"Wendy," she said, entering her daughter's room.

"Yes, Mother?" said Wendy, looking up from the book she was reading in bed.

Molly closed the door. She took a deep breath. "Do you remember the other day," she said, "when you asked me who the Starcatchers were?"

"Yes," said Wendy, putting down the book, her attention now fully focused on her mother.

Molly sat on the bed and said, "I felt I couldn't tell you then." She stroked her daughter's cheek. "But how quickly things can change. Besides, you're about the same age as I was at the time. You're a thoughtful, intelligent girl. You're more ready than I was."

"Ready for what?" Wendy sat up, eager to hear more. "What *is* it, Mother?"

Molly took a deep breath. "I've so much to tell you," she said.

She spoke for more than an hour. Wendy occasionally asked questions, but mostly listened, fascinated, sometimes barely able to believe what she was hearing.

Molly began by telling Wendy about starstuff, the mysterious substance that, for eons, fell to earth at unpredictable times and places, bringing with it fantastic power; about the Starcatchers, a secret group to which Wendy's ancestors belonged, formed to find the starstuff and return it to the heavens before it could fall into the hands of the evil Others; and about the mighty, but hidden, struggle between these two groups that had gone on for centuries.

Wendy's fascination turned to astonishment when Molly got to her own part in the story—how, when she was about Wendy's age, she found herself aboard a ship carrying a trunk full of starstuff; how she fought to defend it from the Others and a band of pirates, her only allies being some orphan boys and some porpoises.

"Porpoises?" interrupted Wendy.

"Yes," said Molly. "Their leader is named Ammm."

"So," Wendy said slowly, "when I was a girl, and you taught

me to speak Porpoise, and I thought it was just a game . . ."

"It was no game," said Molly. "That's how they speak."

"So I can speak to a porpoise?"

Molly smiled. "You can."

"Excellent!" said Wendy. "Do go on."

Molly told how she and the orphans had been shipwrecked on an isolated island, where they had defeated their foes with the help of the native Mollusk tribe, and where the orphans had decided to stay. She told how the Starcatchers had brought the starstuff back to England, only to find that they had been followed by a hideous, inhuman shadow-stealing creature called Ombra. The smile left Wendy's face as her mother described the terrifying night that Ombra came to her house, looking for her—and how Peter, one of the orphan boys, had flown through her window to rescue her.

"He *flew?*" said Wendy.

"Yes," said Molly, "Peter can fly. He was exposed to enough starstuff to kill him, but instead, it . . . *changed* him."

Wendy noticed that when her mother spoke of Peter, her voice softened and her face took on an odd expression. Wendy wanted to ask more about Peter, but her mother had resumed the story. She told how the Starcatchers defeated Ombra at Stonehenge, with the help of Peter and Wendy's father.

"Father?" said Wendy. "*Father* was there?"

"Yes," said Molly, with an odd expression. Again Wendy

had more questions, but her mother had moved on, speaking quickly now, telling about a strange country called Rundoon, where the Starcatchers had fought a fantastic battle against Ombra and the forces of an evil king called Zarboff the Third—a battle involving a monstrous snake, a flying ship, and a starstuff-filled rocket that had smashed into a desert tomb and destroyed Ombra and his allies forever.

"Or so we thought," she said.

"What do you mean?" asked Wendy.

"James—Mr. Smith, from Scotland Yard—believes Ombra must have survived, and that he has come back, and somehow taken control of . . ."

"Baron von Schatten," said Wendy.

"How do you know that?" said Molly, surprised.

"I heard Mr. Smith tell you the other night," said Wendy. "When I listened on the stairs."

"Well," said Molly. "You shouldn't have been listening."

"I'm sorry," said Wendy, not sounding sorry at all. "But how does James—Mr. Smith—know about Ombra?"

"He was one of the orphan boys," said Molly. "He decided, in the end, not to remain on the island, so he returned to England with my father and me, along with three of the others—Prentiss, Thomas, and Ted. Peter remained on the island."

Again, Wendy saw the odd expression on her mother's face when she spoke of Peter.

"In any event," continued Molly, "I hadn't seen James, or the others, in years, until he visited the other night to tell me about von Schatten. And now he's gone missing."

"What do you mean, missing?"

"He said he'd return the next night, but he didn't. And I'm quite worried about him. I went to Scotland Yard to inquire about his whereabouts, and I'm quite sure his superior lied to me. And when I . . ." Molly stopped, deciding she would not tell Wendy about the bobby in the Underground. "In any event," she continued, "I'm worried that James is in danger. And if his suspicions about von Schatten are correct, then . . . we're *all* in danger. So I've decided to go see my father. He's quite ill, but he knows so much. I . . . I . . ." Molly looked down. "I just hope he'll know what to do."

"But why can't Father help?"

Molly's head jerked up. "You must not speak to your father about this."

"But why not?"

"He thinks it's . . . well . . . nonsense."

"But you said he was *there*, when you fought them."

"Yes," said Molly softly. "He was there. But he's changed since then." Seeing the look in Wendy's eyes, she quickly added, "Your father is a good man, Wendy. A very good man. And he may be right about James. I hope he *is* right; I hope this really is all nonsense. But just in case it's not, I must go see your grandfather. I'll go tomorrow, when your father is at work. And you will say *nothing*, to *anyone*, about what I have told you. Promise me."

"I promise," said Wendy.

"And you must keep that promise," said Molly. "You're a Starcatcher, Wendy. These are matters of the utmost importance. We guard these secrets with . . ." Molly stopped, not wanting to complete the sentence.

Wendy nodded gravely.

"Good," said Molly. "Now, it's past your bedtime."

"But I've so much to ask you!" said Wendy.

"Not tonight," said Molly, firmly. "Good night." She leaned over to kiss Wendy's forehead, then rose from the bed and started for the door.

"Mother," said Wendy.

Molly stopped. "Yes?" she said.

"If I can't tell anyone, if I can't *do* anything, then why did you tell me any of this?" said Wendy.

Molly hesitated, then said, "I just . . . I *needed* you to know."

Wendy waited, but her mother said nothing more. Finally Wendy said, "But why . . ."

"Wendy," said Molly, "I said, not tonight. You must trust me."

"All right," sighed Wendy.

"Now, go to sleep," said Molly, closing the door.

But Wendy couldn't sleep, not with all these astonishing things to think about. She had so many questions, but one in particular kept popping up in her mind: Why *had* her mother told her about the Starcatchers, after all this time? The more Wendy thought about it, the more she became convinced that her mother was afraid, and had told Wendy of her intention to visit her grandfather so that someone would know, in case . . .

In case what?

Wide awake now, Wendy rose from her bed and began pacing her room, her mind swirling with thoughts. After a few minutes, tired of pacing, she went to her window, which overlooked the street. She parted the lace curtains and peered out. The night was, as usual, foggy, but by the dim glow of the streetlight below Wendy could just make out a lone figure on the sidewalk. Pressing her face to the glass, she saw the distinctive round-helmeted silhouette of a London constable. She couldn't make out his features, but he was facing Wendy's house. To Wendy, it seemed almost as though he were looking straight at her.

After a long moment the bobby turned and began walking, and was quickly lost to the night fog. Wendy returned to her bed and lay down, wanting to sleep, but was prevented from doing so by her mother's warning, echoing over and over in her mind:

. . . *we're* all *in danger.*

CHAPTER 9

THE BISHOP'S MITER

Aachen, Germany

THE FOUR HOODED FIGURES made their way around the exterior of the Aachen Cathedral. It was more than a thousand years old, and had been added to and remodeled so many times that the group had trouble finding the main doors among the confusion of stone facades.

Finally they rounded a corner and saw an open plaza leading to the cathedral's grand entrance. The sound of a boys' choir spilled out into the plaza, where scattered groups of men and women had gathered to listen.

The robed figures had started across the plaza when the Skeleton, in front, raised his hand. The other three—Scarlet Johns and the two large men—stopped immediately. The Skeleton nodded toward two uniformed men—police or military—standing beneath a large tree near the entrance.

The four waited. It was late in the day, nearly six o'clock. The choir, having finished its rehearsal, went silent; the unearthly beauty of the boys' voices was replaced by the more distant sounds of motor cars and the clopping of horse hooves. Several dozen of the listeners, apparently parents, started toward the cathedral's entrance to collect their children.

"Now," the Skeleton rasped.

He and the three others moved forward quickly, joining the mass of parents. They passed the uniformed men and entered the cathedral. It was an awe-inspiring space, the ceiling sixty feet over their heads, an amber light flooding in through a row of high windows. Every sound echoed, so the footsteps and voices of the parents and children merged into a thunderous roar.

Unnoticed by the throng, the four hooded figures moved up the east aisle, using the wide columns to screen themselves. Scarlet was now leading the way. She led them to an odd, freestanding set of stone steps leading to a massive stone chair.

"The throne of Charlemagne," she whispered.

The Skeleton pulled back his hood a bit and studied the throne with his solitary yellow eye. "We will see if the curator told the truth," he rasped.

Scarlet nodded, suppressing a shudder as she remembered what the Skeleton had done to the curator to make him talk.

"Which way?" said the Skeleton.

"Follow me," said Scarlet. She led the group to an unmarked door. "Here."

The Skeleton raised his scarred stump of a hand and, without knocking, opened the door. He went inside, the others following. They found themselves in a small windowless room, dimly lit by an oil lamp. The only furniture was a simple desk, behind which sat an elderly priest in a black robe. He looked up, his face reflecting mild annoyance at the intrusion but no fear or shock, even at the sight of the Skeleton's disfigured face.

"Good day," the priest said calmly, in German.

The Skeleton ignored the pleasantry. "Where is it?" he said, also in German.

"What is it you seek?" said the priest.

The Skeleton moved close, leaning over the desk so the priest could smell the foul breath escaping from the lipless hole of his mouth.

"You know what we seek," he said.

"I do not," said the priest.

"We shall see," rasped the Skeleton. He moved around the desk so that he was standing behind the priest. As he did, Scarlet moved in front of the desk.

"Long ago," she said, "Charlemagne, uniter of Europe, faced death in the Palatine Chapel. He was saved by a miracle."

"A myth," said the priest. "A fairy tale." Behind him, the Skeleton moved closer. The priest felt his presence but did not turn, keeping his eyes on Scarlet.

"It is no myth," she said. "There was a miracle, and a part of that miracle was never found. We have reason to believe it is still here. We seek to recover it, and to make it part of the whole again."

"I know the story," said the priest. "But you must believe me. It is only a story."

The Skeleton put the claw that was his right hand on the priest's neck. The priest flinched.

"I don't believe you," rasped the Skeleton.

"It will be much easier for you if you tell us," Scarlet said softly.

"I can't tell you what I don't know," said the priest.

The Skeleton's claw-hand moved, ever so slightly. The priest screamed as his body was racked with searing pain, starting at his neck but suddenly everywhere at once. It lasted for several eternal seconds. Then the Skeleton's hand lifted, and the priest slumped forward, gasping. Slowly, he raised his head. When he spoke, his eyes were on Scarlet, but his words were directed to the Skeleton.

"I will tell you nothing," he gasped.

The Skeleton's hand went to the priest's neck again. The priest closed his eyes. His lips began to move. He spoke in Latin, praying.

The Skeleton began to move his hand. Then, suddenly, he lifted it.

"We are wasting time," he said. "Pain will not work on this one. He is strong."

"The strength is not mine," the priest said softly. "It is the strength of my faith."

"Yes," said the Skeleton, thoughtfully. "Your church is more important to you than your life." He said to Scarlet, "We will take him to the chapel. See that the way is clear."

Scarlet left, returning a few minutes later. "It's empty," she said.

"Bring him," said the Skeleton, following Scarlet out the door. The two men took the priest's arms and half carried him out the door. Scarlet let them into the cathedral's central nave, and from there through a series of passages into the Palatine Chapel, its stained-glass windows lit by the fading evening sun. The only other illumination came from a bank of candles.

The two men shoved the priest forward. He stumbled to his knees on the chapel floor. The Skeleton stood over him. "We know that you would sacrifice your life to protect the secret," he said. "The question is, would you sacrifice your church?"

The Skeleton walked over and plucked one of the candles. He returned to the priest, wax droplets spattering the stone floor. He looked up at the ceiling.

"How well do you think those cross ties and braces would burn?" he asked. "And if they did, how long do you think the walls would last?"

The priest only shook his head.

"Coben," rasped the Skeleton.

One of the two large men, the more wiry of the two, stepped forward quickly. The Skeleton handed him the candle. Coben took it and disappeared through an arch, his footfalls echoing.

"Please," said the priest, softly. "This chapel has stood for more than a thousand years."

"'To everything there is a season,'" the Skeleton said. "Perhaps the chapel has outlived its purpose."

Coben reappeared at the second level of the chapel. He had shed his robe. Placing the burning candle between his teeth, he jumped for the chapel's central chandelier, a magnificent ring of gleaming, golden metal fifteen feet across. He caught it, barely, and managed to hang on as the chandelier swung on its chain. Somehow he also managed to keep the candle burning.

The priest gasped as the man, with amazing agility for his size, began climbing the chain.

"Please," the priest said. "It is a house of God."

"It is a means to an end," rasped the Skeleton.

The priest watched, horrified, as Coben reached the timbers supporting the chains. He looked down, holding

the candle near the wood, waiting for orders.

"You can't," the priest whispered.

"I will," said the Skeleton, "unless you tell me where the tip is."

He gestured to Coben, who moved the candle so that the flame licked the wood.

"No!" shouted the priest. With a groan, he bowed his head and whispered, "I'll tell you."

The Skeleton, gesturing at Coben to pull the candle away, leaned close to the kneeling priest. The priest looked up. "The bishop's miter," he whispered, crossing himself.

"Riddles?" the Skeleton said. "You dare to speak in riddles?" He looked up at Coben. "Burn it!"

"No!" said the priest. "It is not a riddle." Struggling to his feet, he pointed toward the stained glass. "The bishop's miter," he repeated.

"What is he talking about?" rasped the Skeleton.

Scarlet walked quickly toward the window indicated by the priest. The sun's light was almost gone, but she could still clearly see the scene depicted in the window—a bishop wearing his vestments, including a miter, the tall pointed hat.

"Look at the miter," she said, as the Skeleton came alongside her. "It's opaque. It's not glass."

"Not glass," the Skeleton rasped. "It looks like . . ."

"Metal," said Scarlet. "It's metal."

And it was shaped like the tip of a sword.

CHAPTER 10

*T*HE *C*AB

*M*OLLY STOOD ON HER FRONT PORCH, umbrella in hand, frowning at the driving rain. She had planned to walk to her father's house in Kensington Park Gardens, but that was now out of the question: her umbrella would be useless in the gusting wind. There was a District Line station not far from her father's house, but after her disturbing experience, she had no intention of taking the Underground.

That left her with one choice: a hackney carriage. Molly sighed. It wouldn't be easy to find a cab in this weather, when everyone else wanted one, too. She stepped to the edge of the porch and, squinting against the rain, peered down the street. To her surprise, she saw a carriage coming her way. She started to raise her arm, but the driver, his face obscured by a heavy scarf, was already guiding his horse to the curb in front of her.

Molly quickly descended the porch steps and gave the address to the driver, who nodded wordlessly. She climbed into the carriage. The driver twitched the reins, and as the soggy, steaming horse began trudging forward, Molly turned to look back through the cab's rear window at her house. She caught sight of a face pressed against a third-floor window, and realized it was Wendy, watching from her bedroom. Molly waved, but couldn't tell if Wendy saw her. As the house receded behind her, Molly turned away, her mind on the task ahead.

Wendy thought she saw her mother wave, but she wasn't sure. Just in case, she waved back. Her hand then returned to fondling the locket her mother had given her that morning. It was a simple golden orb that her mother had worn as long as Wendy could remember.

"But why?" Wendy had asked, when her mother had put it around her neck. It felt oddly warm against her skin.

"I just want you to have it," said her mother. "In case you ever need it."

"How do you mean, *need* it?" said Wendy.

"Just keep it with you," said her mother.

Wendy held it now, feeling its warmth, as she watched the cab carry her mother away. A few houses down, the cab passed a policeman, who appeared to be watching it intently. He nodded at the driver, who nodded back. Wendy wondered, as the cab disappeared into the rain, if the two men knew each other.

CHAPTER 11

DARKNESS

WENDY LOOKED OUT HER WINDOW many times that gloomy day, each time hoping to see her mother returning, each time disappointed.

Over and over Wendy told herself that nothing was wrong, that her mother had simply been delayed. But her worry deepened with each passing hour.

What if something happened to her?

As night fell, Wendy finally saw someone approaching the house—but it was her father. As he trudged up the front steps, Wendy turned away from the window, her knees weakening with dread.

What shall I tell him?

She listened, cowering in her room, as he entered the house and went from room to room downstairs, calling his wife's name. He came up the stairs, still calling, his tone increasingly irritated. Finally, getting no response, he knocked on Wendy's door.

"Come in," she said. The door opened. Wendy was sitting on her bed.

"Where is your mother?" said George Darling.

"I don't know," said Wendy.

"What do you mean, you don't know?"

"She went . . . out," said Wendy.

"At this hour?"

"No. This morning."

"This *morning?*" George's tone had changed from irritation to concern. "Did she say where she was going?"

Wendy looked down, saying nothing. Her father strode across the room and stood over her.

"Where did your mother go?" he said sharply.

Wendy put her face in her hands. She didn't want to betray her mother's confidence. But she was scared. Her father was leaning over her now.

"Where did she go?"

Wendy looked up, her face red and tear-streaked. "She went to see Grandfather Aster."

George straightened, his expression shocked, then guarded. "I see," he said.

He doesn't know that I know about the Starcatchers, thought Wendy.

"How did she go there?" said George.

"She took a taxicab," said Wendy.

Her father turned, headed for the door. "Look after your brothers," he called over his shoulder. Moments later, Wendy heard his footsteps pounding down the stairs.

Two heads appeared in the doorway, one below the other.

"Where's Father going?" said John.

"Where's Mum?" said Michael.

"What's for supper?" said John.

"I don't know," said Wendy.

———◆———

Hours later, after she had fed her brothers and—finally—put them to bed, Wendy crept down to the staircase landing and listened to her father talking with two Scotland Yard detectives. They were polite but had nothing positive to report. They had checked with the staff at the Aster house; Mrs. Darling had never arrived there. They had interviewed many hackney drivers, looking for one fitting the description provided by Wendy, but they had found nothing. None of the neighbors or nearby shopkeepers recalled having seen Mrs. Darling on the street. Of course, the detectives noted, people didn't spend much time outside in this weather.

The detectives asked George, several times, why his wife had gone to see her father. Each time he replied that he didn't know. Wendy didn't believe him, and it was obvious that the detectives didn't either. Their questions were making her father testy.

"What difference does it make *why* she went to see her father?" he said. "The point is, she's missing. You should be out looking for her now."

"We are, Mr. Darling," said a detective. "We have men looking right now. But the more information we have, the better we can . . ."

"I've given you all the information I have," snapped George.

A brief, uncomfortable silence followed. Then one of the detectives said, "We'll be going now, Mr. Darling. We'll let you know as soon as we hear anything."

"I would appreciate it," said George, coldly.

The detectives walked to the front door. From her place on the dark landing, Wendy saw them go past; they were accompanied by a bobby. With a shock, Wendy realized it was the same one she'd seen that morning, nodding at the hackney driver who had stopped for her mother. She had forgotten him until now.

Wendy was about to call out, but she caught herself. If the bobby had seen the taxi, wouldn't he have said something to the detectives? Yet apparently he had not.

Why not?

Wendy waited silently as the bobby and the detectives left, and her father closed the door. Then she descended the stairs.

"Wendy," said her father. "Why aren't you . . ."

"I know why Mother went to see Grandfather," she said. "And so do you."

"What are you talking about?" he said.

"The Starcatchers," she said. "I know about them. And about what Mr. Smith found out. Mother told me all of it."

Her father was standing right in front of her now, his face red with fury.

"That is *nonsense*," he said. "Your mother should never have told you that."

"But what if it's why she's gone missing?" said Wendy.

"It's got nothing to do with it!" he shouted.

Wendy flinched, but did not back away. "How can you be sure?" she said.

He didn't answer, and Wendy saw in his eyes that he *wasn't* sure. He took a breath and let it out, calming himself.

"Wendy," he said, "this is a very sensitive matter. If I tell the police some story about some secret group chasing a magical powder, or an inhuman creature inhabiting the body of a royal adviser, I'd be locked up as a lunatic, or a traitor, or both. You must understand that, Wendy. You must say *nothing* about this."

"But Mother . . ."

"I am as worried about your mother as you are," he said. "And I will do everything in my power to find her. And right now I believe our wisest course is to let the police do what they are trained to do. They're very good, Wendy. They will find your mother."

"Maybe they already have," Wendy said softly.

"What do you mean?"

"The bobby who was just here," said Wendy. "I saw him this morning." Her father listened intently as she described what she'd seen through her window.

"Are you certain it was the same bobby?" her father asked.

"Yes," said Wendy.

"Perhaps he didn't see your mother get into the taxi," said George, sounding to Wendy as though he were trying to convince himself. He went to a window and looked out. There was nothing to see except the utter blackness of a foggy London night. He stared into it for a few moments, then turned to Wendy.

"Tomorrow morning," he said, "you and your brothers will go visit your uncle Neville in Cambridgeshire."

"But I don't want to! Not if Mother . . ."

"Wendy, *listen* to me." Her father's tone left no room for argument. "If you want to help, you will go to Cambridgeshire, and you will look after your brothers. I can't be worrying about your safety when I'm trying to find your mother."

"But—"

"No. You're going, and you'll stay with Uncle Neville until it's safe for you to return."

"How long will that be?"

Her father looked out the window again, at the darkness.

"I wish I knew," he said.

CHAPTER 12

THE GLOW

IT WAS LONG PAST MIDNIGHT, but Cheeky O'Neal was wide awake, listening. Fighting Prawn, keeping a close watch on his unwanted guests, had posted two warriors outside the hut where O'Neal and his men slept. The warriors had been talking for hours, but in the past few minutes their murmuring voices had stopped.

Silently, O'Neal rose from his sleeping mat. Around him, snoring loudly, lay DeWulf, Kelly, and McPherson. Picking his way carefully past them, O'Neal went to the doorway and looked out. As he'd hoped, both sentries were slumped against the hut's log supports, dozing.

O'Neal left the hut, his huge bare feet silent on the dirt. He quickly crossed the village compound and entered the jungle, finding the path he had scouted earlier. He knew exactly where he wanted to go; he'd been carefully studying the island's geography, and particularly its water supply.

The jungle echoed with the hoots, twitters, screeches, and screams of unseen creatures. In places it was pitch-black, but most of the time just enough moonlight filtered through the thick tree canopy to enable O'Neal to follow the path. In a few hundred yards it led him to the mountainside, where it began to climb steeply. Every few steps O'Neal grunted in pain as his bare feet found sharp lava. To his left he heard water rushing, and after another fifty yards the path turned that way.

He came to the stream and turned right, following it up the mountainside, which was steeper now, sometimes forcing him to use his hands to climb. Finally he saw, in the moonlight ahead, what he was looking for: a cave mouth, nearly as tall as he was, the source of the stream. He stepped into the rushing water and waded to the cave, then inside. The water seemed to sparkle at his feet, like phosphorescence in the ocean, only different. In a few feet he was in pitch blackness, his feet feeling their way forward in the strong, cold current, his hands reaching out for rock walls he could not see. Deeper and deeper he went, his feet now, strangely, no longer sore.

The stream swung to the right. O'Neal felt his way around the bend. Suddenly the darkness gave way to a luminescence; the air was no longer ink black. O'Neal shuffled forward twenty feet. Another bend. He rounded it.

And then, in the distance, he saw it.

A constant, golden glow. Like sunshine. But warmer than sunshine. And coming from somewhere—it seemed from the air itself—he heard . . . *music*.

O'Neal smiled.

CHAPTER 13

$\mathcal{U}$NCLE $\mathcal{N}$EVILLE

ORDINARILY, WENDY WOULD HAVE BEEN thrilled to visit her uncle Neville, a magistrate with a large estate in Cambridgeshire. He was often described as an eccentric, but to Wendy and her two brothers he was the only grown-up they knew who acted more like them than like a grown-up.

Uncle Neville, whose full name was Neville Plonk-Fenster, considered himself an amateur scientist. He was always conducting experiments, some of which blew up buildings. Fortunately he was rich and had plenty of buildings.

He also had a passion for aviation, and had built many flying machines, although so far none had actually flown. His latest effort was an ornithopter, which was a strange contraption consisting of a wooden frame some ten feet tall, on which was mounted a pair of huge wings made from silk and feathers.

The pilot stood on a small platform behind the wings, which were connected to a small gasoline-powered engine. The engine caused the wings to flap up and down rapidly; this, in turn, was supposed to cause the ornithopter to take gracefully to the air. So far, all it had done was fall over and flop around like a fish out of water. But Uncle Neville was sure that, with a few minor adjustments, it would soar like an eagle. Or at least a pigeon.

John and Michael worshipped Uncle Neville, and were thrilled when their father told them they would be going to visit him for a while. Of course, John and Michael didn't know that their mother had disappeared; they'd been told she was visiting an ailing great-aunt in Scotland. Wendy knew better, and despite the many diverting activities to be found at Uncle Neville's estate, she couldn't stop worrying about her mother.

Her father had promised to let her know as soon as he heard anything, good or bad. But the hours had stretched into days, and there was still no word from London. Wendy could picture her father, frantic, making every effort to find his wife, but she also knew he would not mention anything to anyone about the Starcatchers. She was convinced mother's disappearance had to do with her past; with her old friend James, who had visited their home; with the Starcatchers. And the one person who knew the most about the Starcatchers was the man her mother had been going to see that miserable day: her father, Wendy's grandfather, Leonard Aster.

After a near-sleepless night, Wendy could stand it no longer. She came down to breakfast, which Uncle Neville had already started. He was sitting at the head of the table, with John and Michael on either side. In the middle of the table was an odd-looking contraption, with many gears and pulleys. It was connected to a wire, which ran to the wall.

"What on earth is *that?*" said Wendy.

"That," said Uncle Neville, "is an automatic toast-butterer."

"It runs on 'tricity," said Michael.

"*Elec*tricity, you ninny," said John.

"That's what I said," said Michael.

"But," said Wendy, "why do you need a machine to—"

"It saves labor!" said Uncle Neville. "Do you have any idea how many hours the British public spends every year buttering its toast?"

"No," said Wendy. "How many?"

"I have no idea," said Uncle Neville. "But I suspect it's a lot."

"Ah," said Wendy. "Well, I was wondering if I could ask you something."

"Yes, of course," said Uncle Neville. "Would you like to see how it works?"

"I, ah, certainly," said Wendy. "What I wondered was—"

"The butter goes here," said Uncle Neville, dumping the butter dish into a hole at the top of the machine. "And then the toast goes here." He put a slice of bread into a slot on the side. "Then you turn it on with this switch." He flipped a switch. The machine started to clank and whirr, its gears and pulleys turning.

"I was wondering if I could take the train to London today," said Wendy.

"What's that?" said Uncle Neville, eyeing the machine, which was clanking louder now and starting to smoke.

"I was wondering if I could take the train to London today, to . . . to visit someone. I'll be back this evening, and I promise to—"

BANG

The automatic toast-butterer belched a smoke cloud and ejected a piece of toast burned to the consistency of charcoal, which flew straight up with such force that it hit the ceiling and shattered into a small black cloud of particles, which floated gently down onto the table. The machine then emitted a geyser of melted butter, which spurted up, then fell back, causing the machine to emit a shower of sparks, and then, with a loud POP, to stop running altogether. It now sat silent, a smoking ruin.

"Brilliant!" said John.

"Is the 'tricity gone?" said Michael.

"It needs a bit of adjustment," said Uncle Neville.

"So," said Wendy, "is it all right, Uncle Neville?"

"What?" said Uncle Neville.

"What I asked. Is it all right?" said Wendy, deciding not to mention the train trip again.

"I suppose so," said Uncle Neville, looking at his machine. "Why not?"

"Thank you," said Wendy.

She hurried out of the room before Uncle Neville thought to ask exactly what he'd given her his permission to do.

CHAPTER 14

*C*HE *P*RIZE

*C*HE SKELETON AND SCARLET JOHNS watched intently as Coben and the other man, whose name was Mauch, worked by the flickering light of the chapel candles. Mauch and Coben had just returned from a foray in to the city of Aachen, where they had broken into several closed stores to gather the materials they needed.

"How much time?" rasped the Skeleton, his lone eye glowing yellow in the candlelight.

"Less than an hour," said Scarlet. "The altar boys replace and relight the candles at nine o'clock."

"Faster!" hissed the Skeleton at Mauch and Coben, the word distorted by his lipless mouth.

"It will be working soon," came the reply. Mauch was holding a small tin pan over a bundle of lighted candles. The pan held a lump of wax, which shrank as it melted. "A few more minutes is all."

"Coben?" said the Skeleton

"Almost there." Coben was building a scaffold from tables, chairs, two large wooden crosses, and a long bench that he'd confiscated from the choir. The teetering makeshift structure rose high off the chapel's marble floor, parallel to and alongside the central stained-glass window.

Scarlet left the chapel to check on the priest. They had left him tied up and gagged inside a large, cedar-lined closet used to store the vestments worn by the clergy during services. They had propped a chair against the closet door to prevent the priest from opening it if he escaped his bonds. Scarlet removed the chair and opened the door.

The priest, propped against the wall, squinted at the light. He seemed to be all right, although he was pale and trembling. Scarlet knelt next to him.

"You have two options," she said, her voice a soothing whisper.

He nodded.

"The first is that my colleague delivers you into heaven perhaps sooner than you would wish."

The priest's eyes widened slightly.

"That's right," said Scarlet. "It would not be a pleasant journey for you, though my colleague would much enjoy it. The second option, and the one I strongly recommend, is that you remain tied up here, that you make no attempt to be found until morning. When you are found, you must make no mention of what happened here tonight. We are not alone, Father. We have eyes and ears here. If you betray us, we will know, and we can be back here from Mun . . . from our headquarters in a matter of hours. And if we do come back, we will destroy you *and* your precious chapel."

The priest shook his head.

"I will do everything in my power," she continued, "to grant you the second option. But first I need your word, as a priest, that you understand and agree to my conditions. Nod your head if you do."

The priest nodded.

"A wise choice," said Scarlet. "We have an agreement. I will trust you, and you will trust me to make good on my promises. *All* of my promises."

She closed the door and propped the chair against it. She returned to the chapel, where the Skeleton was still watching Mauch and Coben. He turned to Scarlet and said, "The priest?"

"He will not be a problem."

"A pity," said the Skeleton. "I would have enjoyed breaking him."

"It won't be necessary," said Scarlet. "We'll be miles from here before he's found. And if he does send anyone looking for us, it will be in the wrong direction. I slipped up and mentioned Munich."

"Good," said the Skeleton. If his face had been willing,

he might have smiled. He returned his attention to Mauch and Coben.

Coben had finished working on his wobbly scaffold, which looked as though it would collapse at any moment. Mauch was pouring melted wax through a piece of silk, allowing the resulting paraffin to drip into the chamber of a small brass blowtorch.

When he was finished, he screwed the chamber back onto the blowtorch, then held it over two burning candles. When he was satisfied that the paraffin had vaporized, he turned the valve and held a match to the torch tip. A tongue of blue flame shot out. Mauch adjusted the valve, then quickly went to the scaffold and handed it to Coben.

"The tip?" said Coben.

Mauch reached into his pocket and pulled out a triangular piece of metal, which he handed to Coben. Mauch had made it from a pewter plate he'd found on the altar, carving the soft metal into the shape of the bishop's miter.

Coben stuck the pewter tip in a pocket and, holding the burning blowtorch carefully, climbed the rickety scaffold. The other three watched anxiously as he reached the top and trained the blue flame onto the outline of lead that held the bishop's miter in the window. For a minute and more the chapel was silent, save for the hissing of the flame.

"How much time?" asked the Skeleton.

Scarlet pulled a watch from her pocket. "Less than twenty minutes."

"Faster!" the Skeleton rasped up to Coben.

"The edges are melting," Coben called down.

As he spoke, the bishop's miter separated and sagged forward slightly from the window. Coben, using a cloth to protect his hand from the heat, carefully took hold of the piece and pulled it free. He quickly substituted the pewter piece. It wasn't a perfect fit, but he melted the lead edging to make up the gaps. From a distance, the window looked barely different from when he'd started.

Coben climbed down quickly and handed the prize to the Skeleton, who held it up in his clawlike hand.

"The tip of Curtana," he rasped. "The Sword of Charlemagne. The Sword of Mercy."

Despite the need for haste, the four stood for a few moments, examining the tip. It was made of silver-colored metal that glinted in the candlelight like steel, but to the Skeleton it felt heavier. The tip was pointed at one end; the opposite edge jagged and at an angle, as the tip had not broken from the sword evenly. It was only a few inches long, about the length of his hand.

The Skeleton tested the edge by gently touching a scarred finger nub to it. He jerked his hand back: it was bleeding.

"Seven hundred years," he said. "And still razor sharp."

Coben leaned closer, peering at the gleaming tip. "All that effort," he said, shaking his head. "All that searching, for . . . that. Nothing but a small piece of metal."

The Skeleton looked at Coben, then back at the tip.

"This small piece of metal," he rasped, "is about to change the world."

CHAPTER 15

$\mathcal{A}$LONE

"$\mathcal{W}$ENDY DARLING! What a fine surprise! Come in and let me give you a hug!"

Wendy stepped into the Aster mansion and was squeezed to breathlessness inside the ample embrace of Mrs. Bumbrake, in her late seventies but still formidable. Mrs. Bumbrake had been employed by the Asters for decades, having originally been hired as governess for Leonard and Louise Aster's only daughter, Molly.

When Molly had married and left home, Mrs. Bumbrake had remained with the Asters. Following the death of Louise, Mrs. Bumbrake had taken over the management of the household, and heaven help any staff member who failed to live up to her high standards. But for the Aster family, she was soft as pudding.

Having finally finished her hug, she stepped back and said, "I thought you were staying with your uncle in Cambridgeshire."

"I'm just in London for the day," said Wendy, hoping this vague answer would be enough. Fortunately, Mrs. Bumbrake's mind was on other things.

"Is there any word of your mother?" she said.

"I'm afraid not," said Wendy. "But Father is doing all he can, and the police . . ." Wendy trailed off, not sure how to finish that sentence.

"It's a terrible thing," said Mrs. Bumbrake, shaking her head. "Your father and I agreed not to tell Lord Aster. Weak as he is, I don't know that he could take the news."

Wendy hoped Mrs. Bumbrake was wrong about that. "I wondered if I could see him," she said.

"I suppose so," said Mrs. Bumbrake. "It would do him some good to see a pretty face! He gets so few visitors these days."

She led Wendy upstairs to the room where Leonard Aster lay in bed. Wendy gasped when she saw her grandfather—his face, once so handsome and alert, now gaunt and deathly pale, his skin like old parchment, his mouth open, his eyes closed.

"Lord Aster," said Mrs. Bumbrake softly. "You've a visitor."

The eyelids fluttered open, and Leonard's eyes fell on Wendy.

"Molly," he said.

Mrs. Bumbrake turned away, hiding her tears.

"No, Grandfather," said Wendy. "It's me, Wendy."

Leonard blinked. "Ah, so it is," he said. "You look more like your mother every day."

"Thank you," said Wendy.

"And to what do I owe this pleasure?" said Leonard. His voice quavered, but he still spoke with the authority of a man who had been a leader for most of his life.

"I . . . I just wanted to talk to you about something."

"Yes . . . I see," said Leonard, giving Wendy an odd look. He turned his head toward Mrs. Bumbrake and said, "If you will please excuse us, Mrs. Bumbrake."

"Of course," said Mrs. Bumbrake, reluctantly. With a stern look, she said to Wendy, "Now, don't you go getting him excited."

Wendy only nodded; she could make no such promise.

Mrs. Bumbrake left, and Wendy closed the door. She returned to her grandfather's bedside. The old man was watching her intently.

"Something's happened to your mother," he said.

Wendy gasped. "But how did you know that?"

Aster raised a bony finger and pointed it at her throat. "You're wearing her locket," he said. "She would not have given it to you unless something was wrong. What is it?"

"Grandfather, I'm so worried about mother. She . . . she . . ." Suddenly Wendy was sobbing, her face pressed into her hands, tears pouring through them. "I'm sorry," she said, finally.

"It's all right," he said softly. "Sit on the bed. Now take a deep breath and tell me what happened. Start at the beginning."

And so she did. She told him about James's visit to her house, and what he had told Molly about Baron von Schatten and the king. Leonard stopped her repeatedly to ask questions. He was particularly interested in the conversation James had overheard between von Schatten and Simon Revile in the king's chambers.

Wendy then told of James's disappearance, and her mother's futile trip to Scotland Yard. She told how her mother had revealed to her the existence of the Starcatchers, and the centuries of struggle against the Others for control of starstuff, culminating in the cataclysmic explosion in the Rundoon desert. Then, fighting back tears, she told of the morning her mother had given her the locket, then had left to go see Leonard, and also disappeared. She told of the hackney driver's nod to the bobby, and of the bobby's reappearance with the two Scotland Yard detectives. Leonard asked her more questions, some of which she could answer, some of which she couldn't. Finally he fell back on his pillow, his face slack with exhaustion.

"I was afraid of this," he said. "We were too confident. We let our guard down. Now they've come back. And they're after the Cache."

"The what?"

"The Cache," said Leonard. "A large quantity of starstuff, hidden here in London centuries ago."

"Hidden by whom?"

"By the original Starcatchers," said Leonard.

"But I thought . . . Mother told me that the Starcatchers returned the starstuff to the heavens," said Wendy. "So the Others wouldn't get it."

"We returned most of it," said Leonard. "But in those early days the Others were much more powerful. The Starcatchers worried constantly that if the Others managed to get their hands on a major starstuff fall, they would have an insurmountable advantage. They decided to create the Cache as a reserve, so that they could defend themselves. They put a large quantity of starstuff into a gold-lined chest, and they hid it in a vault, deep underground, here in London. The vault is protected by a very special lock, made from a metal that has been infused with starstuff. The only way to open that lock is to insert a sword—a very special sword, also infused with starstuff. It is called Curtana."

"Curtana?"

"Yes. It is also known as the Sword of Mercy," said Leonard. "In any event, it was never needed. Eventually it changed hands, more than once. It was used in an attempt on the life of Charlemagne, during which the tip was broken off—by an angel, according to legend. When it broke, it was like the key to the vault breaking. The starstuff was sealed forever. I've no doubt that tip of the sword is the 'missing piece' James overheard von Schatten talking about in the palace. It has been lost for centuries, somewhere in Belgium or Germany. I have a hard time believing . . ." His voice trailed off.

"What about the rest of the sword?" asked Wendy.

Grunting with effort, Leonard raised himself up and looked at Wendy, his gaze intense. "It is now part of the Crown Jewels," he said. "And that is what worries me."

"But why? The Crown Jewels are very well protected, aren't they?"

"Yes. Locked and guarded in the Tower of London," said Leonard. "Completely safe. But they are brought out on certain special occasions."

Wendy gasped. "The coronation," she said.

"Yes," said Leonard. "The jewels will be brought out, including Curtana. Von Schatten, or Ombra, or whatever he is, intends to get hold of the sword and reattach the missing tip. Once Curtana is whole again, it can be used to open the Cache. There have been no starstuff falls since Rundoon, Wendy. That means the Cache is one of only two large stores of starstuff left on earth. If von Schatten gets hold of it . . ."

"Where is the other one?" said Wendy.

"Mollusk Island. Deep inside. It fell into a crevice from

the flying ship. I don't know if von Schatten knows about that one; we must pray that he doesn't. But somehow he found out about the Cache."

Leonard gripped Wendy's arm. His hand was cold. His breath was coming in gasps.

"Wendy," he said. "They must not get that starstuff. They *must* be stopped."

"But how?" said Wendy.

"You must be very careful," gasped Leonard. "They must control at least some of the Metropolitan Police. They captured your mother because she was asking questions. They'll be holding her somewhere. We cannot risk endangering her further. Or you!" He paused, gasping. "You must *not* go to the police. You must go . . ." Leonard winced in pain, groaned, and fell back onto the pillow.

"Go *where*, Grandfather?"

Leonard fought for breath. "Peter," he whispered.

"The flying boy? On the island?"

"Yes."

"But where is the island? How can I get there?"

Leonard raised a shaking hand and pointed toward the locket.

"It has power," he said. "Great power."

Leonard gripped her hand, stopping her. He was trying to say something, but fast losing strength. Wendy leaned close to hear the old man's whispered words.

"He must come . . . Tell him . . ." Leonard's eyelids fluttered shut.

"Grandfather, what? Tell him *what?*"

"Confess," whispered Leonard.

He groaned again, and his hand went limp, releasing Wendy's arm. His face was ashen.

"Grandfather!" said Wendy. He did not respond. Wendy ran to the door and yanked it open. "Mrs. Bumbrake! Please come! Hurry!"

Moments later Mrs. Bumbrake bustled in. She felt Leonard's pulse, then bustled to the doorway and bellowed downstairs, ordering the maid to summon Dr. Sable, the Aster family physician. Then she glared at Wendy and said, "I told you not to get him excited."

"I'm so sorry, Mrs. Bumbrake. I didn't meant to. But . . ."

"Sorry doesn't do any good now," said Mrs. Bumbrake, turning away. She went to Leonard's bedside. Wendy, her eyes burning, went downstairs. She sat in the parlor, weeping, refusing the maid's offer of tea. Twenty minutes later, Dr. Sable arrived; he was in Leonard's room for the better part of an hour. When he came back down, Wendy was waiting at the bottom of the stairs.

"Will Grandfather be all right?" she asked.

"I don't know," Dr. Sable said softly. "His will is strong, but his heart is weak. Right now he's stable, and sleeping. He needs rest, and he needs your prayers, Wendy."

Wendy nodded. Tears streaked her face. Dr. Sable put a hand on her shoulder.

"It's not your fault, Wendy," he said. "I'm sure that seeing you did him good." He turned to Mrs. Bumbrake, at the top of the stairs. "Call me if there's any change. Otherwise I'll be back tomorrow morning."

"Yes, doctor."

Dr. Sable left. Mrs. Bumbrake descended the stairs. Without a word, she pulled Wendy into her arms and gave her a massive hug.

"I'm sorry I snapped at you," she said. "It's just that, with Mrs. Aster gone, he's all I have left." She sobbed into Wendy's shoulder.

Wendy hugged her back, hard. "I know," she whispered.

"You'd best go now," said Mrs. Bumbrake. "Catch your train back to Cambridgeshire. Your uncle will be worried."

"Right," said Wendy.

"I'll send word of your grandfather," said Mrs. Bumbrake, getting Wendy's coat. "I'm sure his condition will improve with rest."

"Thank you," said Wendy.

A minute later she was back outside. She walked north, reaching busy Bayswater Road as the late afternoon deepened into dusk. She considered taking a taxicab to the train station. She saw one clopping her way, and almost raised her hand to signal the driver. But then she glanced behind it and saw, amid some pedestrians, a bobby. He was walking toward her.

She turned around and started walking quickly in the other direction. She came to a busy intersection and turned right. She glanced behind her. She saw a taxicab turning right; was it the same one? She saw the bobby reaching the corner. He seemed to be looking around. Wendy started walking again, even faster, not looking back. She came to an alley and turned into it. Trotting now, she followed the alley to another street, where she turned left, then right into another alley. She kept this up, turning and turning, avoiding main roads, working her way toward the train station, hoping she would get there in time to catch the last train to Cambridgeshire.

And then what? The questions nagged at Wendy as she trotted along. Why had her grandfather said "confess"? And how would she find Peter? She had no idea where this mysterious island was. Even if she did find him, how could a boy—even a flying one—stop von Schatten and the Others from reaching the Cache? For that matter, where *was* the Cache? Wendy realized that her grandfather had told her only that it was in London, somewhere underground.

The more Wendy thought about her situation, the more hopeless it seemed. As far as she knew, only four people understood the danger that faced England, and for that matter the world. Two of them were James and her mother, who had both disappeared, presumably captured by the Others. The third was her grandfather, who lay on his bed with death hovering near.

That left Wendy, an eleven-year-old girl, afraid to trust the police or hardly anyone else. She thought about her mother, who at about Wendy's age had also found herself alone, trying to protect a trunk of starstuff on a ship far out at sea. She had been strong, Wendy knew. But she had also found allies.

Wendy's hand went to the locket around her neck. She would try to be strong, too. She owed that to her mother. But where would she find allies?

Who will help me?

Her hand still on the locket, she hurried on, alone in the deepening London night.

CHAPTER 16

"For Good"

$\mathcal{P}$ETER TOOK OFF FROM THE MOLLUSK VILLAGE at dusk, carrying a coconut. Tinker Bell, as always, flew at his side.

Fighting Prawn watched them soar skyward, a frown of concern on his face. "Be careful," he called.

"I'll be fine," Peter answered, leveling his body as he began to swoop across the village compound. He passed over the hut that housed the shipwrecked sailors, who were seated on rough stools outside, eating supper. Their leader, the huge Cheeky O'Neal, shouted up, "Where are you going, Peter?"

Bad men, chimed Tink, as she always did when she saw the sailors.

Peter nodded, ignoring O'Neal. The big man was always asking questions, lately more and more of them about the island's water supply. Peter didn't trust him any more than Tink and Fighting Prawn did. He'd be glad when the sailors were off the island.

116

That was the purpose of the coconut. On its shell was a message, composed by Fighting Prawn and etched in squid ink by Fighting Prawn's daughter, Shining Pearl. The message read:

CAPTAIN HOOK:
 I PROPOSE A DEAL. MY MEN WILL REPAIR YOUR SHIP AND PROVISION IT SO YOU CAN LEAVE THE ISLAND PERMANENTLY. IN RETURN YOU WILL TAKE FOUR SHIPWRECKED SAILORS WITH YOU. SEND A MAN TO OUR VILLAGE AND WE WILL ARRANGE A PARLEY.
                              FIGHTING PRAWN

The plan was for Peter to fly over the pirate fort and drop the coconut. Peter was confident he could handle this task. Over the years, he had dropped many items on Hook, among them ripe mangoes, dead fish, and vast quantities of bat poop. He generally flew these missions at suppertime, when the pirates were outside, eating and enjoying the evening cool. Peter loved watching them scatter to avoid his missiles. He never tired of tormenting them, especially Hook. Hook, for his part, never tired of thinking up revenge schemes, none of which had ever worked.

Peter, leaving the Mollusk village behind, swooped low

across the jungle canopy, his body only a few feet from the treetops. In seconds he reached the side of the steep volcanic mountain that divided the island in two. He shot upward, Tink at his shoulder, the two of them zooming up the mountain face, reaching the top in minutes. From here, looking back, Peter could see the mermaid lagoon and the smoke from the Mollusk village cooking fires curling into the reddish-gold sunset sky. Looking ahead, he could see the high log walls of the pirate fort. Beyond that, he saw the masts of the sailing ship that, kept aloft by starstuff, had flown Hook, Peter, and others back from Rundoon. It now sat on the sandy bottom of Pirate Cove, a large hole in its hull.

From somewhere on the mountainside below him, Peter heard the mournful trumpet of a conch shell. The pirates, copying the Mollusks, had learned to communicate with one another over great distances by blowing into the shells.

Peter angled himself downward and began his long, swooping descent. Because of the massive mountain's shadow, night fell quicker on this side of the island, and as Peter closed in on the pirate compound, the darkness was almost complete.

As he crossed over the top of the fort wall, well above it, Peter frowned. He saw no pirates below; in fact, he saw nothing but blackness, because there was no cooking fire and no torches or lamps—no lights of any kind. Peter wondered if the pirates had gone somewhere.

Be careful, chimed Tink.

"I *am* being careful," he answered. Flying about a hundred feet above the ground, he circled the compound, peering down: nobody. Peter frowned. He wanted to be sure Hook, or at least one of his men, saw the coconut when he dropped it. He swooped lower.

Careful.

"Quiet, Tink," said Peter, peering into the darkness below. He descended slowly, warily, his eyes darting this way and that. Forty feet above ground, now. Thirty. Twenty. Now he was almost even with the top of the fort walls, and still he saw nobody. He stopped his descent and drifted toward the fort's big log gate, slowly, slowly . . .

Get away! chimed Tink.

"NOW!" roared an unmistakable voice.

Peter lunged upward. For an instant he thought he would soar free.

Then he hit the net.

It was made of vines braided into thick ropes by skilled sailor hands. The net had been attached to two tall palms that grew just outside the fort gate. Had it been light, Peter would have seen that the tops of the palms had been pulled to the ground and attached to stakes with thick ropes. The palms thus became giant springs, to which the net had been attached. When the signal came from the lookout on the mountain—that had been the conch sound Peter had heard—the pirates had run outside and taken their positions. Then they had waited and watched as Peter flew over, his silhouette just visible against the sky. When he was low enough, Hook had given the command, and the men had yanked the loose vine ends, untying the slipknots and unleashing the palms, which snapped up and flung the huge net high into the sky over Peter. There were rocks tied around the circumference of the net; these, plus the weight of the net itself, quickly dragged Peter to the ground. He slammed into the hard dirt of the compound, the breath leaving his lungs, pain shooting through his body.

Hurry! chimed Tink. *They're coming!*

Wheezing for breath, Peter struggled, trying to stand, but the net held him fast. He felt for the dagger he wore in his belt, hoping to cut himself free of the thick braided vines. But as he pulled the dagger out, a boot came down heavily on his hand. Peter yelped in pain and dropped the dagger.

He saw a shape looming over him. A pirate trotted up with a torch, and Peter saw Captain Hook staring down at him, dark eyes gleaming in the flickering torchlight.

"Got you, boy," he said. He leaned over, his face close enough that Peter could smell his foul breath.

"And this time," hissed Hook, "I've got you for *good.*"

CHAPTER 17

A FAMILIAR FACE

MOST OF THE TIME, Molly's captors kept her in a small, damp cell. There was a barred window in the door, through which Molly could look out into a passageway lit every twenty feet by bare electric bulbs, the dim light from which provided the only illumination for the cell.

She was somewhere close to the Underground—that much she knew from the rumble and screech of trains in the distance—but where exactly, she had no idea. Her last memory had been of aboveground when the hackney driver had swerved suddenly into an alley, and three men, their faces hidden behind scarves, had grabbed her, pulled a hood over her head, and carried her roughly into a building, then down some stairs, and still more stairs, then through a maze of dank corridors, and finally into this awful cell.

Once established here, she had pleaded with her captors, then shouted at them, but to no avail. They told her nothing, refusing to speak a word. Three times a day they brought what passed for food—bread as hard as bricks, a slimy potato or carrot—sliding a wooden plate under the bolted door. Molly had learned to eat quickly, and to then slide the plate back out when she was finished, because the rats would come looking for it. A few times a day the men took Molly down the hall, where she was allowed the use of a crude toilet; this was her only time outside the cell.

Twice each day—Molly assumed it was morning and evening, though she had no way to keep track of time—prisoners were herded past her cell door. There were eleven of them, by Molly's count, all men, chained together at their ankles, the chains clanking on the corridor's stone floor as they shuffled past. They were covered from head to toe in dirt and grime, as though they'd been digging.

The first time they'd passed, Molly had spotted James immediately, seventh in line. She had called out his name. He looked at her and quickly shook his head. The guards, big men who carried pistols, shouted at Molly to be quiet and roughly shoved the prisoners forward, causing them to stumble into one another.

After that, the prisoners knew better than to try to talk to Molly. But some of them, always including James, glanced in her direction each time they passed, their expressions ranging from exhaustion to desperation. Molly watched them, her face pressed to the bars, trying wordlessly to communicate some comfort and to receive some in return.

Because of the filth covering the men, it was difficult for Molly to make out their features. But two of them, aside from James, seemed familiar to her. One of them looked like the missing Underground passenger whose picture had appeared in the newspaper the day James had come to her house. The other was the man who was always fourth in line. He always looked at Molly intently, as if he wanted to say something. Each time he passed, Molly became more certain that she knew him from somewhere. But from where? Another picture in the paper? A neighbor? A businessman or friend of her husband's? Who was he?

For long, bleak hours in her cold, cramped cell, Molly pondered this question, along with others: Why had she been kidnapped? Why brought here along with the others? Why was she still being held? Certainly it had something to do with the Starcatchers, with everything James had told her; but why the Underground? Why were men being captured to dig?

The questions multiplied in Molly's mind, but no answers came. One thing she knew and clung to: her absence would be noticed. George would be frantic by now. She felt awful for him, and the children—how worried they must be. There would certainly be people looking for her. Half of Scotland Yard, if she knew George! They were looking, and they would find her.

Wouldn't they?

Molly pulled her coat tight around her, shivering against the unrelenting chill of the cell. She heard the scratching of a rat in the corridor.

Please let them find me.

CHAPTER 18

UNCLE TED

WENDY HAD A PLAN. Actually, it was more of a desperate hope than a plan. But at the moment it was all she had.

It had come to her on the train ride back to Cambridgeshire. Searching her memory, trying to remember everything her mother and her grandfather had told her about the Starcatchers, she'd convinced herself that there was indeed someone she could turn to: the flying boy, Peter. He was more than just his mother's friend. He was an ally of the Starcatchers. He had joined forces with her mother and grandfather more than once. Wendy prayed that he would help her now.

If only she could find him.

Her mother had told her about the island. But what island, and where? And how would she get there? Again, Wendy scoured her memory. Her mother and James had spoken of the other orphan boys who'd been on the island, then returned to London. James had said that one of them was now a fellow at Cambridge. What *was* his name? Wendy had almost given up in despair when it finally the name came to her: *Pratt.*

The next morning, Wendy hurried downstairs in search of her uncle, only to be told by Mrs. Blotney, Uncle Neville's long-suffering housekeeper, that Uncle Neville and her brothers had already eaten breakfast.

"They've gone out to the barn," sighed Mrs. Blotney. "He's going to try to fly that ornithopter contraption again. I've already sent for the doctor."

"Oh dear," said Wendy. Ignoring the plate of food Mrs. Blotney had set out for her, she ran out the door and down the gravel road to the barn. In the big meadow behind it, she found John and Michael watching excitedly as Uncle Neville, screwdriver in hand, tinkered with the gasoline motor on his flying contraption, which looked like a large, ungainly headless bird.

"Uncle Neville," she began.

"Just a moment," said Uncle Neville, frowning as he turned a screw.

"It's going to fly!" said Michael. "It's a . . . a . . . ornihopper!"

"Orni*thop*ter, you ninny," said John.

"That's what I said," said Michael.

"Uncle Neville," Wendy repeated, "I just wanted to . . ."

"There!" said Uncle Neville, setting down his screwdriver.

He grabbed the motor's starter crank and shouted, "Stand back!"

"But . . ." said Wendy, but Uncle Neville was already turning the crank.

With a loud *BANG* the motor emitted a cloud of smoke and sputtered to life, clacking and rattling. The ornithopter's giant silk-and-feather wings slowly moved up, then down, then up again.

"It's going to fly!" shouted Michael over the engine clatter.

"Yes!" shouted Uncle Neville, admiring the sight. "I believe it is!"

The wings were beating faster now.

"Uncle Neville!" shouted John, as the ornithopter began bouncing up and down on its wheeled carriage.

"What is it, lad?" shouted Uncle Neville.

"Aren't you going to get on it?" shouted John.

"Oh my goodness!" cried Uncle Neville. He scurried around the side of the ornithopter, forced to take a long route to avoid the huge wings, now beating quite rapidly. Having cleared the wing, he lunged toward the pilot platform attached to the ornithopter frame.

Too late. With a mighty downsweep of its wings, the ornithopter leaped off the ground, its wheels just shooting clear of Uncle Neville's grasping fingers. He watched helplessly as his invention rose into the air and, gaining altitude, began to flap its way across the meadow. Uncle Neville began to run after it, puffing hard; he was followed by John and Michael, both whooping with delight.

The three of them had gone about twenty yards when Uncle Neville, looking up at the ornithopter, failed to notice a molehill in front of him. He tripped on it and fell on his face with an *oof*; John and Michael, right behind, went down on top of him in a tangle of arms and legs. The three of them were struggling to their feet when the ornithopter emitted several loud bangs, then a series of wheezes. Then the engine went silent, and the wings stopped.

"Oh dear," said Uncle Neville, as the ornithopter began to come down. It descended in a gentle spiral, then picked up speed before crashing into the meadow with a *whump* and pitching over forward, very much as its inventor had. Uncle Neville, followed by John and Michael, puffed over to it. Wendy caught up with them a minute later. Uncle Neville was examining the frame, which was bent; one of the wings had broken off.

"Nothing serious," Uncle Neville said cheerfully. "I'll have it ready to fly again in a day or so." He looked sheepish. "This time, I'll remember to get on."

"Uncle Neville is going to fly on the ornihopper!" said Michael.

"Orni*thop*ter," said John.

"That's what I said," said Michael.

"Uncle Neville," said Wendy, "do you think it's wise to get on? I mean, it *did* come down rather hard."

"Nothing to worry about," said Uncle Neville. "It just needs some adjusting."

"I see," said Wendy. "Um, I was wondering if it would be all right if I went to the university today, to see an old friend of . . ."

"The carburetor," said Uncle Neville.

"I beg your pardon?" said Wendy.

"That's what needs adjusting."

"I see," Wendy said doubtfully. "So would it be all right if I went to see him?"

"See who?"

"The old family friend."

"Is he here?" said Uncle Neville, looking around the meadow.

"No," said Wendy. "He's at the university."

Uncle Neville looked thoughtful for a few moments. Then he said, "I'll need the screwdriver."

"I'll get it!" said John, racing toward the barn.

"I'll get it, too!" said Michael, running behind his brother.

Wendy stood watching Uncle Neville, who looked at his ornithopter, then at her.

"We're very close," he said.

"So it's all right if I go to see him?" said Wendy.

"Who?" said Uncle Neville.

"The family friend," said Wendy. "I'll be back for supper."

"Oh, it's far too early for supper," said Uncle Neville. "I've just had breakfast."

"Right," said Wendy. "Then I'll see you later, when I get back from the university, all right?"

Uncle Neville seemed not to hear her. He was looking at the ornithopter again.

"Very close," he said.

⊷⊶

Wendy was lucky: Uncle Neville's groundskeeper was taking his wagon into Cambridge that morning for supplies, and he agreed to let Wendy ride along. He dropped her off in Trumpington Street, near the town center; they arranged to meet there in three hours for the return trip.

As the wagon rumbled away, Wendy realized she faced a daunting task: the University of Cambridge consisted of many colleges, and many more buildings. But again luck was with her, in the form of a young male student walking past.

"Excuse me," said Wendy. "I'm trying to find a Mr. Pratt."

"Would that be Dr. Theodore Pratt?" the student said.

"Yes!" said Wendy, now remembering the first name. "Is his office nearby?"

"Couldn't be much nearer," said the student. "He's a history fellow at Peterhouse. Go right through there; his office

130

is in the second building on your right, third floor."

Wendy thanked him and found her way to the brick building. She climbed the stairs to the third floor and found Dr. Pratt's office. The door was open; inside she saw a stocky man with a genial round face reading a book. He sat at a desk covered with books, many open; more books—hundreds more—lined the floor-to-ceiling shelves covering two walls. Still more books were stacked in piles on the floor and on two old overstuffed chairs.

Wendy tapped on the door and said, "Dr. Pratt?"

"Yes?" said the man, looking up from his book. When he saw Wendy, he gasped.

"Young lady, forgive me for staring," he said. "But you look *exactly* like a girl I used to know."

"Molly Aster Darling," said Wendy. "I'm her daughter."

With a roar of delight, he rose from his desk, knocking several books to the floor, and lumbered over to Wendy. He started to hug her, but realizing that was a bit informal, he settled for vigorously shaking her hand.

"How delightful!" he said. "Last I saw you, you were just a baby, but here you've turned out every bit as beautiful as your mother!"

"Thank you, Dr. Pratt," said Wendy, blushing.

"You must call me Uncle Ted," he insisted. "It has been a while, but your mother and grandfather will always be family to me. How are they?"

Wendy said nothing, but the look on her face gave Ted his answer.

"Oh dear," he said. "Something's wrong."

Wendy nodded, fighting back tears.

Ted closed the door and ushered Wendy to one of the overstuffed chairs, sweeping the books to the floor so she could sit. He then did the same with the other chair and sat down.

"All right," he said. "Tell me."

It took a while; Wendy broke down crying when she talked about the disappearance of her mother, and as the rest of the story unfolded, Ted often interrupted her with questions. He became particularly excited when Wendy told him her grandfather's story about Curtana.

"The Sword of Mercy!" he exclaimed.

"You're familiar with it?"

"Indeed I am," said Ted. "One of the history fellows here, a close friend of mine named Patrick Hunt, is an authority on it. He'd be quite interested to learn that the missing tip has been found, after all these centuries. But if your grandfather is right—and I have rarely known him to be wrong—this is a very serious matter indeed."

"Yes," said Wendy. "If the Others *have* found it, they'll be able to open the Cache."

"And you're certain your grandfather didn't tell you where this . . . Cache is located?"

"Only that it's in London," said Wendy. She hesitated, then added, "And he said something about 'confess.'"

"Confess what?"

"I don't know. He just said 'confess,' and then he lost consciousness."

Ted nodded, then said, "Who else have you told about this?"

"Aside from you, nobody," said Wendy.

"Why not your father? He's an influential man, and I'm certain he's as worried about your mother as you are. And he's dealt with the Others—he knows the danger."

Wendy shook her head. "He insists that this is best handled by the police."

"But you say the police are in on it!"

"I'm sure they are, at least some of them. But Father trusts them. And he's very reluctant to say anything about starstuff, or the Others, or this Ombra. He says it's ghost stories. He's concerned about what people will think."

Ted nodded, smiling ruefully. "That sounds like George," he said.

"That's why I've come to you, Dr. Pr— I mean, Uncle Ted," said Wendy. "Mr. Smith said you were on that island, with mother and the flying boy, Peter."

"Yes," Ted said softly. "There were five of us from the St. Norbert's orphanage—Peter, James, Prentiss, Thomas, and me. Four of us came back to England. But Peter chose to stay on the island."

"But he came back to England once," said Wendy. "To help my mother."

Ted nodded. "That he did."

"I want to ask him to help her again," said Wendy.

"*What?*" said Ted.

"I must go to the island," said Wendy. "I must talk to Peter."

"But you can't!"

"Why not?"

"Because . . . Well, for one thing, how will you get there?"

"I don't know," said Wendy. "I'll find a way." Her hand went to the locket around her neck.

"But you don't even know where the island is!" said Ted.

"No," said Wendy. "That's why I've come to you. You lived there once, for a long time, didn't you?"

"But . . . Never Land. I don't know exactly where . . ." said Ted. "It's just a speck in the ocean, and it has been so *many* years . . ."

"Well, *somebody* must know," said Wendy. "A ship's captain? One of the others: Thomas . . . Prentiss?"

Ted stared at Wendy, then said, "I must say, you don't just *look* like your mother. You have her . . . tenacity . . . as well."

"I'm sorry," said Wendy. "It's just that—"

"Don't apologize," said Ted. "I always admired your mother's spirit. It's to your credit that you have the same qualities."

"So you'll help me?" said Wendy.

Ted frowned in contemplation. Finally he said, "There may be someone who knows how to get to that island."

"Who is it?" said Wendy eagerly.

"It's someone I haven't seen in many years," said Ted. "Someone who may not even still be living."

"But he or she might be?" said Wendy. "Alive? Able to help us?"

"He . . . yes. He just might be, yes," said Ted. "But even if we can locate him, there's the question of how we will communicate with him."

"What do you mean?" said Wendy.

"You may not believe this," said Ted, "but he happens to be a porpoise."

Wendy smiled.

"Is something funny?"

"*You* may not believe *this*," said Wendy, "but I happen to speak Porpoise."

135

CHAPTER 19

$\mathcal{A}$ $\mathcal{T}$INY $\mathcal{S}$HOOTING $\mathcal{S}$TAR

"$\mathcal{H}$OLD HIM TIGHT!" ROARED HOOK, as five pirates disentangled Peter from the net. "If he gets loose, I'll feed the lot of you to the crocodile!"

Five pairs of rough hands gripped Peter even tighter. He struggled, but it was hopeless, one boy against five men.

"Smee, fetch me his dagger," said Hook. The short, round first mate plucked the dagger from the ground and scurried over to hand it to Hook. Hook waved it at Peter as the sailors dragged him past.

"You won't be needing this anymore, boy," he sneered, tucking it into his belt.

The pirates shoved Peter into a cage made of rough wooden slats. They secured the cage door from the outside with heavy rope; from inside, Peter couldn't reach the knots. The cage was too small for him to stand in; he crouched on the floor, peering through the cracks between the slats, looking for . . .

There she was: a sparkle of light on top of one of the pirate huts, looking like one of the many stars dotting the now-black sky. Peter knew Tink would try to get help for him. But how?

"What have we got here?" Hook said, picking the coconut off the ground. "Thought you were going to drop this on me, did you, boy?" He examined it by the torchlight.

"What's this?" he said, peering at the writing. "'Cap . . . tain . . . Hook . . .' Say! That's me!" He read on. "'I porpoise a . . .'"

"Um, Cap'n," said Smee, on tiptoe, looking over Hook's shoulder. "I b'lieve it says *propose*."

"I know that, you idjit!" said Hook.

"Yes, Cap'n."

"You think I'm some idjit who never learned to *read*?" said Hook, who in fact never had learned to read, as he had begun a full-time pirating career at an early age.

"No, Cap'n," said Smee.

"Porpoise, indeed," said Hook. "I was making a *joke*, Smee. But since you think you know so much about reading, then *you* read it."

Hook shoved the coconut into Smee's hands. Hook and the other pirates gathered around and listened intently as Smee, squinting at the squid-ink letters, read Fighting

Prawn's message aloud. Everyone's eyes then turned to Hook.

"Read the part about the ship again," Hook said.

Smee read: "'My men will repair your ship and provision it so you can leave the island permanently.'"

"*Permanently.*" Hook inhaled through his nose, filling his lungs, then exhaled so hard that the few wisps of hair on Smee's head blew backward. The smell of fish lingered in the air.

"Repair the ship," Hook muttered.

"It's almost too good to be true!" said Smee.

"For once you're right, Smee. It *is* too good to be true. Has to be trap. A clever trap, cleverly designed by the cunning savages to lure us into . . . a trap. They think I'm a fool, Smee."

"But a request for a parley," Smee said, studying the coconut. "Don't we have to honor that, Cap'n? Isn't that the Code?"

"I *know* the Code, Smee," said Hook.

"Aye, Cap'n."

"Don't be telling *me* the Code."

"No, Cap'n."

"But since you're so . . . *particular* about the Code," said Hook, "I suppose you'd be volunteering to go arrange the parley."

Smee gulped and looked around. The other pirates had all backed away, leaving Smee alone.

"I . . . ah . . ." he began.

"Good!" said Hook. He looked over at Peter's cage, thinking. After about a minute, he said, "Now, here's what you do, Smee. You tell the savage Prawn that I'll parley with him. Tell him we each bring three men, no more. But tell him I want to have the parley at sea, out past the reef off the lagoon, because I don't want any of his savages sneaking up. Tell him that for insurance, I'll be bringing the flying devil boy with me on the raft, in a cage, and if the savages try anything, the boy gets my hook across his throat."

"But, Cap'n," said Smee. "If you hurt the boy, Fighting Prawn will kill you. He'd kill us all."

"I KNOW THAT, YOU IDJIT!"

"Yes, Cap'n."

"When I go for the parley, I'll listen to what Prawn has to offer. Then I'll tell him that before I make any agreements, I need to consult with my crew."

"That's very thoughtful of you, Cap'n," said Smee.

Hook rubbed his forehead with his non-hook hand.

"Smee," he said. "You have the brains of a clam."

"Yes, Cap'n."

"No, that is unfair to clams, Smee. Compared to you, a clam is a genius. A clam is Aristotle."

"Yes, Cap'n."

"I'm not *really* going to consult with the crew, Smee. I'm going to tell Prawn to wait right there while I go back to talk with you lot. Then, on our way back, when we're at a spot where Prawn can see us but he's too far away to help, the raft will just happen to have a slight disagreement with the reef, and the lashing, which will be made loose before we depart herewith, will come untied, resulting in the purely accidental tragedy of all hands going overboard, along with the cage holding the flying boy. Boggs and Hurky and I will be able to swim ashore, but the cage, alas, will go straight to the bottom, dragged down by the rocks inside."

"But there's no rocks in the cage," said Smee.

"There will be," said Hook.

"But the boy will . . ."

"Drown?" said Hook. "Alas, he will, Smee. But the savages will clearly see that it was an accident, no fault of mine. Why, I will barely be able to save my own self."

Smee looked troubled.

"Do you grasp the plan?" said Hook. "Are we catching the breeze, Mr. Smee? Are both oars in the water? Is the compass trained to north?"

"We are. I am. It is. . . ."

"The raft will have an encounter with the reef. Boggs and Hurky and I will swim to shore. The boy—sadly—will not make it. Prawn, heartbroken by a chain of events that *he himself* set in motion, will abandon whatever savage trap he had planned to spring on us. It's a brilliant plan, Smee, if I do say so. Perhaps my most brilliant ever. In one bold stroke

I rid myself of the savage's scheming, and the flying devil boy. Is it not masterful, Smee?"

Smee said, "But the boy . . ."

"That's life on the sea," snapped Hook. "Dangerous place, the open water." He spat at the cage, then aimed a glare at Smee. "First light of dawn, you go talk to Prawn. Then you get back here quick, before I change me mind and kill the boy right here."

"Aye, Cap'n," said Smee, his eyes on the cage.

Inside the cage, Peter's eyes were on the sky behind the pirates. A speck of light was streaking from the fort toward the jungle and up the mountainside, like a tiny shooting star.

CHAPTER 20

ꟻoo

ꞀHIS TIME, WENDY AVOIDED UNCLE NEVILLE altogether. He wouldn't notice that she was gone, anyway; he was utterly preoccupied with repairing his ornithopter, with the "help" of John and Michael.

Mrs. Blotney was another matter: she would definitely notice if Wendy was gone overnight. After much thought, Wendy reluctantly decided she would have to lie to the housekeeper. She hated dishonesty, but as long as her mother was missing, she would do whatever she had to do.

"Going somewhere?" Mrs. Blotney asked as Wendy came downstairs holding a small suitcase.

"Yes," said Wendy. "I've spoken to Uncle." That much was true; she *had* spoken with her uncle, though not about leaving. "I'm off to spend some time with my father," she continued. "I'm not certain what his schedule will allow, so I may be gone only for a day, but it could be longer, possibly even a week. I'll post a letter to you if I'm to be back later than tomorrow evening."

"A letter to me?"

"Yes, to you. I don't want to trouble my uncle with the details when he's so busy fixing his flying machine."

Mrs. Blotney nodded. "Just between us," she said, "I hope he continues with the fixing and doesn't get around to the flying, if you know what I mean."

Wendy smiled. "I do," she said. "Well, I'll be off now. Good-bye, Mrs. Blotney."

"Good-bye," said Mrs. Blotney, "and be careful."

"I will," said Wendy, wondering if this was another lie.

The groundskeeper gave Wendy a lift to the Cambridge train station. There she met Ted, who also had a suitcase. The two of them boarded a train for Harwich, an old port city on the North Sea, about sixty miles northeast of Cambridge.

After the conductor punched their tickets, Ted looked around to make sure there were no passengers close enough to overhear, then said, "I have some rather troubling news."

"What is it?" said Wendy.

"Well," said Ted, "after you left yesterday, I decided to try to speak to Thomas and Prentiss. We've been out of touch for some time—they both live in London—but I wanted to find out if either of them knew anything about James's disappearance. We've just had a telephone system installed at the university, and I was able to reach Prentiss at the architectural firm where he works. He had not heard about James. But he had disturbing news of his own."

"What?" said Wendy.

"Thomas has also gone missing."

"Oh dear," said Wendy. "Are you certain?"

"Quite."

"When?"

"Several months ago," said Ted.

"Several *months?*" said Wendy.

"Yes, I'm afraid so," said Ted. "After he failed to appear at work for a full week, his employer finally notified the police. Thomas lived alone; the police said they found no evidence of foul play. But there has been no word from him since. He simply disappeared."

"Did you tell Prentiss about James's suspicions?" said Wendy. "About von Schatten and the Others?"

"No," said Ted. "The telephone operators could have overheard us. I didn't want to risk it."

"So now," said Wendy, "of the four of you who came back from the island . . ."

". . . two of us are missing," said Ted. "I couldn't tell Prentiss much on the telephone, but we're planning to meet soon. I told him to take precautions for his safety."

"As should you," said Wendy.

"I fear so," agreed Ted.

A man sat down across from them. Ted and Wendy, not wanting to be overheard, lapsed into silence, pondering worrisome thoughts for the rest of the trip to Harwich. They arrived just before noon. Since the weather was good, they decided to walk to the harbor, a short distance away through the compact village.

They reached the harbor, where a dozen ships were tied alongside the quay, tended by a ragtag group of dockworkers. Wendy and Ted walked to the end of the quay and stopped, looking out toward the North Sea.

"Now what?" said Wendy.

"Now you call out to them," said Ted. "In Porpoise."

Wendy eyed the murky dark green water doubtfully. "Are you sure they're here?" she said.

"Oh yes," said Ted. "I confirmed it with a biologist at the university. The common harbor porpoise is sighted here regularly."

A red-faced, white-haired man, apparently a dockworker taking a break, ambled up, puffing on a pipe.

"If it's the ferry you want," he said, "you don't get it here."

"Thank you, but we're not waiting for the ferry," said Wendy. She hoped the man would go away, but he simply stood there, watching them and puffing.

"Go ahead, then," Ted urged Wendy.

With a sigh, Wendy turned to the water. She had

145

practiced the sequence of sounds the night before. If she remembered her mother's lessons correctly, what she would be saying, in Porpoise, was: *Please come. Friend.*

She took a breath, then emitted a series of squeaks, chirps, and chitters. When she was done, she stared at the water, praying the dockworker had left.

"What's she doing there, mate?" said the man, who had, in fact, moved closer and was also staring at the water.

"She's calling a porpoise," said Ted.

Wendy moaned in embarrassment.

"A porpoise?" said the man.

"Yes," said Ted. "Try again, Wendy."

"But . . ."

"Go on," said Ted. "We've come all this way."

Wendy again squeaked, chirped, and chittered at the water. Again, nothing happened. Now, to Wendy's further embarrassment, a second dockworker, apparently a friend of the first, ambled up.

"What's this?" he asked his friend.

"This girl," said the first man, pointing at Wendy, "is talking to the porpoises."

"Is she, now?" said the second man. "I do that myself sometimes."

"True," said the first. "But only when you've been drinking."

Ignoring this, the second man looked at the water

and said, "They don't seem to be answering."

"Apparently not," said Wendy, now utterly mortified. She turned to Ted and said, "Please, let's go."

"But don't you think we should—"

"*No,*" said Wendy, turning away. "Let's just go."

"All right," sighed Ted, following. "I suppose it was—"

"Ahoy, there! Here, now," said the first man, looking at the water.

Ted and Wendy stopped.

"What is it?" said Ted.

"It's a porpoise, is what it is," said the first man.

"Hello, porpoise!" said the second man.

Wendy and Ted hurried back to the edge of the quay and looked down. Directly below them was the grinning face of a harbor porpoise, its sleek silver-gray body almost halfway out of the water.

"Wendy!" said Ted. "You did it!"

"I did!" said Wendy, amazed. "Hello!" she called to the porpoise.

"I tried that," said the second man. "He don't answer."

"Oh, right," said Wendy. She took another breath, concentrating hard, and emitted a brief series of sounds that meant—she hoped—*Hello.*

The porpoise looked at her with interest, then, sounding much like Wendy, responded, *Hello.*

"Uncle Ted!" she cried. "He answered me!"

"Excellent!" said Ted.

"What did he say?" asked the first man.

"Please, let me think," said Wendy.

"Why would he say that?" said the second man.

"No, I . . . never mind," said Wendy. She frowned, concentrating on the dialogue she had practiced. It was important, with porpoises, to observe certain formalities.

Pointing at herself, she said, *Name Wendy.*

The porpoise said, *Name Foo. Wendy want fish?*

No thank you, said Wendy. She then tried to say "Wendy not want fish," but she put three clicks where there should have been two, so what she said was *Wendy not jellyfish.*

Wendy not jellyfish, agreed Foo, adding, *Foo not jellyfish.*

Wendy took a deep breath. This was the important part. *Wendy want talk porpoise,* she said.

Foo porpoise, said Foo.

No, said Wendy. *Wendy want talk porpoise name . . .* She turned to Ted and said, "I've forgotten the porpoise's name."

"Ammm," said Ted.

Wendy told Foo, *Wendy want talk porpoise name Ammm.*

Ammm, repeated Foo.

Yes, said Wendy. *Foo know Ammm?*

No, said Foo.

Wendy's shoulders slumped.

But then Foo said, *Foo find Ammm?*

Yes! said Wendy. *Foo find Ammm!*

148

Foo find porpoise find porpoise find porpoise find Ammm, said Foo.

Thank you, said Wendy. *Foo bring Ammm here?*

Yes, said Foo. *Two suns, come here.*

Wendy frowned, and was about to say something. But Foo, with a flash of his powerful tail, was gone.

"Oh dear," said Wendy.

"What?" asked Ted and both dockworkers simultaneously.

"Well," said Wendy, "he said he would find Ammm. Actually, what he said was he would find porpoise find porpoise find porpoise find Ammm, but I think he means that's how they communicate over distance, one porpoise calling to another."

"Excellent!" said Ted.

"But I'm not sure what he meant at the end," said Wendy. "I asked him if he would bring Ammm here, and he said something about 'two suns.' Could he have meant Sunday after next?"

"Porpoises don't have Sundays," said the second dockworker, sounding quite sure of himself.

Reluctantly, Wendy said, "I imagine that's true."

"Day after tomorrow!" said Ted. "The 'next sun' is tomorrow, so two suns is day after tomorrow."

"That makes sense," said Wendy. "But what *time* day after tomorrow?"

"Porpoises don't have watches," noted the first dockworker.

Ignoring him, Ted, said, "I suppose we'll just have to come in the morning and wait."

"I suppose so," sighed Wendy. "I wish I could do something to make things go faster."

"Don't be so hard on yourself, Wendy," said Ted. "You've done amazingly well. Speaking Porpoise! Very clever! You really do remind me so much of your mother. But I suppose you hear that all the time."

Wendy stared at the water, her heart suddenly heavy.

"Yes," she said softly. "All the time."

———◆◆◆———

Ted found them rooms at a nearby seaside inn. He spent the next day exploring Harwich, but Wendy was in no mood for sightseeing. In the morning she posted a letter to Mrs. Blotney, saying that she was well, and unsure of her plans, but planning to be away at least another night. (It occurred to her that the letter would be postmarked Harwich, rather than London; she could only hope that Mrs. Blotney wouldn't notice.) The rest of the day she sat in her room, staring out the window at the gray North Sea and wishing that the endless minutes would tick past faster.

The following morning, after tea and toast, she and Ted were mildly annoyed to find the two dockworkers already waiting for them at water's edge. Their annoyance turned to excitement when the first man announced, "He's here. And he's brought a friend."

"But they won't talk to me," said the second man.

"That's because you can't speak Porpoise," said the first.

"It's my accent," said the second.

"No, it's that you're speaking English," said the first.

Pushing past the two arguing men, Wendy and Ted went to the quay's edge. Wendy called out:

Foo! Hello!

Almost immediately, Foo's blunt snout poked out of the water.

Hello, Wendy, he said. Remembering his manners, he added, *Wendy want fish?*

No thank you, Wendy not jellyfish, Wendy answered. At risk of sounding rude, she plunged ahead, asking, *Foo find Ammm?*

Ammm here, said Foo, and as he spoke, a second snout appeared. It belonged to a larger and clearly older porpoise, his body marked by old scars.

Hello, said Ammm.

Hello, said Wendy.

Ammm was looking at her. He uttered a short whistle, then a lyrical chirp. Wendy gasped.

"What did he say?" said Ted.

Wendy, still staring at Ammm, answered, "He said, 'Molly.'"

Molly, repeated Ammm.

Name Wendy, said Wendy. *Daughter.*

Daughter Molly, said Ammm.

Yes, said Wendy.

Ammm emitted some squeaks that Wendy recognized as porpoise laughter. He said something that Wendy didn't understand—something about teeth being green—and laughed some more. Then he turned to study Ted. After several seconds, he said, *Peter friend*.

"What did he say?" Ted asked Wendy.

"He said you're Peter's friend."

"My goodness!" said Ted. "He remembers me after all these years! Hello, Ammm!"

Hello Peter friend, said Ammm, who apparently understood some English. He turned back to Wendy.

Molly here? he asked.

No, said Wendy. *Molly trouble.*

Bad men, said Ammm.

Yes, said Wendy. *Bad men.*

Ammm help, said Ammm.

Foo help, said Foo.

Thank you, said Wendy. *Thank you.* She thought about how to say the next part. Her mother had never taught her how to say "Neverland," so she said, *Ammm know island?*

Island, said Ammm, and then he made a sound Wendy

152

was not familiar with, which she decided must mean "Neverland."

Yes, she said. *Ammm know island?*

Yes, said Ammm.

Ammm take Wendy island?

Island far, said Ammm.

How far? said Wendy.

Ammm was silent for a moment, apparently calculating. Then he said, *Loud boat four suns.*

"Oh dear," said Wendy. "I was afraid of that."

"What?" said Ted.

"He says by loud boat—I assume he means a steamship—it takes four days to get to the island."

"Well, it *is* a good distance," said Ted. "I know we sailed for weeks."

"But we don't *have* a steamship," Wendy pointed out.

"True," said Ted. "We'll just have to see about hiring one. Although I suspect that will be rather a difficult . . ."

Wendy was shaking her head. "No," she said. "I've wasted enough time already. My mother needs me. I need to get to the island and persuade Peter to come back with me, *now*."

"But how, Wendy?" said Ted. "Be realistic! You can't very well *fly* there, now, can you?"

Wendy's hand touched her mother's locket.

"Can't I?" she said.

CHAPTER 21

ONLY BLACKNESS

BEYOND THE OUTERMOST REEF guarding Mollusk Island, a ramshackle raft plowed through the dark blue sea, which reflected the shimmering afternoon sun like a million mirrors. The raft was made of bamboo and palm-tree trunks, lashed together with ropes woven from jungle vines. It was rowed, awkwardly, by two of Hook's men, using oars carved from driftwood; at the stern, a third man steered with a driftwood tiller.

In the center of the raft stood Hook, who, being captain, neither rowed nor steered; his role was to give orders and be generally dissatisfied with how they were carried out. In his non-hook hand he held a spear. Its shaft was bamboo; its tip was fashioned, Mollusk-style, from a piece of shell honed razor-sharp. It would pierce flesh as well as any steel.

Next to Hook stood the pot-bellied Smee, wearing pants shredded at the knees and a blue-and-white-striped shirt he'd worn so long that both the blue and the white were almost an identical shade of gray.

Behind them rested a wooden cage. Inside it was Peter, and a heavy load of rocks. Peter hated being in the cage, staring at the rocks designed to drag him to the sea bottom. He was certain Tink would do all she could to warn Fighting Prawn about Hook's plan. But he wasn't certain she would succeed. Meanwhile, he was trapped with the rocks, just a few inches above the waiting sea.

The pirates were looking toward the island, where an outrigger canoe was just emerging from Mermaid Lagoon. At the center of the canoe sat Fighting Prawn, his dark-eyed gaze on the pirate raft. Around him, paddling the canoe with quick efficiency, were four Mollusk warriors; two of them, Bold Abalone and Brazen Starfish, were Fighting Prawn's sons.

The Mollusks quickly reached the rendezvous point, a fairly calm patch of sea just inside the outer reef. Fighting Prawn watched as the pirate raft zigzagged clumsily toward them. He spoke to the others in the Mollusk language, which to English speakers sounded like strange grunts and clicks.

"It's a wonder they can navigate a ship," he said.

"Is Peter in the cage?" said Brazen Starfish.

Fighting Prawn squinted. "Yes, I see his red hair," he said. "Give the signal."

Brazen Starfish, sitting on the side of the canoe away from the pirates, slapped the water with his paddle four times. Fighting Prawn saw a swirl of water, like a small rogue wave, near the edge of the reef. He nodded. His eyes then turned skyward, and, with effort, picked up a tiny bright speck shooting toward the pirate raft, approaching it from an angle such that if the pirates looked toward it, they would be blinded by the sun. But the pirates' attention was focused on the Mollusk canoe; none of them saw the speck dart into the cage.

Tinker Bell landed in the crook of Peter's elbow. He smiled, enormously relieved to see her; it was all he could do to keep from speaking. She darted to his head, nestling into his bushy red hair. She moved to his right ear and chimed quietly so the pirates wouldn't hear.

We have a plan, she said.

"Good," whispered Peter. "What is it?"

Instead of answering, Tink burrowed into his hair. He looked up and saw why: Hook had his face pressed to the cage.

"Who are you talking to, boy?" he said.

"A rock," said Peter. "And it's smarter than you."

The rowers giggled. Hook shot them a silencing glare. Turning back to Peter, he said, "That's a funny joke, boy. You can tell that one to the fish when you get to the bottom of the sea. Meanwhile, here's a joke for *you.*" He spat a foul gob at the cage; Peter turned away in disgust as it spattered him through the bars.

"Now, listen, boy," said Hook, leaning close. "I'll have this spear by your neck during the parley. If you say one word to the savages—if you so much as *sneeze*—I will bring the spear down, and your head and body will no longer be acquainted."

Smee said, "Approaching the canoe, Cap'n."

"*Not one word*," Hook snarled at Peter. To the rowers he said, "Keep us at a comfortable distance."

As the two vessels neared each other, Tink dropped back to Peter's arm, holding a tiny finger to her tiny lips to remind him not to speak. He made a shrugging gesture to ask her *What's the plan?*

No time, she chimed back, and in a flash she was gone, unobserved by the pirates, whose attention was on the Mollusk canoe, now only about fifteen feet away.

"Don't come any closer!" said Hook. He held the spear up so Fighting Prawn could see it, then held it over the cage, its deadly tip pointed at Peter. "If I see anything tricky from you savages, I'll run the boy through, savvy?"

"There is no need to hurt the boy," said Fighting Prawn. "I am offering you a chance to leave the island."

"So your coconut said," replied Hook. "But why would you make such an offer?"

"We don't like you," said Fighting Prawn.

"Fair enough," said Hook. "I don't like you, either. But I've been here twenty years and more. Why make this offer now?"

"Because some other white men came ashore, shipwrecked," said Fighting Prawn. "We want them gone. You will take them with you."

Hook thought about that. "Say the rest," he said.

"My men will repair your ship and supply it with food and water," said Fighting Prawn. "We will provide you with four seaworthy canoes for lifeboats. I give you my word we will make no attempt to harm you or your men. In return, you give me your word that you will leave and never come back."

"Cap'n," whispered Smee, "it sounds like a good bargain."

"Shut up, Smee," said Hook.

"Aye, aye," said Smee.

Hook studied the Mollusk chief across the short expanse of water. His face was calm, but his mind was racing. He had realized, to his surprise, that the Mollusk chief was sincere: he actually intended to help the pirates leave the island. That was good. But Hook did not want to give up on his plan to drown the boy. He had waited too many years for his moment of sweet revenge. He would have to handle this just right. The savage had to believe that the boy's death was an accident. That way he would still allow Hook to leave unpunished.

It was perfect, Hook decided. He would rid himself of the

boy forever, *and* get off this wretched island. A brilliant plan. Hook was only sorry that everyone around him was too stupid to admire it.

He smiled at Fighting Prawn. "All right, then," he said. "We have an accord. If you don't mind, I won't shake your hand on it, so we'll have to do with a nod." Hook nodded.

Fighting Prawn nodded back. "So now you can let the boy go," he said.

Hook shook his head. "Sorry, chief," he said. "The boy is my insurance. I don't plan on letting him go until you've completed your end of the deal. When the ship is ready, the boy goes free. Not before."

Fighting Prawn said nothing, his eyes on the spear tip at Peter's neck. After a moment, Hook barked an order to his men to turn the raft around. Peter pressed his face to the cage slats, his eyes meeting Fighting Prawn's. Peter couldn't read the expression on the Mollusk chief's face. Didn't he know what Hook planned to do? Hadn't Tink warned him? Or did he actually believe the pirate was telling the truth?

Is he going to just let Hook take me away?

The raft was moving away now. The canoe began to turn. Peter started to cry out to Fighting Prawn, but Hook, expecting this, touched the spear tip to Peter's neck. Peter felt blood trickle.

"One word, boy," said Hook, "and you die right here and now."

Desperately, Peter weighed the situation. If he shouted to Fighting Prawn, Hook would spear him. But Hook planned to drown him soon, anyway. His only hope was that the plan Tink told him about would work. But what *was* the plan?

He watched helplessly as the Mollusk canoe, propelled by the paddles of the four strong warriors, pulled swiftly away, growing smaller in the distance. Fighting Prawn was still looking back toward the raft but had made no move to rescue Peter. The pirates, meanwhile, were paddling the raft toward the outer reef and the deep water just beyond it. Peter heard the crashing of waves against the reef, and felt the ocean swells lifting and lowering the raft. He imagined the depths beneath him and what it would feel like to plunge into them, imprisoned by the weighted cage.

Hook, seeing the fear on Peter's face, cackled. "You can shout all you want now, boy," he said. "The savage can't hear you. The primitive fool actually believed I'd let you live."

With a glance at the receding Mollusk canoe, Hook casually curled the toes of his bare right foot around a rope and pulled it; a knot came loose. Hook used his left foot to loosen another. The raft shifted. Water gushed up into Peter's cage. The spaces between the logs were getting wider.

"Oh dear," said Hook. "Looks like we're having a spot of trouble." He smiled at Peter, his black eyes glittering.

"Good-bye, boy," he said.

"Mr. Smee," Peter pleaded. "This isn't right."

Smee could not bring himself to look at Peter. He shuffled his bare feet on the raft, his head bent.

"Okay, boys," said Hook. "Make it look good, now. Put her into that surf at the edge of the reef."

Peter looked back toward the Mollusk canoe. It was still heading away. He was desperate now, moving from wall to wall in the cage, looking for some way out, knowing there was none.

The raft was almost on the reef. The gaps between the raft logs increased. Smee's leg slipped through a gap, and he went down. A wave lifted the raft, and suddenly it broke apart, now just a loose tangle of logs and boards.

"HELP!" bellowed Hook. "HEEEELLLLLPPP!"

Peter's cage was precariously balanced between two logs. It began to slip off. Peter looked frantically back toward the island and saw that the canoe, now little more than a speck in the distance, was turning around. They were coming back.

Too late.

Peter screamed as his cage slipped off the logs and into the sea. As it went under, Peter gulped a last breath. The surging water surrounded him; underwater, he heard the dull roar of the waves, saw the pirates' legs kicking above him as the heavy rocks dragged him down, down . . .

A wave broke above him, clouding the water with foam and air.

Down, down . . .

He jammed his hands, painfully, through the cage, fumbling for the knots holding it together. It was no use. There were far too many knots, and far too little time. His lungs were starting to burn.

Down, down . . .

The water grew darker; the light and sound of the surface far above now.

Down, down . . .

Only blackness now. His lungs were on fire. He swallowed water. He was losing consciousness.

He felt something tug on the cage, pulling it through the water. He looked around desperately but could see only blackness.

And then there was nothing.

———

Peter! Peter!

The voice was urgent. Peter tried to answer but could not. He rolled sideways, vomiting seawater, then coughing violently, his throat raw. He blinked, but could see little. Wherever he was, it was dark and damp. He was lying on rock. He could hear the roar of waves nearby. He could make out the outline of a woman's head, her hair long and wet.

You are safe, Peter.

He realized that the voice, unlike the sound of the waves, was coming from inside his head.

"Teacher?" he croaked.

I'm here, responded the mermaid, her thoughts becoming his thoughts.

"Where am I?" he said.

A cave in the reef. You are safe.

"Thank you."

I'm sorry it took so long to reach you. Chief didn't want the pirate to see.

Peter understood. Fighting Prawn wanted to make sure Peter and the mermaid were safely out of Hook's murderous reach.

"Can I go back now?"

Chief wants you to wait here until the pirates return to their side.

Peter nodded, seeing the cleverness of Fighting Prawn's plan: let Hook think he had succeeded in killing Peter. Let him think he had outwitted the "savage." Then get him off the island.

"All right," he said. "I'll stay here until Hook's gone."

Good. Teacher smiled, revealing her sharp, pointed teeth. *You need to rest.*

Peter lay back on the rock, resting. For the first time, he thought about what the island would be like without Hook.

He wondered if his life would become boring.

CHAPTER 22

DANGER COMING

'EACH DAY MOLLY FOUGHT A GRIM BATTLE against loneliness and despair.

Nobody spoke to her. She called out to the guards,
pleading with them for information, or even just human
conversation, but they never answered. And so she sat, day
after day, in the tiny, dank, foul-smelling cell, sometimes
sobbing quietly, sometimes talking to herself, finding it
harder and harder to keep out the awful thought:

I will never get out of here.

She had no way to mark the passage of time save by
the delivery of the awful food and the wretched, twice-
daily spectacle of the exhausted prisoners trudging past. She
dared not call out to them, for fear the guards would hurt
them. But she waited for them eagerly, listening for the
clanking of their chains in the hallway, pressing her face
to her cell bars in anticipation of the only real human

contact in her otherwise relentlessly bleak day.

As the prisoners passed, she and James always met eyes, each trying to cheer the other up, to communicate the simple message: *I'm still here, still alive.*

But James was not the only prisoner with whom she exchanged looks. She was now certain that she knew the fourth man in line, the one who had looked at her so intently when she arrived. It took her several days to recognize him, but once she did, she was sure.

It was Thomas.

He had clearly been down in the tunnels longer than the others. His face was gaunt, his arms and legs bone-thin, his filthy clothes nothing but shreds and tatters. But it was Thomas.

Molly had spent a great deal of time—time was all she had—thinking about what his presence meant. She understood why she and James had been taken captive; they had learned von Schatten's secret. But as far as Molly knew, Thomas knew nothing about von Schatten. Yet he had apparently been taken captive before either James or Molly.

Why?

The more Molly thought about it, the more certain she became that the reason had to be the island. Very few people even knew of its existence; Thomas had actually lived there. Molly believed that that was why he had been captured: von Schatten, or Ombra, or whatever he was, wanted Thomas's knowledge of the island. If Molly was right, there was a connection between the island and the strange activity in the Underground.

What was it?

Molly didn't know the answer. But she knew that whatever it was, it could only mean trouble for the island and her dear friends who lived there. She wished there were some way she could send a warning to let Peter and the Mollusks know that they were in danger. But she couldn't even get a message to the streets of London above her, let alone to an island far out at sea. She could only clutch the bars of her tiny, dim cell, waiting for the next brief glimpse of James and Thomas, her next brief chance to exchange the unspoken message that had become the only thing that any of them had left to cling to.

I'm still alive.

CHAPTER 23

SIGNPOSTS IN THE SEA

*W*ENDY HATED HERSELF for what she was about to do to Uncle Neville.

It's for mother, she kept telling herself. But that didn't make her feel any better.

She'd returned the evening before. Uncle Ted, who'd stayed in Harwich, had tried to talk her out of her plan, but Wendy could not be budged. His last words to her as he put her on the train were "Wendy, you're every bit as stubborn as your mother. I just hope you're also as resourceful."

"I hope so, too," replied Wendy.

She took a taxicab from the Cambridge train station to Uncle Neville's estate. Nobody seemed suspicious; apparently Mrs. Blotney hadn't noticed the Harwich postmark on the letter Wendy had sent.

The next morning Wendy awakened early and filled a cloth bag with supplies—bread, cheese, three apples, and a bottle of water. An hour later, at breakfast, she peppered Uncle Neville with questions about his ornithopter. He was happy to answer them; in fact, the ornithopter was all he wanted to talk about. He was giddy with anticipation, having finally finished repairing the odd-looking craft. He intended, despite Mrs. Blotney's heartfelt pleadings, to make a test flight after breakfast.

John and Michael were so excited they could barely stay in their chairs. Every few seconds, Michael would shout, "Uncle Neville's going to fly the ornihopper!" Each time, he emitted a spray of toast crumbs, and each time John corrected him, saying, "It's orni*thop*ter, you ninny." But they were both too excited to get into serious quarreling.

Meanwhile, Wendy kept pressing for information. She had gotten Uncle Neville to explain the controls, which were quite simple—a lever for up and down, and another for steering. But the next issue was more worrisome.

"So . . . the motor," Wendy said. "It uses gasoline?"

"Yes," said Uncle Neville. "It's quite a reliable motor. It has two cylinders and a four-stroke—"

"I see," said Wendy. "And how long does the motor keep going before it runs out of fuel?"

Uncle Neville looked at the ceiling and scratched his cheek, thinking. Then he said, "I don't know, actually, since it has never operated under flight conditions for more than a brief while without . . . ah . . . without . . ."

"Crashing," said Mrs. Blotney.

"Quite so," Uncle Neville agreed cheerfully. "But I imagine that with a full tank of fuel, it would run for, I should think, three or four hours."

Wendy gulped. "Will the tank be full today?" she asked.

"Yes, I always fill it, just in case," said Uncle Neville. "Although I'm planning just a short flight today. I won't be going to France, at least not yet, ha-ha!"

Wendy tried to smile, but her mind was buzzing with troubling thoughts. Three or four hours. That didn't sound like nearly enough time, but it would have to do.

"All right, then!" said Uncle Neville, wiping his mouth, then tossing his napkin onto the table as he rose. "Wind is down and the sun is up! It's time to fly!"

With a whoop apiece, John and Michael were racing to the front door. Uncle Neville was right behind, followed by Wendy, who was holding her cloth bag. A very unhappy Mrs. Blotney brought up the rear.

Two minutes later, Uncle Neville and the boys were swinging open the big barn doors. Just inside, the ornithopter was waiting, its feathered wings arching out on both sides like enormous eyebrows.

Uncle Neville and the boys took hold of the ornithopter frame and began rolling it out of the barn on its four small, wire-spoke wheels. Wendy went to help them, and as she grasped the wooden frame, she was struck by how flimsy it was—just sticks, really. The wings looked especially frail, literally made from feathers (ostrich, her uncle had told her). They were connected by wire cables to the two large control levers mounted next to the platform where the pilot stood. There was a smaller lever there also, connected by a cable to the motor. Wendy assumed this was the throttle.

The motor itself looked a bit more substantial than the rest of the craft, but Wendy knew nothing about what made it work; its wires, belts, and hoses were a mystery. She did note, with relief, that the fuel tank was on the side of the motor facing the pilot's platform.

When the ornithopter had been wheeled into place, Uncle Neville lugged a red metal can out of the barn. Wendy, touching her golden locket, watched closely as he unscrewed the cap on top of the fuel tank and filled the tank with gasoline. He put the cap back on, tightened it, and wiped the tank with a rag. Then he spent a few minutes inspecting the motor and making some small adjustments.

"All right, then!" he said at last. "It's time!"

"I'll go call the doctor," said Mrs. Blotney, turning back toward the house, unable to watch.

"You boys stand back!" said Uncle Neville, shooing John and Michael a few feet farther from the ornithopter. The instant he was done shooing, they moved right back to where they had been. Uncle Neville, busy with the starter crank on the front of the motor, wasn't watching the boys.

He also wasn't watching Wendy, who, clutching her bag, had stepped around the back of the ornithopter and moved next to the platform.

"Ready?" said Uncle Neville.

"Ready!" shouted John and Michael.

Uncle Neville grabbed the starter crank in both hands and gave it a yank. The motor coughed, then sputtered to life. The boys cheered. The giant wings started moving, rising slowly, then descending. Uncle Neville was making one last adjustment to the motor.

Now, thought Wendy. She climbed up onto the platform.

The engine roared as Uncle Neville finished his adjustment. The big feathered wings swept up and down, kicking up dust. On each downbeat, the ornithopter jumped a foot off the ground, then settled back onto its little wheels.

"Hurry, Uncle Neville!" shouted John.

Uncle Neville was already bustling around the side of the ornithopter, avoiding one of the huge flapping wings. He stopped suddenly when he saw Wendy.

"Wendy!" he shouted over the sputtering of the motor. "Get down from there!"

"I'm sorry, Uncle Neville," she shouted back. She put her hand on the throttle lever.

"No!" shouted Uncle Neville.

Wendy pushed the lever all the way forward. The motor

belched black smoke and then roared much louder. The big wings beat faster. With a *whoosh*, the ornithopter shot gracefully forward and upward.

Despite his concerns, Uncle Neville could not help but pause for a moment to admire the brilliance of his invention—with a child at the controls, it was actually flying! Then, remembering the danger, he lunged toward the ornithopter. He managed to get a hand on one of the wheels, but the next downbeat of the wings knocked him back, and the ornithopter shot upward and forward, gaining altitude.

Another flap of the wings, and it was well out of reach, rising steadily as it flew across the open field. Uncle Neville ran behind, trailed by Michael and John, all three shouting and jumping. But Wendy couldn't hear them over the sound of the motor and the pounding of her own heartbeat in her ears. She was *flying*.

The ornithopter was now fifty feet in the air. It began to lean to the right, first slightly, then more sharply. Suddenly it was losing altitude. Wendy grabbed one of the levers and pulled it; this corrected the tilt for a moment, but then sent the ornithopter in the other direction, so far to the left that Wendy nearly fell off the platform. After several seconds of panic, she managed to get the craft level again. It resumed its rise, its big wings swooshing.

She was getting the hang of this.

Her uncle's field was well behind her now; she was

crossing over a line of trees and still gaining altitude. She looked down and felt a wave of nausea as she realized how high up she was on this fragile, creaking craft, standing on a platform barely larger than a step stool. She became aware of how hard her heart was pounding.

Concentrate, she told herself. *Find the train tracks.*

She glanced back over her shoulder at her uncle's mansion, now small in the distance. Off to the left, she could see the spires of Cambridge. She adjusted the altitude lever so that the ornithopter was no longer climbing. Then, carefully, she leaned to her right, peering around the motor, squinting against the wind into the distance ahead. She stayed that way for several minutes, crossing a field, then another, then another. From time to time she thought she heard shouting below, but she did not look down, instead keeping her eyes on the horizon, looking for . . .

There. Beyond the next field, the train tracks ran along a raised bed, perpendicular to Wendy's present course. As she approached the tracks, she put the ornithopter into a gentle right turn until she was flying directly over them, in the direction of Harwich.

Or so she hoped.

She followed the tracks, clutching the ornithopter's frame, passing over towns and villages, listening to the whoosh of the wings and the roar of the motor. Occasionally the motor would cough and Wendy's heart would stop; but then it would resume roaring. She prayed it was as reliable as Uncle Neville had said.

She had no watch, so she didn't know exactly how long she'd been flying—it felt like an eternity, but she knew it was probably less than an hour—when she saw the sea in the distance. She followed the tracks into Harwich, comforted somehow by the sight of the train station. She adjusted her course slightly to take her toward the harbor, reducing her altitude as she drew close to the quay.

It was bustling with dockworkers. One of them caught sight of the ornithopter; soon all of them were pointing and shouting, some in fear, as the strange flying craft bore down on them. Wendy ignored them, her eyes searching the quay. Her heart leaped when she saw the bulky form of Uncle Ted at the very end, jumping up and down and waving both arms over his head to get her attention. As she drew close they made eye contact, and he pointed vigorously toward the harbor. Wendy looked in that direction and saw the sleek silver shape of a porpoise poking out of the water. She altered course slightly, heading toward it. The moment she did, the porpoise flashed its tail and dove, then resurfaced farther away, clearly leading her toward the harbor's mouth.

Wendy followed. In a few moments, she realized with alarm that she was flying much faster than the porpoise could swim. As she passed over it she looked down frantically, wondering what she was supposed to do. Then she glanced up, and there it was, a hundred yards ahead: another grinning porpoise, poking high out of the water, waiting for her. Wendy aimed for it, followed it as far as she could, and then found the next porpoise, then the next, then the next, each one holding its grinning snout high, guiding her forward, like signposts in the sea.

For several minutes Wendy was so focused on finding the next porpoise that she didn't look back. When she did, she saw that she had passed over the harbor breakwater and was already well out over the open sea; Harwich was receding rapidly behind her. Ahead lay only water, formless and dark. Wendy, for the first time, noticed the chill of the sea wind; the water, she knew, would be colder.

The engine coughed once, then resumed its steady roar. Wendy's hand gripped the steering lever. Shivering in the wind, she again looked back toward Harwich, toward land, toward safety.

"No," she said, out loud. Then she turned forward, looking for the next silver signpost in the endless dark green sea.

CHAPTER 24

BREAKTHROUGH

SCARLET JOHNS FOLLOWED THE ROBED form of the Skeleton down the dank and dimly lit corridor. Ahead of the Skeleton was a guard, who walked quickly, not looking back. He had briefly glimpsed what remained of the Skeleton's face, and did not want to see it again.

From somewhere close came the rumble, screech, and clank of a train. The corridor was narrow and claustrophobic, the air stale, as if already breathed too many times to be of any use. The only light came from a string of widely spaced, flickering bulbs hung from a wire that snaked along the tunnel wall. It was cold down here, eighty feet below the London streets; muddy water dripped constantly from the earthen walls and ceiling, held up by what looked like hastily erected wooden braces.

They passed a cell to the left. The Skeleton ignored it, but Scarlet paused to peer through the barred window. She saw a figure huddled in the corner, wrapped in filthy clothes. The figure looked up. Scarlet, expecting to see a male prisoner, inhaled sharply: It was a woman, kept in cage that a dog did not deserve. The woman's dirt-streaked face was gaunt and pale, but still quite beautiful; her eyes shone with both defiance and fear. The woman's gaze held Scarlet's for a moment. With an abrupt turn of her head, Scarlet looked away. She resumed following the Skeleton. She did not want to think about the woman.

In another dozen yards the tunnel widened into a space that was apparently being used as an office of sorts. A table had been improvised from wooden planks; on it sat a flickering lantern and a jumble of large sheets of paper that appeared to be architectural drawings and mechanical plans.

"Wait here," said the guard, keeping his eyes averted from the Skeleton. He left quickly the way they had come.

The Skeleton and Scarlet waited in silence. Scarlet, restless, looked down the corridor every few seconds. The Skeleton stood utterly still, his face obscured by the hood of his long robe. Five long minutes passed.

Suddenly the Skeleton rasped, "He is coming." Scarlet again looked down the corridor. She saw nothing. She was about to speak, when she felt something.

The air, already cold, was growing colder.

Molly felt it, too. She was standing next to the cell window, her face pressed against the bars, looking to her left, trying to get another glimpse of the two strangers who had just been led past by the guard—a hooded man, and the woman who had stopped to look in at her.

She felt the chill and turned to look to her right. She could see only a few feet down the corridor. She heard footsteps approaching. The air grew colder still, the footsteps closer . . .

And then Molly screamed.

She hadn't meant to scream, but she couldn't stop herself. It was as if the past twenty years hadn't happened and she was a girl again, trapped in her room while the hideous shadow-thing seeped under her door, coming for her. She had felt the same chill that night, and as she felt it now, the horror came back, overpowering her thoughts.

She clapped a hand over her mouth, forcing herself to be quiet. She backed quickly away from the cell window. A dark shape appeared outside. The footsteps stopped. Molly didn't want to look at the window, but she couldn't look away. Her hand still to her mouth, she watched as a tall figure in dark clothing and a top hat stepped toward the cell and bent to look inside. A face appeared in the window, long and thin, impossibly pale. The lips were thin, bloodless. The eyes were hidden behind wire-rimmed glasses with lenses black as coal. Molly had seen von Schatten once before, at a banquet. He had looked strange then. Down here, in the gloom of the tunnel, he looked inhuman.

He was silent for a few seconds, staring at Molly. She did not breathe.

"Greetings, *Starcatcher*," he sneered. His voice was different from the one he had used at the banquet. Now it sounded like a moan from a tomb. Molly knew that voice well.

Somehow she found words of her own. "What do you want?" she said.

A pause, and then the hideous voice: "What we have always wanted."

Molly started to speak again, but von Schatten was gone. Molly sank onto the hard wooden planks that served as her bed. She was grateful that von Schatten, or Ombra, or whatever this creature was, had not entered her cell. But his words filled her with despair.

What we have always wanted.

⟫━◆━⟪

Scarlet watched the tall, thin man with the dark eyeglasses as he approached the table. The Skeleton had told her to speak to von Schatten only if spoken to, so she offered no greeting. Von Schatten ignored her, addressing his words to the Skeleton.

"Give it to me," he said.

From somewhere in his robe, the Skeleton produced a bundled rag with a string of rawhide holding it tight. With the gnarled nub of his right hand, he set it on the table.

"The tip of Curtana," he rasped. "As promised."

Von Schatten looked, unafraid, at the hideous face of the Skeleton, then down at the bundle. He reached down and untied it with quick motions of his long, bony fingers. The cloth came away, and he picked up the piece of metal, which seemed to glow in the lantern light.

Von Schatten's bloodless lips twitched in what might have been an attempt at a smile. He turned to the Skeleton.

"Where was it?" he said.

"The cathedral at Aachen," rasped the Skeleton. "It was in a stained-glass window, disguised as a bishop's miter. In plain view, all these years."

"You have done well," said von Schatten. "Both of you." He turned in Scarlet's direction. A sense of dread overcame her; she felt as though the air had been sucked from her lungs. She was greatly relieved when von Schatten was distracted by the arrival of one of the guards, who came puffing down the corridor from the direction opposite the way Scarlet and the Skeleton had arrived.

"Baron von Schatten," he began, as he reached the table.

"We have . . ." He stopped, catching sight of the Skeleton's face.

"Out with it!" snapped von Schatten.

"Yes, Baron," said the guard, tearing his eyes away from the Skeleton. "You said to inform you when the prisoners have broken through. We believe they have."

"Stop the digging immediately," von Schatten said. "I will be there shortly."

"Yes, Baron," said the guard. He scurried back down the corridor.

Von Schatten turned to the Skeleton, and once again his thin lips writhed into a ghastly smile.

"It appears you arrived at an opportune time," he said. "You bring the tip of Curtana, and now we appear to have broken through to the chamber. That give us two legs of the tripod. We now need only the third leg, and we shall have it soon enough, thanks to our friend in the palace."

"Still," rasped the Skeleton, "you run the risk of discovery here, so close to the Underground."

"We are well hidden," said von Schatten. "We are protected by powerful friends in the police force. No one knows of our efforts here except, of course, the guards, who are well aware that their lives are worthless if they betray us."

"What about the prisoners?" said the Skeleton.

"We will not need them much longer," said von

Schatten. "When their usefulness expires, they will be eliminated."

"Perhaps," said the Skeleton, "you will allow me to carry out that task."

Von Schatten's lips twitched. "You would enjoy that, wouldn't you?" he said.

"Yes," rasped the Skeleton, and Scarlet shivered for reasons that had nothing to do with the cold.

"Very well, then," said von Schatten. "When their work is done, they will be yours. Now let us observe as they finish digging their graves."

Von Schatten and the Skeleton started down the corridor. Behind them, Scarlet hesitated. She had been promised great deal of money for her expertise, which had been critical in finding the tip of Curtana. But now that the tip was found, had her usefulness also expired? She thought about the woman in the cell only yards away. Suddenly she was seized by the urge to run, to forget the money and get out of this underground hell. Could she escape? Would she be able to get past the guards? And even if she did, would they . . .

"Scarlet!" the angry rasp of the Skeleton's voice jolted her back to the moment. She saw that von Schatten and the Skeleton had stopped and were looking back at her.

"Are you coming?" rasped the Skeleton.

Scarlet half-turned toward the exit corridor, her body tense, on the edge of running. But she could not get past that edge. She sagged, then slowly turned and began walking toward the two dark figures.

"Yes," she said quietly. "I'm coming."

———◦———

Molly had heard every word; a trick of acoustics carried sound perfectly from the wooden table to her cell. Molly had listened with increasing dismay to von Schatten's conversation with the two visitors. Now, as they walked away, she tried to piece together the meaning of what she had overheard.

The strangers had brought von Schatten the tip of something, the name of which Molly did not recognize. But she recognized the name of the city it had been found in: Aachen. That triggered a memory in Molly. James said he had overheard von Schatten talking about a "missing piece" that had something to do with Germany. Aachen, Molly knew, was in Germany. Apparently the strangers had brought von Schatten his missing piece.

Whatever that piece was, it was one of three things von Schatten needed—the "legs of the tripod," he called them. Apparently he also had the second leg—a chamber, close by, which must be what James, Thomas, and the other prisoners had been digging for. As for the third leg, Molly had no idea what it was, other than that von Schatten expected to have it soon.

That was bad enough. Much worse was the discussion about the fate of the prisoners.

When their usefulness expires, von Schatten had said, *they will be eliminated.*

Molly wondered how soon that would be. Tomorrow? Today? In the next hour?

She peered through the cell window. She had done this a thousand times, but this time she focused her attention on the wooden supports that held up the tunnel. Her gaze then went to the boards that formed her cell floor. She went to the wall of her cell and dug her finger into the dirt, grabbing the end of the widest board. She grunted and pulled with all her strength. With a sucking sound, the end of the board came up. Spiders and centipedes, disturbed by the board being moved, scurried across the mud. Molly jumped back. The board was oak, thick and sturdy.

Molly again moved to the door and examined the tunnel supports outside her cell. They appeared to have been constructed hastily, for temporary use. She looked down again at the loose floorboard, then at the steel bars across the cell window.

Molly looked both ways down the corridor. She saw nobody. She lifted the floorboard, slipped it quietly through the bars, and went to work.

CHAPTER 25

LIFELINE

THE ORNITHOPTER'S MOTOR was coughing more often now. Sometimes it belched three or four times, the big feather wings jerking in hesitation, before finally the engine roared back to life.

Each time this happened, Wendy worried the engine might not come back. Her mood was not helped by her discomfort. Her legs ached from standing on the tiny platform; her hands ached from gripping the ornithopter control levers. She was thoroughly cold now, shivering almost constantly in the chilly, damp ocean air. She had managed to eat some bread and cheese, but when she'd tried to drink some water, the bottle had slipped from her aching hand and fallen into the sea far below.

Again and again she peered ahead, blinking into the rushing wind, searching the horizon for the dark shape of land. Again and again she saw only the dark green sea, stretching away. Her only reassurance came from the sight of the porpoises. Thank goodness: there was always one below, and always another waiting for her ahead.

The day was cloudy, so most of the time she could not tell the location of the sun, nor her direction of travel. From what glimpses of the sun she did manage, she figured that the porpoises were now leading her southwest. Uncle Neville had guessed that the motor had three or four hours' worth of fuel. Wendy didn't know exactly how long she'd been aloft, but she was quite sure it was already longer than four hours. She glanced constantly at the fuel tank, each time patting the locket around her neck.

The engine coughed again, this time longer than ever, and when it started up again the roar was more of a sputter. Then more coughing. The wings hesitated and jerked. The ornithopter, though still flapping, was starting to descend.

This is it, thought Wendy.

She leaned forward and grabbed the filler cap on the top of the fuel tank. She gave it a counterclockwise twist. The cap did not budge.

The engine coughed again, and again, and this time it kept coughing. The ornithopter, its wings beating very slowly now, began descending at a steeper angle.

Fighting panic, Wendy gripped the cap and twisted it as hard as she could. Still it did not budge. She let go of the control lever and put both hands on the filler cap. The engine's sputter was more silence than combustion now. Out of the corners of her eyes Wendy saw the dark sea below drawing closer and closer. She gritted her teeth and with a desperate grunt yanked at the cap. This time it gave.

The engine stopped, belched, and then sputtered again ever more weakly. Wendy could hear the waves below. She spun the cap off and tucked it into the pocket of her coat. She braced herself against the ornithopter frame. With cold-stiffened fingers, she reached behind her and fumbled with the clasp of her locket. The wave tops were near. From somewhere below came the urgent chitter of a porpoise: *Up! Up!*

The engine wheezed and shuddered violently, clearly about to die. With a jerk, Wendy pulled the locket from her neck, breaking the chain. She leaned forward, holding the locket toward the fuel tank's opening. With her thumb, she flicked the locket open.

Instantly the air was filled with light, and Wendy was no longer cold, or scared, or anything bad at all. In fact, despite her desperate predicament, she felt wonderful. The source of this feeling was a radiant golden sphere of light that now enveloped the locket and her hand, from there infusing her whole body with a sense of calm and well-being. And that melodious sound . . . Was that *bells?*

Up! Up!

The urgent warning brought her back to the moment.

She saw the porpoise now, directly below her, only yards away. The sputtering ornithopter was in free fall, its wings barely moving. Forcing herself to concentrate, Wendy tilted the locket over the fuel tank. A thin stream of golden light poured into the hole. A second later, the sputtering engine came to life. But this time, instead of the clackety roar she had been listening to for hours, it emitted a smooth, almost pleasant, hum.

Up! Up! Up!

Wendy snapped the locket closed with one hand and pulled the altitude lever with the other. The ornithopter responded instantly, swooping upward as its big wings beat in powerful whooshes. As it rose, Wendy carefully pushed the locket down into her coat pocket. She retrieved the fuel cap and tightened it over the tank opening. The ornithopter, its motor humming happily, continued rising swiftly and easily, flying far faster now than it had before. Soon Wendy was again soaring high above the limitless sea. Below and well behind her was the porpoise that had warned her to stay up. She waved; the porpoise leaped high in response, then was gone. Wendy looked ahead and found her next guide, waiting patiently.

She allowed herself a tiny smile. As she'd hoped, the starstuff had held her aloft. And she felt fantastic; the warmth still filled her; a vibrant energy had replaced her exhaustion.

But it would not last. She could already feel the effects of the starstuff diminishing. In time she would have to pour more into the fuel tank. How soon would that be? How much starstuff was left in the locket? How far away was the island? And what would she do when night fell? How would she see her porpoise guides? Assuming that she made it to nightfall . . .

As each new question popped into Wendy's mind, her confidence diminished. She put her hand into her pocket and gripped the locket, feeling its reassuring warmth. Her eyes went back to the horizon, searching for a hint, a promise of land. She saw nothing.

She tightened her grip on the locket, her lifeline, her only hope.

$\mathcal{T}$UG-O'-$\mathcal{W}$AR

$\mathcal{P}$IRATE COVE LOOKED LIKE a giant spiderweb. Arranged around its shore were eleven pulleys, some suspended from palm trees, others from ropes stretched tightly between trees and rocks. Connecting these were long runs of rope, strung through the pulleys and coming together in the middle of the cove, where Mollusk divers had tied the ropes together beneath the hull of the sailing ship *De Vliegen*. The ship, which had a huge hole in its hull, had sat on the bottom for more than twenty years, with only its masts sticking out of the water.

From the shore, a cry went out: "All hands prepare to heave!"

This was followed by a similar command in the Mollusk language, which loosely translated to "Pull until you grunt like a warthog!"

Hook and Fighting Prawn, longtime enemies brought

together for this effort, stood side by side on a tall rock overlooking the water. Surrounding the cove were Mollusks and pirates, working side by side but as wary of each other as their leaders were. The men had formed into groups and were gripping the ropes with callused hands, the same hands that had spent days rigging the massive network of pulleys.

"On three?" Hook asked Prawn. It was understood the pirates and Mollusk warriors would take orders only from their own leader.

"On one," Prawn corrected, as this was the Mollusk system. Before Hook could protest, Fighting Prawn counted, "Three . . . two . . . *one.*" On "one," both men raised their arms and shouted, in their separate languages, for their men to go to work. The men heaved; the slack ropes tightened; the palm trees bowed; the pulleys creaked and cried; the men grunted and dug their heels into the sand as if locked in a giant game of tug-o'-war.

For several excruciatingly long seconds, nothing happened. The only signs of the intense effort were concentric circles of ripples dancing around the taut ropes where they entered the water. The pulleys groaned. The ropes stretched. The workers gritted their teeth. Sweat poured from their straining bodies.

"It ain't moving," said Hook. "Your men need to pull harder."

Fighting Prawn shot Hook a look, but said nothing.

And then: bubbles. Just a few at first, but soon the cove was boiling with them. The water became milky, clumps of seaweed mingling with clouds of sand. And then, slowly, the masts wobbled and began to rise. The main deck railing poked through the surface, and then came a great rushing sound as the ship's deck appeared, water cascading off the sides.

There the ship seemed to waver, the dripping ropes trembling with the strain of holding the massive weight of the ship. One of the pulleys broke; pieces of it whistled over the ship and flew far out over the cove before splashing into the water. Two men—one pirate, one Mollusk—collapsed.

Urged on by Hook and Fighting Prawn, the other men kept heaving on their ropes, backing step by agonizing step away from the water, up the beach, toward the jungle. With each step more of the ship's dripping hull appeared. Finally the hole in the hull was visible. Water gushed from it as it cleared the cove surface. Now they could patch it.

Fighting Prawn and Hook ordered the men to stop. The ropes were tied off to trees, and a cheer rang across the cove. And the men fell silent, as they got their first good look at the ship that had been mostly underwater for more than two decades.

It looked impossibly well-preserved. Yes, there was a bit of slime on the hull, and there were fish flopping on its deck. But except for the hole, the ship looked sound. It looked almost *new*. None of the wood had rotted, not even the smallest piece of a rail. More incredible: all of its rigging was still intact. Every pulley and rope. Only the sails were missing.

"That ain't possible," said Hook. "A ship can't look like that after sitting on the bottom."

"A ship can't fly, either," said Fighting Prawn.

Hook would never admit it, but the Mollusk chief had a point. The *De Vliegen* had once carried a huge quantity of starstuff, which had enabled it to fly across the ocean. The starstuff had fallen out, dumped into the island's water supply. But clearly it had left the ship permanently changed.

"So she will sail again," said Fighting Prawn. He read the name carved across the ship's broad transom. "The *De Vliegen*."

"Yes, she will sail again," said Hook. "And soon. But not as the *De Vliegen*."

Fighting Prawn raised a questioning eyebrow.

"It's a pirate ship now," said Hook. "Her name is the *Jolly Roger*."

———✦———

From high above the cove, on the side of the steep mountain ridge that divided Mollusk Island, Cheeky O'Neal, Frederick DeWulf, Rufus Kelly, and Angus McPherson had watched the raising of the ship.

"They did it," said DeWulf. "Didn't think they could, but they did."

O'Neal, his eyes on the ship, nodded.

"How long d'you think it'll take them to repair it?" said Kelly.

"Shouldn't take long," said DeWulf. "Dripping wet, and she looks like she just came out of the yard. Look at that rigging! She appears to have been under maybe a day or two, discounting the slime that's suggesting more like ten or twenty *years*. Any of you want to explain that to me?"

"There's a lot on this island can't be explained," said Kelly.

"Looks like they're already gettin' started with the repairs," said McPherson, pointing at the cove, where men, Mollusks and pirates alike, were climbing from canoes onto the ship. "Guess they really want us off this island."

"What if they finish the repairs before we're ready?" said Kelly. He addressed the question to O'Neal. All eyes were on the big man, waiting for an answer.

O'Neal continued staring at the ship for a few more seconds. When he spoke, his voice was a deep, determined rumble.

"It doesn't matter what they want," he said. "We stick to our plan."

With a glare at the other three, he spat on the ground, turned, and started back up the ridge.

CHAPTER 27

The Last Bit

Dusk had turned the gloomy sky a darker shade of gray. Wendy knew night would come soon, blending sky and sea into blackness.

She peered ahead, feeling the familiar brief pang of anxiety until she caught sight of the next porpoise. How many had there been? Wendy had long since lost count. For what seemed like the thousandth time, she shifted her position on the tiny platform, trying to give her aching legs some relief.

She reckoned she had been standing for at least twelve hours. The porpoises had led her many miles south. The air was distinctly warmer now, though Wendy was hardly comfortable. Aside from being exhausted, she was hungry, having finished the last of her bread and cheese hours earlier. Her throat was parched; she thought often of her lost water bottle.

But what gnawed at her most, more than hunger or thirst, was worry. Three times the humming of the motor had dropped suddenly in pitch, and the beat of the ornithopter's big wings had slowed. Each time Wendy quickly unscrewed the fuel-tank cap, opened the locket, and carefully poured in some more starstuff. Each time the motor hummed back to life.

But the last time this happened, the flow of starstuff had been barely a trickle. When Wendy had snapped the locket shut, she wasn't sure there was anything at all left inside.

She would find out soon enough.

The sky was much darker now. Wendy gently pushed the altitude lever, nosing the ornithopter down so she could fly closer to the sea. Her eyes were fixed on the porpoise currently guiding her. She could barely see its gray body. She wondered how she would follow the porpoises when darkness fell.

Wendy passed over the guide porpoise and, straining to see through the gloom, found the next one. With each passing minute the sky grew darker. She took the ornithopter lower, then lower still. She passed over her guide and anxiously searched the water. The darkness was almost total now. Where was the next porpoise?

Then she saw it: a strange greenish glow in the sea ahead. As she swooped closer, she realized that the glow was coming from the water itself. It formed an inverted "V," created by the wake of the next porpoise, which itself was barely visible. When she passed over it, Wendy saw another ghostly "V" in the distance ahead. She didn't understand why the water was glowing like this, but she was very grateful that it was.

She passed from "V" to "V," each one an arrow pointing to the next. The motor hummed; the wings whooshed. Minutes became a half hour, which became an hour. Wendy's legs ached; her eyes stung, peering ahead into the darkness.

And then the hum sank lower in pitch.

Wendy reached frantically to unscrew the fuel-tank cap. She was close to the water and could not afford to let the ornithopter descend much farther. She reached into her coat pocket, pulled out the locket, and held it over the fuel tank. With a silent prayer she flicked it open.

There was a momentary flash of golden light, raising Wendy's hopes. But they fell immediately when the glow flickered and dimmed. Wendy shook the last bit of starstuff into the fuel tank. The engine resumed its high-pitched humming, but only for a few seconds.

Then it died.

Its wings having stopped, the ornithopter began to descend rapidly. Wendy pulled back hard on the altitude lever. The ornithopter swooped up a few feet, then stalled and went into a downward spiral. Wendy fought to control it, but the levers were useless. She was going into the ocean. She looked down in panic, but in the darkness could see nothing. She heard rushing water.

With the sound of cracking wood, the ornithopter slammed into the sea. Wendy felt a stab of pain as her head struck the ornithopter frame. Before she could hold her breath she was dragged under water. Dazed by the blow to her head, she took several seconds to understand that her coat was caught in the wreckage of the frame, which was being dragged down by the weight of the motor. She kicked furiously, blindly in the black water. She felt her coat rip and suddenly she was no longer going down. Lungs burning, she thrashed the water, struggling to swim to the surface, but not sure which way it was.

Then she felt pressure on both sides, and she began moving swiftly. *The porpoises.* A few seconds later, her head broke the surface. She gasped for breath, coughed up salt water, gasped some more. There were porpoises all around her; three were holding her up, using gentle pressure from their sleek bodies. Others swam close by, chittering and squeaking urgently.

Wendy tried to understand them, but she could not concentrate. She felt dazed; her head throbbed viciously. She reached up to touch her scalp and recoiled as her fingers found a deep gash. She felt blood trickling down her forehead, into her eyes.

She needed to find out where she was, where the island was. Whether she would live. She tried to concentrate, to remember her Porpoise vocabulary. Nothing came. She felt an overwhelming sense of fatigue. She struggled to keep her eyes open.

I can't fall asleep, she thought. *Not here. I can't . . .*

Her eyes closed; her body went limp. The porpoises repositioned themselves under her; others formed a protective ring around her. Then they began moving, taking the waves as gently as they could, painstakingly keeping Wendy afloat while her hand dragged lifelessly in the sea.

CHAPTER 28

ONE LAST PUSH

*T*HE TRAINS HAD STOPPED.

Because she was cut off from the outside world, Molly's sense of time had come down to two factors: the workers' schedule and the trains. She'd lost track of the schedule because von Schatten had ordered the work halted. That left the trains. She'd not heard one for over an hour. She knew the Underground stopped at midnight, which meant it was now past one in the morning.

That, in turn, meant there would likely be fewer guards on duty—and those who were on duty were likely dozing.

Carefully, Molly pushed the stout plank out her cell's barred window. By the dim light from the bare corridor bulbs, she managed to fit the plank into a space she had made between the corridor's clay wall and the closest vertical wooden support post.

Creating the space had required painstaking effort. Molly had hovered by the cell window, waiting for the rumble of a train to cover her efforts. When she heard one coming, after checking each way to see that there were no guards about, she would ram the end of the board into the clay and rock, chipping away what little she could before the train noise subsided.

The guards had nearly caught her. Despite the trains, they apparently heard her pounding and came looking. Fortunately, she was able to pull the board back into the cell before they arrived, and they had failed to spot the small hole she'd dug behind the post, hidden in shadow.

That had made her nervous enough to stop her work, at least during the day. But her digging had shown her that the corridor wall—which was also the wall to her cell—was not particularly strong. If she could move the post, the wall behind it would crumble. And that would leave a hole.

A way out of the cell.

She wasn't sure exactly what she would do when she got out. Somehow she would have to get to James and the others, to try to free them before von Schatten decided to kill them. She would worry about how to do that later. First, she needed to escape.

She punched the board repeatedly into the small hole she'd carved behind the post. A tiny bit of clay and rock dislodged. At this rate, it was going to take forever.

But, she thought, if there was one thing she had a lot of, it was time.

Patience, she reminded herself. She stabbed the board into the hole.

And again . . .

And again . . .

CHAPTER 29

NOWHERE ELSE

WENDY'S LEFT EYE BLINKED OPEN. Her right eye felt glued shut. Her head pounded with pain. Her parched throat screamed for water.

But it was daylight. And she was still alive.

She felt the porpoises' powerful bodies beneath her; felt the motion of the heaving sea. She was seized by a very unpleasant feeling in her stomach. She turned sideways, vomiting seawater onto one of the porpoises. She tried to say "I'm sorry" in Porpoise, but it came out as more of a croak. In any event, the porpoises didn't seem to mind.

One of them surfaced close to Wendy's face.

Fish? it said. It opened its mouth to reveal a dead cod.

Wendy nearly threw up again.

No thank you, she said. *No fish. Water?*

The porpoise regarded her for a moment. Then pirouetted full-circle, as if indicating the sea.

Water, it said.

No, said Wendy. She tried to think how to say "fresh water," but the words didn't come. Even if they had, she didn't know how the porpoises would find fresh water out here. Wherever "here" was.

She leaned over and splashed some seawater on her face, trying to clean off the dried blood. She got her right eye open and gingerly felt the gash in her forehead. It was still painful, but the bleeding had slowed down to an ooze. That was something.

The porpoises carried her onward, taking shifts in groups of three or four. The sun rose swiftly in a blue, cloud-free sky; with it rose the temperature. The heat only made Wendy more thirsty. She took off her ripped coat and used it to form a crude pillow. In an hour, despite her thirst and discomfort, despite the sun's glare, she fell back asleep, rocked on the backs of the porpoises.

She awoke with a start. The porpoises were making a lot of noise. She opened her eyes, then quickly closed them to block the glare of the sun, now nearly overhead.

She felt a shadow cross her face. Slowly, using her hand as a shade, she opened her eyes. She blinked, and saw him.

The flying boy.

He hung suspended over her, perhaps ten feet in the air. He wore tattered clothes, the pants and sleeves cut short, a knife tucked into his belt. His hair was a wild tangle of reddish-orange; his face a mass of freckles around an upturned nose and sparkling blue eyes.

"Hello, Peter," Wendy croaked.

Instead of answering, he descended slowly, his feet crossed Indian-style, until he was hovering right next to her. When he spoke, his voice was barely a whisper.

"Molly," he said.

"No," she said. "I'm Wendy, Molly's daughter."

Peter nodded, and Wendy saw a flash of sadness in his eyes. "I guess I know that, after all this time. It's just that you look so much—"

Like a cow, said Tinker Bell, from deep inside Peter's hair.

"Be quiet," said Peter.

"What?" said Wendy.

"Ignore her," said Peter, pointing toward his hair.

Wendy eyed Peter's hair doubtfully, seeing nothing. "All right," she said. "But . . . how did you find me?"

"The porpoises," said Peter. "They sent word to the island that there was a girl sent by Ammm. Ammm's a porpoise."

"I know," said Wendy.

"They said the girl was in trouble," continued Peter. "So I flew out here. Since they said 'girl,' I figured it probably wasn't Mol—your mother. But I thought maybe . . ." He stopped, clearly embarrassed.

"Anyway," he went on, "the Mollusks will be here soon with a canoe. They'll have you on the island in a couple of hours. Meanwhile I brought you this." From inside his shirt he pulled out a coconut, with a hole plugged by a piece of wood. He unplugged it and handed it to Wendy.

"Water," he said.

Without a word she grabbed the coconut and gulped until there wasn't a drop left. The water was warm, but she had never tasted better.

"Thank you," she said, finally. "And thank you for rescuing me."

"It's nothing," said Peter, blushing.

"No," said Wendy. "It's not nothing. Mother said you were very brave."

"Did she?" said Peter. "Molly said that?"

Wake me up when this is over, said Tinker Bell.

"What *is* that sound?" said Wendy. "Like bells."

Peter pointed to his head again. "It's Tinker Bell," he said. "She likes to sit on my head."

Wendy peered at Peter's hair and saw a tiny, exquisitely beautiful face poking out of the curls with a deeply unhappy expression.

"A fairy!" Wendy exclaimed.

Tink emitted a burst of bells that Peter chose not to translate literally.

"She prefers the term 'birdwoman,'" he said.

"I see," said Wendy. "She's quite lovely."

Yes, I am, agreed Tink. *And you are a cow.*

"She says thank you," said Peter. "But you were saying about Molly . . ."

Wendy's face grew somber.

"My mother is in trouble," she said.

"What kind of trouble?"

"Years ago," said Wendy. "Some very bad men came to your island, I'm told."

Now Peter's face was somber, too.

"Yes," he said.

"Peter, they're in England."

"But they can't be! They were destroyed! I was there when it happened!"

"That's what everyone thought. But they weren't destroyed. They're in England, and they've got my mother."

Peter only stared at her.

"I've come to ask you to help me find her," said Wendy.

"You . . . you want me to go back to England?"

"Yes."

"But can't her father . . . Can't the Starcatchers . . ."

"My grandfather is very ill," said Wendy. "The Starcatchers have disbanded. He told me to come here and get you, Peter. There's nobody else."

"But if I go to England, what would I do?" said Peter.

"I don't know," said Wendy.

That's quite a plan, said Tink.

"And he said something else," said Wendy.

"What was it?"

"He said 'confess.'"

"Confess what?"

"I'm afraid I don't know that, either," said Wendy.

Does she know anything? said Tink.

"Be quiet, Tink," said Peter. He stared into the distance for a minute, then another. Finally he said, "I'll have to think about it."

"I see," said Wendy, her voice suddenly cool.

"No," said Peter, stiffening. "I don't think you do. I've been on this island for more than twenty years. I've heard nothing from Mol—from any of you Starcatchers. And now, suddenly, when there's trouble, you ask me for help."

"Yes," said Wendy. "I'm asking you to help your friends."

"Who I haven't seen for twenty years," said Peter.

"I didn't know there was a limit on friendship," said Wendy.

Peter didn't answer that. He stared out at the sea. A minute passed, and then Wendy spoke.

"Please," she said, softly. "I've nowhere else to turn."

Peter looked at her, then out to sea again. His mind went back to another time at sea, long ago, before he could fly, when he had been hurled into a raging sea. He would have drowned for certain had it not been for a brave girl who leaped from the deck of a ship, risking her own life to save his.

That was Molly, the mother of this girl, who had come all this way to ask for his help.

He nodded his head once, then again more emphatically.

Oh no, said Tink.

CHAPTER 30

(T)HE (C)ALL

(G)EORGE DARLING IMPATIENTLY PACED the hallway outside the door to Chief Superintendent Blake's office in Scotland Yard. George was not accustomed to being kept waiting.

The call from Uncle Neville about Wendy had turned George's already troubled world completely upside down. First his wife had disappeared, now his daughter. In a *flying machine*. George was furious at himself for entrusting his children to his batty relative Neville, with his lunatic inventions.

George's first act had been to order Neville to bring John and Michael back to London, *immediately*. His second act had been to contact the Cambridgeshire police to have them organize a search for Wendy. They had been scouring the countryside, so far without success. George was pressing them hard to widen the search. He wanted desperately to go organize it himself, but felt he had to remain in London, to keep pressure on Scotland Yard to find his wife. That was what had led him to request—actually, demand—an appointment this morning with Blake.

And so he paced, exhausted, sick with guilt and worry, nagged incessantly by questions about both his wife and daughter. *Where had the flying machine come down? Why hadn't anyone . . .*

"He will see you now, Mr. Darling," Blake's secretary announced.

"About time," muttered George. He squared his shoulders and marched into Blake's office. The secretary closed the door behind him.

"Mr. Darling," said Blake, rising from his desk. "To what do I owe the pleasure of—"

"Spare me the pleasantries," said George. "I haven't the stomach for it today."

Blake sat back down.

"Of course, I understand," he said, with a calmness that George found very irritating. "I heard about your daughter. Terrible thing. A girl on a flying contraption . . ."

He stopped there, but George saw the rest of the thought in Blake's eyes—contempt for a father who would let his daughter get into such a predicament.

"Terrible thing," Blake repeated. "If there's anything we can do here at the Yard . . ."

"I am working with the Cambridgeshire authorities," said George. "And I am confident they will find my daughter. What I wish to know is what progress you have made in locating my wife."

"As my men have told you a number of times, Mr. Darling, we are doing—"

"I *know* what they've told me, Chief Superintendent. They've told me they're doing everything they can. But I fail to understand how, with all the resources of Scotland Yard, they have produced nothing. *Nothing.* My wife was . . . my wife *is* a respectable woman, from a good family. She is not a beggar; she is not a criminal. Such people don't simply disappear."

"Oh, but they do," said Blake, again with that irritatingly calm voice. "People disappear all the time."

"So you're saying there's nothing more you can do."

"What I am saying," said Blake, "is that everything that can be done is being done."

George felt as though his head was going to explode. He had gotten virtually no sleep since his wife had gone missing. Now his daughter was missing as well. And this smug, pompous man, sitting behind a desk . . .

George realized that he had moved close to that desk. He was now leaning over Blake, unable to stop himself from blurting out what he was thinking—what he had been thinking for days now.

"Perhaps you don't *want* to find her," he said.

Blake stiffened. "What did you say?"

George leaned closer. "Before my wife went missing, she came to see you," he said.

"Did she?" said Blake. "I meet so many—"

"She came to see you," interrupted George, "to discuss certain concerns she had about one of your men, James Smith. And about the Palace."

Blake's eyes narrowed.

"My wife told me that after she left that meeting with you," continued George, "she was almost grabbed by a police officer in the Underground. Two days later she disappeared."

"What are you suggesting?" said Blake quietly.

"I'm not suggesting anything," said George. "I'm *telling* you this, Chief Superintendent. I want my wife found. And I no longer believe your department is trying to find her."

"That's a serious accusation, Mr. Darling."

"Yes it is," said George. "And I intend to make sure it is investigated. I have friends in the government, Chief Superintendent. Powerful friends. I will bring this matter to their attention."

"Do you really think that's wise?" said Blake, his voice still calm. "Making accusations? A man in your position? A man with a career?" He paused, then added, softly, "A man whose wife could be . . . vulnerable?"

George recoiled. "Is that a *threat*?" he said.

"No," said Blake. "It's merely a description of your situation. I shouldn't think you'd want to make it any worse."

For a moment the two men stared at each other. George started to say something, then decided against it. He spun on his heel, went to the door, yanked it open violently, and stalked out.

When he was gone, Blake stared at the empty doorway for a moment, drumming his fingers on his desk. Then he picked up the telephone and made a call.

CHAPTER 31

THE PLAN

MOLLUSK ISLAND WAS THE most beautiful place Wendy had ever seen.

When she first caught sight of it, from the Mollusk canoe, it was a dark speck on the horizon. But as the canoe drew closer, escorted by porpoises and propelled swiftly through the sea by eight strong warriors, the speck turned into a spectacular sight—a rugged volcanic mountain rising steeply from the blue water, the dark green of its jungled slopes occasionally broken by the white foam of a cascading waterfall.

The mountain's volcanic peak rose steeply overhead as the canoe passed through a series of reefs and into the calm water of a lagoon, embraced by a long, curved white-sand beach fringed with palm trees. A group of people stood on the beach, apparently waiting for the canoe, but they were too far away for Wendy to identify them. Closer at hand, near the middle of the lagoon, was a small, rocky island; Wendy saw some figures lounging on a big flat boulder by the water's edge. As the canoe drew closer, she saw that they were beautiful young women. Several of them waved at the canoe, and Wendy, hesitantly waved back. Then, with a chorus of giggles, the beautiful young women slid from the rock and dove into the water, flashing their long graceful . . .

Tails?

Wendy gasped as the mermaids disappeared below the lagoon surface. One of the Mollusk warriors said something to the others in their odd-sounding grunt-and-click language; all eight warriors chuckled.

This is definitely not England, thought Wendy.

The canoe was fast approaching the beach. Wendy was relieved to see that Peter was one of the people standing there. After making sure she was safely aboard the canoe, he'd flown back to the island, saying he needed to speak to somebody. Wendy thought he'd said the person's name was Fighting Prawn, but that seemed unlikely.

The canoe reached shallow water and glided onto the sand. Wendy turned and waved her thanks to the porpoises, who headed back toward the open sea. Then Wendy climbed out of the canoe and stepped onto the sand. She staggered, her legs wobbly, her body weak from her harrowing ordeal. Peter ran to her, grabbing her arm to keep her from falling.

As he helped her up the beach, Wendy heard bell sounds coming from his hair. They sounded displeased.

Waiting for her with open curiosity was a group of about two dozen Mollusks. Standing slightly apart from the others was a tall, powerfully built man with deep-bronze skin, jet-black hair, and piercing dark eyes. Wendy had no doubt, as Peter led her to him, that he was the leader. When they reached him, Peter said, "Fighting Prawn, this is Wendy Aster."

"Darling," said Wendy.

"What did you say?" said Peter.

"My last name is Darling," said Wendy.

Peter frowned. "Darling?" he said. "But wasn't that . . . I mean, isn't that *George's* name?"

"Yes," said Wendy. "George Darling is my father."

"George is your father," said Peter softly.

"Yes," said Wendy.

"So George . . . married Molly."

"Why, yes," said Wendy.

"Oh," said Peter. He reddened and looked down.

"Is there something wrong?" said Wendy.

"No," said Peter, recovering. "Anyway, Fighting Prawn, this is Wendy *Darling*."

Wendy didn't like the way he said her name, but decided to ignore it.

"Pleased to meet you," she said to Fighting Prawn.

Fighting Prawn studied her face for a moment before speaking.

"Peter was right," he said. "You look remarkably like your mother. You must also have her courage, to have come all this way alone."

"I had help," said Wendy. "From the porpoises. And of course, Peter. But now I need to . . ."

Wendy's voice turned to a moan as she staggered forward, faint from lack of food, water, and sleep. Fighting Prawn caught her and picked her up easily.

"Tell us later," he said. "First you need to eat and rest."

Wendy tried to protest, but lacked the strength. Holding her in his arms, Fighting Prawn turned and carried her toward the path to the village. Peter followed, still trying to digest the news that Molly had married George, and wishing this fact did not bother him so much.

———•◆•———

Wendy slept the rest of the day, and all night long, in a hut in the Mollusk village. When she awoke, two of Fighting Prawn's daughters, Shining Pearl and Little Scallop, brought her coconut milk and a wooden platter covered with fruits, berries, and some kind of broiled chunks on skewers. She ate ravenously.

"What *is* this?" she said, holding up a skewer. "It tastes quite interesting."

"It's one of our favorites," agreed Shining Pearl. "We only get it a few times a year."

"What is it?" asked Wendy.

"Our word for it is—" Shining Pearl made an odd-sounding noise.

"What does that mean?" said Wendy.

"Giant scorpion," said Shining Pearl.

"Oh," said Wendy, quickly putting down the skewer.

"Don't worry!" said Little Scallop. "We take out the poison parts."

"Thank you," said Wendy, "but I'm quite full." She gulped down some coconut milk, then said, "Can I see your father now?"

"He's waiting for you," said Shining Pearl. "With Peter."

They led Wendy out of the hut into a spectacular island morning, the sun rising in a cloudless blue sky, turning the jungled mountainside a million shades of green. The Mollusk village was bustling—adults cooking, eating, talking; children running, playing, laughing. Wendy was struck by how healthy and happy they all seemed; there was no sign of suffering or discontent. The whole village—the whole island—seemed somehow magical. Wendy was beginning to see why Peter was not keen on leaving.

Fighting Prawn and Peter were sitting on stools made from logs in the shade of a sort of lean-to. As Wendy approached, they rose, and Fighting Prawn invited her to join them.

"You seem to be feeling better," said Fighting Prawn, once they were all seated.

"Much, thank you," said Wendy.

"How'd you like the scorpion?" said Peter, smiling. A raucous burst of bells pealed from somewhere inside his wild mass of hair.

"I found it *delicious*," lied Wendy, silencing Tink and wiping the smile from Peter's face. Turning to Fighting Prawn, Wendy said, "I am very grateful for your hospitality, Mr. . . . Prawn. Unfortunately, even though I've just arrived, I need to arrange for Peter and me to get back to England. It's most urgent."

"So Peter tells me," said Fighting Prawn. "I will of course do what I can. Both your mother and grandfather were friends to my people. If they are in trouble . . ."

"I'm afraid they are," said Wendy. "Grandfather is very ill, and I don't even know where Mother is. I fear she's been kidnapped."

"Did you go to the police?" said Fighting Prawn.

Wendy shook her head and said, "I think they're involved."

"*What?*" said Peter.

She told them everything she knew about the trouble in London. They were stunned by the news that Ombra apparently had returned in the form of von Schatten, and had worked his way into a position of great power. Peter was also shocked to learn that, in addition to Molly, both James and Thomas were missing. This news erased whatever doubts he'd had about going back to England to help the Starcatchers.

"So," concluded Wendy, "I've come all this way to ask Peter to come help rescue my mum."

Pathetic, chimed Tink, from Peter's hair.

"What did she say?" asked Wendy.

"She said she and I are at your service," said Peter.

"Thank you," said Wendy, giving Peter's arm a light touch that turned his face as red as his hair. "But how are we to get back? I mean, I suppose you can fly, Peter, but I think I've had enough flying for a lifetime."

"I'm not sure I could find my way to England flying," said Peter.

"So how will we get back?" said Wendy.

Peter and Fighting Prawn exchanged a look; they had been discussing this when Wendy walked up.

"We've got a ship," said Peter.

"You mean a canoe?" said Wendy. "Because I don't think . . ."

"No," said Peter. "It's a ship, quite a large one. It brought Mol—your mum to this very island once, back when it could fly. It's being repaired and should be ready to sail tomorrow."

"But that's wonderful!" said Wendy.

"There is one problem," said Peter.

"What's that?"

"The captain and crew."

"What about them?"

"They're pirates."

"*What?*"

It took Peter and Fighting Prawn several minutes to explain their plan to get Hook and the suspicious "shipwreck" victims off the island.

"So you're going to ask this . . . Hook person to sail Peter and me back to London?"

"Actually," said Peter, "we're not going to mention me."

"Why not?" said Wendy.

"Hook thinks I'm dead," said Peter.

"Why would he think that?" said Wendy.

"Because he killed me," said Peter. "At least he thinks he did."

This required several more minutes of explanation.

"So you see," concluded Peter, "if Hook saw me on the ship, he would try to kill me again. He hates me."

Peter seemed quite proud of this.

"So you're *not* going on the ship with me?" said Wendy.

"Oh, I'll be on the ship," said Peter. "I'll hide in the sails. I've done it before."

And it was horrible, noted Tink.

"And what makes you so sure that this Hook person will actually take me back to London?" said Wendy. "He sounds dreadful."

"He is dreadful," said Fighting Prawn. "But he will take you back, for two reasons. First, I will make him give me his word."

"And he is a man of his word?" said Wendy.

"Of course not," said Fighting Prawn. "But the second reason will be convincing. I will explain to him that if you are *not* returned safely to England, I will find him, wherever he is, and feed him to Mister Grin."

"Mister who?" said Wendy.

"Grin," said Fighting Prawn. "A very large crocodile."

"With a very large appetite for Hook," added Peter.

"Oh my," said Wendy.

For a moment, the three of them were silent. Then Wendy said, "So if I understand this correctly, you propose to send me to England on a ship captained by a murderous pirate, with a crew of cutthroats, and fellow passengers who are probably here on false pretenses and up to no good, with my only guarantee of safety being a threat of death by crocodile, and a flying boy hiding in the sails?"

Fighting Prawn and Peter looked at each other, then nodded.

"Yes," said Fighting Prawn. "That is what we propose."

"When do we sail?" said Wendy.

CHAPTER 32

ICE COFFIN

$\mathcal{B}$EWILDERED, FRUSTRATED, ANGRY, George Darling walked the streets of London, oblivious to the gusting wind and the hard, cold rain streaming down his face, soaking his clothes. He didn't want to go home to his empty house. He couldn't sleep anyway, not when he knew that both his daughter and wife were out there, somewhere, in need of help.

His help.

He understood now that the police were not going to find them. He'd placed yet another a call to Cambridgeshire, only to be told the search for Wendy had been called off because of darkness and the same horrible weather that was assaulting London. It was a rainstorm of biblical proportions, made worse by the fog that oozed up from the Thames, blanketing the streets like a thick smoke, making it impossible to see more than a few feet.

The blackness around George matched his mood. Utterly helpless, unable to think of any way to find his wife and daughter, he was spiraling downward to despair. He walked the streets of Knightsbridge like a zombie, without direction or reason.

Despite the weather, he was not alone. A few determined souls braved the deluge, some darting into pubs, others simply trying to get home. They walked quickly, heads bent, leaning into the gale, splashing through the slop that overflowed the gutters and sanitary ditches meant to carry the city's stinking waste to the sewers, the river, and eventually out to sea.

George plodded along, sometimes pinching his nose to block out the foul smells, paying scant attention to the few pedestrians he encountered. He had been walking for two hours, maybe more, when he realized that he was close by the entrance to the Sloane Square Underground Station. He turned toward it, a vague plan forming in his mind. His wife—why hadn't he believed her?—had told him a bobby had tried to grab her in the Underground. Perhaps there was something down there, some clue. . . .

It wasn't much, but it was better than aimless wandering. George turned toward the Underground. From close behind he heard the *clop-clop* of horse's hooves splashing on the cobbled street. He glanced back and was surprised to see, emerging through the fog, the familiar white boxy shape of an ice cart. Strange to see one so late—the ice men usually came around in the morning, delivering to the better homes of the neighborhood.

The cart was heading directly toward him, as if the driver did not see him in the fog. George stepped aside at the last second. The cart brushed him, knocking him backward.

"Mind your way, driver!" he shouted, recovering his balance.

He heard splashing behind him. He started to turn, then felt powerful hands grip his arms and lift him off his feet. A man on each side. Big men, and very strong. They lifted him without apparent effort.

"Let go! LET ME GO!" shouted George, struggling to free himself. It was useless. The men swiftly carried him to the ice cart, where a canvas tarpaulin had been pulled back, revealing blocks of ice stacked so that there was a space between them just wide enough for . . .

A man's body.

He struggled harder, kicking with all his strength. But the big men overpowered him easily, shoving him headfirst into the space between the ice blocks. A third man—apparently the cart driver—helped them to pin him down. George heard a grinding sound and realized that the men were sliding heavy blocks of ice across the space over him. He tried to raise himself up, only to bang his head painfully on the cold, hard block above. He shouted for help, but

heard nothing in response except the grunting of the men imprisoning him, and the howl of the unrelenting storm.

He continued to struggle as more blocks were dragged into place above and behind him. Finally the men stopped holding him. They didn't need to: he was imprisoned in an ice coffin, cold and pitch black. He shouted once more but he knew it was useless: the ice imprisoned the sound as it imprisoned him.

He felt a rumble.

The cart was moving.

George, his arms pinned to his sides, his face pressed against the rough wooden cart floor, shivered violently in his sodden clothing. His only hope was that the men who had captured him were the same men who had captured his wife. If that was so, maybe he would see her. Maybe he could find a way to help her . . .

If he could find a way to stay alive.

CHAPTER 33

WORRIES

THE SHIP FORMERLY KNOWN AS the *De Vliegen* and now as the *Jolly Roger* was ready to sail. The sails themselves looked a bit odd—the Mollusks had made them by tightly weaving fibers stripped from the stems of a hardy, thick jungle plant they called the salamander vine. The resulting sails were strong and supple, but Hook was not happy with the color. Not happy at all.

"Pink?" he said, upon first seeing them. *"PINK?"*

The sails were, in fact, an especially bright shade of pink.

"Yes, Cap'n," said Smee, "I think they're lovely."

Hook slowly turned to face his first mate. This was usually a bad sign.

"Smee," Hook said calmly.

"Yes, Cap'n."

"We are pirates, are we not?"

"Yes, Cap'n."

"So this is a *pirate ship*, is it not?"

"Yes, Cap'n."

"And when we, as pirates, bear down upon our victims at sea, what emotion do we want them to feel?"

Smee frowned. "I don't know, Cap'n."

"FEAR, YOU IDJIT!" bellowed Hook, nearly knocking Smee over. "We want them to be terrified of us, do you understand?"

"Yes, Cap'n."

"We want them saying 'Oh no! Pirates! We're doomed!'"

"Yes, Cap'n."

"We do not want them saying 'Oh, look at the lovely pink sails!'"

"Yes, Cap'n. I mean, *no*, Cap'n."

Hook went to Fighting Prawn to complain about the sails. Fighting Prawn informed Hook that the sails could not be changed.

"But what pirate ship has pink sails?" demanded Hook.

"Yours, apparently," said Fighting Prawn, displaying not the tiniest hint of a smile.

Aside from this issue, the renovation and provisioning of the ship went smoothly. On the day it was to sail, Fighting Prawn and all his warriors crossed the island's mountain ridge to gather at the pirate lagoon. They brought with them the shipwrecked men—Cheeky O'Neal, Frederick DeWulf, Rufus Kelly, and Angus McPherson. The Mollusks had been keeping the four under close watch, lest they try to avoid being put aboard the ship.

The Mollusks also brought Wendy. Fighting Prawn had told Hook earlier that he would be taking her to London. Hook reluctantly agreed—Fighting Prawn gave him no choice—but this was the first time he had seen his passenger. Like everyone else, he was struck by her resemblance to her mother. Unlike everybody else, Hook did not find this appealing.

"Your mother caused me no end of trouble," he said. "And now *you're* causing me trouble."

"I'm so sorry," said Wendy, not sounding a bit sorry.

Hook, turning to Fighting Prawn, said, "It's bad luck, you know. A woman on the ship."

"If you fail to take her safely to London," said Fighting Prawn, "your luck will be very bad indeed. She will send me word when she arrives home. If I do not hear from her"—he stepped closer, lowering his voice so that only Hook could hear—"I will hunt you down. Wherever you go in this world, I will find you. You know me, Hook; you know I will do as I say. I will find you and bring you back here, and Mister Grin will finally finish his meal."

Fighting Prawn nodded toward the jungle, which sometimes echoed with the roars of the giant crocodile that for more than twenty years had craved Hook's flesh.

Hook pulled away. "I gave you my word, Prawn," he snapped. "I'll take her back."

Fighting Prawn nodded. It was not Hook's word he trusted; it was the fear he'd seen in Hook's eyes.

The *Jolly Roger* was loaded with the final barrels of water and baskets of food. Then the passengers were ferried to the ship in Mollusk canoes. Fighting Prawn rode with Wendy. As they neared the ship, he nudged her gently, glancing upward. Following his eyes, she saw one of the sails furled at the top of the mainmast. Poking out of one of the pink folds, just barely visible, was a thatch of orange hair. She looked at Fighting Prawn and nodded.

Once aboard the ship, they went below to Wendy's cabin. It was small, but comfortable enough. Fighting Prawn, after making sure nobody was listening, said, "You will be safe, Wendy. Hook will not dare harm you; the rest of the pirates are not such bad men. And you will not be alone. You have your friend in the sails, and Ammm assures me that the porpoises will stay close by the ship all the way to England."

Wendy gave the embarrassed Mollusk chief a quick hug. "Thank you," she said. "For everything."

They went back up on deck. The four shipwreck survivors were just coming aboard. Cheeky O'Neal looked around the ship, pausing to smirk at the pink sails. He walked confidently up to Hook, his huge frame towering over the pirate. They exchanged stares, each man taking an instant dislike to the other.

"So, *Captain*," said O'Neal, "where might our cabin be?"

Hook smiled unpleasantly. "Allow me to show you," he said. He led O'Neal and the other three men down below, then down farther still, to a dark hold in the lowest and most forward part of the ship, below the water line.

"You can't be serious," said O'Neal, looking at the cramped, dark space. "I can't even stand in there."

"How unfortunate for you," said Hook.

"We won't go in there," said O'Neal.

"Yes you will," said a third voice.

O'Neal turned and saw that Fighting Prawn had followed them below. With the Mollusk chief were a half-dozen warriors, spears at the ready.

"After you," sneered Hook, pointing into the hold. One by one the four men went inside. O'Neal was last. As he ducked his head to squeeze through the doorway, he turned to give both Hook and Fighting Prawn a look of pure hatred.

Fighting Prawn felt glad to be getting this man off the island.

When the four were in the hold, Hook closed the door and slid a heavy iron bar across the front of it. The men were now prisoners.

The door had a small barred opening. O'Neal pressed his faced against it and said, "How long do you plan to keep us in here?"

"Until I decide to let you out," said Hook.

"Far from here," added Fighting Prawn.

"Oh yes," said Hook. "You'll be in there quite a while."

Hook turned to go back up on deck. He was followed by the Mollusks. Fighting Prawn was the last to leave. As he did, he glanced back at the hold. O'Neal still had his face pressed against the opening.

But now he was smiling.

———◆◆◆———

An hour later as dusk approached, the ship, with Hook at the wheel, set sail, its pink sails turned dramatically red by the setting sun. Fighting Prawn stood on the shore of the lagoon, watching the pirates as they scurried about the ship, responding to Hook's commands. A wiry figure appeared high in the sails, out of sight of the pirates below; Peter caught a glimpse of Fighting Prawn, waved quickly, then disappeared.

Another figure stood on the deck, next to the rail—Wendy, looking small and very much alone. She also waved.

Fighting Prawn waved back. He believed he had done everything possible to ensure her safe passage. But he could not rid his mind of worries. Would Hook do as he'd said? Could Peter stay concealed? Would Wendy be all right?

And why had O'Neal been smiling?

CHAPTER 34

It's Here

$\mathcal{F}$OR THE THIRD TIME, Neville pressed the doorbell button of the Darling house. As before, he heard the chimes echo inside. And as before, nobody came to the door.

"Odd," he said. He turned to John and Michael, who stood behind him on the doorstep. "Your father said he'd be here."

"What about Mum?" said John.

"Yes," agreed Michael. "Where's Mum?"

Neville frowned. He had forgotten that neither John nor Michael knew that their mother was missing.

"Your mother is, er, abroad," he said.

"What's abroad?" said Michael.

"Abroad is France, you ninny," said John.

"I'm not a ninny!" said Michael.

"Are too."

"Am not!"

The two boys continued arguing, which for once was fine with Neville, as it distracted them from the question of where their mother was. What bothered Neville was the absence of their father. George had been very insistent that Neville return his sons to London immediately. Why wasn't he here?

After several more futile stabs at the doorbell, Neville put the boys back into the taxicab, whose driver had been ordered to wait. Neville gave him an address on Kensington Park Gardens.

"Where are we going now?" asked John.

"We're going to your grandfather Aster's house," said Neville.

"Will Father be there?" said John.

"I don't know," said Neville. "We'll see. If all else fails, you can wait there until your father picks you up."

In ten minutes he was ringing the door of the Aster mansion. It was opened by Mrs. Bumbrake, whose face lit up at the sight of her visitors.

"Why, Mr. Plonk-Fenster, this is a surprise!" she said. "And John and Michael! What brings you here at this hour?"

"We're looking for George," said Neville. "He's not at his house."

"George is our dad," explained Michael. "But we don't call him George, 'cause we call him Dad."

"She knows that, you ninny," said John.

"I'm NOT a—"

"All *right*, you two," snapped Neville, who had been listening to basically this same argument for several hours. "You boys go play somewhere while I talk to Mrs. Bumbrake."

"There's tin soldiers in Lord Aster's study," said Mrs. Bumbrake.

The boys, delighted, scampered off. Mrs. Bumbrake turned a worried face to Neville. "George isn't home?"

"No," said Neville. "I don't understand it—he told me to bring the boys home immediately. He's quite upset with me about Wendy going missing."

"I don't blame him," said Mrs. Bumbrake, with a stern look. "How could you? Putting a girl on a flying machine!"

"I didn't *put* her on it!" protested Neville. "She *jumped* aboard and flew off before I could stop her. But you should have seen how it flew! I had no idea it could . . ." He stopped, seeing Mrs. Bumbrake's disapproving look. "In any event," he went on, "I had hoped to find George here."

"He's not here," she said. "I expected him—he's been coming by regularly to see Lord Aster—but he didn't come today."

"Where could he be?" said Neville.

"I don't know," said Mrs. Bumbrake. "But I'm worried. With Molly missing, and now George . . ."

"Now, wait," said Neville. "You don't *know* George is missing."

"That's just it," said Mrs. Bumbrake. "I don't know *anything*. So many strange things are happening"

"What strange things?" said Neville.

"I'll make some tea," said Mrs. Bumbrake. Tea was Mrs. Bumbrake's solution to everything.

In a few minutes they were sitting in the parlor over a pair of steaming cups. Mrs. Bumbrake told Neville about Wendy's visit, during which she apparently had told Lord Aster something that made him very upset.

"Upset about what?" said Neville.

Mrs. Bumbrake considered her answer. Finally she said, "Do you know about the Starcatchers?"

Neville frowned. "A little," he said. "A secret society fighting evil. Magic and hocus-pocus. Very unscientific. Leonard approached me about joining years ago, but I declined. Said I was too busy. To be honest, I thought it was silly."

"It's not silly," said Mrs. Bumbrake. "It's real."

"What do you mean?"

"The evil," said Mrs. Bumbrake. "It's real. I've seen it, and Lord Aster has been fighting it his whole life. He thought he'd won, but now it's come back. It's *here*, in London. I think that's why Molly's missing, and George as well. And Lord Aster . . . he's . . ."

Mrs. Bumbrake buried her face in her hands, stifling a sob.

"What about Lord Aster?" Neville asked softly.

Mrs. Bumbrake looked up. "He's . . . dying," she said.

"Oh dear," said Neville. "Is there anything—"

"Dr. Sable said at this point it's no use taking him to the hospital. He doesn't want to go anyway."

"How much time?"

"Days. Maybe hours." Mrs. Bumbrake sobbed again. "I fear he's going to die without ever seeing his family again. And the worst of it is, he keeps calling for Molly . . . actually, sometimes Molly, sometimes Wendy. Whichever it is, he wants to tell her something. He seems obsessed with it."

"Tell her what?"

"I honestly don't know. He's delirious, and he's very weak, so his words are unclear. But he keeps saying something about a sword."

"A sword? Does he own a sword? Perhaps something he wants to bequeath to his heirs?"

"Not that I know of. And there's one other thing."

"What?"

"Something about a meteorite."

"A *meteorite*? Are you quite certain?"

"Yes. He's said it quite clearly several times."

"What about a meteorite?"

"I don't know. As I say, he's delirious. He just keeps repeating Molly's name, or sometimes Wendy's, then something about a sword, and a meteorite. When I ask him what he means, he becomes agitated, and then I lose him."

"Odd," said Neville.

"Whatever it is," said Mrs. Bumbrake, "I think it's connected with the Starcatchers."

"But you can't possibly—"

"Yes, I can. I know what I know. It has to do with the Starcatchers I tell you, and Wendy's visit, and Molly's disappearance, and now George's. The evil is back, Mr. Plonk-Fenster. It's here." She glanced toward the parlor window, then added, "It's around this very house."

"*What's* around this house?" said Neville.

"I think we're being watched," she said. "I've seen men outside."

"It's London. There are lots of—"

"No, these men are watching us. Bobbies, some of them. Watching at all hours."

Neville nodded, but he was unconvinced. He was about to say something when John burst into the parlor, followed by Michael, who had his hand over his face.

"Michael put a soldier in his nose," announced John.

"Only his head," protested Michael.

"More like his whole body," said John. "And it's stuck."

"Is not!" said Michael.

"Then pull it out if it's not stuck," said John.

"I don't *want* to pull it out," said Michael.

Neville and Mrs. Bumbrake exchanged a look. He

lowered his voice and said, "We can discuss this later. For now, the question is, what do we do with the boys, until we find Geo—until matters are straightened out?"

"The boys will stay here," said Mrs. Bumbrake firmly. "And so will you."

"But I had planned to—"

"Mr. Plonk-Fenster," said Mrs. Bumbrake, "*surely* you do not intend to leave me in this house with these two children and Lord Aster in his current condition."

Neville blinked. "Of course not," he said.

"Good," said Mrs. Bumbrake. "Now let me see about the soldier in Michael's nose." She rose from the table and headed toward the boys. Neville also rose. He went to the window, parted the curtains, and peered out into the London night. The fog had crept in as usual, obscuring most of the street. The lone illumination came from a gas streetlight, casting a ghostly pale cone of light down to the sidewalk.

In the cone, facing the Aster house, was a bobby.

CHAPTER 35

DEASY'S TALE

CAPTAIN HOOK STOOD AT the starboard rail of the *Jolly Roger*, a happy man. At last—at *last*—he was where a pirate belonged, at sea, in command of a ship. Granted, the ship had pink sails; Hook could barely bring himself to look at them. But he intended to fix that problem by stealing the sails of the first ship he encountered, along with anything else of value. Why, he'd take the whole ship if he liked it better than the one he commanded now.

Hook spat into the dark blue water. He smiled, imagining the terrified looks on the faces of those aboard the first ship he attacked. The word would spread quickly, he was sure of it. *Hook was back.* The world would quiver in fear.

"Cap'n!" shouted the helmsman.

Hook turned and said, "What is it?"

The helmsman pointed to port.

"Smoke," he said.

Hook quickly crossed the deck and squinted into the distance. It took him a moment, but then he saw it: a black smudge on the horizon.

"Steamer," he said.

"Aye," said the helmsman at the wheel. "Heading northeast."

Hook rubbed his chin, careful to use his non-hook hand. He was surprised to see a steamer this far out to sea; in his pirating years, steamers had mainly been slow and fairly small coastal vessels. But no matter. Whatever had brought this ship out to the open sea, it was going to be Hook's ship soon. Its cargo, his cargo.

He studied the wind a moment, the direction of the smudge on the horizon, noted the position of the sun, then shouted some orders. His men adjusted the sails; the helmsman altered his course a few degrees.

"Smee!" bellowed Hook.

The spherical first mate appeared a minute later, puffing from the exertion of climbing the ladderway.

"Aye, Cap'n?"

Hook pointed at the smudge. "Y'see that ship, Smee?"

Smee squinted. "No, Cap'n," he said. "But I do see smoke."

"That's the *ship*, you idjit. It's a steamer. That's coal smoke you see. I've put us on a course that will intercept her after sunset. Cover of darkness, Smee. A sneak attack. They'll never know what hit them."

Smee nodded, frowning doubtfully at the smoke.

"Now, listen, Smee, I want you to go below and check them prisoners, make sure they're secure. Don't want 'em getting loose in the fray."

"Aye, Cap'n."

"And check that pesky girl, too. Tell her to keep to her cabin until it's over."

"Aye, Cap'n."

Smee was still frowning at the smoke smudge. There was something troubling about this plan, but he couldn't quite think of what it might be.

"Don't stand there gaping like a grouper!" bellowed Hook. "Get below!"

"Aye," said Smee, waddling away, still frowning.

Hook turned back to look at the smoke smudge once again. It had already grown noticeably larger.

Hook grinned.

"They'll never know what hit them," he said.

<hr>

Peter, hidden high in the sails almost directly over Hook's head, had seen the steamer and heard the pirate's plan.

"Tink," he whispered. "When you go to Wendy's cabin tonight, I'm going with you."

246

Tink had been visiting Wendy after dark to get food and water. Wendy saved it from her rations, and Tink carried it, a bit at a time, up to Peter.

You can't go, chimed Tink. *They'll see you.* She didn't mention her other reason, which was that she liked having Peter to herself, away from that girl.

"I have to go," said Peter. "I need to warn Wendy that Hook's planning to attack that ship."

Why? said Tink.

Peter didn't actually have a good reason. He was bored from being stuck in his cramped hiding place, and he wanted to see Wendy.

"In case something happens," he said.

Tink made a disgusted face and chimed, *You just want to see that girl.*

"Don't be silly," said Peter.

I'M not being silly, said Tink. *YOU'RE the one who's going get himself killed by Hook.*

Peter smiled and said, "He's already killed me, Tink. Remember?"

Tink made a disgusted sound, turned her back, and refused to talk to Peter again until nightfall.

———— ◆◈◆ ————

Samuel Deasy walked unsteadily to the starboard rail on the main deck of the steamship *Lucy,* a two thousand-ton liner carrying one hundred eighty-five passengers across the ocean in considerable luxury.

Most of the passengers, including Deasy's wife and her family, were still in the dining hall, finishing a lavish dinner. But Deasy had consumed a bit too much wine—*quite* a bit too much wine—and was feeling queasy. He was also annoyed by the disapproving looks he was getting from his in-laws, particularly his mother-in-law, who was not fond of him. So he had announced that he wanted to get some fresh air, and made his way unsteadily to the main deck.

The sun had set, and the moon had risen full and bright. Deasy leaned heavily on the rail, listening to the deep *thrum-thrum-thrum* of the ship's engine and watching the water whoosh past far below. He raised his head and looked out at the vast expanse of ocean, utterly empty except for . . .

A sailing ship.

It was running without lights but was visible in the moonlight, ahead and just a bit to starboard. To Deasy, it appeared to be on something of a collision course. At the least, it would pass very close to the *Lucy*. He was not worried; he assumed that the ships were aware of one another. The helmsmen would adjust their courses accordingly.

What Deasy didn't know was that the helmsman of the *Lucy* had also had a bit too much to drink this night. He was half asleep at the wheel, unaware of the dark and far smaller sailing ship to starboard, a ship on a heading certain to cross his course.

———•◦•———

"Cap'n," said Smee.

"What is it?"

The two stood on the foredeck of the *Jolly Roger*, watching— along with every other pirate on the ship—as the steamship, ablaze with lights, churned toward them, looking taller and more massive every second.

"Well," said Smee, "I was just thinking that the ship . . . that is, it's . . . it's . . ."

"It's *what*, Smee?"

"It's big, Cap'n. It's quite big."

Hook had been thinking the same thing. He had never seen a ship quite so large as the one bearing down on him, nor one that moved so fast. The smudge of smoke had turned into a towering, billowing plume.

"I was wondering," said Smee, "if perhaps we should plunder a different ship. One that's not so . . . big."

Hook turned around and saw that his men were listening with great interest, awaiting his response to Smee's suggestion. In his heart, he wanted to agree with Smee. If he could have thought of a good piratical reason for not attacking the steamship, he would have done so. But to simply *quit*—to turn tail and run like a scared dog—Hook could not bring himself to do that. He was *Captain Hook.* Captain Hook did not run.

"Smee," he said, speaking loudly so all the crew could hear.

"Aye, Cap'n."

"What are we?"

"Nervous, Cap'n?"

"WE ARE NOT NERVOUS," bellowed Hook, nearly bowling Smee over. "WE ARE PIRATES!"

"Aye, Cap'n."

"AND WE ARE GOING TO PLUNDER THAT SHIP!"

"Aye, Cap'n."

Hook turned to face the crew. "Any man who feels otherwise," he said, "is welcome to jump overboard now."

He glared at them. Nobody moved.

"Good," said Hook. "Prepare to board."

He turned to face the oncoming *Lucy,* which looked like a mountain moving through the sea.

———

"Do you hear that?" said Cheeky O'Neal.

"Hear what?" said Rufus Kelly.

The two were sitting slumped against the walls of their cramped and stinky cell. Frederick DeWulf and Angus McPherson were sprawled on the filthy floor, snoring.

"Ship's engine," said O'Neal. "Close by."

Kelly listened. "I hear it," he said, after a moment. "Sounds like a big 'un."

O'Neal rose and went to the cell door. He grabbed it with his massive hands and shook it. It didn't give; it never did. He cursed, then turned and kicked at the two sleeping men. They woke up, grumbling.

"What is it?" said DeWulf.

"Ship," said O'Neal. "Nearby."

"What good does that do us, locked in here?" said DeWulf.

"I don't know," said O'Neal. "Maybe they'll board us. Maybe the fool Hook will try to board them. Maybe nothing. But I want us to be ready. If we get out of here, we make for the lifeboat, starboard side. Don't waste a second. Kill any man tries to stop you."

The men nodded. Now they could all clearly hear the *thrum* of the other ship's engine.

"Very close," said O'Neal.

———◆———

On the deck of the *Lucy*, Samuel Deasy watched with increasing fascination as the liner bore down on the sailing ship. Neither ship had altered course. They were now close enough to each other that in bright moonlight Deasy could clearly see men standing on the deck of the sailing ship. He could also see that the ship's sails were an odd color—pink, it looked like.

It was evident now that the ships were going to collide. Deasy wondered if he should shout a warning. But to whom? He looked around: There was no one else on deck. There was nothing he could do.

Deasy turned back to the rail, unable to look away from the disaster about to take place below.

<hr />

Peter and Tink dropped to the deck at the stern of the *Jolly Roger*, unseen by Hook and the crew, all of whom were staring with various degrees of fear at the monstrous looming steamship hull.

"Where is she?" Peter whispered.

This way.

Tink, a streak of light, shot down a ladderway. Peter was right behind. Tink zoomed along a passageway and stopped in front of a door. Peter yanked it open. Inside it was dark. Somehow, Wendy had slept through the excitement.

"Wendy, wake up!" Peter said.

"Peter?" she said, her voice sleepy. "What is it?"

"We've got to get out now!" said Peter, tugging at her arm.

"Get out?" she said. "Why?"

Fine, chimed Tink. *Let's leave her here.*

"We're about to be hit by a ship!" said Peter. "A very large ship."

"WHAT?" said Wendy.

Not very bright, is she? observed Tink.

"A ship!" said Peter, dragging Wendy into the passageway. "Hurry! We have to get on deck before—"

But it was too late.

———

What saved the *Jolly Roger* from being instantly crushed by the massive hull of the *Lucy* was that at the last possible instant, Hook lost his nerve. With the steamship's sharp prow only yards away, he suddenly turned and—in a surprisingly high, almost girlish, voice—screamed at the helmsman, "HARD TO STARBOARD! HARD TO STARBOARD!"

With all his strength, the helmsman spun the wheel right. It was not nearly enough movement to get the *Jolly Roger* out of the steamship's path, but it was just enough to turn the smaller ship so that the larger one, instead of hitting head-on, scraped it at an angle.

But it was a tremendous collision for those aboard the *Jolly Roger*—a thundering crash, then a horrendous grinding sound, as the *Lucy*, herself barely affected, pushed the smaller ship violently sideways as if she were a scrap of driftwood, hurling Hook and his men to the deck. The *Lucy* surged past, raking the length of the *Jolly Roger*'s port side, ripping away pieces of her deck and hull. The pirates hung on to whatever they could grab to keep from sliding overboard as the *Jolly Roger* leaned sideways at a sickening angle.

———•———

Belowdecks, Peter and Wendy were hurled sideways, slamming into the passageway wall. Peter's head hit something, and he fell to the floor, dazed.

Tink was at his ear instantly.

Up! Up! she chimed. *Out! Out!*

Peter groaned, his head throbbing. He felt blood trickling down his face. He struggled to get to his feet. It was difficult because he felt woozy, and something seemed to be wrong with the floor. He felt Wendy pulling him up.

"Peter," she said, "are you all right?"

"I think so," he said, staggering sideways. "The floor . . ."

"The ship is listing," said Wendy. "We have to get out of here."

As I already told you, noted Tink.

Holding on to each other, with Tink lighting their way, a wounded Peter and a determined Wendy headed toward the aft ladderway.

———•———

"What's happened?" said McPherson, struggling to his feet, his voice on the edge of panic.

"We collided," said DeWulf. "And we're taking on water. Hear it?"

From somewhere near their cell came the sound of rushing water.

"We'll drown!" shouted McPherson.

"Be quiet!" snapped O'Neal. He grabbed the door and shook it, but it still held firm. His eyes scanned the cell, stopping at a corner to his right. Where the walls had once met flush, there was now a gap of about an inch.

"Come here!" he shouted to the others. They stumbled over, and he positioned them against one of the walls.

"On three, push like your lives depend on it," he said, "because they do. One . . . two . . . THREE!"

The four heaved against the wall, and the gap widened by several inches.

"Again!" said O'Neal. "One . . . two . . . THREE!"

With a crash, the wall gave way. The men stumbled into the passageway.

"The lifeboat," said O'Neal. "Nobody stops us."

———◆———

Peter and Wendy climbed onto the deck. The *Jolly Roger* had righted itself somewhat but was still listing. The steamship's long hull had just finished passing; its stern loomed high above, bearing the name *Lucy*.

Peter looked forward on the deck of the *Jolly Roger*.

Hook, Smee, and the rest of the pirates were regaining their footing, turning to watch the ship that had almost crushed them.

And then Hook saw Peter.

For a moment he stood utterly still, staring.

"You!" he shouted. "You're *dead*. I *killed* you."

"He don't look very dead to me, Cap'n," said Smee.

Hook ignored Smee, keeping his glittering black eyes on Peter. Had the boy's ghost come back to haunt him? But no: he appeared perfectly real. Hook started walking aft.

"I killed you once, boy," he said. "And I will kill you again."

"Peter," said Wendy. "Fly away. *Now*."

Yes, said Tink, in a rare moment of agreement. *Fly*.

Peter wiped some blood from his eyes, trying to force his woozy brain to think.

"Peter, he'll *kill* you!" said Wendy. "Fly!"

Hook was only yards away, his razor-sharp hook held high.

"Wendy," said Peter. "Hang on."

She started to speak, but her words became a scream when Peter reached behind her, grunted, and picked her up.

"NO!" screamed Wendy.

NO! chimed Tink.

"NO!" bellowed Hook.

Ignoring them all, Peter turned, took two staggering steps, and with a desperate effort leaped with Wendy over

256

the stern rail of the ship, eluding by inches the furious arc of the pirate captain's lunging hook.

⟞⟝

On the main deck of the *Lucy*, Samuel Deasy had trotted the entire length of the starboard rail from bow to stern, trying to stay even with the drama below, watching with fascinated horror as the steamship's hull brushed aside and swept past the sailing ship.

Incredibly, the smaller ship had not sunk. And now, as it tossed in the wake of the *Lucy*, Deasy saw an amazing scene unfold. Two children—a boy and a girl—stood on the moonlit aft deck as a tall man charged toward them, shouting, with something—a knife?—glinting in his hand. Just as he was about to reach the children, the boy swept the girl into his arms and, as Deasy gasped, *leaped off the stern.*

What happened next was so astonishing that Deasy nearly fell over the rail. The boy and the girl, instead of falling into the sea, began to . . . *rise.* Their ascent was wobbly; it seemed to require great effort on the boy's part. But after a few moments they had gained enough altitude to be level with Deasy. They continued to rise as they flew toward the *Lucy*, passing a good fifty feet over Deasy's head, preceded by a strange streak of light, like a tiny shooting star.

"Hello!" shouted Deasy, this being the only thing he could think of to say.

The boy and girl did not respond; they swooped toward the bow of the *Lucy*, passing the tall, red-and-black smoke-belching funnel. Then they were gone, leaving Deasy struggling to comprehend what he had just seen—if he'd seen it at all.

He heard a shout, and turned to look astern. The sailing ship was rapidly disappearing behind; it would soon be out of sight. But Deasy could see that the tall man was still standing at the stern rail, shouting in the direction of the *Lucy*. He seemed very, very upset.

———✦———

O'Neal, DeWulf, Kelly, and McPherson crept along the starboard rail, unseen and unheard. The pirates were all on the port side of the *Jolly Roger*, some assessing the damage inflicted by the steamer, some watching Hook, who was still screaming curses at the hated flying boy.

It took less than a minute for the four men, experienced hands all, to untie the lifeboat and lower it over the side. With O'Neal rowing as quietly as he could, they slipped quickly and silently away from the *Jolly Roger*, undetected by the pirate crew and their furious captain.

———✦———

Samuel Deasy, red-faced and disheveled, stumbled into the elegant main dining room of the *Lucy*, shouting incoherently. He was quickly surrounded by a curious crowd, which included the steamship's captain, an experienced, dignified-looking seaman named Alfred Hart, who'd been dining with invited passengers at his table.

It took several minutes for Deasy to calm down enough to get his story out. And quite a story it was, starting with an account of the *Lucy* colliding with a sailing ship. This drew doubtful looks from the crowd, as nobody had felt anything. A few guests went out on deck and returned quickly to report that they saw nothing. Captain Hart declared that such a thing would not happen, especially not on a bright moonlit night.

But Deasy was adamant: not only had they struck another ship, but that ship had pink sails!

Now the doubtful looks turned to amusement: clearly this man was drunk. Deasy's wife and her family, mortified, tried to pull him away, but he yanked himself free and began shouting that two children had leaped off the sailing ship and . . . *flown over the steamship.*

At this absurdity, the crowd roared with laughter. Deasy's in-laws, furious, were pulling him away as he continued to insist that he had seen these things with his own eyes. He was still shouting as he was dragged out of the dining room.

The passengers returned to their tables, still laughing. Now they'd have a fine story to tell, about a drunk who claimed he'd seen a pink-sailed ship and flying children.

Of all the silly tales!

CHAPTER 36

A Second Bowl

$\mathcal{M}$OLLY LAY SHIVERING in the grim darkness of her cell, listening to the endless *drip-drip-drip* of water in the tunnel outside. Aside from being cold, she was weak from hunger and aching from the effort she'd put into using the plank to pry the tunnel support.

Over the past two days she'd loosened it a good deal. She stopped when she felt that the next hard yank or two would bring down the post and, in turn, the overhead beam. She had set her trap; now she had to be patient, to wait for the opportunity to use it as a means to escape. She prayed it would come soon, before she was too weak to take advantage.

She heard footsteps in the tunnel. She stood, grunting with the effort, and peered through the bars into the yellowish light cast by the string of electric bulbs. A guard was coming, carrying a bowl. Mealtime: lukewarm brown slop, perhaps some moldy bread. She thought this might be breakfast. Or was it dinner? She'd lost track.

She prepared to take the bowl. If she didn't grab it as it came through the slot, the guard allowed it to fall, dumping it into the mud. More than once, compelled by aching hunger, she'd eaten a meal with pebbles and sand crunching between her teeth.

The tin bowl pushed through. Molly grabbed hold tightly.

"Thank you," she whispered to the guard, desperate in her loneliness to engage in conversation with *someone*, even her captors.

The guard, as always, ignored her. Talking was not permitted. She watched him leave, and was about to sit and eat her meager meal when she noticed something unusual: the guard turned and went on down the hall. After delivering the food, the guard always went back the way he'd come. But this time he continued along the tunnel to her right. Molly pressed her face against the bars to follow his progress. She caught a glimpse of something in the guard's hands.

A second bowl.

She watched intently as the guard stopped about thirty feet down the hall. He turned toward the wall and pushed the bowl forward. When he pulled his hands back, the bowl was gone. The guard came back along the tunnel, passing Molly's cell, then disappeared around the corner.

Molly sat on the floor, chewing the spongy slop and thinking about what she'd seen. Clearly there was another cell. And clearly it was now occupied by a prisoner. Was it one of the workers, being punished? Or someone new to the tunnels? If so, who?

She didn't dare shout out; that would only draw the guards.

She looked around the cell and found a rock. When she was a girl, her father had taught her, among many other specialized skills, Morse code. She'd complained that it was boring, but he had insisted. "You never know when something like that could be useful," he said.

Molly closed her eyes and searched her memory, recalling the dots and dashes that represented letters.

She raised the rock to the cell bars and began tapping.

h - e - l - l - o . . .

CHAPTER 37

A BIG PUFF

CHEEKY O'NEAL WORKED THE OARS, keeping the lifeboat steady as it rode a wave onto Mollusk Island. As the wave broke and surged onto the moonlit beach, McPherson, DeWulf, and Kelly jumped out and heaved, skidding the lifeboat up onto the sand. With O'Neal's help they quickly hauled the boat into the jungle and covered it with palm fronds. DeWulf returned to the beach and swept the sand smooth, eliminating any trace of their arrival.

They were thirsty, hungry, and tired, but O'Neal would not let them rest. He grabbed some low-hanging bananas from a tree at the edge of the jungle and tossed a few to each man.

"We'll eat on the move," he said.

He plunged straight into the thick, nearly pitch-black jungle, hoping to run across a path. The going was difficult; they had to fight for each step through the dense tangle of branches, leaves, and vines. Finally, after an exhausting hour, they reached a moonlit footpath. DeWulf sprawled on the ground, panting.

"Get up," growled O'Neal.

"I need a rest," said DeWulf.

"There's no time," said O'Neal.

"Why not?" McPherson said defiantly, as he and Kelly dropped to the path next to DeWulf. O'Neal glared down at the three mutinous men.

"I'll tell you why not," he growled. "The ship was expecting the signal yesterday at sunset, and we weren't here to give it. They'll think we're captured or dead. Maybe they'll turn transom and leave us here. Or maybe they'll come looking for the starstuff themselves. Either way, it's trouble. If they leave, we're stuck here, and sooner or later the natives will find us, and this time they'll kill us for sure. Or if the ship sends men for the starstuff, not knowing the island, they'll be spotted, and there will be a fight. And I for one would not want to fight these natives on their island."

O'Neal stepped forward, leaning over the three.

"So those are the choices," he said. "We keep moving and send the signal. Or we die."

Grumbling, the three men rose to their feet.

"How do we know they'll see the signal?" said Kelly.

"We make sure it's a big one," said O'Neal.

"A big puff," said Kelly.

"A very big puff," said O'Neal.

CHAPTER 38

GOOD NEWS AND BAD

$\mathcal{A}$T DAWN, A STEWARD ABOARD the *Lucy* found Peter and Wendy dozing fitfully on deck chairs. Although they were both tired from their ordeal on the pirate ship, and, in Peter's case, from flying them across to the steamer, the chilly sea air had prevented them from getting much sleep.

Peter had nearly overshot the ship, and had been forced to descend too fast. They'd landed clumsily, pitching forward and sprawling onto the deck. Tink had found this highly amusing; Peter and Wendy had not. After determining that neither of them had been badly hurt, they'd decided to simply stay where they were and wait to be discovered.

When the steward approached, Peter quickly tucked a complaining Tinker Bell into his shirt. He and Wendy made no effort to run away as there was nowhere to go. The steward, realizing that the two disheveled children were not paying passengers, took them to Captain Hart's cabin. The captain was unhappy to be awakened so early, and much more unhappy to learn he had two stowaways aboard. When he saw Peter and Wendy, he frowned, suddenly remembering the drunken passenger who'd claimed to see a pink-sailed ship, and two children flying over the *Lucy*.

Could it possibly be?

He shook his head. *Nonsense.* The passenger had been seeing things; children did not fly. But then how *had* these two gotten aboard, and where had they been hiding?

For the next half-hour, an increasingly frustrated Captain Hart tried to get information from Peter and Wendy—*any* information. But they told him nothing, not even their names, having agreed to reveal as little as possible for fear word of their mission would somehow reach the Others.

Finally, Captain Hart gave up. He summoned two large crewmen and ordered that the children be locked up in the brig.

"You'll stay there until we get to London," he said. "After that, the police can deal with the both of you."

Peter and Wendy exchanged looks. The captain had given them good news and bad. The ship would take them to London; that was a lucky break, indeed. But they could not allow themselves to fall into the hands of the police.

As the crewmen herded them belowdecks, Wendy leaned closer to Peter and whispered, "We can't trust the police. . . ."

"I know," whispered Peter, glancing at the crewmen. "We'll have to escape."

"How?"

"Don't worry," said Peter.

Wendy looked doubtful. Peter didn't blame her. From inside his shirt came the soft sound of muffled bells.

You can just fly away, you know, said Tink.

"What did she say?" whispered Wendy.

"She said we'll think of something," answered Peter.

CHAPTER 39

The Signal

"Hurry!" bellowed Cheeky O'Neal. "We're running out of time!"

He and his men had spent the past few hours dragging jungle vegetation up to a lava pool near the top of the massive volcano that formed the center of Mollusk Island. Above them was the rim of the volcano's crater, a smoldering cauldron nearly a quarter-mile across. This morning the crater was belching steam. O'Neal hadn't seen it do that before. It gave him an uneasy feeling.

Below them was the jungle. It was shrouded in the dense morning fog that covered most of the island. But dawn had started to redden the horizon. In minutes the sun's glare would fill the sky; it would quickly burn off the fog.

O'Neal needed to send the signal soon, because when the fog cleared, the Mollusks would see the smoke from their village far below. O'Neal looked out at the vast dark sea, praying that the ship was still close enough to spot the signal when the sun came up. This was the only hope that he and the other three had of completing their mission and getting off this island alive.

McPherson, DeWulf, and Kelly, exhausted from climbing and working all night, were now throwing vegetation into the lava pool to create the signal. Their efforts did not satisfy O'Neal.

"Faster!" he shouted. He stomped over to the vegetation pile, grabbed a bunch of palm fronds in his huge hands and threw them into the lava pool. A thick cloud of smoke billowed upward.

"I want to see more smoke like that," O'Neal said, "or I'll throw *you* into that hole."

McPherson, Kelly, and DeWulf, tired as they were, jumped to it. They had seen O'Neal do some scary things when he got mad. One time he'd pulled out most of a man's hair by the roots. He'd reached into another man's mouth and yanked out a gold tooth. They figured he was perfectly capable of using their bodies as fuel for smoke signals.

The three heaved palm fronds and chunks of jungle wood onto the pool. Soon a thick column of smoke rose into the sky, now turning a bright blue. O'Neal grabbed a cluster of huge palm fronds and waved them through the column, interrupting it. He stopped, then waved the fronds again, repeating this process over and over. The result was a broken line of smoke rising ever higher, like dark thread stitched in blue fabric.

Suddenly the ground shuddered. O'Neal staggered and almost fell into the lava. The main crater blew a huge blast of steam. The men looked up and saw molten rock coursing down the hill like honey down the side of a jar, a thick finger of death pointing right at them.

"Run for it!" said McPherson.

"NO!" shouted O'Neal. He needed the signal a little longer and higher, high enough to clear the top of the mountain, long enough to be seen from any side of the island, for he had no idea where the ship was.

For a second, the other three looked as if they might run. But the fire in O'Neal's eyes was hotter than anything the lava could produce. The three men frantically threw the rest of the jungle plants into the lava as O'Neal used the big fronds to break the smoke into dashes. Up, up it rose.

"All right," O'Neal shouted. "Go!"

The four men started down the slope, into the jungle, half-running, half-sliding down a steep ravine. But the thick jungle slowed them down, and the lava was gaining. They felt its heat behind them.

"We'll never outrun it!" Kelly shouted.

O'Neal glanced back and saw McPherson was right; the glowing wall of lava was gaining on them, igniting the jungle as it went, causing trees to explode in flames. O'Neal looked around frantically. A few yards below he spotted a thick moss-covered log, the remains of what had once been a huge jungle tree. He stumbled down to it, and, using his massive strength, spun it so it was pointing down the steep ravine.

"Come on!" he shouted to the other three. They stared at him, not understanding.

"GET ON THE LOG, you imbeciles!"

McPherson, Kelly, and DeWulf clambered onto the log, their legs straddling it. The hissing, roaring wall of lava was right behind them.

"Hold on!" shouted O'Neal. He put his shoulder to the back of the log and lunged forward with all his strength. The log started sliding down the ravine, quickly picking up speed. As it shot ahead, O'Neal managed to dive forward and wrap his arms around the trunk, hanging on for his life; in front of him, Kelly, McPherson, and DeWulf were doing the same. The men screamed as the big log bucked and bounced, crashing through the thick jungle vegetation like a runaway buffalo. After a steep, terrifying, thirty-second drop, the men felt a violent jolt as the log hit a rock, flipping up on its end and catapulting them forward. They landed, sprawling, in a clearing—somehow still alive, somehow not badly hurt. From above them they could hear the lava still coming, but they had enough of a head start now to outrun it.

O'Neal looked up at the sky, now bright blue. The

271

volcano had sent up a billowing cloud of ash and smoke. But above that, still clearly visible, was the dashed line of smoke he and his men had created. It was a clear signal, visible from long way off.

O'Neal smiled. He was sure of it now: the ship would come.

CHAPTER 40

*T*HE *P*LAN

*T*HE *Lucy* STEAMED IN TO THE Royal Victoria Dock in
East London. From their side-by-side windowless cells deep
belowdecks, Wendy and Peter couldn't see anything, but
they could hear the blasts of the ship's horn and feel the
shudder of the docking maneuvers. Tink, far too tiny to be
imprisoned by the cell bars, had already left the brig and
was elsewhere in the ship, carrying out her particular
mission. Peter and Wendy sat fidgeting on their hard bunks,
too nervous to rest, waiting for someone to come fetch them
so they could put their plan into action. They'd had plenty
of time to discuss it; the question now was whether it would
work.

Finally they heard heavy footsteps in the corridor, then
saw the two crewmen sent down to escort them out—the
same two burly men who had brought them to the brig. The
men opened the cells and herded Peter and Wendy up

through the ship, one in front and one behind. Peter and Wendy were relieved to note that the men didn't bother to tie or shackle them; evidently they didn't expect any trouble from children.

When they reached the main deck, Peter saw that night was falling over London. That was good; darkness would help with his plan. Both the deck and the dock were bustling with debarking passengers and porters pushing carts piled high with luggage. Most of the ship's traffic flowed down a long gangway from the deck to the dock, where Peter and Wendy spotted their welcoming committee: two London bobbies.

As they reached the top of the gangway, Peter and Wendy exchanged looks.

Ready? his eyes asked.

Ready, hers answered.

"Don't be getting any ideas, you two," growled one of the crewmen. He gripped Peter's arm in his meaty hand; the other man gripped Wendy as well. The four of them joined the throng of passengers heading off the ship. The crowd moved slowly; that was good. Still, by the time they were a third of the way down, Peter was worried.

Where's Tink?

Halfway down, Peter paused to look down at the cold, dirty water of the Thames, in the narrow space between the dock and the ship.

"Keep moving!" barked the crewman holding Peter, jerking him forward. Wendy shot Peter a look: *Where is she?* Peter shrugged: *I don't know.*

They trudged forward several more steps. By the dock lights they could see the faces of the waiting bobbies, looking up at them. A worrisome thought knotted Peter's stomach: Tink had failed.

Then he heard screams. They started at the top of the gangway and quickly spread downward. People lunged this way and that, trying to escape something, but on the crowded gangway, suspended over the water, there was nowhere to escape.

"Get ready," Peter whispered to Wendy. The panic spread quickly. They were shoved forward by the mob behind them. The men holding Peter and Wendy tightened their grips. Wendy bit down on her lip to keep from crying out in pain. The crowd surged, nearly knocking them over. The only thing keeping them up was the dense mass of people in front of them. The screams intensified. Then Peter saw the cause of the panic: first one, then a dozen gray shapes slithered down the gangway between the passengers' jumping feet.

Rats.

A blur of light appeared and, moving almost too fast to see, circled the crewman holding Peter, then the one holding Wendy. The rats converged into a river of gray, matted fur. Before the two crewmen had any idea what was happening, a dozen rats scurried up their pants. The crewmen screamed and let go of their captives, jumping up and down in a frenzy and swatting at the animals clawing at their legs. Peter and Wendy were now free of their captors, but imprisoned ahead and behind by the dense mob of panicked passengers.

Now came the tricky part of the plan.

"Trust me," Peter shouted to Wendy. Putting a hand on the gangway railing, he vaulted over, disappearing as he fell.

"MAN OVERBOARD!" shouted somebody from the main deck. More screams arose as passengers leaned over the railing, peering into the darkness below. Wendy took a deep breath and slung her left leg over the railing. She was lifting her right leg over when her crewman guard, still swatting at the rats in his pants, saw her, bellowed in rage, and reached for her. He caught her foot and pulled hard, trying to return her to the gangway. She drew back and kicked out with all her strength. Suddenly her shoe came off in his hand and she fell backward over the railing, her cry joining those of the gangway throng. She felt herself tumbling through darkness, then slammed into something

"OOF!" exclaimed Peter. He'd caught her five feet above the water, and was able to slow her fall, but not stop it. The two of them plunged into the ice-cold Thames. After a few awful, disorienting seconds in the icy, pitch-blackness underwater, they came up gasping and sputtering. From above came a chorus of shouts and screams, and the sound of feet pounding on the dock.

"Hang on!" said Peter, positioning Wendy behind him and gathering her arms around his shoulders. With a grunt, he lunged upward, slowing lifting her clear of the river, water cascading off them both. The effort weakened him, making him dizzy; he knew he could not fly her far.

This way! This way!

Peter saw Tink hovering to his left, leading him toward the massive looming stern of the *Lucy*. He flew after her, wobbling from side to side, unable to gain altitude, his toes brushing the water. The shouts receded behind them. They cleared the stern of the ship and flew another hundred yards along a stretch of empty dock before Peter, his strength gone, veered to the right and splashed back into the water next to a piling. It was covered with slime and barnacles, but he wrapped both arms gratefully around it and clung to it, sucking air into his burning lungs.

"Are you all right?" said Wendy, holding on to his back.

"I've been better," said Peter. "You?"

"Likewise," said Wendy.

The sound of chimes came from a few feet away.

Are you going to stay in the water all night, or are you going to climb up this ladder?

"Tink says there's a ladder over there," said Peter.

Wendy let go and swam to the ladder. Peter, too tired to fly, followed. A minute later they were on the dock, dripping wet and shivering cold.

"Well," said Peter. "Here we are."

"Yes," said Wendy.

You're welcome, said Tink.

"Thank you, Tink," said Peter.

"Yes, Tink," said Wendy. "Thank you."

You fly like a dead pelican, said Tink.

"She says, you're welcome," said Peter.

"How did she get them to do that?" said Wendy.

"Get who to do what?" said Peter.

"Get the rats to crawl up the men's trousers."

"She told them the men had cheese in their pockets," said Peter.

"She can talk to rats?" said Wendy.

"Oh, yes," said Peter. "Not just rats."

They're smarter than you, said Tink.

"What did she say?" said Wendy.

"She said we'd better get going before we freeze to death."

They started trudging toward the lights of London, clothes dripping, Wendy walking on one bare foot.

"Where exactly *are* we going?" said Peter.

"To my house," said Wendy.

"Is it far?" said Peter.

"I don't know," said Wendy.

Wonderful, said Tink.

"What will we do when we get to your house?" said Peter.

"I'm . . . I don't know that either," said Wendy. "But I'm sure we'll figure it out when we get there."

"I see," said Peter.

They trudged a few more steps.

Definitely not as smart as the rats, said Tink.

CHAPTER 41

AN ODD REPORT

"EXCUSE ME, SIR." The secretary stood nervously in the doorway to Chief Superintendent Blake's Scotland Yard office.

"What is it?" snapped Blake. He was signing the last of the day's correspondence and planned to be on his way to dinner in five minutes. He did not appreciate anything interfering with his dinner.

"It's Superintendent Shroder, sir," said the secretary. "He says it's of the utmost importance."

"It had *better* be," said Blake. "Send him in."

The secretary scurried away and a stocky, sweating man entered, holding a piece of paper.

"Sorry to interrupt, sir," he said. "But a matter has come up which I believe is of the utmost—"

"Yes, the utmost importance," said Blake, drumming his fingers on his desk. "What is it?"

"Sir, you may recall that you gave special orders that you wanted to be advised immediately if any officer reported any . . . *unusual* activity involving children meeting certain descriptions."

Blake's fingers stopped drumming. "Go on," he said.

"Well," said Shroder holding out the piece of paper, "a short while ago, two officers turned in an odd report from Royal Victoria Dock. I would go so far as to say it is quite unbelievable, sir. However, since the children involved are . . ."

"Let me see it," said Blake, snatching the report from Shroder's hands. He read it quickly, rubbed a hand through his hair, and read it again. Then he handed it back to Shroder.

"You are to take this report to Buckingham Palace immediately," he said.

"The palace?" said Shroder. "But . . ."

"*Immediately*," snapped Blake. "You are to hand it personally to Baron von Schatten's assistant, Simon Revile, and no one else. You will then await his instructions. Do you understand?"

"Yes, sir."

"Go!"

Shroder scurried out the door.

Blake sat still for a few seconds, then pounded his fist on his desk, thinking about the dinner he would not be eating anytime soon.

CHAPTER 42

SOMEPLACE SAFE

"I THINK WE'RE GETTING NEAR MY HOUSE," said Wendy.

"You *think?*" said Peter, a bit testily, through chattering teeth.

"I'm sorry," said Wendy, also a bit testily. "I'm doing the best I can."

It's not very good, said Tink, from inside Peter's shirt.

"Oh, be quiet," said Peter.

"What?" said Wendy.

"I wasn't talking to you," said Peter.

"I should hope not," said Wendy.

I WAS talking to her, said Tink.

After a few more steps, Wendy said, "Listen, if you don't like walking with me, you can fly."

Excellent idea! said Tink.

But Peter shook his head. He didn't like walking, but he couldn't leave Wendy alone. The truth was, he wasn't enthusiastic about being on his own in London at night. He'd had more than his share of bad experiences in this vast, confusing city.

They slogged on in silence. Their physical condition was as miserable as their mood. They'd been walking for hours—Peter in short pants and sleeves, Wendy on one bare foot—through the fog and chill of the London night, made all the chillier by the fact that they were soaking wet. They'd taken a zigzag route through a maze of dark streets, avoiding people as much as possible, and hiding whenever they saw, or thought they saw, a bobby. They were hungry, tired, and cold. And, at the moment, lost.

They rounded a corner; ahead was a busy, well-lit street. As they drew closer, Wendy said, "I think that's Old Brompton Road!"

"Is that good?" said Peter.

"Yes," said Wendy. "We're near my house."

It's about time, said Tink.

They reached Old Brompton Road and turned left. In a few blocks they turned left again, and walked halfway down a residential street. Wendy stopped and said, "I don't understand."

"What?" said Peter.

"This is my house. But there are no lights."

"It's late. Maybe George . . . I mean, maybe *your father* is asleep."

"Even if he were, there would be lights front and back."

Wendy climbed the front steps, tried the doorknob, then rang the bell several times. No answer.

"Where could he *be?*" said Wendy, her voice quavering. She'd been counting on seeing her father again, being held in his strong arms, letting him take the burden of making decisions. And now . . .

She put her face in her hands.

Now she's going to cry, said Tink, not sympathetically, but accurately. Wendy stifled a sob; a tear, then another, leaked through her fingers and spattered on the porch. Peter wanted to put his arm around her, but couldn't quite get up the nerve, so he patted her twice on the back and said, "There, there." It felt like a stupid thing to say, but it was all he could think of at the moment.

After an awkward moment, Wendy raised her head and sniffed, regaining her composure. "All right," she said. "We'll go to Grandfather's house."

MORE walking? chimed Tink.

"Is it far?" asked Peter.

"Less than a mile, I should think," said Wendy.

If only you COULD think, said Tink.

"What did she say?" said Wendy.

"She said let's go, it's cold," said Peter.

They trudged back up the street and continued north, crossing Kensington Road and entering Hyde Park. Wendy led the way, sticking to a footpath. There were few lampposts here; most of the time they could see only a few feet in the fog.

We were here, said Tink. *Bad men chased us.*

"I remember," said Peter.

"Remember what?" said Wendy.

"Tink and I were in this park," said Peter. "With Mol— your mother. I flew her out of Lord Aster's house when Ombra was after her."

She nearly got us killed, said Tink.

"What did she say?" said Wendy.

"It was a scary night," said Peter. "We escaped through this park. That was the night I met your father. We hid in his room."

"Really? His *room*?" said Wendy.

"I'd rather not talk about it," said Peter.

They hid me under the bed, fumed Tink.

"What did she say?"

"She'd rather not talk about it either," said Peter.

They walked some more in silence, passing by the looming shape of Kensington Palace, its lighted windows barely visible off to the right. They were approaching, from the back, a row of grand homes on a grand street called Kensington Palace Gardens. Wendy pointed to a particularly large house off to the right.

"There it is," she said.

"I know," said Peter. He would never forget that house.

They started trotting toward it, energized by thoughts of warmth and food. Suddenly Tink made a low sound. Peter grabbed Wendy's arm.

"Wait," he whispered.

"What is it?" she whispered back.

"Men," he said.

Wendy peered toward the house. "I don't see anybody," she whispered.

Of course you don't.

Peter led Wendy into a stand of trees. It was pitch-black there, save for Tink's glow.

"What do we do?" whispered Wendy.

"I'll have a look," said Peter. "You and Tink stay here."

I'm not staying with her.

"Yes you are," whispered Peter. "If you go with me, they'll see you glow."

Put me in your shirt.

"No. They still might see you."

Hmph, said Tink, this being the closest she ever came to saying "I suppose you're right."

"I'll be right back," whispered Peter. Before Wendy could say anything more, he launched himself straight up, his body brushing against tree branches. In a moment he was a hundred feet in the air, hidden by fog. Flying felt good after all the walking. When he figured he was close to the house, he descended slowly until he could see that he was over the large back lawn. He first studied the service entrance at the back of the mansion, which had an electric light glowing over the door; he saw nobody near it. Upstairs from the entrance and to the right was a large window revealing a well-lit room. Inside, Peter saw two children—one small, one medium—and a stout man with a red face and white hair.

As Peter watched, a large, red-faced woman entered the room and said something to the children. Despite the tension of the moment, Peter smiled as he recognized Mrs. Bumbrake. He was about to swoop forward for a better look when he heard a cough almost directly below. He froze, then slowly leaned forward, straining to peer through the darkness. Finally he saw the shape, standing against a bush.

A bobby.

Peter's eyes swept the lawn, but he saw no other men. Slowly, silently, he flew straight up into the fog, then forward over the high roof of the Aster mansion, stopping when he could see the street in front. This time the bobby was easier to spot: he was across the street, using the shadow of a large tree to keep out of what little light was cast by the streetlamp.

Peter turned and headed back toward the park. It took him a few minutes, flying through the fog, to locate the stand of trees where he'd left Wendy and Tink.

"Well?" whispered Wendy.

"Two policemen are watching the house," he answered. "One in front and one in back."

"Did you see anybody inside the house?"

"Mrs. Bumbrake," said Peter. "Two boys, one little and one maybe seven or eight."

"Michael and John!" said Wendy. "My brothers!"

"And an older man, sort of heavy, with white hair."

"That's Uncle Neville," said Wendy. "Did you see my father? Tall man? Handsome?"

"No, nobody else," said Peter, annoyed at himself for resenting Wendy's description of her father.

"Maybe he was in another room," said Wendy.

"Maybe," said Peter.

"Well," said Wendy, "whoever's in there, we need to get them out."

"We do?" said Peter. "Why?"

Because she's crazy, said Tink.

"Because the police are here," said Wendy. "That means they're in danger, especially if von Schatten finds out we're in London. We need to get everyone out of that house, so we can all go to someplace safe, and then we can figure out what to do next."

"Someplace safe?" said Peter. "Where?"

"I don't know," admitted Wendy.

She is just full of good ideas, said Tink.

CHAPTER 43

NO WORSE FATE

HOLDING SOME PAPERS AND sweating despite the chill in the air—a chill he felt whenever Baron von Schatten was near—Simon Revile hesitated at the door to the king's bedchamber in Buckingham Palace. He raised his hand and rapped twice on the door.

"Enter." Von Schatten's moaning voice sounded, as always, as if it came from somewhere distant. Revile stepped inside. Except for the light coming through the open doorway, the bedchamber was dark. Von Schatten and the king occupied facing chairs in the middle of the room. The king sat utterly still, seemingly unaware of Revile's entrance. Von Schatten turned his head slowly until his dark glasses faced Revile.

"What is it?" he said.

"I apologize," said Revile. "I know your orders were that you were not to be disturbed. But I felt that, in this instance—"

"*What is it?*" snarled von Schatten, in a voice that chilled Revile's blood.

"Chief Superintendent Blake," Revile said quickly. "He's just sent a man here with a police report."

"Concerning?"

"A few hours ago, two officers were called to Victoria Dock to meet a ship and take custody of two stowaways."

"Why would that interest me?"

"They were children," said Revile. "A boy and a girl."

"The world is full of children," said von Schatten, turning his head toward the king.

"The boy escaped by flying."

Von Schatten's head snapped back toward Revile. "Flying? The police are certain?" he said.

"Not exactly. The boy jumped off the gangway, followed by the girl. It was dark. Neither child was seen again. The bobbies commandeered a small boat and searched the harbor, but found nothing."

"Perhaps the children drowned."

"Perhaps. But witnesses, including one of the officers, said they saw something flying away from the ship."

"A bird."

"Much bigger than a bird. The story has already caused quite a stir in London, sir."

"What are the names of these children?"

"We don't know. The ship's captain questioned them, but they told him nothing."

"How did they get aboard the ship?"

"Nobody knows that, either. They were discovered when the ship had been at sea for more than a week."

"They just appeared on the ship? Out at sea?"

"Yes."

For a few moments von Schatten was silent. Then, in a voice so low Revile could barely hear it, said, "He's come back."

"But how would he know? All those years on the island . . ."

"The Darling girl must have gotten word to him," said von Schatten.

"The girl who disappeared," said Revile.

"Yes," said von Schatten. "We should have taken her when we took her parents." He thought for a moment, then said, "How many men does Blake have watching the Aster house?"

"Two, sir. Front and back. 'Round the clock."

"Tell him to send ten more of his best men right now. Tell him they must surround the house, but they *must not be seen*. Let the boy and the girl think it's safe. Let them go inside, where the boy can't fly. Then take them. Do you understand?"

"Yes, Baron," said Revile, turning to go.

"Wait," said von Schatten. "Where is the Skeleton?"

"In the Underground. He's been asking when he may, ah, *interview* the prisoners."

"Not yet. I still need them alive. Tell him I would appreciate his help in apprehending the boy and the girl."

"Are you sure?"

"Yes. He has skills that can be useful in this situation. But tell him I want the boy alive. Make that very clear: the boy is *mine*."

"And the girl?"

"He can do what he wants with the girl. Go."

"Yes, Baron," said Revile. He backed out of the room and closed the door, leaving von Schatten once again alone with the king, who still had not moved a muscle. Revile hurried down the long palace hallway to carry out von Schatten's orders. Revile was not one to feel concern for others, but even he could not help but feel a twinge of pity for the two children. He could imagine no worse fate than to fall into the disfigured hands of the Skeleton—unless it was to become the prey of von Schatten.

CHAPTER 44

ALMOST HERE

PETER FLEW OVER THE HIGH WALL along the back of the Aster property and settled gently on the ground. He walked to the wall's iron gate and found the latch; as Wendy had promised, the gate could be opened from the inside without a key. He carefully lifted the latch and pushed the gate open so Wendy could come through. They left the gate ajar.

Peter pointed toward the bushes where the bobby was concealed. Wendy nodded. They split up, Peter going toward the bobby, and Wendy melting into the shadows along the wall in the other direction. In the pocket of Wendy's skirt, and not happy about it, was Tinker Bell; Peter didn't want her with him, for fear her glow would give him away.

He walked on tiptoe until he could just make out, by the faint light from the service entrance, the profile of the bobby, who was facing the house. Peter crept toward him, closer, closer, until he was barely two yards away. He took a deep breath, then in one quick motion lunged toward the bobby, grabbed his hat, swerved away, and started running.

"HEY!" shouted the bobby. "COME BACK HERE! STOP!" Peter glanced back to make sure the bobby was chasing him. He was; in fact he was quite close. Peter picked up speed, sprinting through the gate. The bobby was right behind, still shouting "STOP!" This is what prevented him from hearing the click of the gate closing and locking behind him.

It was darker on the other side of the wall, dark enough that Peter could cheat a bit; he was more flying than running, his feet barely touching ground. Increasing his lead but remaining close enough to be visible, he led the bobby to the same clump of trees where he and Wendy had stood a few minutes earlier. He stopped, made sure the bobby could see him, then put the hat on his head, grabbed the trunk of a large oak, and shot up it, moving his arms and legs to make it appear that he was climbing. In seconds he was high up in the tree, concealed in the darkness by the mass of branches.

The bobby puffed up to the base of the tree.

"YOU COME DOWN RIGHT NOW!" he shouted. "AND GIVE ME MY HAT!"

"I don't think I will," Peter called down. "I rather *like* your hat."

Enraged, the bobby grabbed the tree trunk and tried to hoist himself up, only to fall to the ground in quite an undignified manner. He jumped to his feet and ran around the tree, looking for a way up but finding none; there were no branches low enough for him to reach. Still, he ran around the tree several times, like a dog chasing an invisible squirrel. Peter found this quite amusing.

"PARKER!" a voice called from the dark.

"Over here!" shouted the bobby under Peter's tree.

A second bobby came trotting up; Peter recognized him as the one who'd been guarding the front of the house.

"What's happened?" he said. "I heard shouting."

"Some wretched boy stole my hat," said the first bobby.

"How'd he do that?" said the second.

"He ran up and snatched it. Now he's up this tree."

"He climbed *this* tree?"

"Yes, and I'm going to go up there and strangle him with me bare hands!" He looked up into the tree and shouted: "D'YOU HEAR ME BOY? WITH ME BARE HANDS!"

"How're you going to climb this tree?" said the second bobby.

"I can if he did! Give me a hand."

Reluctantly, the second bobby clasped his fingers together so the first bobby could use his hands as a foothold. The first bobby again grabbed the tree and, putting his weight on the second bobby's hands, lunged upward. This time both bobbies fell ingloriously to the ground.

Peter laughed out loud. This made the second bobby as

angry as the first. The two of them struggled to their feet and resumed their furious, but fruitless, effort to climb the tree and strangle the boy. They were so focused on their task that neither of them noticed the dark shape that darted out of the top of the tree and swooped back toward the house. A tiny light shot toward him; in a second Tink was at his ear.

Her dress smells like seaweed, she said.

"Did she get into the house?" said Peter.

They let her in. She left the back door open.

"Good," said Peter. "I think those two will be trying to get up the tree for a while, but keep an eye on the neighborhood in case anybody else shows up."

Would you like me to fix your dinner, too?

"That would be nice," said Peter.

Tink made an impolite sound and zoomed off. Peter landed by the service door and went into the house. He ran through the staff kitchen and up the stairs, where he found a scene of emotional turmoil. Mrs. Bumbrake, sobbing with joy and relief, was embracing the long-lost Wendy from the front, while Michael and John were hugging her from behind. Close by, looking happy but not quite up to joining the hug, was Uncle Neville. Peter hesitated in the doorway, unnoticed, reluctant to disturb the emotional reunion.

"Wendy!" Mrs. Bumbrake was saying. "Where have you *been*? We've all been so worried!"

"I know, and I'm sorry," said Wendy, extricating herself

from the hug. "I promise I'll explain." She turned to Neville and said, "Uncle Neville, I'm *so* sorry I took your ornithopter, but I had to . . ."

"Nonsense!" said Uncle Neville, waving the apology away. "You did brilliantly! How did you get it to fly so well?"

"Well, I, ah . . ."

"And how far did it go? A mile? Two?"

Wendy smiled. "It went a good deal farther than that," she said.

"Really!" said Uncle Neville. "You must tell me how . . ."

He was interrupted by Mrs. Bumbrake, who had just spotted Peter.

"Peter!" she exclaimed. "Is that *you?*"

"Hello, Mrs. *mmph,*" said Peter, as he was swept into Mrs. Bumbrake's embrace.

"Who is Peter?" asked Uncle Neville.

"He's a family friend," said Wendy.

"I see," said Uncle Neville, clearly not seeing.

"We have to go," said Peter. "Right now."

"What?" said Mrs. Bumbrake and Uncle Neville together.

"Peter's right," said Wendy. "There's no time to explain. We must go immediately."

"Go where?" asked Uncle Neville.

Peter and Wendy looked at each other.

"We don't know," said Wendy. "But we—"

"What is *that?*" said John, pointing at a blur of light as it zipped across the room and stopped on Peter's shoulder.

"That's Tinker Bell," said Peter.

"My word," said Uncle Neville, gaping.

"It's a fairy!" said Michael.

Tink made an unhappy sound.

"She prefers the term 'bird woman,'" said Peter. Tink chimed rapidly into his ear. He nodded, frowning.

"How far?" he said.

Tink chimed some more.

"Keep an eye on them," said Peter, and Tink zoomed from the room.

"What is it?" said Wendy.

"Police," said Peter. "A lot of them. At the bottom of the big street out front, headed this way."

"That's it," said Wendy. "We have to go *right now*."

"But if it's the police," said Uncle Neville, "why would we—?"

"I'll explain later," said Wendy. "But right now you must trust me. Everyone in this house is in great danger. We must get out *now*, before those men arrive. *Please*, Uncle Neville."

Neville blinked once, then said, "All right."

"Thank you," said Wendy. "We'll leave by the service entrance. Michael, John, come along." She took her brothers by the hand and started for the stairs. Neville was right behind.

Peter looked at Mrs. Bumbrake, who had not moved.

"Come on, Mrs. Bumbrake," he said.

"Can't," she said.

"Mrs. Bumbrake," Wendy called over her shoulder. "Please! The men will be here soon!"

"I don't care, miss," said Mrs. Bumbrake. "I'm not leaving Lord Aster."

Wendy stopped and turned, her face white.

"Oh dear," she said, "I'd forgotten."

"Can he walk?" said Peter.

"No," said Mrs. Bumbrake. "He's much too weak."

Peter and Wendy exchanged a look: *What do we do now?*

Tink zoomed back into the room, chiming urgently.

"What did she say?" asked Wendy.

"The men are almost here," said Peter.

CHAPTER 45

A WHISPER DOWN THE TUNNEL

*M*OLLY WAS GROWING DESPERATE. For two days, when she thought it was safe to do so, she'd tapped her rock against the bars of her cell, sending *h-e-l-l-o* in Morse code, and sometimes *s-o-s*. But she'd gotten no answer. There was definitely someone in the cell farther down the tunnel; the guard delivered food there. But whoever it was didn't respond. Molly concluded that the other prisoner either didn't understand Morse code or simply didn't care to respond to her messages.

She decided to risk calling out. She waited until there had been no guard noise in the tunnel for a quite some time, then pressed her face to the bars, turning toward the other cell. Keeping her voice to a whisper, and cupping her hand to her mouth, she called out, "Psst! Hello!"

Nothing.

She raised her voice: "Hello! *Can you hear me?*"

Still, nothing. Molly slumped to the cell floor and put her face in her hands, sobbing. She had resigned herself to the fact that she would never see her family again; that she was going to die in this cold, miserable, filthy place. All she had left to hope for was a stolen moment of communication with another human being. And now even that hope was gone.

Then she heard a voice, a forced whisper from down the tunnel.

"Molly? Is that you?"

Molly sprang to her feet, her face pressed against the bars. *Could it possibly be . . .*

"George?" she called out, much too loudly.

"HERE NOW!" shouted a guard's gravelly voice from down the hall. "SHUT YER GOB OR I'LL COME DOWN THERE AND SHUT IT FOR YOU!"

Molly didn't dare say any more. She could barely speak anyway. She clung to the bars with both hands to keep from falling as sobs racked her body, an outpouring of the emotion pent up over so many lonely days and nights.

Several long minutes passed. Then the whisper came again.

"Molly," George said, "is that really you? Are you all right?"

It was several seconds before Molly had regained control enough to answer. Finally she whispered, "It is me, my love. I'm . . . I'm alive."

George groaned. "Oh, Molly," he whispered, "Please forgive me. I should have believed you . . . I . . ."

"Are the children all right?" interrupted Molly, fearing the guard would stop their conversation.

After a moment, George whispered, "They're . . . fine." His hesitation troubled Molly. She was about to probe when she heard footsteps coming rapidly down the tunnel.

"George," she whispered urgently, "do you know Morse code?"

"Of course. Learned it from a friend of my father's, chap named Robert Baden-Powell. Served in Her Majesty's cavalry in . . ."

"*George*," she hissed. "I've been tapping to you in Morse code for *days*."

"Oh," he said, sheepishly. "I thought that was the pipes."

"No! It was—"

"I said SHUT YER GOBS," bellowed the guard, stomping into view. "And since you didn't listen, YOU'LL GET NO FOOD TODAY. If I hear ANOTHER WORD from either of you, you'll get ME BOOT IN YOUR FACE." The guard stomped off, but this time not far. He was clearly waiting, listening. George and Molly remained silent in their cells.

Hungry as she was, Molly didn't care about the food. She'd survive a day without eating. She felt hope stirring again, after so many nights of despair. She was no longer alone. George was nearby, and even though they couldn't talk, they could communicate. They would find a way to get out of this horrible place, to get back to their children. They had to.

Molly picked up the rock again and began tapping.

CHAPTER 46

ONE LIGHT AND ONE DARK

"GRANDFATHER! CAN YOU HEAR ME?" Wendy bent over Leonard Aster's gaunt, gray, apparently lifeless face. Peter, standing next to Wendy, was shocked to see this frail old man in place of the strong and courageous Starcatcher leader he once knew.

"Grandfather, *please*, wake up!" said Wendy.

"It's no use, child," said Mrs. Bumbrake softly. She stood in the doorway, dabbing at her eyes. "He's been like this for days."

From downstairs, they heard pounding on the big front door, and muffled shouts.

Neville appeared in the doorway, panting from hurrying up the stairs.

"I've locked all the doors," he said. "The police are trying to get in."

The pounding got louder.

"Sooner or later they'll break down the door," said Neville.

"Or come through a window," said Peter.

"We've got to move Grandfather," said Wendy.

"How will we get him out?" said Peter.

"Through the back door," said Wendy.

"They'll be waiting for us back there," said Peter.

"What we need," said Uncle Neville, "is a diversion."

"A what?" said Peter.

"Mrs. Bumbrake," said Uncle Neville, "do you have any flour?"

"Any *what?*" said Mrs. Bumbrake.

"Flour," said Uncle Neville. "The kind you bake with."

"There's a sack in the kitchen, downstairs," said Mrs. Bumbrake. "But why . . ."

"What about candles?" said Uncle Neville.

"Also in the kitchen," said Mrs. Bumbrake. "But . . ."

"No time to explain!" said Uncle Neville. To Wendy and Peter, he said, "Bring Leonard down to the rear door." Then he was gone. As he left, Tink zoomed into the room.

Bad man, she chimed to Peter.

"I know," he said. "The police."

Not the police, she chimed. *A very bad man.*

Peter wanted to ask more, but Wendy was tugging his arm.

"We'll have to carry Grandfather," said Wendy.

"No," said Mrs. Bumbrake. "He's too weak!"

A crashing sound echoed through the house.

"We have to try!" said Wendy, slipping an arm under Leonard's shoulders. "Take hold of his legs." As Peter and Mrs. Bumbrake stepped forward, Leonard moaned.

"He's waking up!" said Mrs. Bumbrake. Leonard's eyes fluttered open, focused on Wendy, then Peter and Tink, then back on Wendy. The faintest of smiles formed on his lips, and in a voice so weak they could barely hear it, he said, "You found him."

"Yes, Grandfather," said Wendy, tears welling in her eyes. "I found him."

They wouldn't be here without me, chimed Tink.

"Yes, of course," whispered Leonard, who was the only human being other than Peter who understood Tink. "Thank you, Tinker Bell." He reached a thin, bony hand toward Peter. "We need your help," he said. "Don't let them . . ." He coughed, then with effort regained his breath. "The Cache. Confess . . ." He coughed again, unable to stop this time, his body curling up in pain.

Another crash downstairs, louder than before. Footsteps on the stairs. John appeared in the doorway, breathless.

"Uncle Neville says you must come down to the kitchen right now!" he shouted, then turned and ran back downstairs.

Wendy leaned over her grandfather and said, "Grandfather, the police are here."

His eyes widened. "No," he whispered. "You must go." There was another crash, and the sound of wood splintering.

"Lo . . . Lock . . ." said Leonard, his trembling hands reaching under the neck of his nightgown. Wendy saw a bit of fine gold chain in his fingers.

"He's got a locket!" she said. She helped her grandfather pull the locket out from under the nightgown. It was identical to the locket her mother had given her. "It's starstuff!" she cried.

"Use it," gasped Leonard. "Now. Get away." His shaking hands fumbled with the clasp.

"Here, let me," said Wendy, taking the locket in her hands. She undid the clasp. A glowing sphere of light surrounded her hands, and everyone in the room—despite the peril of the situation—felt a sense of exhilaration and well-being.

"Are you going to use it?" said Peter.

"No," said Wendy firmly. "Grandfather is."

Hearing this, Leonard reached his hand out to stop Wendy, but he was too late. With a flick of her wrist she overturned the locket. Instantly the room blazed with brightness as a shower of brilliant light poured onto the old man's face and chest. Wendy, Peter, and Mrs. Bumbrake turned away, closing their eyes, hearing strange and wonderful music in the air. It was ten seconds before they were able to reopen their eyes, and when they did, Leonard was no longer in the bed; instead he stood before them in his nightgown. He was as gaunt as ever, but his once-pale skin now glowed with ruddy health, and his eyes were clear and alert.

"That starstuff wasn't for me," he told Wendy. "That was for *you.*"

"We're not leaving you here," she said.

"I appreciate that, Wendy, but my time is done, and you must . . ."

He was cut off by a resounding crash downstairs, and the sound of splintering wood.

"Maybe we should argue about this later," said Peter.

"All right," said Leonard, once again in command. "Let's go." He started for the door, stopped, and said "Just a moment." He went to his massive oak wardrobe, opened it, and pulled out a sword. He brandished it, his eyes shining.

"Now we're ready," he said. "Like old times, eh, Peter?"

"Yes, sir!" said Peter.

"Come on, then," said Leonard, moving quickly out the door, followed by the other three. At the bottom of the stairs they stopped to look toward the front door. As they did, it shuddered with a loud crash and the men outside heaved against it.

"It won't hold much longer," said Leonard. "Tink, go outside and have a look at the back door. We'll meet you down in the kitchen."

Yes, sir, chimed Tink, streaking to the main fireplace and up the chimney.

Leonard shepherded Mrs. Bumbrake, Wendy, and Peter onto the kitchen stairs. He followed them, stopping on the top step to push a heavy door closed, then lock it.

"I had this door installed long ago, when I thought I might need to barricade the family in the basement," he said. "Never needed it until now. It's stronger than the front door. They won't get through it any time soon."

There was a thunderous crash from the other side of the door, and the sound of shouting and heavy shoes tromping on the wooden floors.

"They're in the house," said Leonard. "We'd best get down to the kitchen."

In the kitchen they found John and Michael with Uncle Neville, who had set a large cloth sack of flour in the middle of the floor.

"Hello, Leonard," said Neville. "You're looking well."

"Thank you, Neville," said Leonard. "Nice to see you. Why have you put a flour sack on the floor?"

"To make a bomb," said Neville.

"Oh dear," said Mrs. Bumbrake.

"Uncle Neville's gonna splode the kitchen!" said Michael.

"It's *explode,* you ninny," said John.

"That's what I *said,*" said Michael.

There was pounding on the door at the top of the kitchen stairs.

"What do you mean, a bomb?" said Leonard.

"Flour particles," said Neville. "If you get enough of them suspended in the air, then introduce a flame"—he waved an unlit candle and a box of matches—"you get quite a dramatic explosion. I've done some experiments on my estate. Lost a building, in fact. Fortunately, no one was in it at the time."

"Oh dear," repeated Mrs. Bumbrake.

The pounding on the stairway door intensified.

"So your plan is to set off the explosion *here?*" said Leonard, peering down at the flour sack.

"Precisely," said Neville. "We tromp on the flour, like so." He brought his right foot down on the flour sack, which blew out a cloud of flour directly onto Leonard, covering him head to toe in white.

"Sorry!" said Neville.

"Quite all right," said Leonard, brushing at the flour ineffectively. "Go on."

"Yes," said Neville. "By tromping on the sack, we fill the air with flour particles. Then we nip into the pantry over there and toss a lighted candle into the kitchen. This will cause an explosion. In the ensuing confusion, we make our escape!"

Neville looked around the room, pleased with his plan. The others were less enthusiastic.

"I'm not sure," said Wendy, "exactly how . . ."

She stopped as Tink zoomed in through the kitchen-fireplace chimney, chiming excitedly.

"Interesting," said Leonard.

"What is it?" said Wendy.

"The policemen," said Peter. "There's only three upstairs, pounding on the door." He pointed toward the stairway, which echoed with the sound of continual pounding. "The rest are all waiting outside the back door." He pointed toward the hallway that led to the back door.

"Why aren't they trying to get in by the back door, then?" said Wendy.

"It's a trap," said Leonard. "They *want* us to run out the back door, into their clutches."

"Should we try to go upstairs?" said Wendy.

"There are three men that way," said Leonard. "We *might* be able to fight our way through, but . . ." He trailed off, looking at Mrs. Bumbrake and the two boys.

"So what do we do?" said Wendy.

"We open the back door," said Leonard.

"We *do*?" said Peter.

"We do," said Leonard, with a small smile. "Now, listen closely." It took him several minutes to explain the plan. The others listened in silence, except for Mrs. Bumbrake, who said "Oh dear" four times.

When Leonard was done, he dragged the flour sack into

the hallway next to the back door, then stomped on it until the air was thick with flour dust. He was now totally, completely white. He returned to the kitchen, tucked his sword under his arm, and took the candle and matches from Neville. The pounding from the stairway door continued unabated.

"All right," he said. "Go to your positions."

Mrs. Bumbrake, Neville, John, and Michael headed for the pantry. Wendy and Peter, with Tink inside Peter's shirt, started for the stairway. Leonard put out a white hand, stopping them.

"When you get out of here," he said, "go straight to a hotel in Sloane Square called the Scotland Landing."

"But you'll be with us!" said Wendy.

Leonard put his hand on her shoulder. "I shall try," he said. "But this starstuff is going to wear off, and when it does, I shall be as bad off as I was before. Worse, in fact."

"But . . ."

"No, Wendy," said Leonard. "I've had my time. This is your time. Don't fail us." Leonard's voice was breaking. "Don't fail the Starcatchers," he said. He pushed Wendy gently toward the stairway, then turned away, toward the flour-filled hall. Wendy was about to call out to him; there was so much more she needed to know. But it was too late. Leonard was opening the box of matches.

The policemen out back—seven large, tough men—were growing impatient.

"Why don't we just break the door down?" said one. Several others murmured agreement.

"Our orders are to wait here," said another man. He lowered his voice and tilted his head. "Does anybody want to tell *him* that we're going to disobey orders?"

All seven man looked toward the corner of the house, where they could just make out the dark shape of a man in a hooded cloak, standing where he could see both the street and the rear entrance to the Aster mansion. None of the bobbies wanted anything to do with the cloaked man. They would follow their orders. They turned back toward the door.

Ten seconds passed. Twenty.

Then the night erupted.

The earsplitting blast blew the rear door off its hinges so hard that it shattered against the garden wall fifty feet away, exploding into burning shards. A huge tongue of flame came right behind it, blasting across the lawn, turning a wide swath of it black.

Fortunately for them, none of the bobbies was directly in front of the door when it blew, although all of them were thrown violently backward and onto the ground. It was several seconds before they were able to get to their feet. They stared, ears ringing, at the gaping, smoking hole where the door had been, trying to understand what had happened.

It was then that they saw the ghost.

⟞⬦⟝

When the flour bomb went off, Peter and Wendy, as Leonard had instructed them, were kneeling at the top of the stairway, facing the door with their eyes closed and their hands clamped tightly over their ears. After the explosion, they waited a few seconds, then opened their eyes to see that the stairway was thick with dust and smoke. They stood up, coughing. The pounding on the door had stopped, but now it resumed, more frantic than before.

"Ready?" said Peter.

"Ready," said Wendy.

Peter pulled Tink out from under his shirt.

"All right," he said.

Tink flew halfway down the smoke-filled stairway and hovered there. Wendy went down and stood next to her. Peter stepped to the side of the stairway, pressing himself against the wall.

"Don't forget to close your eyes," he said.

"I won't," said Wendy.

Peter unlocked the door and turned the handle. It was

several seconds before the pounding men on the other side realized it was unlocked.

"It's open!" shouted a voice.

The door was pushed open. Peter was now concealed behind it. A bobby stepped onto the stairs, followed by two more.

"There's the girl!" shouted the first, spotting Wendy in the smoke. All three men started toward her. She closed her eyes, and as she did, Tinker Bell flashed her brightest light, filling the stairway with a blinding glare. The instant it was gone, Wendy opened her eyes and grabbed Tink, who was so weak from her effort that she could barely fly. Wendy turned and ran to the bottom of the stairs, where Mrs. Bumbrake, Neville, John, and Michael were waiting. Wendy made it to the bottom and jumped out of the way just as the three bobbies, yelping in pain and fear, tumbled after her. Peter had shoved the first from behind; he had taken the other two down, like bowling pins. They sprawled onto the floor, moaning and still temporarily blind, unaware of the group of people now quickly climbing the stairs.

"Hurry!" whispered Peter, as they reached the top. "This way." He led them toward the smashed front door, and out into the night.

⸺⸱⸺

Four of the seven bobbies in the back simply ran from the ghost. They had already been terrified by the explosion;

the sudden appearance of a bizarre white figure flying over them—*flying*—and waving a sword was more than they could stand. They ran to the rear gate, opened it, and took off into Hyde Park.

The other three bobbies tried to do battle with the ghost, but they had no chance. It swooped and darted above them, back and forth, easily evading their clumsy efforts to hit it with their nightsticks while skillfully slashing at them with its sword. In less than a minute they, too, were running into the park to escape the flying fiend.

The little group stopped by an oak a few dozen yards from the Aster mansion, in an area dimly lit by one of the street-lamps on Kensington Palace Gardens.

"Is she okay?" said Peter.

"I think so," said Wendy, handing Tink to Peter. Tink's eyes were closed, but she was glowing. He held her for a moment, nodded, then gently put her into his shirt. "We need to get away from here," he said.

"To where?" said Neville.

"Lord Aster said we should go to a hotel near Sloane Square," said Peter.

"I believe that would be . . . that way," said Neville, pointing down the street. As he did, the clang of a fire-truck bell came from the other direction.

"We'd better get going," said Peter.

Wendy hesitated, looking back toward the house. "What about Grandfather?" she said.

"I'll go back and see," said Peter.

"I'll go with you," said Wendy.

"No," said Peter, with a firmness that surprised even himself. "He's just done everything he could so that you could escape. All that would be for nothing if you got caught now."

Wendy nodded reluctantly. "I suppose you're right."

"I'll fly over the house and see," said Peter.

Then he heard a soft, urgent chime from Tink.

And then he screamed in pain. Without knowing how he got there, he realized he was on his knees. The awful pain had receded from his body, but it had left him too weak to stand. He was aware that Wendy had screamed, and that Michael and John were crying. He felt something on his neck, something rough and repellant, and he knew that whatever it was had caused the pain, and might cause it again. He desperately hoped it would not. He would do anything—anything—to keep from feeling that pain again.

He turned his head as much as he dared. A man in a black cloak stood next to him. He had apparently come from the shadows by the tree. Peter hadn't heard him approach.

"Don't move, unless you want to feel that again," said the Skeleton, his voice a harsh rasp, his words distorted.

"Let him go!" said Wendy. The Skeleton turned toward her, and suddenly she saw his face by the dim streetlight. She screamed again.

"Here now!" said Neville, stepping toward the Skeleton. "Let the boy . . . *unnh.*"

The Skeleton's movement was so quick that nobody actually saw it. He merely reached out and touched Neville's forearm, then withdrew his hand. But the touch sent an agonizing shock up Neville's arm into his shoulder. He stumbled away, groaning, toward Mrs. Bumbrake, who was staring in horror at the Skeleton as she clutched the whimpering John and Michael to her.

From the ground, Peter whispered urgently, "Get away! All of you! Run!"

The others hesitated, not wanting to spend another second near the Skeleton but not wanting to leave Peter.

The Skeleton broke the silence. "If you run away, any of you, this boy will feel a pain so unbearable that it will never leave him, however long he lives. Something far worse than this." His gnarled stump of a hand moved slightly on the back of Peter's neck. Peter collapsed to the ground, unable to scream or even breathe, his entire body jerking in agony.

"Shall I proceed?" said the Skeleton, reaching his stump down toward Peter.

"No," whispered Wendy. "Please." As she spoke, some-

318

thing in the sky behind the Skeleton caught her eye—a white figure, soaring over the house.

Like an angel, she thought.

The Skeleton saw Wendy's reaction, and turned to see what had caused it. He whirled as Leonard Aster, still covered head to toe in flour, landed ten feet in front of him, sword in hand. He started carefully toward the Skeleton. The Skeleton shifted a bit to his right, angling his body sideways.

"Don't let him—" began Wendy, but before she could get the warning out, the Skeleton, cat-quick, had lunged toward Leonard, his claw of a hand darting out. Leonard, with starstuff-heightened senses, saw it coming. He vaulted into the air, just avoiding the Skeleton's touch as he thrust out his sword to force the Skeleton backward.

Leonard landed a few feet away, putting himself between the Skeleton and the others. "Wendy," he said over his shoulder. "Help Peter up and get away. Go where I told you. Do it now."

"But—"

"*Now!*" There was a note of desperation in Leonard's voice, and Wendy suddenly understood why: the starstuff was wearing off. She went to Peter, who was still on the ground, moaning. With Neville's help, she got him to his feet. Draping his arms over their shoulders, they started down the street as quickly as they could manage, trailed by

Mrs. Bumbrake and the two boys. Behind them, the sound of the fire-truck bells grew louder. After they had gone about fifty yards Wendy glanced back. Flames were erupting from the roof of the Aster mansion. By the light of the fire, Wendy could see two shapes near the big oak, one light and one dark, circling each other, each looking for an advantage.

She turned back, hurrying with Peter down the dark street, away from the horror behind them. She clung to the hope that her grandfather would somehow prevail, that she would see him again. She tried not to think about how weak he had been without the starstuff.

They were almost to the end of the street. Ahead were the lights of Kensington Road.

From somewhere behind her, Wendy heard a scream.

CHAPTER 47

THE LAUNCH

THE ENGINE CREW OF THE STEAMER *Nimbus* had seen
their captain only once on this voyage. He was a last-minute
replacement for Captain Peale, a fair and well-liked seaman
who had commanded the *Nimbus* for twelve years.

But just before sailing, Mr. Peale and his regular officers
and deckhands had all taken ill with a strange sleeping
sickness. Only the four engineers working far belowdecks
remained from the original crew. The *Nimbus* was lucky to
have them: its twin engines were quirky, prone to problems
that only the four engineers understood how to fix. They
came to wonder if they were spared the illness because of this
knowledge.

The one time they'd met their new captain had been
enough. It was just before casting off; he'd come down to the
engine room and told them, in a brief, snarling speech, that
he didn't want them associating with the rest of the crew.

That was fine with them; they wanted no part of the new crew if it was anything like the new captain.

He was old, with a weather-ravaged face and dark eyes set in a permanent glare. The worst was his nose—or lack of one. He wore a beak of gray wood tied around his head, covering a hole in the center of his face. Sometimes when he spoke the hole emitted a deep whistling noise, like the hooting of an owl. The captain's name was Nerezza.

After the *Nimbus* left port, the engine crew had almost no contact with anyone else on the ship. Their only communication with the captain came in the form of orders barked down the voicepipe from the bridge to the engine room. Occasionally the engineers ventured up on deck, but the new crew made it clear they were unwelcome, so they never stayed long. They were not told where the ship was going, or why.

One day, in midocean, the *Nimbus* stopped. Through a porthole, the engine crew caught a glimpse of a small dinghy being lowered, with four men aboard. After that, for many days, the *Nimbus* seemed to travel in a huge circle, many miles in diameter. They were out of sight of whatever they were circling, but the men in the engine room had spotted a small, persistent cloud on the horizon. They figured they were circling an island, day after day. But why?

"Some kind of smuggling," was Chief Wilkie's guess. The other three were inclined to agree. This Nerezza was a bad one, that much they were sure of. One of the men said he'd once heard a story about a Captain No Nose, who sailed to England with a ghost as cargo. The other insisted they didn't believe in ghosts. But the story stayed with them, and more and more, they avoided the upper decks. All they wanted was to get off this ship alive.

But when? Endless day followed endless day, with the *Nimbus* always circling, circling.

And then one day some black smudges of smoke appeared in the sky, and the ship came alive. The crewmen readied the odd launch that had been loaded aboard the *Nimbus* just before she sailed—a sturdy-looking six-oar rowboat with a cargo space amidships. The engine crew had wondered what its purpose was. Even more mysterious was the launch's cargo—four crates hauled up from the forward hold. The engine crew speculated on what was in the crates. Gold, was one theory.

At sunset, the ship turned toward the cloud on the horizon, and Nerezza's command came down the voice-pipe.

"All ahead one-quarter," he rasped. "Run her quiet, and no new coal."

The engine crew knew what this meant. Nerezza had let the boilers build up heat; now they could propel the ship forward at a slow pace without so much as a puff of smoke from her stacks.

Night fell. Hours passed. The ship steamed quietly forward, all her lights out.

Then she stopped.

The engine-room crew, hearing activity above, went to the portholes. By the dim moonlight, they watched as the launch was lowered. There was a man at each oar, and one at the tiller.

"Take a close look at the tillerman," said Wilkie.

The others squinted through the portholes and gasped. The man at the tiller was Captain Nerezza. He gave a hand signal. The six men pulled smoothly on the oars. The launch slipped away from the *Nimbus*, into the night.

"That's two boats we've lowered now," said one of the engine crew. "Where are they going?"

"I don't know," said Wilkie. "But wherever it is, there's going to be trouble."

CHAPTER 48

THE SCOTLAND LANDING

THE DRIVER OF THE HORSE-DRAWN TAXICAB was initially reluctant to take the odd-looking passengers, especially Peter, wearing island rags, and Wendy, missing a shoe. But when Neville handed the driver a pound note, he quickly relented, allowing the six of them to squeeze into the cab, with John and Michael, terrified from their encounter with the Skeleton, sitting on Mrs. Bumbrake's ample lap. Peter, still in pain, needed Wendy's help to climb in. He sat in silence, looking down.

The taxicab rumbled through the dark streets for fifteen minutes, then stopped in front of a narrow three-story building on a quiet street near Sloane Square called Draycott Place. Neville looked at the building doubtfully. It was completely dark, not a glimmer of light showing in any of its windows. "Are you certain this is it?" he asked the driver.

"I am, guv'nor," said the driver. He pointed toward a small sign by the door that said:

SCOTLAND LANDING HOTEL
NO VACANCY

"I've passed this hotel a thousand times," said the driver. "It never has a vacancy."

"Really," said Neville.

"Are you sure this is where you want to go?" said the driver.

"We are," said Wendy, before Neville could answer.

They piled out of the taxicab, and Neville paid the driver, who flicked his reins and disappeared into the night. Wendy approached the door and tried the knob. It was locked. There was no doorbell button or pull rope, so she knocked three times. There was no answer. She tried again, and again, each time pounding harder, but still getting no response.

"I'm cold," said Michael, huddling close to Mrs. Bumbrake.

"Me too," said John.

"Perhaps we should try to find another hotel," said Neville.

"Grandfather told me to come *here*," said Wendy. "We need to be someplace safe, with the police looking for us."

"They'll find us anyway if we're standing out here in the street," observed Mrs. Bumbrake.

Wendy knocked again. Still no answer. "There must be *somebody* here," she said. "Why don't they answer the door?"

Just then the door opened, and out poked an enormous head. It belonged to an equally enormous man, with a wild mane of white hair flowing into a bushy white beard. Peter was sure he'd seen this man before, but he couldn't quite think where.

"Can't you see the sign?" the man growled. "There's no . . ." His eyes fell on Peter. "Hold on." He stepped outside; his shoulders were so wide they barely fit through the door. He was barefoot, wearing only a nightgown the size of a tent. He moved close to Peter, peering down into his face, then nodded. "You're the boy who was at Stonehenge," he said. "Remember me?"

"You were at Lord Aster's country house," Peter said. "You're the man with the animals."

The man grinned, his beard parting to reveal a set of huge white teeth. "That I am. Magill's my name. And you are . . ."

"Peter."

"That's right, Peter," said Magill. "And still a boy after all these years." He did not appear to be surprised by this. Glancing around at the others, he said, "Who are your friends, Peter?"

"My name is Wendy Darling," said Wendy. "I'm Leonard Aster's granddaughter."

Magill's eyes brightened. "And how is Lord Aster?" he asked.

Wendy hesitated, then said, "There's been some trouble."

Magill's smile disappeared. "Come right in," he said.

They entered the hotel, and Magill, after bolting the door, led them down a hallway into a drawing room. It had a pungent, musky aroma and was quite dark, the only light coming from a few glowing coals in the fireplace. In the far corner a massive figure, even larger than Magill and remarkably hairy, dozed in an overstuffed chair, snoring loudly.

"Don't mind Karl," said Magill.

Karl, thought Peter. Somehow he knew that name. . . .

Uncle Neville stepped closer to the sleeping form and peered at it for a moment.

"My word," he said. "Is that a . . ."

"A bear!" said Peter, remembering.

"Oh dear," said Mrs. Bumbrake, pulling Michael and John close.

"You have a *bear* in your hotel?" said Wendy.

"It's not really a hotel," said Magill. "We've no guests. After Lord Aster became too ill to travel to his country house, he brought me here to London, to be close by. Just in case, he said."

"And you brought Karl," said Peter.

"Well, of course I did," said Magill. "I couldn't very well leave him up there alone, at his age, now could I?"

"But . . . he's a *bear*," said Wendy.

"He's better behaved than a lot of Londoners," said Magill.

"You keep him inside?" said Peter. "All the time?"

"No, I take him out sometimes," said Magill. "At night. He wears a coat and hat, and we stick to the darker areas. Sometimes we visit with the wolves in Hyde Park."

"The *wolves?*" said Wendy and Peter together.

"They come down occasionally from Salisbury Plain to visit," said Magill. "Although they wouldn't want to live here."

In the corner chair, Karl, apparently awakened by the noise, shifted his massive form and opened his eyes. He looked around the room at the visitors, then emitted a deep, rumbling growl.

"It's all right, Karl," said Magill. He made a growling sound of his own, and Karl, apparently satisfied, resumed dozing. Magill turned to Wendy. "We've talked enough about my situation," he said. "Tell me about Lord Aster, and this trouble you mentioned."

As quickly as she could, Wendy summarized what had happened—the suspicions about von Schatten; the mysterious disappearances; Leonard Aster's concern that the Others

330

intended to reattach the missing tip to the Sword of Mercy, then use it to open the Cache of starstuff.

"Grandfather said we must stop them," said Wendy. "That's why I went to get Peter. But now that we've returned"—Wendy's voice quavered; she took a breath and went on—"it seems my father's gone missing, too. Mrs. Bumbrake said he's not been in touch for days. We can't go to the police; von Schatten controls them. Just now we barely escaped Grandfather's house. The police came with a . . . a horrible *creature*, who very nearly killed Peter. Had it not been for Grandfather's fighting him, we'd not be here."

"Lord Aster fought him?" said Magill.

"Bravely. And he saved us," said Wendy, glancing at Peter, who was looking down. She decided not to tell Magill about the scream.

For a moment the room was silent, save for a long rumbling snore from Karl. Then Magill said, "If Lord Aster sent you here for help, it's help you'll get. What do you need?"

Wendy looked at Peter, then back at Magill. "We don't really know," she said.

"That makes it more difficult," said Magill.

Uncle Neville, who had been listening intently as Wendy explained the situation, cleared his throat. "It seems to me," he said, "that if we want to stop this von Schatten from opening the Cache, it would be helpful to know where the Cache is, so we could try to prevent him from getting to it."

"We don't know where it is," said Wendy. "All we know is that Grandfather said something about 'confess.'"

"Confess what?" said Neville.

"We don't know," said Wendy.

"I see," said Neville. "Then the other way to stop von Schatten would be to prevent him from using the sword as a key."

"How?" said Wendy.

"If I understand you correctly," said Uncle Neville, "the sword will open the Cache only if the tip has been re-attached."

"That's what Grandfather said."

"Then perhaps we can get the tip ourselves," said Neville.

"But we've no idea where it is," said Wendy. "And von Schatten may have it already."

"Yes, I assume he does," said Neville. "But until the coronation, the Sword of Mercy will be locked away in the Tower with the other crown jewels. Meanwhile, the tip is likely somewhere here in London, awaiting reattachment. Perhaps we could get it first."

"How?" said Peter.

"I don't know," admitted Neville. "I'm just looking for

areas of weakness that might be attacked. It would help if we knew something about the tip and how it would be reattached. Would it be a job for a blacksmith?"

"I don't know," said Wendy, frowning, "but I know somebody who might: Uncle Ted."

"Ted?" said Peter.

"His colleague, actually," said Wendy. "A fellow at Cambridge. Uncle Ted said he was an expert on the Sword of Mercy, and knew about the missing tip."

"It sounds as if it might be a good idea to get in touch with that fellow," said Neville.

"We could call Uncle Ted on the telephone," said Wendy, "if we had a telephone."

"There's a telephone here," said Magill.

"*Here?*" said Wendy.

"In the parlor," said Magill. "Lord Aster had it installed. 'Just in case,' he said. Never used it myself. Don't know how."

"What's a telephone?" said Peter.

"Marvelous device," said Neville. "Sound causes a metal diaphragm to vibrate; this in turn causes fluctuations in an electrical current passing through carbon granules. Clever, eh?"

Peter turned to Wendy. "What's a telephone?" he said.

"I'll show you," said Wendy. She and Peter, followed by Uncle Neville, headed for the parlor, leaving Mrs. Bumbrake, John, and Michael nervously watching the still-dozing Karl.

After a minute of silence, John asked Magill, "What does he eat?"

"He used to eat mostly berries, nuts, insects, the occasional small animal," said Magill. "But since we moved to London, he's become quite fond of fish and chips."

"How does he get them?" said John.

"I buy them from a local chippy," said Magill. "Karl can eat a dozen orders at a time and still want more. In fact, one night I left the door unlocked and he went out *looking* for more. Good thing I found him before he found the chippy." Magill laughed heartily. Seeing the non-amused expression on Mrs. Bumbrake's face, he stopped abruptly, then said, "It seems you'll be staying here at the Scotland Landing. What sort of room do you prefer?"

"I prefer a room," said Mrs. Bumbrake, "that is as far as possible from the bear."

CHAPTER 49

THE MISSION

"*Escaped?*"

The word hissed like steam from von Schatten's bloodless lips. His anger further revealed itself in the dull redness that seeped from the edges of his dark eyeglass lenses, forming two glowing circles in the darkened palace chamber.

Simon Revile took an involuntary step backward on fear-weakened legs.

"I'm afraid so, Baron," he said.

"*How?* Did you not send the Skeleton?"

"Yes, Baron. And he had the boy. But Leonard Aster—"

"*Aster?* I was told he was seriously ill."

"He was, sir. Apparently he used starstuff. He flew over the house. He attacked the Skeleton, and during the fight, the boy and the others escaped."

"Why did the police not stop them?"

335

"From what I gather, they were also, ah, *thwarted* by Lord Aster."

"Incompetent fools," hissed von Schatten. "Did Aster also escape?"

"No. The Skeleton prevailed."

"But the boy is gone."

"Yes, Baron. But Chief Superintendent Blake says his men are scouring the city. He assures me that the boy and the others will be caught."

The redness around von Schatten's eyeglasses glowed more brightly. "Tell Blake," he said, "that if they are *not* caught, he will answer to me personally."

"Yes, Baron," said Revile, turning for the door, eager to leave.

"Wait."

Reluctantly, Revile turned back. "Yes, Baron?"

"I want none of this to distract the Skeleton from tomorrow night's mission."

"Yes, Baron."

"The escape of the boy irritates me greatly. But it does not affect our plans. Tomorrow night is crucial. You will stress this to the Skeleton. He must not fail me."

"Yes, Baron."

"Go."

Revile scurried from the room.

CHAPTER 50

THE THIRD ELEMENT

HAVING RECEIVED A TELEPHONE CALL from Wendy and Peter, Ted was on the first morning train from Cambridge to London. With him was his colleague, the historian Patrick Hunt, a smiling, perpetually enthusiastic man with long blond hair. When they arrived at the Scotland Landing Hotel, they were met at the door by Magill, who looked around to see if they'd been followed, then quickly brought them inside, where Peter, Wendy, and Uncle Neville were waiting.

"Peter!" cried Ted, quickly crossing the room to embrace the friend he had not seen for twenty years. Peter hugged him somewhat awkwardly; he barely recognized this portly man as the sidekick who had joined him on so many long-ago adventures. There was a muffled chime of protest from Peter's shirt. Peter pulled back, and Tink—still resting from her efforts of the previous night—stuck her head out.

"Tinker Bell!" exclaimed Ted. "How delightful to see you!"

You're still fat, chimed Tink.

"She's delighted to see you, too," said Peter.

"My word," said Patrick, staring at Tink. He looked at Ted and said, "I had honestly wondered if you made all this up."

"None of it," said Ted. He quickly introduced Patrick to the others. "When I told Patrick this was a matter involving the Sword of Mercy," he said, "he insisted on coming."

"I've long been fascinated with the sword," explained Patrick. "To think that, after all these years, the missing tip may have been found! Although I understand that this could be a very big problem."

Wendy gave Ted a sharp look. "How much have you told Mr. Hunt?" she said.

Ted looked sheepish. "Everything," he said. "He kept asking questions, and one thing led to another. . . ."

Seeing Wendy's doubtful look, Patrick said, "You have my word that I will keep this matter in the strictest confidence. I'm here only to help you, Wendy. And from what Ted has told me, you need as much help as you can get."

"He's right, Wendy," said Peter.

"I suppose he is," sighed Wendy. "And if Uncle Ted vouches for you . . ."

"So that's settled," said Ted. "Now, where shall we start?"

"If I may," said Neville. "Since the Cache cannot be opened without the sword, it would appear that our best hope is to prevent von Schatten from reattaching the tip to the sword. The question is, how might we do that?"

All eyes turned to Patrick.

"I've an idea about that," he said, "although it may take a bit of explaining."

"By all means," said Neville.

Patrick cleared his throat. "Nobody," he said, "at least nobody that I'm aware of, really knows how the Sword of Mercy, or Curtana, came to be. Its origins, as the expression goes, are shrouded in mystery. But there are legends, and one of the more prevalent ones holds that the sword was made from a very unusual metal."

"Unusual in what way?" said Neville.

"It came from space," said Patrick.

Neville frowned. "Wait just a moment," he said. He went to the stairway and called up: "Mrs. Bumbrake, could you please come down for a moment?"

A minute later Mrs. Bumbrake had joined the others. Neville introduced her to Patrick, then said, "Could you please repeat for Mr. Hunt what you told me the other night, about what Lord Aster talked about in his delirium?"

"Well," said Mrs. Bumbrake, "he kept mumbling something about a sword."

"And wasn't there something else?" prodded Neville.

"Yes," said Mrs. Bumbrake. "Sometimes he talked about a meteorite."

"What did he say about it?" Patrick asked eagerly.

"Nothing that I understood," said Mrs. Bumbrake. "I'm sorry."

"No need," said Neville. "You've been very helpful."

As Mrs. Bumbrake climbed back up the stairs, Patrick said, "Lord Aster's words support the legend—that the sword was made from a strange metal rock that fell from the sky."

"Strange in what way?" said Neville.

"For one thing, it sometimes glows," said Patrick.

"It's starstuff!" said Peter.

"Not exactly," said Wendy. "A large lump of pure starstuff would kill whoever came near it. Grandfather Aster said the sword was made from metal that was *infused* with starstuff."

"What does that mean?" said Peter.

"It means the metal has some starstuff in it," said Wendy. "Grandfather said the vault that contains the Cache is made from the same metal."

"In the legend, this particular metal is called 'heaven-stone,'" said Patrick. "It has some unusual properties, among them great strength. Not even diamond can cut it; only another piece of heavenstone will do."

"This is all quite interesting," said Neville. "But I fail to see how it helps us stop von Schatten."

"I'm getting to that," said Patrick. "Let's assume that von Schatten has gotten hold of the tip to Curtana. On

Coronation Day he'll be able, through his control over the king, to obtain the sword itself. So he'll have both the tip and the sword. But I believe that to put them together, he must have a third element."

"What?" said Wendy.

"More heavenstone," said Patrick. "Essentially, he has to weld the tip to the sword at high temperature. But to do that, he needs a filler material, to fuse the two pieces. He cannot use ordinary metal. I believe he must use heavenstone."

"With all due respect," said Neville, "I still fail to see why this is relevant."

"It's relevant," said Patrick, "because other than the tip and the sword, there is only one known piece of alleged heavenstone on earth. I say 'alleged' because there are reputable scientists who scoff at the legend."

"What do *you* think?" said Wendy.

"I believe it's heavenstone," said Patrick. "It's almost certainly of extraterrestrial origin, and it exhibits unusual properties. All attempts to analyze it have failed. It was found by a British archaeologist named Mansfield in a cave in the Aquitaine region of France, where Charlemagne rose to power, and where the Sword of Mercy was made. The age of other artifacts Mansfield found in the cave suggests that the stone—which is known as the Mansfield Stone—was placed there at around the time of the sword's creation. Perhaps it was excess heavenstone, not needed for the sword and therefore placed in the cave for safekeeping. In any event, if my theory is correct, von Schatten cannot repair Curtana without the Mansfield Stone. At some point, he will have to try to acquire it."

"Where is it now?" said Peter.

Patrick smiled and said, "Less than a mile from here."

For a moment there was a shocked silence. Then Peter, Wendy, and Neville simultaneously exclaimed *"What?"*

"The Mansfield Stone," said Patrick, "currently belongs to the Natural History Museum, right here in London. The stone is not on exhibit; as I say, some authorities believe it's a fraud, and the museum has chosen to keep it out of public view until its experts can agree on what, exactly, it is. It's stored in a specimen room, under lock and key."

"If what you say is correct," said Neville, "we need to appropriate this stone as soon as possible."

"Appropriate?" said Peter.

"Steal," said Wendy.

Peter nodded.

"For the greater good," said Neville.

"I was thinking," said Patrick, "that we might steal . . . I mean *appropriate* it tonight."

"We?" said Wendy.

"I can get us into the museum," said Patrick.

"Then 'we' it is," said Wendy. "Tonight."

CHAPTER 51

ONLY DARKNESS

THEY LEFT THE SCOTLAND LANDING HOTEL at 7 p.m., when the dark, fog-filled streets were virtually empty of homebound pedestrians.

Peter, with Tink tucked into his coat, led the way. The chilly air made him grateful for the warm clothes and shoes he was wearing, courtesy of Patrick, who'd gone shopping for Peter and Wendy that afternoon. He'd also picked up some special materials Neville had requested.

Peter kept to the shadows and peered around each corner, scouting for bobbies or anyone else of concern. Following a half-block behind were Wendy, Ted, and Neville, who was carrying a small satchel. Wendy had initially suggested that her uncle not accompany them, but he would not hear of it.

"I believe my expertise may prove useful," he said. "And I do not fear danger. I have faced danger many times."

Most of it caused by your own experiments, thought Wendy. But she didn't argue.

The little party avoided the main roads, working its way through the maze of streets and alleys east of Sloane Square, Peter relying on Tink's flawless sense of direction. Just after 7:30, Peter cautiously emerged from Queensberry Place onto Cromwell Road. Looming out of the fog across the street was the Natural History Museum, a massive, ornate brick structure.

Peter watched the street and sidewalk for several minutes, keeping an eye on the occasional pedestrian and the dwindling Cromwell Road traffic. When he was convinced that there was no trap awaiting them, he turned and opened his coat. Tink emitted three brief flashes of light. A minute later, the other three joined them.

Wendy pointed to the left and said, "That's Queensgate Mews. Patrick said we go around that way, then knock on the door at the back corner of the museum."

"Right," said Peter. "We'll wait until the road is clear, then cross." Ted and Neville nodded. A smile twitched Peter's lips; Ted was a grown man, but Peter, at least at this moment, was still the leader.

When they saw a break in traffic, they ran across Cromwell Road, Neville in the rear, puffing to keep up. They went up Queensgate Mews, along the side of the museum. When Peter was sure there were no guards about, he led them onto the museum grounds. As Patrick had told them, there was an unmarked door near the corner in back of the huge main building. Peter rapped on it three times. There was the sound of a deadbolt sliding, and the door opened.

"Welcome to the museum," said Patrick, smiling broadly.

They stepped into a long corridor lit by overhead electric lights. Patrick closed the door. "It went as planned," he said, keeping his voice low. "I identified myself to the museum staff as a Cambridge fellow, giving a false name, and said I wanted to do some research in one of the restricted areas. They weren't a bit suspicious, as they get many such requests. Just before closing I made a show of announcing I was leaving. Instead I hid in a storage room until the staff had gone for the day."

"Is there anyone else here?" asked Peter.

"At least one watchman, who is currently snoring loudly at his post in the main hall. There may be one or two others. But I don't think they'll be a problem for us. We're going to a specimen room on the third floor here in the rear of the building. The stairway is this way."

He led them up the stairs to a long, dimly lit marble hallway lined on both sides with heavy oak doors. About halfway down he stopped in front of one on the left-hand side with a sign that said MINERALOGY.

"It's in here," said Patrick.

"All right, then, stand back," said Neville, starting to

345

open his satchel. Patrick stopped him. "No need for that yet."

"Then how are we going to open the door?" said Neville.

"With this," said Patrick, pulling a key from his pocket. "The museum staff keeps the specimen-room keys hanging on a board downstairs. I happened to brush against it as I walked past." He smiled proudly.

Ted stared in amazement at his light-fingered Cambridge colleague. "You actually *enjoy* being a criminal," he said.

"Immensely!" said Patrick. "I think I'm rather good at it." He used the key to open the door, and the group entered. Patrick found the light switch and flicked it on, revealing a large, musty room with four massive tables in the center, littered with books, scientific instruments, and mineral specimens. Along the walls were rows of cabinets and display cases filled with more mineral specimens of all shapes and sizes.

"There's thousands of rocks here," said Wendy. "How are we supposed to find the one we're looking for?"

"I hadn't thought of that," said Patrick. "We'll just have to—"

He was interrupted by a chime from Tink, who was hovering next to a massive steel cabinet at the far end of the room.

"She says it's in that box," said Peter.

"But how would she know that?" said Patrick.

"She knows," said Peter.

346

"All right, then," said Neville, bustling over with his satchel. He examined the cabinet, then said, "I don't think I can get enough explosive into the lock mechanism itself. But I can blow the hinges. The door should come right off." He opened the satchel and set to work.

The others waited in silence. The minutes crept past.

Tink emitted a low chime.

"What?" said Wendy, looking at Peter.

"She hears somebody downstairs," said Peter.

"I didn't hear anything," said Patrick.

"Tink has very good ears," said Peter.

"Maybe we ought to leave," said Ted.

"Not without the stone," said Wendy. "We might not have another chance to get it. Uncle Neville, how much more time do you need?"

"Almost done," said Neville, working furiously.

Peter opened the door, stuck his head out and looked both ways. "There's nobody in the hallway," he said. "Not yet, anyway."

"I say we light the fuse, get the stone, and run," said Wendy.

Nobody argued.

"There are two stairways," said Patrick. "The one we used, and another at the far end of the hall. The explosion will bring them running. Whichever hallway they come up, we'll go down the other."

Peter, Wendy, and Ted nodded.

"Shall I light the fuse?" said Neville.

"Yes," said Wendy.

"Gather in the far corner, then," said Neville. "I'll join you in a moment."

They huddled in the corner near the door. Peter tucked Tink into his coat. Neville struck a match and touched it to the fuse. A shower of sparks erupted. Neville rose and, carrying his empty satchel, puffed across the room, dodging the big tables. As he reached the others, he shouted, "Turn around and cover your ears!" They did, and waited.

And waited.

And . . .

BOOM!

The concussion knocked them over as the room roared with deafening noise, then filled with smoke. Peter was the first back on his feet. He stumbled through the acrid-smelling haze to the metal cabinet. As Neville had promised, the door had been blown off its hinges; it lay bent on the floor a good ten feet from the cabinet. The rest of the cabinet was also blackened and badly damaged. But inside it, looking unharmed, was a lump of metal. It was roughly the shape of a potato but about twice the size, with an uneven silvery surface that seemed to shimmer in the smoke.

Peter reached in and picked it up. It seemed unusually heavy. Peter's fingers tingled where they touched it.

"Is this it?" he asked the others, who had come up behind him.

"That's the Mansfield Stone," said Patrick.

Tink, emerging from Peter's coat, chimed urgently.

"Somebody's coming up the stairs," said Peter. He grabbed the satchel from Neville and dropped the stone into it. "Who's going to carry this?" he said.

"You should," said Wendy. "If the rest of us get caught, you can fly away."

"I'm not going to leave anybody," said Peter.

"*Yes you are*," said Wendy firmly. "If we don't keep the stone from von Schatten, all of this will have been for nothing."

Tink chimed again.

"We have to go," said Peter. Holding the satchel, he ran for the door, with the others right behind. When they reached the hallway, it was still empty, but they could hear loud footsteps coming from the hallway to the right, the same one they had used to come up to the third floor.

"This way," said Peter, running to the left, with Tink zooming ahead.

As he reached the far stairway, Peter looked back. Three figures had reached the top of the other stairs. In the dim lighting, Peter couldn't see them clearly, but somehow he knew they weren't museum guards. Whoever they were, they had spotted Peter and the others and were running toward them.

"Hurry!" Peter shouted, starting down the stairs. He

glanced back. Wendy and Patrick were right behind, followed by Ted, followed by Neville, who was moving more slowly on the stairs. Peter turned back to help, joined by Ted; each took one of Neville's arms so he could move a little faster. But the three pursuers were gaining. Peter heard footsteps thundering close behind as he and the others reached the ground floor. Two corridors met here; Patrick pointed at one and said, "This way!"

The other four followed him as he ran down the corridor. He jogged right, then left; Peter realized he was leading them along the rear of the building, back toward the door through which they had entered. Peter stayed at the rear, the heavy satchel banging against his legs.

They rounded a corner, and Patrick, still in the lead, stumbled over something. Peter heard gasps, then saw what had tripped Patrick: a museum guard. He lay on the floor, hands and feet bound, eyes wide with fear. He was trying to say something, but all that came out was "He . . . he . . ."

Wendy knelt to untie the guard. The sound of running feet grew louder.

"Wendy," said Patrick urgently, "we don't have time."

Reluctantly, Wendy rose. Patrick started running again, followed by the others, with Peter the last to leave the terrified guard. The man looked in the direction Peter's group was going, then met Peter's eyes, shook his head, and said, "No. No." Peter hesitated.

"Peter, come *on*!" called Wendy.

Peter turned and ran, haunted by the look in the guard's eyes.

They continued to follow Patrick through the maze of hallways, turning left, then right, then left again. The last turn brought them into a long corridor. Peter's hopes rose as he recognized this as the corridor they'd been in when they first entered the museum. At the far end was the exit door—and escape.

Led by Patrick, they started running toward it.

Tink, flying just above Peter, emitted a sharp chime.

Suddenly, Patrick stopped.

Peter froze as he saw the reason. A dark figure had just stepped out of a shadow at the far end of the corridor. It was a man wearing a cloak with a hood that shrouded his face. But Peter had seen that awful face, and felt the excruciating pain that the man could inflict with the merest touch of his clawlike hands. Remembering that agony, he felt his legs weaken, his stomach roil.

The hooded man started walking toward the group. Behind them, they heard the sound of their pursuers, getting closer in the maze of corridors.

"What do we do?" said Ted.

"There's only the one in front of us," said Patrick. "We can rush him. He can't stop us all."

Yes he can, thought Peter. But he kept silent, ashamed to show his fear.

"The important thing is the stone," said Wendy. "Peter, you must escape. Fly if you can. Leave us behind if you have to. Just don't let him get the stone."

Peter nodded, staring at the oncoming figure.

There were shouts behind them. Peter looked back. The pursuers had entered the long corridor. Peter saw there were two large men and a woman.

"Now!" shouted Patrick. He started running toward the hooded man, followed by the others. Behind them they heard the shouts of the three pursuers. As they neared the hooded figure, Peter caught a glimpse of the face—more skull than face—and the lone yellow eye. Somehow Peter knew the eye was looking straight at him.

They were twenty feet from the hooded man . . . Ten . . .

The man's left claw-hand shot out, reaching for something on the wall.

The corridor went completely dark.

Peter ran into Ted, who had stopped. They both stumbled forward. An urgent chime came from Tink. Peter felt Ted's body stiffen, then heard Ted scream, his voice impossibly high-pitched. Peter knew why. He turned and crawled the other way in the blackness, still holding the satchel. Footsteps—the three pursuers—clattered toward him, past him, the pursuers missing him in the blackness. He huddled against the wall. Behind him he heard shouts, grunts, yells, the sounds of struggle. He could make out Patrick's voice, and Neville's. He debated what to do. He remembered Wendy's words. *Leave us behind if you have to. Just don't let him get the stone.*

He started to crawl back the way he and the others had come, away from the struggle. Slowly, he rose to his feet and shuffled forward, feeling for the wall in the utter blackness. Behind him the shouts continued. He heard Wendy scream. And then an odd sound, a deep rumbling, then a fearsome roar. The sounds of struggle increased, a confusing mix of shouting and banging. Peter listened for a minute, paralyzed, then again started shuffling away from the noise.

STOP!

Tink's urgent chime was right in his ear. Peter froze.

Close your eyes.

Knowing what was coming, Peter shut his eyes tight. Through his eyelids he saw the brilliant flash. He opened them just as the flash ended, and saw the reason for Tink's alarm.

The hooded man was in front of him, not three feet away.

His back was to Peter.

Either he had been looking the wrong way, or he had somehow known that the flash was coming. It had not blinded him.

He was turning around. . . . As the last of Tink's light faded, Peter saw the gaping hole where a mouth should have been, the empty socket, the lone yellow eye . . .

The claw-hand reaching out . . .

353

Peter screamed, and turned. In the blackness, he stumbled away from the hideous thing. He started running blindly. He fell over something; it moaned, and he realized it was a person. He struggled to his feet. Strong hands grabbed him, and he screamed.

"It's all right, Peter," said a gruff voice. "It's me."

Magill.

The big man held Peter's arm and half pulled, half carried him down the corridor, then through the door.

"This way," said Magill, taking off at a run. He led Peter away from the museum through a maze of streets, Peter running behind, his mind too numb to think about anything except putting one foot in front of the other. After ten minutes they ducked into an alley so dark that at first Peter didn't realize there was anyone else there. As his eyes adjusted, he could just barely make out the silhouettes of five figures—Wendy, Patrick, Neville, Ted, and the huge, hairy figure of Karl, in an overcoat and hat.

"Found him," said Magill.

"Thank goodness!" said Wendy. "Peter, we were so worried!"

"A very close thing," said Neville. "If Magill here hadn't appeared . . ."

"I thought I'd follow you—just in case, as Lord Aster would say," said Magill. "But it was Karl here, old as he is, who turned the tide."

"Indeed!" said Patrick. "Karl is a good man—that is, bear—to have on your side in a fight."

"But who *were* those people?" said Ted. "They clearly weren't museum staff. What were they doing there?"

"I've been thinking about that," said Wendy. "I think they were there for the same reason we were."

"To get the Mansfield Stone?" said Patrick.

"Precisely," said Wendy. "They must have been sent by von Schatten."

"If that's true," said Ted, "we got there just in time."

"Yes," said Wendy. "It was a near thing, but the stone is ours."

Peter cleared his throat, and when he spoke, he could barely choke out the words.

"I . . . I don't have it," he said.

"*What?*" said Wendy.

"The stone," said Peter. "I dropped it when he . . . when he . . ." He looked down, his eyes burning.

The dark alley fell into a silence that, to Peter, seemed to go on forever. It was Ted who finally spoke. "Don't be hard on yourself, Peter," he said softly. "I felt just a little of the pain that *thing* could cause, and I screamed like a baby. Nobody blames you. You're a brave person; you've shown that many times."

Not tonight, thought Peter. *Tonight I was a coward.* He looked around at the group. He saw that Wendy was looking at him, but in the darkness he couldn't see her expression. He looked down again, willing himself not to cry in front of everyone.

There was another uncomfortable silence, and then Patrick, trying his best to sound cheerful but not quite succeeding, said, "I suppose we should make our way back to the hotel. We'll get some rest, and we'll come up with a new plan in the morning."

"Follow me," said Magill. He started toward the entrance to the alley, the others following.

"Wait a moment," said Peter. "Where's Tink?"

"Isn't she with you?" said Wendy.

"She was," said Peter, "but she . . . that is, I thought she must have . . ."

"Must have what?" said Wendy. "She's always with you, isn't she?"

Peter's mind went back to the terrifying moment when Tink had flashed in the museum. The flash would have left her weak, perhaps unconscious. *Of course.* He should have grabbed her, should have protected her the way she had protected him. But he had been too terrified to think of saving her, or the stone. He had thought only of himself.

"Oh no," he whispered.

"Tink's a strong little lady," said Ted, patting Peter's shoulder. "I'm sure she'll turn up."

"Nothing to be done about it now," said Magill. "We have to go."

They started out of the alley, Ted holding Peter's arm. All the way back, Peter's eyes searched the sky, looking for the familiar darting point of light. He saw only darkness, and the occasional streetlamp, blurred by his tears.

CHAPTER 52

THE VELVET SACK

REVILE, HIS WIDE FACE CLAMMY with the sweat of fear, stood outside the door to the king's chamber. His left hand was in his coat pocket. He raised his right hand toward the door, made a fist, then let it fall. He took several deep breaths, trying to work up the courage to knock.

"Enter."

Revile jumped. Somehow von Schatten had known he was outside the door. There seemed to be nothing von Schatten *didn't* know.

Revile entered the chamber. As always, it was almost dark, lit only by a candle burning on the king's writing table. Von Schatten stood next to the table. The king was nowhere to be seen.

"Do we have the stone?" said von Schatten.

"Yes, Baron," said Revile. "The Skeleton and his people took it to the Underground. But there was a . . . That is, we *did* get the stone, but there was an unexpected development."

Von Schatten took a step closer, almost touching Revile. Revile felt a horrible coldness creep into his chest. He tried to step back, but found he could not.

"What unexpected development?" said von Schatten. By the flickering light of the candle, Revile saw his own terrified face reflected in von Schatten's coal-black eyeglass lenses.

"There were other people at the museum. They got there before the Skeleton. And they had the stone."

The dull-red glow appeared at the edges of von Schatten's glasses. "Who were they?" he said.

"Five of them. Three men—we don't know who they were—and two children. The Darling girl . . . and the flying boy."

The glow around von Schatten's glasses intensified. Revile felt the cold deepen.

"Was the boy captured?" said von Schatten.

"N . . . No, Baron, they . . . *uhh*." Revile was unable to finish, as a searing pain shot through him. He realized he was *feeling* von Schatten's anger. It lasted a moment, and then subsided. Revile desperately wanted to step backward, but still could not.

"They *what?*" said von Schatten.

"They escaped, Baron. There was a struggle; others arrived and set upon the Skeleton's men. It was dark;

apparently they had some kind of animal, which wounded the Skeleton's men. But the Skeleton *did* get the stone."

There was a long and, for Revile, exceedingly uncomfortable silence. When von Schatten spoke, his tone was measured, though Revile could still feel his fury.

"If they were after the stone," said von Schatten, "then they know about the sword. They must know the entire plan."

"Yes, Baron."

"Tell Superintendent Blake I want him to intensify his search for the boy and the others. Tell him to concentrate on the neighborhood around the museum. They have to be staying *somewhere*."

"Yes, Baron."

"What is the situation at the Tower?"

"All is in readiness, Baron. We have three men in place, posing as representatives of the king. The Beefeaters weren't happy about this, but they could hardly argue with a direct request from His Majesty. Officially, our men are there to oversee the safeguarding of the jewels as they are transported from their cases and prepared for the coronation next week."

"Do these preparations involve Curtana?"

"As it happens, Curtana is to be polished tomorrow, Baron, along with the Sword of Spiritual Justice and the Sword of Temporal Justice."

"I see," said von Schatten, looking away, thinking. Seconds passed, stretching out to a minute. Finally von Schatten turned back to Revile and said, "Tell our men at the Tower I want the substitution to be made tomorrow, when the sword is being transported."

Revile was stunned. "Tomorrow?" he said. "But—"

"*Tomorrow*," said von Schatten. "Inform the Skeleton there has been a change of plan. And arrange for the train. We will reunite Curtana with its tip tomorrow night. We must act quickly, before the boy and his allies can make any more mischief."

"Yes, Baron."

"And tell the Skeleton to be on guard. We *cannot* allow the boy to thwart us. I am disappointed that the Skeleton has failed twice now to capture him."

"He did not fail completely, Baron."

"What do you mean?" said von Schatten.

Revile pulled his left hand from his pocket. He was holding a black velvet sack, tied tightly at the top with a double-knotted silver cord.

"What is that?" said von Schatten.

"Something very dear to the flying boy," said Revile. He handed the sack to von Schatten. "I suggest you open it carefully."

Von Schatten swiftly untied the knot with long, bony fingers. Keeping a firm grip on the top of the bag, he opened it just a bit. From within came a faint glow, and then a lone mournful chime. Von Schatten retied the knot and looked at Revile. He did not smile—von Schatten never smiled—but there was a look of grim satisfaction on his hatchet-thin face.

"This pleases me," he said, his bony forefinger tapping the velvet sack. "The boy will never leave England without her."

"No, Baron."

"Which means," said von Schatten, "the boy will never leave England."

CHAPTER 53

*U*NTIL *T*ONIGHT

*P*ETER SAT SLUMPED IN A CORNER chair in the drawing room of the Scotland Landing Hotel. He had barely spoken a word since the night before, when he and the others had returned from their ill-fated trip to the museum.

Mrs. Bumbrake fixed breakfast for everyone—Peter hadn't touched his—then retired upstairs with John and Michael. Karl was asleep in front of the fireplace, periodically emitting massive bear snores. Magill was out buying food for his new guests. Wendy, Neville, Ted, and Patrick were seated in the center of the room, discussing what to do next.

"We have no choice now," Wendy was saying. "If we can't stop them from fixing the sword, we have to stop them from getting to the Cache."

"That's going to be difficult," said Neville, "without knowing where it is."

"Then we're just going to have to find it," said Wendy.

"Tell me again," said Patrick, "exactly what your grandfather told you about the Cache."

"He said it's in London," said Wendy. "In a gold-lined chest, in a vault deep underground. But he didn't tell me *where* in London. He was very ill."

"Underground in London," said Neville. "That doesn't narrow it down much."

"No, it doesn't," agreed Patrick.

Ted was frowning at Wendy. "Wasn't there something else?"

"What do you mean?" said Wendy.

"Something else Lord Aster told you about the Cache."

"I don't think so," said Wendy. "He said something odd about 'confess,' but . . ."

"Yes," said Ted. "You told me he said somebody should confess."

"He did," said Wendy, "but I think he meant that for Peter. I don't think—"

"That's it!" said Patrick, leaping to his feet.

"I beg your pardon?" said Neville."

"The Sword of Mercy!" said Patrick. "Do you know what it's also known as?"

"Curtana," said Wendy.

"Yes, that," said Patrick. "But it's also called Edward the Confessor's sword."

"Interesting," said Neville, "but how does that . . ."

"Edward the Confessor's tomb," said Patrick, "is in Westminster Abbey. In fact, it was he who constructed the original abbey on the site, in the eleventh century."

"I see," said Ted. "So you're suggesting . . ."

"If Edward the Confessor's sword opens the Cache," said Patrick, "it stands to reason that the Cache is in, or near, Edward the Confessor's tomb. That's what Lord Aster was trying to tell Wendy!"

"It does seem to make sense," said Wendy. She looked around. "Does anybody have a better suggestion?" Nobody spoke. "Then we'll go to Westminster Abbey and have a look at this tomb," she said.

"Um," said Patrick, "That's a bit of a problem."

"What is?" said Wendy.

"We don't know where the tomb is."

"We don't?" said Ted. "I thought it was a great big thing right there in the middle."

"Not quite," said Patrick. "That's the *shrine* to the Confessor; his remains were moved there centuries ago from his tomb. But the shrine is above ground, so if the Cache is buried, as Lord Aster said, it can't be in the shrine. The Confessor's original *tomb* is underground, but unfortunately nobody knows precisely where. Over the centuries, the abbey has seen many changes, and records were not always well kept. The location of the Confessor's tomb is one of the abbey's enduring mysteries. In fact, it's believed that there are quite a few lost tombs, chambers, and vaults beneath the abbey."

"So how on earth are we supposed to find it?" said Neville.

"It could be a problem," admitted Patrick.

"We'll just have to see when we get there," said Wendy.

"As good a plan as any," said Patrick.

The front door of the hotel creaked open; the group listened to the thumping of heavy footsteps in the hall. Magill appeared in the drawing room, his arms laden with packages.

"It's a good thing the lot of you stayed here," he said.

"Why?" said Ted.

"Police," said Magill. "All about. Hundreds, looks like. Going door to door, asking questions. Especially interested in a girl and a boy. 'An unusual red-haired boy,' is the description they're using."

Wendy glanced over at Peter, still slumped in the corner chair. He hadn't reacted to Magill's news; hadn't moved at all. She turned back to Magill.

"Do you think we can get past the police?" she said. "We need to go to Westminster Abbey."

"We can get past them," said Magill. "But not in daylight."

"All right, then," said Wendy. "Tonight."

The group dispersed, leaving Wendy and Peter in the

drawing room, alone except for the snoring Karl. Wendy took a breath, exhaled, and walked over to Peter's chair.

"Peter," she said.

He didn't move.

"We're going to need you tonight," she said.

His head snapped up. His eyes were red, his face tear-streaked.

"Why?" he said. "So I can fail again?"

"Peter, it wasn't your fault. That man, or that *thing*, whatever it was, would have been too much for any of us."

"I *ran away*, Wendy. I left the stone. And I left Tink. *I left Tink*. Because I was afraid of him. I *am* afraid of him."

"I'm afraid of him, too, Peter," she said. "But we have to try to stop them. And we need your help. We need your special abilities."

"I never asked to be special!" shouted Peter. "I don't *want* to be special!" He looked away. Wendy reached out and touched his arm. He pulled away from her.

"Peter," she said, "I never asked to be a Starcatcher. I'd rather be a regular English schoolgirl, sitting in my regular English home having a regular English supper with my regular English family. But come to find out, that's not what or who I am. I have to accept that. I'm a Starcatcher now, and I don't know where my parents are, and the police are after me, and somehow I'm supposed to save England from evil with the help of some Oxford fellows and a dotty uncle and an old snoring bear. Do you think I asked for this? Do you think I want it?"

Suddenly, Wendy was sobbing, her face in her hands, her body shaking.

For few moments, Peter stood still, listening to Wendy cry. Then he turned toward her. Slowly he reached out a hand and rested it on her shoulder.

"For what it's worth," he said, "you also have the help of an unusual red-haired boy."

Wendy turned and flung her arms around him. For a few moments she held him as tightly as she could. Then she let him go, and they both looked away, blushing.

"Well," said Wendy, "I'd better get some rest. I don't suppose we'll get much sleep tonight."

"I don't suppose so," agreed Peter.

"Until tonight, then," said Wendy, heading for the stairs.

"Until tonight," said Peter.

CHAPTER 54

$\mathcal{A}$ $\mathcal{M}$INOR $\mathcal{M}$ISHAP

$\mathcal{R}$EVILE'S MEN WAITED until after the three swords had been polished, so that the counterfeit would not be subject to close scrutiny. Acting as the king's official representatives, they solemnly observed as the Crown Jeweler and his staff worked on the swords in a subterranean room in the Tower of London's Jewel House. When the work was done, they joined the procession of Yeoman Warders, or "Beefeaters," transporting the swords back upstairs to their secure cases. Two of Revile's men—a small man, and a tall man who walked a bit stiffly—went in front of the Beefeater who was carrying Curtana. The third man fell in behind.

The procession entered a long, narrow hallway. The Beefeaters' mood was serious, but not tense. The last place they expected trouble was here, in the bowels of the best-guarded building in the Tower complex.

Halfway down the tunnel, the short man in front of the

Beefeater holding Curtana stumbled, or so it appeared. What happened next took place so quickly that it would have taken the eyes of a career pickpocket—which is precisely what Revile's men were—to follow it. The short man fell to the floor, sprawling in such a way that he took out the feet from under the Beefeater. The Beefeater fell forward hard, his body obeying the defensive instinct to break his fall by thrusting out his hands—and losing his grip on the sword. Both the Beefeater and Curtana were deftly caught by the tall man in front, who righted the Beefeater and, with a flourish, handed him the counterfeit sword he had been concealing in a special sheath inside his coat—a sheath that now held Curtana.

The men ahead in line didn't see any of this; they were facing forward. The view of the men behind was blocked by the third man in Revile's team. Everyone quickly concluded that it had been a minor mishap; the important thing was that the sword had not been dropped. The procession continued on its way, and in ten minutes, the swords were back in their cases.

A few minutes later, the king's three observers were leaving the Tower. The tall one was still walking a bit stiffly.

CHAPTER 55

CTHE WHITE STARFISH

"WE SHOULDN'T BE DOING THIS," whispered Little Scallop.

"Shh!" hissed Shining Pearl, momentarily silencing her little sister. The two girls, having slipped out of their sleeping hut, were creeping along a moonlit path leading away from the Mollusk village.

After a few steps, Little Scallop said, "But Father says—"

"I *know* what Father says," said Shining Pearl. Their father, Fighting Prawn, the Mollusk chief, had told the girls more than once that they were never to leave the village alone at night. "But that rule was from before, when there were pirates here. Now the pirates are gone, so there's nothing to worry about."

"It's still a rule," said Little Scallop.

"Yes, but this is a special situation. We need to surprise Father for his birthday. How can we do that if he knows what we're doing? And we'll only be gone a little while. And the boys will be with us."

"I don't see what's so special about a smelly starfish anyway. Why couldn't we just have made him a conch necklace?"

"Because we've made him necklaces for the last I-don't-know-how-many birthdays. And it's not just a starfish. It's a *white* starfish, and those are good luck."

"What if it isn't a white starfish?"

"It is, and I know exactly where I saw it."

"Why didn't you get it then?"

Shining Pearl rolled her eyes. "I told you. I couldn't get to it when the tide was high. But now it's low, so it will be easy. Just wait: tomorrow morning we're going to give it to Father and he's going to be so happy he's going to give us one of those hugs where you can't breathe."

Little Scallop smiled; she loved those hugs. But her frown returned as she said, "But what if we get caught?"

"We won't, if you'll be quiet. Now look for the boys. They were supposed to—"

"There!" said Little Scallop, pointing ahead on the path. By the moonlight, Shining Pearl saw a face peering around the side of a large rock. As she came closer, she saw it was Nibs. He stepped onto the path, followed by the rest of the Lost Boys: Curly, Tootles, Slightly, and the twins.

"Are you sure you want to do this?" said Nibs.

"Of course," said Shining Pearl. "Why wouldn't we?"

"Look at the sky," said Nibs.

Shining Pearl looked up and saw that a third of the stars had been blotted out by a vast, low cloud bank, which at the moment was creeping toward the island, covering more and more of the night sky.

"It's going to rain," said Nibs.

"A *lot*," said Slightly.

"We should go back," said Little Scallop.

"Not without the starfish," said Shining Pearl. "Who cares if we get a little wet?"

Without waiting for an answer, she set off down the path. The others followed with various levels of enthusiasm. Shining Pearl led them to the water trail, which ran along the coast all the way around the island, winding its way past lookout points, beaches, and tidal pools. It was one of the island's most-used trails, so it was wide and well-worn. The children made good progress, and soon were a good distance from the Mollusk village.

As they walked, Nibs kept glancing at the sky, watching the cloud mass draw ever closer. Gusts of wind had started to reach the island, causing the trees in the dark jungle to thrash about. The wind carried a few drops of rain.

"Are you *really* sure you want to do this tonight?" said Nibs.

"Yes," said Shining Pearl. "Tomorrow's Father's birthday, and I want to give him that starfish."

"But why d'you need all eight of us, for one starfish?" said Nibs.

Shining Pearl tried to think of something to say.

"It's because she's scared," said Slightly.

"I am not!" said Shining Pearl, not convincingly.

"Can't blame her," Slightly went on. "The pirates made this part of the island scary for all of us. Been out of bounds the whole time we've lived here. I wanted to come along just so I could see stuff I haven't seen before."

"Can't see much of it in the dark," said one of the twins. No one could tell them apart.

"Here we are!" shouted a relieved Shining Pearl. She ran down to the water, where a semicircle of rocks had created a tidal pool, protected from the increasingly rough sea. Little Scallop joined her, as did the twins. The rest of the boys stayed back at the edge of the jungle, where the tree canopy protected them from the ever-more-persistent rain.

"All this for a starfish," said Slightly. Nibs, Curly, and Tootles, eyeing the deteriorating weather, muttered in agreement.

"I'm going up there, where it's drier," said Tootles. He started making his way deeper into the jungle. "OWW!" he cried.

"What?" said Slightly.

"There's something here!" said Tootles. He started

pulling away a pile of leaves and branches, revealing . . .

"A boat!" he shouted.

The others ran over and stared.

"What's a boat doing here?" said Curly.

"Those leaves were meant to hide it," said Slightly. "They were cut recently. They aren't even brown."

"Shipwrecked," Curly said. "It's shipwrecked sailors."

"Then why hide the boat?" said Slightly. "They'd want help, wouldn't they?"

"Maybe they want to lie low until they see who else is on the island," said Nibs. "To make sure they're friendly."

"Or maybe they're not shipwrecked," said Slightly.

"Then who are they?" said Curly.

"I don't know," said Slightly. "But we should tell Fighting Prawn."

"No!" said Shining Pearl. She had come up behind them with Little Scallop and the twins. She held a wet clump of seaweed, which was wrapped around the prized white starfish. "If we tell Father, he'll know we broke the rule. We're not supposed to even be here."

The boys considered that. They weren't supposed to be there, either.

"But we need to tell him somebody's on the island," said Slightly. "We can't just ignore this boat."

It was starting to rain harder. The wind was bringing ever bigger waves, roaring as they pounded the shore. A bolt of lightning lit the jungle nearby, followed almost immediately by a deafening crash of thunder.

"I wish we never came here," said Little Scallop, speaking for everybody.

"I have an idea," said Nibs. "We'll go back home tonight. Tomorrow we'll come back here and pretend we discovered the boat. Then we can tell Fighting Prawn."

"I don't know," said Slightly. "What if whoever brought this boat . . ."

"Whoever it is," interrupted Nibs, "they can't do anything tonight, not with this storm coming."

"All right," said Shining Pearl. "We'll go back now, then come out here tomorrow first thing."

They started back the way they'd come on the water trail, but stopped after only a few dozen yards. Directly ahead, a huge wave crashed over the trail, followed by another, then another, the vicious surge slamming into a mountain cliff too steep for the children to climb around. The children waited for an opening, but the massive waves kept thundering in.

Finally, Slightly stated the obvious: "We're not going to get through this way."

"We'll have to take the mountain trail," said Shining Pearl.

"In this weather?" said Nibs.

"It's the only way back," said Shining Pearl, who

knew the island better than any of the others. She turned back on the water trail, which met the mountain trail farther down the coast, past where they'd discovered the boat. "Come on!" she urged.

The rest started after her, except for Curly, who hung back.

"What about the boars?" he said.

The others stopped. They'd forgotten about the boars.

"They come out at night, you know," said Curly. "That's when they hunt."

"And that's when they get hunted," said Slightly. Everyone knew what he was talking about. A shudder passed through them all.

For a few seconds, the group stood in silence. Then Shining Pearl said, "We can't stay out here. We have to get back."

"She's right," said Nibs. "We'll stick together and listen sharp. If anyone hears anything, give a shout, get up a tree fast as you can."

He and Shining Pearl started walking, followed by the others. Curly was last in line. He was still unhappy about taking the mountain trail. But he definitely didn't want to be left alone. Not on a night like this.

CHAPTER 56

$\mathcal{A}$ $\mathcal{F}$LASH OF $\mathcal{L}$IGHTNING

JUST DOWN THE WATER TRAIL, where it converged with the mountain trail, Cheeky O'Neal, Frederick DeWulf, and Rufus Kelly were crouched behind a pile of huge rocks at the edge of a beach, getting what protection they could from the rain. They'd been there for hours, listening to the thundering sound of big waves crashing on a reef a hundred yards offshore.

"Don't see how they can land a boat in this," said DeWulf. "Don't see how they'll get past that reef."

"You don't know Nerezza like I do," said O'Neal.

"Of all the nights for a storm to come up," said Kelly.

"It works in our favor," said O'Neal, staring into the sheeting rain. "There's no way the Mollusks will see them coming in this." He turned to DeWulf and said, "McPherson's been on watch long enough. Go relieve him."

"But it hasn't even been an hour!" protested DeWulf.

O'Neal, leaning his huge frame close to DeWulf, growled, "I said *go relieve Angus.*"

"All right," grumbled DeWulf, rising to his feet. "But I don't see how—"

"They're coming!" shouted McPherson, soaking wet, running around the rocks from his lookout post on the beach. "I saw 'em just now in a flash of lightning, riding a wave over the reef. Looks like they're struggling."

O'Neal was on his feet, running around the rock, followed by the others. In a moment they were on the beach, surf surging to their knees, then waists, almost knocking them over. They peered into the driving rain. There was a flash of lighting.

"There!" shouted McPherson, pointing.

The others saw the boat then, sliding down the face of a huge wave, its oarsmen rowing frantically. Then the lightning was gone, and the boat disappeared.

"This way," shouted O'Neal, running toward the area of the beach where the boat had been headed. Another flash, and he picked it up again; it was riding the last push of the wave surging onto shore, spinning sideways and leaning, but still upright.

As he sprinted toward it, O'Neal smiled grimly. He'd been right.

Nererzza had made it.

CHAPTER 57

PRISONERS

SHINING PEARL CLUNG TO THE white starfish wrapped in wet seaweed as she and the others struggled through the mud, which was ankle-deep and getting deeper every minute in the torrential rain. She followed Nibs, who led the way; behind them came Slightly, Little Scallop, then Curly, Tootles, and, well back, the twins.

It was very dark, and the windblown rain was coming down so hard that the fat drops actually hurt. The children held banana leaves over their heads, but these gave them little relief from their misery as they slogged along the water trail toward the place where it met the mountain trail.

Nibs stopped so suddenly that Shining Pearl nearly bumped into him.

"What is it?" she said.

"I heard shouting ahead," he said. "Maybe the shipwrecked sailors. Everybody keep quiet."

"What are we going to do?" said Slightly.

"You're all going to stay here while I go have a look," said Nibs.

"I'm going with you," said Shining Pearl.

"Oh, all right," said Nibs. He tried to sound reluctant, but Shining Pearl could tell he was glad to have company.

The others huddled under a tree as Nibs and Shining Pearl crept ahead. Now they could both hear shouting over the sound of the rain and crashing waves. They rounded a curve; the trail now overlooked a beach, but they couldn't see anything in the darkness.

A bolt of lightning struck the jungle nearby, and suddenly the beach was filled with brilliant light. It lasted only two seconds, but that was long enough for Nibs and Shining Pearl to see the boat rocking in the surf, with men struggling to hold it steady. Other men were unloading a large, obviously heavy crate. Three other crates sat farther up the beach.

The lightning flickered out. The two children stood for a moment in stunned silence, broken by Shining Pearl.

"We need to tell Father," she said. "He'll want to know about this. I wonder what's in those boxes."

"Maybe we can find out," said Nibs. "Let's get a little closer."

Shining Pearl thought about that. Maybe if she found out what the men were up to, her father wouldn't be so angry at her for leaving the village at night.

"All right," she said. "But be careful."

They crept closer, reaching a clump of trees just above where the boxes sat. They waited in the rainy darkness for another flash of lightning.

When it came, they both gasped. They could see some of the men clearly now, and *three of them were castaways*—the same men who had boarded Hook's ship and sailed off.

Another lightning flash. Shining Pearl grabbed Nibs's arm and pointed. Farther down the beach, two men were talking. One of them was the huge African, Cheeky O'Neal. The children looked at each other.

All four castaways had returned to the island.

Why?

"We need to tell Father *now*," whispered Shining Pearl.

They were about to leave the protection of the trees when there was another flash of lighting.

"Oh no!" whispered Shining Pearl, pointing. Little Scallop and the other children were coming toward them, the lightning making them clearly visible on the path.

"What are they *doing*?" whispered Nibs.

"They must have gotten worried about us," said Shining Pearl. "Let's just hope we can get to them before . . ."

Too late. A series of brilliant lightning flashes turned the nighttime into daylight. From the beach, a man shouted, then another. The children had been spotted. Suddenly a half-dozen men were sprinting toward them. The children turned to flee, but it was too late. Shining Pearl started toward them, but Nibs gripped her arm, keeping her hidden behind the trees. She watched helplessly as the men pulled her sister and the others off the path onto the beach, prisoners now.

———•———

The children were dragged up to Cheeky O'Neal and Nerezza. They recognized O'Neal from his stay on the island, but recoiled when a lightning flash revealed Nerezza's face, and the wooden beak strapped to it. Peter had told them stories about a vicious sea captain with no nose.

O'Neal scowled at the children. "You should have minded your own business," he said.

"You know them?" said Nerezza.

"I do," said O'Neal. He pointed at Little Scallop. "That's one of the chief's daughters."

Nerezza thought about that. He stepped toward the soaked, terrified children. "I should kill the lot of you right here," he snarled. "But you might come in handy. Especially you." He pointed at Little Scallop. "Tie 'em together!" he barked. "Then hide the boat. We'd best get off the beach before more trouble shows up."

The crew made quick work of it. They tied the children together, then hauled the launch up the beach and concealed it in a ravine. They checked to make sure the rain had erased all traces of their activities from the sand. Then they lashed the crates to poles and headed off, two men per crate, and two more herding the string of children. Nerezza and O'Neal walked in the lead.

⤙⬥⤚

From their hiding place, Shining Pearl and Nibs watched the caravan head into the jungle, in the direction of the mountain trail. When they were sure the men had gone, they stepped out.

"We should have done something!" said Shining Pearl.

"Such as?"

"I don't know," she admitted.

"Well, I do," he said. "We get to the village and tell your father. They're heading for the mountain. We can take the shortcut to the other side of the mountain trail. From there, there's nothing between us and the village. They'll be well behind us."

Shining Pearl knew this was a good plan, though she didn't want to say so.

"All right," she said, starting for the jungle. At the very least, she intended to go first.

384

$\mathcal{V}$ISITORS

$\mathcal{F}$IGHTING PRAWN PACED ANXIOUSLY around the fire ring. The hot rocks steamed from the rain.

"Did you check the food cave?" He spoke in the Mollusk language, grunts and clicks that could convey many subtle meanings.

"We did."

His son, Bold Abalone, did the talking for the group of six warriors, all nervously watching their angry chief.

"The mermaids?" he snapped.

"Have not seen either of them."

"The boys?"

"They are also missing. Their hut is empty, and so is their underground hideout."

"Which means they're probably with the girls, leading them into mischief."

Bold Abalone said nothing. Everyone knew it was

usually Shining Pearl leading the boys into mischief, but Fighting Prawn wouldn't want to hear that right now.

"If I might speculate, Father?" he said cautiously.

"Yes?"

"It being your birthday tomorrow, I think it's possible they went off in search of a gift to please you."

"They would have pleased me much more by obeying the rules."

"They might have been caught in the storm," Bold Abalone said quietly.

Fighting Prawn softened, his anger at his daughters' disobedience far outweighed by his concern for their safety.

"Whatever they've done, we need to find them," he said. "In this rain . . ."

He didn't finish, but they all knew what he was thinking. When the rain was heavy, it caused problems for the wild boars that roamed the central part of the island, slowing the usually nimble creatures down, sometimes trapping them in mud holes. This in turn attracted Mister Grin, the monstrous crocodile, who in heavy rains ventured much farther inland than usual. He loved the taste of boar almost as much as he loved the taste of Captain Hook. During the last rain he'd gotten four of the creatures, their skeletons found by the Mollusks a few days later, stripped of all meat.

Mister Grin would be out hunting again tonight.

"Search the island," Fighting Prawn said grimly. "Three

groups. One on the mountain trail, one on the north water trail, one on the south. You'll meet on the far end, by Skull Rock, and then come back up the center, if necessary, taking the smaller trails. If they show up back here, we'll sound the conch."

Bold Abalone stepped forward and placed a hand on his father's shoulder.

"We will find them, Father."

Fighting Prawn grabbed his son's forearm with an unusually strong grip.

"You will," he said, his voice catching in his throat.

"Chief!" a voice called out. "A ship!" Fighting Prawn turned and saw Wandering Crab, a tall warrior currently on beach watch, beckoning urgently.

With a nod Fighting Prawn sent Bold Abalone off to organize the search. He followed Wandering Crab out of the village and down onto the beach. Night and fog still shrouded the coast, but in the distance he could make out the running lights of the ship.

"It may just be a passing freighter," he said, although he knew this was unlikely. Big ships never came near the island, which was far from any shipping lane and guarded by treacherous reefs.

"I thought so at first," said Wandering Crab. "But it's not passing. It's going back and forth, just outside the reef."

"For how long?"

"That's its fourth pass."

Fighting Prawn frowned. Ordinarily he would challenge any ship that came so close to the island. But he didn't like the idea of sending out canoes in the dark, and in a storm like this.

"Perhaps it's looking for the men who were here," Fighting Prawn said. "The castaways. That might explain it. Maybe some of their men were picked up by this ship, and now it's searching for other survivors."

"Then why stay offshore?" said Wandering Crab. "Why not send a landing party?"

Fighting Prawn nodded. He didn't like visitors in any event. He especially did not like visitors whose intentions were not clear.

"Double the watch on the beach," he said. "If this ship is still there at first light, we send canoes. With weapons. If anything changes, I want to hear about it immediately."

"Yes, chief." Wandering Crab loped back toward the village to get the additional men. Fighting Prawn trudged behind, thinking about the ship, and the missing children. At the moment he could see no connection between the two. It seemed to be a coincidence.

In his long life, Fighting Prawn had learned to be very suspicious of coincidences.

CHAPTER 59

ᴄᴛHE CAVE

ᴄHEEKY O'NEAL STOPPED in front of the cave. Water gushed from the mouth and tumbled down the mountainside.

"It's in there," he told Nerezza. "About a hundred feet. The stream curves to the right, and then there's a pool. It glows. It's at the bottom of the pool."

Nerezza nodded. "We'll set up here," he shouted to his men, the hole beneath his wooden nose whistling. "Put the crates over there. You two, put on the suits. Make sure every inch of your skin is covered, if you want to come back out of the cave."

The men, though exhausted from climbing the mountainside in the mud and rain, set to work.

"The pool is deep," O'Neal said quietly to Nerezza. "Fifteen, twenty feet."

"We have rubber hoses," said Nerezza. "They can breathe through those."

"It won't be easy for them, working in those suits," said O'Neal. "And if a hose kinks while they're down there . . ."

"We have more men," said Nerezza.

"What about the children?"

Nerezza turned his attention to Little Scallop, Slightly, Curly, Tootles, and the twins. They were wet, mud-covered, exhausted, and thoroughly miserable from being half dragged, half shoved up the mountainside, tied together like mules.

"They could still be of value to us. Have the men tie them to that tree over there. Nice and tight. That way, they'll be close at hand if we need them. If we don't, we can deal with them later."

"You mean let them go?"

Nerezza looked at O'Neal.

"I didn't say that," he said.

CHAPTER 60

ANOTHER WAY

"I DON'T THINK I CAN KEEP GOING," Shining Pearl said.

Nibs hated to admit it, but he felt the same way. The trail was a river of muck. They were sinking up to their shins; each step was an exhausting effort. In the last few minutes they hadn't gone more than ten feet. At this rate, they could take days to reach the village.

"And," said Shining Pearl. "There's that."

She pointed to a pile of brown lumps at the edge of the path. Fresh boar dung.

Nibs nodded. He'd been noticing it, too.

"If Mister Grin gets a whiff of that," said Shining Pearl, "he's going to come hunting."

Nibs shuddered, thinking about the massive beast with jaws that opened wider than a man was tall. If it came prowling down this trail, with the two of them stuck in the muck . . .

"Father says Mister Grin can smell it for miles," said Shining Pearl.

"Really?" said Nibs.

"Really. And he'll come looking for it in the rain, because he knows the boars move slowly."

Nibs stared at the dung for a moment. Then he turned around.

"What are you doing?" she said. "The village is that way."

"Yes, but those men took our friends—and your sister—back *that* way, up the mountain trail."

"Which is why," she said, "we're headed *that* way, to the village, to get help."

"But we're not making any progress, are we."

"No," admitted Shining Pearl.

"So," said Nibs, "maybe we can get help another way."

And then, to Shining Pearl's horror, he bent down and scooped up a lump of boar dung.

CHAPTER 61

*T*HE *S*ANDAL

*B*OLD ABALONE STOOD ON THE BEACH, staring out into the foaming sea, holding a woven grass sandal. It had been brought to him by one of the warriors searching the edge of the jungle by torchlight.

Bold Abalone recognized the sandal. It belonged to his sister, Little Scallop. His heart was knotted in his chest. He prayed that his sister was safe on the island somewhere, not out in the raging water. He could not bear the thought of having to tell his father.

He was interrupted by a shout from one of the warriors, waving at him from down the beach. Bold Abalone sprinted to him, hoping for word of his sisters. Instead, the man told him that the searchers had found a boat.

"Show me," said Bold Abalone.

They ran along the beach to the mouth of Fire Creek. Bold Abalone waded up the creek bed to where some men were waiting. They showed him the launch, partially covered with leaves and ferns; the rain had washed some away, enabling the searchers to spot it. It was a good-sized boat, capable of carrying a dozen men. It had obviously taken a lot of effort to drag the boat into the creek. Whoever had put it there clearly did not want their presence known.

Bold Abalone ordered his men to search the jungle nearby. Then he stared at the launch, his mind swarming with questions. Who had brought the boat, and where were they now? Did this have something to do with the strange ship patrolling offshore near the village? Was it connected to the disappearance of the children?

A shout from the jungle; his men had found tracks. Bold Abalone ran to look. Like all Mollusk warriors, he was expert at reading tracks. A glance by torchlight told him that a large group had passed through recently. It included men, some of whom were carrying something heavy, causing their shoes to sink deep into the mud.

The group also included children, one of whom was missing a sandal.

Bold Abalone shouted orders. Two men were to stay and watch the launch. Two others—his fastest runners— would return to the village to inform Fighting Prawn. Bold Abalone would take his best tracker and follow the intruders up the mountain trail. As they started into the jungle, Bold Abalone thought about his sisters somewhere on the mountain, and about Mister Grin, who was likely to be prowling tonight.

Bold Abalone clutched the sandal tightly in his hand, and quickened his pace.

CHAPTER 62

*T*HE *C*AVE

*T*HE CREATURE WAS RIGHT BEHIND THEM.

Nibs and Shining Pearl could hear him coming through the jungle, his giant tail swinging back and forth, taking down full-grown trees with a single swipe.

Sometimes he roared, a sound that froze the children's blood.

They were on the mountain trail, following the track of the men who'd come ashore on the boat. Mister Grin, in turn, was following Nibs and Shining Pearl—or, more accurately, the scent of the boar dung they were carrying. They'd each started out with an armful of the smelly lumps; Shining Pearl had tucked her precious white starfish into the pocket of her dress. They'd been hoarding the dung carefully, dropping a lump here and there, just often enough to keep the gigantic crocodile coming. The roars meant Mister Grin was getting frustrated— tired of finding boar dung, when it was flesh he craved.

He was hungry.

And he was after them.

Another roar.

"He's getting closer," said Shining Pearl.

"Yes," said Nibs.

"I don't think we can keep outrunning him," said Shining Pearl.

Nibs stopped. "We don't have to," he said.

"What do you mean?"

Nibs pointed ahead. Shining Pearl peered through the leaves and the torrential downpour. They had reached a clearing. Fifty feet ahead was the mouth of a cave, illuminated by torches burning inside. A man stood guard outside.

"How many lumps do you have left?" he whispered.

"One," she said.

"Me, too," he said. "All we have to do is get them close to the cave. Mister Grin will do the rest. Come on."

He started forward.

"Wait!" said Shining Pearl, grabbing his shirt.

"What?"

"Look," said Shining Pearl, pointing. "Just past the guard."

Nibs squinted through the rain and, by the flickering light of the torches inside the cave, saw Little Scallop and the other children, huddled together, heads down, next to a tree.

"They're tied up!" said Little Scallop.

"Oh no," said Nibs.

Behind them a tree crashed to the ground.

"Listen," said Shining Pearl, handing her dung lump to Nibs. "You sneak up that way and put all the dung near the cave. I'll go the other way and come up behind Little Scallop and the boys. When I signal you, make sure the guard sees you, then run back this way."

"You want me to run *toward* Mister Grin?"

"Make sure you get off the path in time."

"Thanks for the advice," he said.

Ignoring his sarcasm, Shining Pearl said, "When Mister Grin has gone past, circle back and meet us down the hill from here. All right?"

"I don't know," said Nibs. "What if—"

"Good," said Shining Pearl. And she was gone.

CHAPTER 63

THE GLOWING POOL

NEREZZA SHOUTED ACROSS THE glowing pool, his voice echoing in the cave: "Tell them to hurry! It's taking too long!"

Cheeky O'Neal only grunted. There was nothing he could do to speed the process. The men were working underwater in gold suits and breathing through tubes, which was hard enough; on top of that they had to do everything by feel, the brilliant light underwater forcing them to keep their eyes closed. They had to feel around blindly for the starstuff, then use gold buckets to scoop it up and pour it into the gold-lined chest that had been lowered to the bottom. From time to time they surfaced to rest and report their progress. Despite Nerezza's fretting, they were doing well. They believed they'd gotten most of the starstuff off the bottom; the chest was three-quarters full.

And the divers felt wonderful. So did Cheeky, and the

other men in the cave, except for Nerezza. The starstuff-laced water lifted their spirits, erased their aches, filled them with energy. O'Neal marveled at its powers. Nerezza had warned him, however, that any man who was exposed directly to the starstuff without the protection of a gold suit would die within seconds. The men were to make absolutely certain that the chest was securely shut before they hauled it up from the bottom of the pool.

From the looks of things, that time would be soon. The underwater glow had dimmed considerably. O'Neal looked across at Nerezza. The captain—and the people who'd hired him—had gone to enormous effort and expense to get this starstuff. The chest alone must have cost a fortune. O'Neal wondered what the starstuff would be worth, and how a man like him might use it. It was something to keep in mind.

CHAPTER 64

AN AWFUL SCREAM

NIBS CREPT THROUGH THE JUNGLE, approaching the cave from the side opposite from that where the children were tied up. He waited until the guard was facing away, then placed one of the foul-smelling dung lumps just outside the cave mouth. He gently tossed the other into the cave itself.

He crouched behind some rocks and peered out. By the light of the torch in the cave, he could just make out the guard. He was staring out into the rain, looking bored.

Then, just past the guard, Nibs saw a slim brown arm rise out of a bush and wave.

Nibs took a breath.

"Hey!" he shouted.

The guard spun and looked at him.

"Hey!" Nibs shouted again, starting down the path.

The guard looked over at the children tied to the tree. Seeing they were all there, he shouted into the cave,

"There's another boy out here! He's loose!" Then he took off running after Nibs.

The instant the guard was gone, Shining Pearl emerged from behind the bush and ran to the other children. They started to call out, but she shushed them with a finger to the lips, pointing toward the cave. She ran to Little Scallop, who was tied like the others, with her hands behind her back. Shining Pearl fumbled with the knot but the wet rope felt glued in place.

"I have a knife!" Slightly whispered. "My pocket."

Shining Pearl reached into his pocket and pulled out a stick with a sharpened shell lashed to it. She began sawing the part of the rope attached to the tree.

She heard shouts from inside the cave.

And then, from just below in the jungle, the sound of trees going down.

She sawed frantically with the knife. The rope parted. The children were still tied together, but at least they were free of the tree.

"Hurry," she said, pushing them, stumbling, toward the jungle. The twins had just disappeared into the foliage and Shining Pearl was about to follow them when she realized she had dropped the starfish. She turned and saw it lying near the cave mouth. She ran over, picked it up, and turned to race back into the jungle.

A huge hand grabbed her neck from behind.

"What are you doing here?" said Cheeky O'Neal.

Before she could answer, a thunderous roar filled the clearing. They looked downhill and saw the guard emerge from the jungle, running full-speed toward them, a look of utter terror on his face.

Three seconds later they saw why.

The monster crocodile burst into the clearing, his glowing yellow eyes impossibly far apart, his massive maw open to reveal a jagged row of needle-sharp teeth the size of spears. On open ground he moved with amazing speed; he was gaining on the guard, now in a race for his life.

O'Neal didn't wait to see who won. Lifting Shining Pearl easily off her feet, he turned and ran for the cave.

From behind them came an awful scream.

CHAPTER 65

*T*RAPPED

*T*HE COLUMN OF WARRIORS loped up the steep trail, single file, Fighting Prawn in the lead. The old chief gripped his spear in his right hand; a bow and a quiver of arrows were slung across his back. He ran with a steady, efficient stride; the younger warriors knew that he would not tire or stop to rest. Not with his children in danger.

Movement ahead on the trail. Without a word, the warriors melted into the jungle on either side, waiting, spears poised.

Then they heard voices. Children's voices.

Fighting Prawn burst from the jungle and ran forward. Ahead on the trail were Little Scallop and the Lost Boys. The chief dropped to his knees in the mud and embraced his daughter. She was sobbing, her words incoherent. Fighting Prawn saw that, except for Nibs, the children were tied together, their hands behind their backs. He pulled his knife and quickly cut them free, counting them as he did.

"Where is Shining Pearl?" he said.

Little Scallop only sobbed harder.

"The men got her," said Nibs. "She's in the cave." He told the chief what he had seen from his hiding place in the jungle: Shining Pearl cutting the other children loose from the tree, then being grabbed by Cheeky O'Neal; Mister Grin catching one of the men as O'Neal ran back into the cave.

"O'Neal?" said Fighting Prawn. "Are you sure?"

The children assured him that it was indeed O'Neal, as well as the other three men who'd been with him on the island, and some other men as well.

"They brought big boxes," said Slightly.

"And golden suits," added Tootles.

"So they were never shipwrecked at all," said Fighting Prawn. "They were after the starstuff all along. Now we know why that ship is patrolling off the village. They want to draw our attention away while the raiding party removes the starstuff."

He ordered two of his men to take the children back to the village. Then he and the other warriors hurried up the path. When they neared the clearing by the cave, they were met by Bold Abalone.

"They're in the cave," he told his father. "We can see torches. But we can't get any closer, because Mister Grin is waiting outside. I think he got one of their men—we heard a scream—and now he wants more."

"So they're trapped in the cave," said Fighting Prawn.

"Yes," said Bold Abalone. "They can't escape. When Mister Grin leaves, we can go in after them."

"I wish it were that simple," said Fighting Prawn.

"What do you mean?"

"They have Shining Pearl."

CHAPTER 66

"$\mathcal{H}$E SEEMS TO WANT MORE"

$\mathcal{N}$EREZZA GLARED AT SHINING PEARL. "This is another one of the chief's daughters?" he said.

"Yes," said O'Neal. "She freed the other children; they escaped. That means the Mollusks will be up here soon."

"Then we will leave now. We're almost ready." Nerezza nodded toward the pool. His men were hauling ropes, carefully raising the chest from the bottom. It had been filled with starstuff and locked shut. The divers were stripping off their golden suits.

"We can't leave now," said O'Neal.

"Why not?"

"Follow me."

O'Neal grabbed a torch and led Nerezza toward the mouth of the cave. When they were ten feet from it, he stopped.

"Look there," he said, pointing.

"What?" said Nerezza, peering into the darkness outside the cave.

O'Neal took two more steps toward the mouth. From the darkness came a deep growl.

Then Nerezza saw the huge glowing yellow eyes, the massive snout.

"What *is* that?" he said.

"A crocodile," said O'Neal. "A very *big* crocodile. The natives call him Mister Grin."

"Where's the guard I posted?" said Nerezza.

"Inside Mister Grin," said O'Neal. "He seems to want more."

Nerezza stared at the monster, pondering his options. He had no firearms; he hadn't expected to need them. He could order one of his men to make a run for it in an attempt to lure Mister Grin away. But he doubted that any man would be fool enough to follow such an order.

"We'll have to wait, then," he said. "It has to go away eventually."

"By then the Mollusks will be here," said O'Neal. "If they're not here already."

Nerezza pondered that, then said, "I assume the chief is fond of his daughter?"

"Yes."

"In that case," said Nerezza, "she may be useful."

$\mathcal{V}$ERY $\mathcal{W}$ARM

$\mathcal{I}$T TOOK PETER, WENDY, and the others the better part of two hours to reach Westminster Abbey. After leaving the Scotland Landing through the back door, they took an indirect route, Magill leading them south on a zigzag course through pitch-black alleys until they reached the Thames. They then followed the embankment east and north, past rundown buildings and docks. Occasionally they were approached by rough-looking characters, sometimes in groups; but they quickly melted back into the fog upon catching sight of the large figure of Magill, and the even larger figure of Karl shuffling along in an overcoat and bowler hat.

Just as Big Ben tolled eleven, they reached the area of the riverbank below the abbey, which was hidden from them by the dense fog that had settled over the river. As they had agreed, the others stayed there while Peter flew ahead. Launching himself upward into the fog, Peter keenly felt the absence of Tink. Ordinarily she would be flying just ahead of him, leading the way with her reassuring glow. But now he was forced to find his way, flying tentatively with his hands in front of him, almost feeling his way in the fog. Finally, through the gloom ahead, he saw the abbey's two front towers.

He descended carefully, landing on the edge of a steeply sloped roof behind the towers. He listened for a minute, then, hearing nothing aside from the traffic on the street in front of the abbey, lowered himself to the ground. He looked around for police or guards, and, seeing none, began to make his way around the vast building. He found what looked like the front door—a massive thing—but, not surprisingly, it was locked. He kept going, again wishing he had Tink to help him. Slowly he worked his way around the building. He came to another big, locked door. He kept going, and finally, in a dark corner at the rear, he came to a smaller door. It, too, was locked. But it was what he was looking for.

He flew back down to the river, finding the others shivering in the fog. He led them on foot back up to the door at the rear of the abbey. Magill studied it for a moment, then said, "All right."

Magill growled something. Karl lumbered over, rose up on his hind legs, put his massive forepaws against the door, and pushed. The door burst open with a crash and the sound of metal snapping.

"Good boy," said Magill.

Patrick went inside, followed by the others, Magill and Karl bringing up the rear. They were in a hallway, and then a vast, echoing, dimly lit space. Peter gasped at its grandeur—magnificent stone columns in the center, and towering arches leading up to majestic windows and a ceiling that seemed as high as the sky itself.

"Someone's coming!" hissed Wendy.

In fact, it was two someones—a pair of night watchmen, one stocky and one stockier, both clutching electric torches as they trotted toward the group, heavy shoes clomping on the stone floor.

"Here now!" shouted the less stocky one. "Stop!"

This command was unnecessary, as nobody in the group was moving. They stood waiting in the gloom as the watchmen clomped up.

"Here now!" said the stockier one, puffing. "The abbey is closed!"

"We regret the intrusion," said Patrick. "But we're here on an important matter that simply can't wait."

"The abbey is closed!" repeated the watchman. He was very firm on this point.

"How did you get in?" demanded the less stocky one.

"Through that door back there," said Patrick, gesturing.

"That door's locked!" said the watchman. "I locked it myself."

"Indeed you did," said Patrick.

"We'll see what the police have to say about this," said the stockier one.

"We would prefer that you didn't," said Patrick.

"Is that so?" said the watchman, turning. He then emitted a most unwatchmanlike yelp, for he had turned directly into the massive hairy bulk of Karl, who had circled around in the gloom and, on padded feet the size of dinner plates, come up silently behind him. The other watchman then turned and emitted a similar sound. The two men stood staring at the bear.

"Now then," Patrick said reasonably. "Why don't you two gentlemen sit on that bench over there? Karl here will keep you company."

Magill stepped forward and, taking the watchmen by their arms, led them to an oak bench against a wall. He grunted something to Karl, who curled up on the stone floor in front of the watchmen and immediately began snoring.

"You'll be fine, long as you don't move," Magill told the watchmen. "If you move, you'll wake him up. And believe me, you don't want to wake him up." He walked away, leaving the two men frozen as still as the abbey's stone columns.

The group spread out and began the daunting task of searching the abbey's many spaces, large and small—its chapels, statues, monuments, and memorials—hoping to find some clue, some sign of where the Cache might be hidden. But at the end of an hour they had seen nothing that a million tourists had not seen before them. A feeling of hopelessness was beginning to settle over them.

They had left St. Edmund's Chapel and were trudging into St. Benedict's Chapel when Wendy felt a strange sensation on her right-hand side. She reached her hand into her pocket. Then she stopped.

"Wait," she said.

"What is it?" said Peter.

Wendy withdrew her hand. In it she held the locket her mother had given her, the one she had torn from her neck so she could pour its starstuff into the fuel tank of Neville's ornithopter. She had stuck it into her pocket then and kept it with her since.

"It's warm," she said.

"What is it?" said Patrick, peering at the locket.

"It's a starstuff locket," said Peter. "I remember Mol—your mother wore one like it."

"It's that same locket," said Wendy. "She gave it to me. And something's making it warm."

"Let's see if you can make it warmer," said Peter. "Try moving this way." He walked toward the part of the abbey known as Poets' Corner. Wendy followed him.

"No," she said. "It's getting colder."

Peter turned and led her past some columns toward the sanctuary.

"Warmer," she said. "Much."

They reached the sanctuary. "It's very warm now," said Wendy, her voicing rising in excitement. Her eyes fell on the high altar. She turned toward it, then started walking quickly toward it. She drew close, then went around and past it. Ten feet behind the altar, she stopped. She was standing next to a large, ornate shrine.

She held the locket toward it. It glowed like fire.

"It's under here!" she said. "I can almost feel the locket pulling my hand downward."

"Fascinating," said Patrick.

"What is?" said Ted.

"This is the shrine to Edward the Confessor, containing his remains," said Patrick. "Stands to reason it would be located over the Confessor's original tomb."

Ted was studying the area around the shrine. "I see no evidence that this floor has been tampered with, do you?" he said.

The others looked, and agreed that the area appeared undisturbed.

"So if the Cache is, in fact, buried beneath this," said Ted, "it's obvious that von Schatten hasn't tried to get at it from here. It would be an awfully messy job, impossible to do unnoticed."

The others nodded.

"So," said Patrick, "if they're not getting to it from here in the abbey . . ."

"They must be getting to it from underneath," said Ted.

"A tunnel," said Neville. "Clever!"

"But wouldn't that also be a massive undertaking?" said Patrick. "To tunnel beneath the abbey?"

"Indeed it would," said Neville. "It would require a great deal of time and manpower."

"The missing Londoners!" exclaimed Ted.

"What?" said Neville.

"It's been going on for months," said Ted. "People missing from the Underground. All from the District Line."

"Are you suggesting," said Patrick, "that von Schatten is using these missing people to dig a tunnel?"

"I am," answered Ted. "The Westminster Bridge station is a stone's throw from here. And it's on the District Line."

There were a few seconds of silence, as everyone stared at the abbey's stone floor.

"So," said Patrick, "let's have a look 'round the Underground, shall we?"

CHAPTER 68

ᴛONIGHT

Sᴛʟᴇɴᴛ ᴀs ᴀ sʜᴀᴅᴏᴡ, von Schatten glided down the tunnel, followed by the plodding Revile. Molly, gaunt and haggard, watched him through the barred window of her cell. For hours, she and George—they'd gotten very good at Morse code—had been tapping hasty messages to each other when they thought it was safe, discussing the unusual level of activity in the tunnel. Some of it was quite puzzling—especially the men who had passed through an hour earlier, unspooling the two fat black cables that now snaked along the tunnel floor. And now von Schatten had come. Something was up.

As von Schatten reached Molly's cell, he stopped and looked in. Molly stared into his dark lenses, willing herself not to back away.

"Tonight, Starcatcher," von Schatten groaned. "Tonight the struggle finally ends, both here and on your flying friend's

417

precious little island. And when it ends, your pathetic life will no longer be of any use to me. Perhaps you will see the Skeleton later. He has been asking after you."

Molly said nothing, fearing her voice would display the terror she felt. Von Schatten looked at her for a moment longer. At that instant, Molly thought she heard something—a faint sound, like a muffled bell. She thought perhaps she'd heard it before, but couldn't quite place it.

Then it was gone, and von Schatten was moving on, followed by Revile. They passed George's cell without a glance.

When they had passed by, Molly took a rock from her pocket and began tapping.

t-o-n-i-g-h-t she tapped

A pause, and then George tapped: *a-r-e y-o-u r-e-a-d-y*

Molly's eyes went to the floor plank, then the tunnel support outside her cell, the one she had so painstakingly undermined.

y-e-s she tapped. *a-r-e y-o-u*

y-e-s

A pause, then George resumed tapping.

l-o-v-e y-o-u a-l-w-a-y-s

Molly, her eyes burning, began tapping back.

l-o-v . . .

THE FOUR

THE CELL DOOR BANGED OPEN. James, lying huddled on the dirt floor with the other ten prisoners, sat up, squinting as the light of an electric torch flashed across his face.

"I need four," said a distorted, rasping voice. James, realizing that it was the Skeleton, turned away to hide his face, wanting nothing to do with this hideous creature.

Too late.

"That one," the Skeleton said, pointing his claw of a hand at James. A guard yanked James roughly to his feet. The Skeleton selected three more men. The four of them were herded out into the tunnel, where six guards surrounded them. The cell door clanged shut. Skeleton stepped close to the four men, his yellow eye peering out from his hood, inspecting them by the light of a bare electric bulb.

"I have selected you to perform a task," the Skeleton said. "If you do exactly as I say, you will not suffer. If you disobey me, or even hesitate . . ." He reached out his claw and touched the shoulder of the man next to James. The man screamed and fell to the floor.

Without another word the Skeleton turned and started down the hall. The guards yanked the fallen man to his feet and shoved the four prisoners forward. They were shaken, and hunger had weakened their legs, but they did not stumble. They did not dare.

CHAPTER 70

THE TUNNEL IN THE TUNNEL

ONCE AGAIN IT WAS PETER'S JOB to scout ahead. The others remained outside at the rear of the abbey as he took to the air and flew along the river up to Westminster Bridge. He rose several hundred feet, so that he was shrouded by the night fog. Then, following Ted's directions, he flew along Bridge Street until he figured he was above the Underground entrance. Slowly he descended until he could just make out the stairway leading down to the station.

He smiled grimly at what he saw. Although the Underground was not running—it was past midnight—there were four policemen around the stairway, clearly standing guard.

Peter flew quickly back to the others and reported what he'd seen.

"It would appear you guessed correctly, Wendy," said Patrick. "Something's going on down there."

"Yes," she said. "But how do we get past the police?"

"Karl and I can deal with the bobbies," said Magill.

"You don't plan to harm them, do you?" said Wendy.

"Of course not," said Magill, sounding a bit disappointed. He reached into his coat and pulled out a coil of rope. "Give us five minutes."

He grunted something to Karl, and the two of them disappeared into the night.

The others waited, saying little. Finally, Patrick said, "I reckon it's been five minutes."

They walked around to the front of the abbey, then up to Bridge Street, Peter leading the way. They approached the Underground entrance from the opposite side of the street. Where Peter had earlier seen the four bobbies, there was now not a soul.

They crossed the street and looked down the stairway. It was deserted.

"Down here!" Magill's voice came from somewhere below.

They hurried downstairs. At the bottom was a metal security fence that had been broken open, apparently by Karl. Passing through it, they found themselves in the station's ticket hall. Magill stood next to the four bobbies, who were seated on the floor, leaning against the ticket booth, bound hand and foot, with their arms behind them. They were looking warily at Karl, who sat next to Magill, looking back at them.

Patrick approached the bobbies. "Good evening, officers," he said.

"You had better untie us right now," snarled one.

"I'm afraid we can't do that," said Patrick. "But I'm certain somebody will find you down here once the trains start running. Meanwhile, I don't suppose you'd be willing to tell us where we might find the entrance to the tunnel being dug beneath Westminster Abbey?"

The four bobbies glared silently at Patrick.

"Apparently not," he said. "Then we'll just have to find it on our own."

He turned to go, followed by the others.

"You'll be sorry!" shouted one of the bobbies, his words echoing off the concrete walls. "You have no idea what you're getting yourself into!"

The warning stayed in Peter's mind as he and the others passed through the unmanned ticket turnstiles and out onto the gloomy, deserted platform. Peter had never been in an Underground station. He felt confined down here, with little room to fly; he could almost feel the tons of stone and earth above him. The grimy platform they stood on stretched left and right, each side leading to the gaping black mouth of a tunnel.

"I'm a bit turned around," said Ted. "Which way is the Abbey?"

"That way," said Magill, pointing to the left-hand tunnel

with the certainty of a man who always knew exactly where he was.

They trooped down to the end of the platform, where a sign informed them that there was NO ADMITTANCE. Magill reached into his coat and pulled out an electric torch. He flicked it on and shone it into the tunnel mouth. There was a narrow ledge leading to an iron staircase, which in turn led down to a footpath alongside the tracks. Ahead, the tracks, lit by dim electric bulbs every few dozen feet, curved gently to the left, then disappeared.

They went to the staircase, Magill leading the way. As he started down, Neville said, "Mind you don't touch that rail running alongside the track. It carries six hundred volts, for the electric locomotives."

They descended the stairs and started along the footpath, single file, keeping to the wall and away from the electrified rail. Magill and Karl led the way; Peter was at the end, behind Wendy. Every now and then a low, dark shape scuttled past.

"Rats," whispered Wendy. "I *hate* rats."

"Me too," agreed Peter, again thinking of Tink. She didn't like them, either.

They rounded the curve and reached a straightaway. The only sound was the shuffling of their feet. From time to time Peter glanced behind him; he saw nothing but the widely spaced tunnel lights, and the blackness between.

424

Suddenly Magill stopped. He flicked off the torch.

"What is it?" whispered Patrick, second in line.

"Train," Magill said, pointing.

The others inched forward and peered down the tunnel. About fifty yards ahead, silhouetted by a lightbulb, was the boxy shape of an electric Underground car.

"The Underground's closed," whispered Neville. "Why would a train be here, sitting between stations?"

"If you were secretly digging a tunnel in the Underground," said Ted, "how would you carry out the dirt?"

"Ah," said Neville, nodding. "Clever."

"That may not be all they're using the train to carry out," said Ted.

"I don't understand," said Neville.

"The Cache!" said Wendy. "They could carry that out in the train, too."

"Exactly," said Ted.

"So what do we do?" said Peter, staring at the train.

"I suggest we have a look," said Patrick. "But carefully."

They crept forward, staying as close as they could to the wall, torch off, all eyes ahead. As they neared the train, Magill held up his hand, and they stopped. He held up two fingers, which they understood to mean he'd seen two people, although none of them saw anything ahead except indistinct shadows. Magill gestured at them to wait, and, dropping into a crouch, moved toward the train, followed by Karl.

Two minutes passed. From ahead, a short yelp shattered the silence, followed by thuds. A minute later Magill and the bear returned.

"Two of them," he said. "And a tunnel."

"Capital!" said Patrick.

They started forward. As they reached the car, they saw it was connected to two others, forming a three-car train. Peering through the windows, they saw that Ted's theory was correct. The seats had been removed, and the floors had been covered with heavy canvas tarpaulins. The canvas was filthy; clearly the cars had been hauling dirt. But at the moment they stood empty, gates open, as if awaiting passengers.

The two guards lay on the ground against the wall, helpless. In addition to firmly tying them up, Magill had gagged them with strips of canvas cut from the tarpaulins. He stepped over them and pointed ahead, and to the left.

"There's the tunnel," he said.

The entrance was rectangular, about seven feet high and half again as wide, chiseled neatly out of the Underground wall. Leaning against the wall next to it was a piece of plywood the precise size and shape of the tunnel entrance, painted the same color as the wall.

"They use that to cover the entrance when the trains are running," said Ted. "You'd never see it from a train racing past."

426

There were two thick black rubber cables snaking from the tunnel to the train. Neville, frowning, bent over next to the train to get a closer look.

"Interesting," he said.

"What?" said Ted.

"These are electrical cables," he said. "They've been attached to the power rails. Why do you suppose?"

"For lights?" suggested Ted.

"Not with this much voltage," said Neville. He looked into the tunnel, which had bulbs glowing along the wall. "Besides, they've already wired the tunnel for lights."

"Then what are they up to?" said Neville.

"I suggest we find out," said Patrick.

"Karl and I'd better go first," said Magill, peering into the tunnel.

"Lead on," said Patrick.

One by one, they entered the tunnel. As before, Peter went last. He tried to convince himself that he was doing a brave thing, protecting the rear. But he knew better. He wasn't afraid of what was behind him; he was afraid of who— or what—lay waiting ahead.

CHAPTER 71

WHOLE AGAIN

HERDED BY A HALF-DOZEN GUARDS, James and the other three prisoners followed the Skeleton down the familiar tunnel to the excavation site. James noted the two black cables running along the ground; he had not seen them before.

They passed the cells that held George and Molly. The Skeleton led them into the last chamber. The prisoners knew it well; they had excavated it themselves, at the cost of much sweat, exhaustion, and pain. The chamber was considerably larger than the rest of the tunnel, its ceiling ten feet high, braced by beams and planks.

Von Schatten stood with his lackey Revile next to a workbench that had been set up at the center of the room. Next to them was the Skeleton's assistant, Scarlet Johns; next to her were his henchmen, Coben and Mauch. The two men were kneeling on the ground near the bench, doing something with the ends of the two black cables; both wore rubber gloves. James noted that both also had ugly deep scratches on their faces and arms, as though they had been attacked by an animal.

At the far end of the chamber was the strange vault that had been the apparent goal of the excavation project. It was a massive thing, its front face eight feet square. It was made of a mysterious metal, smooth and silvery, creating an odd sensation of warmth when touched. Neither rocks nor shovels scratched it. The face of the vault had a seam running around the perimeter a foot from the edge, forming what appeared to be a tight-fitting square door, although there were no visible hinges. In the center of this door was a vertical slot about three inches long.

When the vault was first uncovered, James and the others had watched as the guards had tried for hours, using crowbars, hammers, chisels, and other tools, to open it. Their efforts had been utterly futile; the vault's gleaming surface was unmarked, the door still precisely in place.

Next to the vault stood a sturdy-looking dolly with a flat bed and four thick rubber tires. James assumed this would be used to transport something—presumably something that was now inside the vault. Something heavy. He further assumed that he and the other prisoners had been brought to the chamber to play some role in this process. But how did they intend to open the vault? His eyes went back to the workbench.

On it lay a sword, its handle golden, its blade shining. The tip was missing.

Next to the sword, on a blue velvet cushion, was what appeared to be the tip. Next to it, gleaming in the electric light, was a lump of silvery metal.

Von Schatten was examining these objects when the Skeleton approached. He pointed to the silvery metal and said, "You are certain this will work?"

"Miss Johns is the authority," said the Skeleton, gesturing toward Scarlet. Von Schatten turned to her.

"All my research suggests it is heavenstone," she said. "It should work."

"It had better," said von Schatten. He turned back to the Skeleton. "And these prisoners?"

"They will retrieve the chest," said the Skeleton.

Von Schatten examined them, his gaze lingering for a moment on James. James felt the familiar, awful coldness creeping into him.

"Appropriate," said von Schatten, "that you should be here to witness this." Then he turned toward the Skeleton and said, "Get on with it."

"Are you ready?" the Skeleton rasped to Mauch and Coben.

"We are," said Coben. He and Mauch put on leather welding goggles with thick dark lenses. Then they bent and, with rubber-gloved hands, carefully picked up the black cables. The rubber insulation had been peeled back from the ends of the cables, revealing thick copper wires. Affixed to the end of each wire was a metal clamp. Keeping the clamps well apart, Mauch and Coben approached the workbench. Mauch carefully attached his clamp to the middle of the sword blade. When it was in place, he lifted the sword tip from its velvet cushion and positioned it at the end of the blade, fitting the two broken edges together. He stepped back.

Coben picked up the piece of silvery heavenstone, studied it for a moment, then attached the clamp to one end. Holding the clamp, he announced to the chamber, "If you don't want to be blinded, you'll want to look away."

Everyone turned away except the two goggled men and von Schatten, who kept his dark lenses fixed on the sword.

Coben bent over the bench and slowly brought the heavenstone down directly over the crack between sword and tip. With a sharp buzzing sound and a brilliant burst of light, electricity arced across the gap, almost instantly heating both to more than 6,000 degrees. The lower end of the stone melted, and the molten metal flowed down along the arc, fusing sword and tip together. It was done in seconds. Coben pulled the stone away; the arc stopped instantly, leaving an acrid smell in the air.

Mauch detached the clamp from the sword; he and Coben set the cables down on the dirt floor, keeping them well apart.

"May I lift it?" asked von Schatten.

"By the handle, yes," answered Coben. "The blade is still hot."

Von Schatten grasped the handle and lifted the sword so it gleamed in the light. The weld was perfect, the seam barely visible.

The Sword of Mercy, broken for so many centuries, was whole again.

Holding it in front of him, von Schatten turned toward the vault.

CHAPTER 72

THE WOMAN LOOKING BACK

KARL, PADDING ALONG JUST BEHIND Magill in the tunnel, emitted a low growl. Magill stopped and signaled for the others to wait. He then crept ahead, disappearing into the darkness past the next dangling light. Several minutes passed, and he returned.

"Men ahead, in a locked cell. Two guards. We took care of them."

They moved forward, walking past the guards, who lay bound and gagged next to the tunnel wall. They arrived at the cell, little more than a cramped cage. Seven filthy, haggard men huddled together on the dirt floor eyeing the visitors warily, saying nothing.

"Who are you?" said Patrick.

No response.

"Who is keeping you prisoner?"

Still no response. Patrick turned to the others. "They're too weak or too scared to answer," he said. "We'll have to tend to them later. We need to move on."

"Agreed," said Ted.

"Can't we at least let them out?" said Wendy.

Magill examined the lock, then the bars. "Might be able to," he said. "But we'd have to pull this wall out, and that might collapse the tunnel."

"Wendy, we'll get them out," said Patrick. "But for now we need to keep going."

They started forward again. After about a hundred feet, Karl growled again, and the group stopped. Magill crept forward to check, returning quickly.

"A woman," he said.

Before anyone could stop her, Wendy had brushed past the others and was running ahead.

"Wait!" called Ted. But Wendy wasn't listening. Reaching the cell door, she grabbed the bars and pressed her face against them. She gasped at what she saw—a gaunt, dirt-smeared face, framed by filthy, matted hair. Wendy would not have recognized the woman looking back at her except for the brilliant green eyes—eyes identical to her own.

"Mother!" she cried, reaching through the bars.

"Wendy! Oh, Wendy," sobbed Molly, grabbing her

daughter's hands and clinging to them to keep from collapsing to her cell floor. "But how . . . how did you . . ."

"There's a group of us," said Wendy. "Peter is here."

"*Peter?*" said Molly.

Peter's head appeared in the window next to Wendy's.

"Peter!" Molly exclaimed. "Oh my . . . It's been so long!"

"Hello, Molly," said Peter, hoping his expression didn't betray his shock at Molly's appearance.

Molly peered through the bars at the others. She knew Ted and Neville, and vaguely remembered Magill. Ted introduced her to Patrick. Surveying the group, she said, "But . . . what are you all doing here?"

Wendy quickly explained the group's search for the starstuff Cache, and how their visit to Westminster Abbey had led them to the Underground and the secret tunnel. Molly listened intently, occasionally interrupting with questions.

When Wendy was finished, Molly said, "Von Schatten is going after the starstuff tonight. They've gathered farther down the tunnel, the whole lot of them. They've got James."

"James!" said Peter.

"Yes," said Molly. "He's one of the prisoners they've been using to dig the tunnel."

There was an insistent tapping sound from farther on in the tunnel. Hearing it, Molly said to Wendy, "That's your father. He's in the next cell, that way. Go and see him, but

435

come back. We've got to make a plan."

Wendy dashed down the tunnel and found her father. His condition was as shocking as her mother's had been: The strapping, well-dressed George Darling was now a skeleton of a man in rags, his face covered by a thick beard. Tears spilled from his eyes as he held her hands through the bars.

"Wendy," he said, his voice breaking, "I'm so sorry to have doubted you. Can you ever forgive me?"

"Oh, Father . . ." began Wendy, but when she tried to say more her words turned into sobs. For a few moments they simply clung to each other through the bars. Then, willing herself to be strong, Wendy wiped her tears and, as quickly as she could, explained the situation to her father, as she had for her mother. When she'd finished, she said, "We're making a plan. I'll be back in a moment." Reluctantly, her father released her hands, and she ran back to the others, who were deep in discussion.

"What are we going to do?" she asked.

It was Peter who answered. "We're going to go down the tunnel and try to stop them," he said.

"How?" said Wendy.

Peter looked around at the others, then said, "We're going to figure that part out when we get there."

"Neatly summarized," said Patrick.

"What about my parents?" said Wendy. "We've got to get them out."

There was an uncomfortable pause, then Molly said, "That will have to wait for the moment, Wendy."

"But why?" said Wendy.

"We've no key, for one thing," said Magill, pointing to the lock on the cell door.

"Karl could pull the door off its hinges!" protested Wendy.

"Indeed he could," said Magill. "The problem is, your mum and dad have been weakening the tunnel walls." He pointed to the support post next to Molly's cell door. "If we pull their doors out, the tunnel will collapse."

"We were planning to bring it down tonight," said Molly. "We were going to wait until von Schatten was coming back out."

"But it would collapse on you, too!" said Wendy.

Her mother said nothing, and suddenly Wendy understood that her parents had been planning to sacrifice themselves to stop von Schatten.

"No!" she cried. "You can't! You—"

She was silenced by the massive right hand of Magill, clamped over her mouth.

"Not so loud," he said, politely. "All right?" Wendy nodded, and he released her.

"You can't . . ." she began again, but Molly—now in the role of mother—raised her hand, and Wendy stopped instantly.

"Wendy," said Molly, "we've worked out a plan that might get us all out of this. It's not ideal, but it's our best chance. It won't help for you to waste time arguing, so please just listen, all right?"

"Yes, Mother," said Wendy.

"Good," said Molly brightly. "Now here's what we're going to do."

ʟɪᴋᴇ Sᴏᴍᴇ Sᴛʀᴀɴɢᴇ Cᴏᴍᴇᴛ

ᴠᴏɴ Sᴄʜᴀᴛᴛᴇɴ, holding the Sword of Mercy, stood with the Skeleton in front of the gleaming vault, where they had been conferring quietly for several minutes. James had heard the word "prisoners" several times, had seen the Skeleton aiming his yellow eye in their direction. Each time, he felt his stomach clench in fear. He glanced toward the tunnel, considering a desperate dash for freedom. But burly guards blocked the way; there was no hope for escape.

Von Schatten and the Skeleton finished their discussion. The Skeleton stepped back. Von Schatten turned toward the gleaming vault. Holding the sword handle in his right hand, he raised the blade with his left, guiding the tip to the slot in the center of the door. Carefully, he inserted the tip. He paused for a moment; there was not a sound in the chamber.

Von Schatten took his left hand off the blade and slowly

pushed the sword into the slot. It slid in smoothly, all the way to the handle.

For several seconds nothing happened. Von Schatten started to turn toward the Skeleton, as if to say something.

Then the vault door started to open. Von Schatten moved away quickly. Suddenly James felt the guards shoving him forward, along with the other three prisoners. They now stood closest to the vault, forming a human shield to protect the others from whatever was inside.

Slowly the massive door, made of metal more than a foot thick, came toward them, pivoting outward on hidden hinges. It opened smoothly, almost soundlessly, as though it had been oiled and opened that very morning, instead of having been shut tight for centuries.

The door reached a right angle, then, with just the faintest click, stopped. The inside of the vault was as smooth and pristine as the outside—its walls, ceiling, and floor all the same smooth, shining metal. Sitting precisely in the center of the floor was a wooden trunk, looking quite ordinary except for its hinges and lock, which were made of the same metal as the vault.

For a moment everyone stared at the trunk. Then von Schatten, apparently satisfied that it posed no danger to him at the moment, pushed past the prisoners for a closer look. He turned back to the Skeleton.

"It's locked," he said.

The Skeleton looked toward Scarlet Johns.

"I suspect," she said, "that the sword will open that lock as well. Although of course it would be very unwise to open it without taking precautions."

Von Schatten nodded. "All right," he said. "Have them take it to the train."

———◈◦◈———

Once again, Peter was acting as scout. When they had spotted the guards in the chamber ahead, the others had stayed back, hidden in the darkness of the tunnel while Peter floated up and glided carefully forward, hoping that if the guards glanced back, they would be looking for people on foot, not somebody pressed up against the ceiling.

At the moment, the guards' attention was on the activity in front of them. As Peter inched closer, he saw that past the guards were some other men, and a woman. He inhaled sharply when he caught sight of the hooded form of the Skeleton. He felt the fear building in him, fought the impulse to turn and fly back down the tunnel as fast as he could, past Wendy and the others, out of the Underground, into the safety of the open skies. Struggling for control, he forced himself to think of Tink.

She could be in that room.

He inched forward. Looking past the Skeleton, he saw four prisoners. He knew one of the ragged, bearded men was

James, but at this distance he could not tell which. Beyond them he saw the vault, the chest . . . and von Schatten. As Peter watched, von Schatten's head turned in his direction. Peter pressed as hard as he could against the tunnel ceiling, praying the darkness concealed him. Von Schatten's dark eyeglass lenses appeared to be pointing directly at him. Did he sense Peter's presence? Peter held utterly still, prepared to turn and flee.

Slowly, von Schatten turned away. He was saying something, apparently giving orders. The four prisoners reluctantly trooped into the vault. They surrounded the wooden chest, preparing to pick it up. All eyes in the chamber were on them. Peter turned and quickly flew back down the tunnel to report.

———◆———

The chest was surprisingly light. This confirmed what James had suspected since he first saw it: there was starstuff inside. He understood now why the prisoners had been summoned to handle the chest. If it were to break open, its contents would kill anyone who was nearby. Von Schatten and the Skeleton were going to let James and the others assume that risk.

"Put it here," rasped the Skeleton, gesturing with his claw hand toward the rubber-tired dolly. The prisoners carefully set the chest down on it, then looked to the Skeleton.

"You two pull; you two push," he said, gesturing. "I want

guards on all sides." As directed, James and another prisoner positioned themselves in front of the dolly, grabbing its handle. The other two went behind it. The guards surrounded them—two in front, one on each side, two behind.

"You will move it cautiously," said the Skeleton. "Or you will die painfully."

"One moment," said von Schatten. He went to the vault door and slid the sword out of the slot. "Ready," he said.

"Go," said the Skeleton.

The prisoners began rolling the dolly toward the tunnel. The guards moved with them, keeping a bit of distance, their wary eyes fixed on the chest. The Skeleton walked behind, followed by Scarlet, Mauch, and Coben, followed by Revile. Von Schatten, holding the sword, was last.

The dolly was almost to the tunnel mouth.

From the darkness came a bone-shaking roar.

The two guards in front had almost no time to react before Karl, coming out of the tunnel with astonishing speed, slammed into them, knocking them hard to the ground. The prisoners, terrified, ducked as Karl hurtled past them to the left, leveling the guard on that side of the dolly. An instant later Magill, coming right behind the bear, leveled the one on the other side with a hard fist to the face, as Karl took out the two rear guards.

The dolly was now liberated; it had taken perhaps three seconds.

Karl and Magill kept right on going. Karl's target was the Skeleton; Magill's was Mauch and Coben. Here the fight was more even. Magill was a powerful man, but Mauch and Coben were both skilled fighters, and they had numbers on their side. Seeing Magill coming, they quickly separated and began to circle the big man, keeping apart, feinting, looking for an opening.

As for Karl, he swiftly discovered that the Skeleton was no ordinary human. The bear charged, but at the last instant the Skeleton shifted sideways, at the same time thrusting a claw-hand deep into the bear's thick hide. Karl roared as he fell forward, his entire body consumed by a searing pain that would have killed a man. He tumbled on the dirt and scrambled to his feet, furious, but also, for the first time in his life, fearful. He turned to face the Skeleton, who stood motionless, waiting. Karl began to move warily toward him.

For the moment, these two struggles provided cover for the group now coming from the tunnel into the chamber. Ted, Neville, and Patrick went straight to the dolly and rolled it into the tunnel. Wendy and Peter grabbed the stunned prisoners and pushed them, stumbling, after the dolly. Three of them went, but James, recognizing his rescuers, stopped.

"Wendy!" he said. *"Peter!"*

Peter waved in acknowledgment, but was moving past his old friend

"Please, Uncle James!" said Wendy. "We have to get out of here!" James started into the tunnel after her. He glanced back toward Peter, who was heading toward the fighting.

For the moment, Karl was holding his own against the Skeleton. But Peter saw that Magill was in trouble. Coben and Mauch had worked their way around to one side, forcing Magill to face them. What the big man did not see, but Peter did, was that von Schatten was coming up behind, drawing the sword back to strike.

"Look out!" Peter shouted, at the same time launching himself into the air.

Magill turned and ducked just in time to avoid the arcing blade. Peter flew over Mauch and Coben, straight at von Schatten, spinning in midair to position himself for a kick. As he reached von Schatten, he shot his right foot out, aiming for the head. Von Schatten, with snakelike quickness, jerked his head back and shot out his hand, grabbing Peter's foot. Instantly Peter felt a horrible sensation of cold creeping into his leg. He had felt it before, long ago; he knew he could not allow it to consume any more of him. With all his strength, he yanked his leg away, the effort sending him tumbling erratically through the air, bumping against the chamber ceiling, almost falling.

He collected himself and turned, hovering. Von

Schatten was now standing next to the workbench in the center of the room. Behind him, the fierce struggles continued—Karl against the Skeleton; Magill against Mauch and Coben. Revile was crouched in a corner, apparently trying to avoid any part of the fight; Scarlet Johns stood next to him, motionless, watching without expression. Out of the corner of his right eye, Peter saw movement along the chamber wall. But his gaze was fixed on von Schatten, who, ignoring the fighting, was reaching into his pocket. Slowly he withdrew a black velvet sack, tied with a silver cord. He held it down on the bench, raised the sword, then brought it down swiftly, cutting off the top of the bag.

Gripping the bag firmly, he lifted it toward Peter.

A tiny head appeared, poking out of the top.

Von Schatten squeezed the sack. Tink grimaced. A high, plaintive chime cut through the sound of the fighting, cut through to Peter's heart.

"No," he said. "Please."

"Come here," said von Schatten.

Peter sank to the ground, his eyes on the tiny head poking out of the sack in von Schatten's hand. Tink looked awful, her usual glowing color replaced by a dull, ashen gray. She saw him starting toward von Schatten.

No, she chimed. *Get away. He will kill you.*

Peter stopped.

Von Schatten held Tink down on the workbench with

his left hand. With his right, he raised the sword over her. He looked at Peter.

"Come here," he repeated.

No!

Ignoring Tink's desperate chimes, Peter took a step, then another. He saw movement to the right, behind von Schatten. Suddenly he realized it was James. Peter forced himself not to react. He took another step forward. Another. He had almost reached the bench. He could see that James was very close to von Schatten, tensing to attack.

With impossible speed, von Schatten spun, bringing the sword around. The flat side caught James in the forehead with a sickening sound. James fell to the ground, blood gushing from his head.

Von Schatten turned quickly back toward Peter. The sword was again poised over the helpless form of Tink.

"Come here," he said, a third time.

Peter hesitated. Von Schatten raised the sword. Peter stepped forward. He had reached the bench.

"Closer," said von Schatten.

Peter edged around the bench. He was now next to von Schatten.

"Put your hand on the bench," said von Schatten.

No! chimed Tink.

"If you don't," said von Schatten, "she will die right now."

Peter put his hand on the bench, next to Tink. He feared von Schatten would cut his hand off, but what actually happened was almost worse. With a sudden motion, von Schatten set the sword down and put his hand on Peter's. Peter's mind told him to pull his hand free, but his body would not allow him to move. He felt the awful cold seeping into him, paralyzing him as he was inhabited by the evil presence he had felt before, during a desperate struggle inside a rocket hurtling over a faraway land.

Ombra.

Peter heard a groaning voice, but it did not come from von Schatten's lips; it came from inside his own mind.

You did not kill me in the desert, the voice said. *You weakened me, so I must inhabit this host, this flesh that was once von Schatten. But you did not kill me, boy, and you did not defeat our cause. When I am finished with you, I will retrieve the chest; have no doubt of that. Do you think your pathetic little band can defeat me? No, I will have the starstuff, from here and from the island you so love. But first I will put an end to you, and your precious little friend. You should have listened to her. You should have escaped. Now you will die. And the last thing you will know is this: you failed.*

Peter tried to pull his hand away, but it would not move, would not even twitch. He felt the cold deepening, felt his consciousness draining away. The room seemed to be getting darker. He was no longer able to hear the sounds of the fighting still going on by the tunnel entrance. His head slumped forward. He could now see only the ground by von Schatten's feet.

Behind them, he saw movement.

It was James.

Somehow, despite the awful wound to his head, James had regained consciousness. He was crawling toward von Schatten. Peter felt a pang of despair, knowing that his brave friend would be killed in this hopeless effort. As the light faded from his eyes, Peter watched James, using his elbows, drag himself forward.

He was holding something. Something in each hand, in fact. Something metal, attached to something black. That was also what Peter saw, before blackness engulfed him.

Von Schatten, his attention on Peter, did not see James; did not see him clench his hands to open the clamps; did not notice anything until James, with his last ounce of strength, lunged forward and attached the clamps to von Schatten's legs.

The underground chamber echoed with an unearthly high-pitched moan that seemed to come from everywhere as von Schatten's body, 600 volts coursing through it, went rigid and fell backward. Peter, suddenly released, groaned and slumped to the ground. He lay there for a few seconds, and then heard a familiar sound—Tink chiming in his ear.

Get up! Get up!

Peter rolled over. He screamed at the ghastly sight only inches from his face: Von Schatten lay twitching on his back, smoke pouring from his clothes as his flesh burned with a stomach-turning stench. The worst was his face. His eyeglasses had melted, forming two black rivers down his gaunt cheeks. Left exposed were his eyes, which were not eyes at all, but two gaping holes in the center of his skull, revealing nothing inside but a red glow. Wisps of smoke drifted upward from the holes.

Peter turned away, trying not to vomit as he struggled to his feet.

This way, chimed Tink. *Hurry.* As always, she was ahead, leading the way, although Peter could see she was weak and flying erratically.

"Wait a moment," he called. "I have to get James."

He bent and grabbed James's hands, pulling him to his feet. His childhood friend was now a grown man a foot taller than Peter, but had been so badly starved that they weighed nearly the same. Peter put James's arm around his shoulder and together they followed Tink. She led them to the right, toward Magill, who was getting the better of Mauch and Coben. Karl was not doing as well. He had tried, over and over, to use his massive size and strength against the Skeleton, but each time he had been rewarded only with a jolt of excruciating pain. The old bear was tiring, and weakening. The Skeleton was coming ever closer.

Magill had just knocked Mauch hard to the ground—apparently for good—and had grabbed Coben in a headlock. He shot a glance at Karl, then yelled to Peter, "Get to the train! I'll help Karl finish this lot, and we'll be right behind."

Peter thought about arguing, but decided that, in their current condition, he and James would be useless against the Skeleton, more hindrance than help to Magill. He glanced back at von Schatten's smoldering body. The two columns of smoke coming from his eye sockets seemed to be thickening. Peter felt a twinge of dread.

Holding James up, he stumbled toward the tunnel, Tink leading the way. Peter noticed that some of the guards who'd been beaten down by Karl and Magill in their initial charge were groaning and shifting on the ground, starting to revive.

"Wait a moment," whispered James.

"What?" said Peter.

"Keys," said James, pointing toward one of the guards. Peter saw he had a ring of keys on a belt hook. "The other prisoners," said James.

Peter bent over, snatched the keys and hooked them onto the frayed piece of rope that served as James's belt. He slung James's arm over his shoulder. As they entered the tunnel, Peter was intensely aware of the sounds of struggle behind them, and Karl's roars of pain. He wondered about his decision to leave, but did not look back.

He had not remembered the tunnel being so long. His

legs were weak, and it was an effort to keep James upright. Twice they stumbled badly. The third time, they fell.

Get up, chimed Tink. *Hurry.*

"Come on, James," said Peter, struggling with his friend.

"I don't think I can," said James. "You go ahead."

"No," said Peter.

"Let me help," said a soft voice, and then Wendy was bending down next to Peter. Tink was right behind her, and Peter realized how weak she was; she hadn't even managed to say anything unpleasant about Wendy.

They managed to get James back to his feet and, supporting both his arms, started down the tunnel again. Tink, too tired to fly farther, settled into Peter's hair.

"It's just ahead," said Wendy. "Next to the cells where they have my parents. We're going to pull the doors free, but we don't dare until everyone is safely through, because the tunnel will collapse. We're hoping to block von Schatten from following us."

"What about the starstuff?" said Peter.

"Neville and Ted have gone ahead with the dolly. They're going to load it onto the train. Neville thinks he can figure out how to drive it. I hope he's right."

In another fifty feet they came to Patrick, standing in the tunnel next to George's cell. He held the end of a plank that George had handed him through the cell window. The other end was wedged behind a tunnel support post next to the door.

"There you are, Peter," he said as they approached. "We're ready to go here."

"But not until Magill gets here," said Peter. "Wendy, can you help James get to the train?"

"I want to stay here with my parents," said Wendy.

"Wendy," said George firmly. "Help James. He needs you."

"All right," said Wendy. "But I'm coming right back." She took James's arm and started helping him down the tunnel toward the train.

"Where are Magill and Karl?" said Patrick.

"They should be here soon," said Peter, trying to sound confident. He looked back up the tunnel, a silent plea in his thoughts.

Please come soon.

———

Magill had defeated Mauch and Coben; they lay in the dirt, unconscious and bleeding. He glanced at Revile and Scarlet; they had not moved from the wall. Magill turned now to help Karl. The big bear was still valiantly trying to attack the Skeleton, but Magill saw he was seriously weakened, and would not last much longer. Magill knew he could not allow himself to get within reach of the Skeleton's claws. He looked around for a weapon. His gaze stopped at the workbench. On it lay the Sword of Mercy.

He ran over and grabbed the sword. Gripping it with both hands, he took three quick steps toward the Skeleton, who was about to make another lunge at the flagging Karl. Magill swung the sword, aiming for the Skeleton's neck. The Skeleton somehow sensed it coming, ducking and whirling with astonishingly quickness, at the same time darting a deadly stump of a hand out at Magill. Thanks to the sword, Magill was just far enough away that it missed him.

The next minute saw a deadly dance—Magill and the Skeleton circling, Magill thrusting the sword, the Skeleton countering with his hands, neither gaining an advantage. As he circled, Magill assessed the situation. He was tiring, and Karl would soon be too weak to be effective. They needed to get out of the chamber. He began to maneuver his way toward the tunnel entrance, growling at Karl to follow. The Skeleton saw what he was doing and tried to block him, but Magill was steadily gaining ground. He and Karl managed to reach the tunnel mouth. Four of the six guards were now conscious, but in no mood to fight; they scrambled away as Karl growled at them. Magill and the bear entered the tunnel, Magill walking backward, still fending off the Skeleton with the sword.

Suddenly the chamber was filled with a furious sound, a groan that seemed to come from the earth itself. The Skeleton stopped and turned. Magill, looking past his foe, saw a chilling sight. The two columns of smoke pouring from the empty eye sockets of von Schatten's body had united into a thick, swirling column, which was now forming unto the unmistakable shape of a dark cloaked figure, with a hooded head and glowing red orbs for eyes. It towered over von Schatten's corpse, yet still seemed to be attached to it.

It groaned again, and with a dark snakelike arm, pointed toward the electrical cables clamped to the feet of the corpse.

The Skeleton understood. He turned and swiftly moved back to the body. Magill knew he should run, but he could not take his eyes off the spectacle.

The Skeleton was beckoning toward Revile and Scarlet. They cowered against the far wall, fearful of the dark thing now filling the center of the chamber. The Skeleton beckoned again, more insistently. Reluctantly, they approached. The Skeleton rasped something to them—Magill couldn't hear it. They looked at each other.

"Do it!" rasped the Skeleton, loud enough for Magill to hear.

They knelt on the floor. Each carefully took hold of one of the thick black electrical cables.

"Now!" the Skeleton ordered.

Scarlet and Revile yanked on the cables, pulling the clamps free of von Schatten's legs.

Instantly the column of smoke began to contract and descend, its two streams swirling back into the eye sockets, like black water going down the drain. In seconds the smoke was gone.

The corpse began to move.

As Magill watched in horror, the hideous charred thing that had once been von Schatten rose to its feet. It turned slowly and looked directly at Magill with eye sockets red as fire.

Magill, with Karl right behind, turned and ran.

———————

"Maybe I should go back for them," said Peter, for the dozenth time.

"I don't think that would be wise," said Patrick. "If Magill and Karl can't handle the situation, then—"

He was interrupted by a chime from Tink, who was still sitting in his hair.

"Someone's coming," said Peter.

"Ready?" said George, gripping the bars of his cell window.

"Ready," said Patrick, his hands on the plank wedged behind the support post.

They stared into the tunnel. They heard running footsteps. Then two figures came into view, and Peter's heart leaped.

"It's them!" he cried.

"Get back, Peter," said Patrick.

Magill, still holding the sword, was almost to them. He was glancing back constantly, clearly frightened. Peter didn't want to think about what it would take to frighten Magill.

"Steady, now," said Patrick, gripping the plank. "As soon as they get here . . ."

Magill and the bear had reached them.

"Keep moving!" shouted Patrick. To George he said, "Now!"

Patrick pulled on the plank, yanking the tunnel support post free. At the same instant George threw himself into the door, which burst free of the now unsupported wall. Immediately huge chunks of earth and rock began to fall from the tunnel roof. A roof beam fell on George, knocking him to the ground.

"GO!" he shouted.

But Patrick and Magill had him by the arms, and were dragging him free of the falling rubble. He staggered to his feet and followed the others, who were already running to Molly's cell. She was waiting anxiously, her face pressed to the bars. She lit up when she saw her husband.

"Oh, George!" she said. "I was so worried!"

"I'm fine," he said. "Now let's get you out."

Tink made another warning sound.

"Someone's coming," said Peter. They looked back toward George's cell. The tunnel had not been fully blocked by the cave-in; there was a space about a foot high at the top.

Hands were frantically scooping away rocks and dirt. Through the opening Peter saw the heads of two guards.

"Faster!" called a voice. Peter recognized the rasp of the Skeleton. Then his stomach clenched as he caught sight of a face looming behind the guards—a hideous face, with blackened flesh hanging off and two glowing eyes looking directly at him.

Peter turned away.

It can't be.

"We'd better hurry," said Patrick. "Mr. Magill, please get the door."

Magill handed the sword to Peter and grabbed the bars in Molly's cell door. Patrick and George wedged the floor plank behind the support post.

"Ready?" said Patrick. The others nodded. "Now!"

Again both door and support post gave way, sending dirt cascading down into the tunnel. As Molly tumbled into the hall, George grabbed her, pulling her free. For a moment they embraced, Molly sobbing.

"I'm sorry," said Patrick, "but we really don't have time for that."

Peter saw he was right. The guards had cleared away enough of the first cave-in to start climbing through the opening. The second cave-in had not brought down nearly as much debris; the pursuers would get through quickly.

"Go!" said Magill, pushing the others along the tunnel.

Nobody argued. They headed for the train—Molly and George, holding on to each other; Peter, still carrying the sword; then Patrick, with Magill and Karl bringing up the rear. Their pace was slowed by Molly and George, who were too weak to move at any more than a fast walk. Peter kept looking back over his shoulder, each time fearing he would see that horrible face. They passed the cage that had held the other prisoners, and Peter was glad to note that it was empty, its door ajar. James had used the keys.

He saw a figure in the tunnel running toward them; it was Wendy, coming back as she'd promised. She quickly embraced her parents and said, "The train's just ahead."

They quickened their pace a bit and soon reached the end of the tunnel, and the waiting train. As before, the doors to all three cars stood open. Ted and Neville stood in the doorway to the middle car; behind them, sprawled on the canvas-covered floor, were James and the other freed prisoners.

"Where's the chest?" said Peter.

"It's right there," said Ted, gesturing toward the front of the middle car. Peter looked and saw that the chest had been taken off the dolly, which lay by the side of the tracks.

"We need to leave immediately," said Patrick. "Neville, can you drive this train?"

"I believe so," said Neville. "The controls have several ingenious safety features, but I . . ."

"Just get going!" shouted Magill, reaching the train with Karl.

Neville scurried forward to the engineer's cab in the first car. The others helped George and Molly climb up into the middle car, a difficult task, as they were weak; and since there was no train platform, the door opening was nearly four feet off the ground. Once they were aboard, Patrick climbed in, followed by Magill and Karl, who was given a wide berth by the prisoners. To Peter, standing anxiously next to the track, it seemed to take forever for everyone to board the train. He wondered why Neville hadn't gotten the train moving yet. He kept glancing into the tunnel.

He saw them even before he heard Tink's chime.

"They're coming!" he shouted.

"Neville!" shouted Ted. "Start the train!"

"Almost there!" Neville called back.

Peter looked back up the tunnel. He counted three . . . no, four guards running toward them. The Skeleton was right behind them.

Behind the Skeleton was the thing that had been von Schatten.

He heard a hiss of air, and turned to see that the train had finally started moving. He took a last hasty glance into the tunnel. The first guard had almost reached the end. Peter flew into the train. It was picking up speed. Peter willed it forward.

Faster.

The first guard emerged from the tunnel. Now the second guard. Now the others.

Faster.

The guards reached the doorway to the third car. One by one, they hauled themselves in. Peter prayed it would be just the guards—Magill and Karl could handle the guards.

Faster, please . . .

Too late. The Skeleton, with an odd slithering motion, almost lizardlike, was in the third car. Then came the Ombra creature, who seemed to glide into the car effortlessly.

Their pursuers were all on the train.

"Close the gate!" shouted Patrick, pointing to the passageway at the back of the car.

Magill ran over and slammed the metal gate shut. It had a latch; he closed it. Seconds later, the guards were attacking it from the other side, delivering powerful kicks. The metal was bending. The gate would not hold.

The train was picking up speed. Peter looked ahead; they were just reaching the Westminster Bridge station, through which they had entered the Underground. Suddenly an idea struck Peter.

"Jump out!" he shouted, grabbing one of the freed prisoners and pulling him to his feet.

"What are you doing?" asked Patrick.

"It's the starstuff they're after," said Peter. "Not these people."

Patrick and Magill, understanding instantly, started grabbing the weakened prisoners and shoving them out the door as the train reached the platform. Some went willingly, some less so. They all stumbled and fell, but in a few seconds they were all safely off the train. The last to go was James, too weak to resist.

"Peter, help me!"

Peter spun and saw Wendy dragging her parents toward the door. They were resisting, but they, too, were very weak. Peter rushed over, and together he and Wendy managed to get them out the door just before the train reached the tunnel. Wendy caught a last glimpse of them rolling on the platform, holding on to each other. Then the train was in the tunnel.

"Thank you," she said to Peter.

"Why didn't you jump off?" he said.

"Why didn't you?"

Before Peter could answer there was a crash at the end of the car. The guards had broken through the gate. One of them started to enter the car, then immediately retreated in the face of a roar and a swipe of the massive paw of Karl, who stood blocking the passageway.

The train was picking up speed.

"What do we do now?" said Ted, over the rumble of the wheels.

"For now," said Patrick, "Karl seems to have them bottled up."

"That won't work for long," said Magill. "He can hold back the guards. But not that thing he was fighting back there. In close quarters like these, it will have its way with Karl. And once that thing is in here with us . . ."

"*Both* of those things," said Peter.

The train was now traveling at its top speed, slightly above sixty miles per hour. It rocketed through another station.

"Could we push the chest out the door?" suggested Ted.

"*No,*" said Wendy. "If it breaks open, it could kill people. Many people. And if doesn't break open, they'll just get it back, and everything we've done is wasted."

They shot through another station.

Tink chimed.

"He's coming," said Peter.

The Skeleton appeared in the passageway between the cars. Karl roared and lunged forward, then jerked violently backward. The Skeleton advanced another step.

"Give me the sword," said Magill.

Peter handed it to him, and Magill rushed toward Karl, trying to help, but there was not enough room to maneuver. The Skeleton's claw lashed out; Karl staggered and fell backward. As the bear gamely struggled to rise again, Magill lunged at the Skeleton, thrusting the sword. This time he miscalculated. The Skeleton, with snakelike quickness, grabbed Magill's wrist. Magill screamed and jerked away. The sword clattered across the floor of the car. Magill stumbled back to the others, his now useless right arm dangling, his face a mask of agony.

Another station flashed past.

Karl was back on his feet, again blocking the Skeleton's path. But he was losing ground an inch at a time, and Magill could no longer fight with him. There was no doubt now: the Skeleton was going to win this fight.

Peter picked up the sword.

"Get into the front car," he said. "Everybody."

"What are you going to do?" said Wendy.

"The only thing that will stop them," he said, looking at the chest.

"Peter," said Wendy, "you can't . . ."

"*Please,*" said Peter. "I'll be all right. This is our only chance. They'll have us in another minute."

There was no argument to that.

"Go to the front, and stay away from the passageway," said Peter. "Mr. Magill, when I tell you, call Karl."

Reluctantly, the others went into the front car. Peter, holding the sword, positioned himself next to the chest. Karl, still snarling, had been backed up halfway through the car. The Skeleton came relentlessly forward, followed by the guards and Ombra. Peter tried not to look at the glowing eyes. He knew they were looking at him.

Another station flashed past.

Peter took a breath, then turned to Magill.

"Now!" he shouted.

Magill growled something. With a roar, Karl reared up on his hind legs, took a massive swipe at the Skeleton, then spun and ran past Peter into the forward car.

Now Peter stood alone next to the chest. He tapped the lock with the sword.

"If you come any closer," he said, "I'll break it open."

The Skeleton hesitated.

Ombra spoke, his groan coming through the charred hole that had once been von Schatten's mouth: "You don't know that the sword will break the lock."

"You don't know that it won't," said Peter.

A moment of silence. Another station flashed past. The train rocked violently as it rounded a curve it was not meant to take at such high speed. Peter staggered sideways, then caught himself.

Ombra moved forward, toward the Skeleton. The guards spread to the sides of the car. Ombra groaned something, too low for Peter to hear. Peter gripped the sword tightly and drew it back.

There was an urgent sound from Tink, and at the same instant the two creatures moved toward Peter, the Skeleton to his right and Ombra to his left. With all his strength,

Peter swung the sword at the lock. The two pieces of metal clashed together in a brilliant cascade of sparks; there was a clattering sound as the tip broke off and fell to the floor. A light whiter than white filled the car. The guards screamed and covered their eyes. The Skeleton staggered backward. A hideous groan escaped Ombra.

The chest, its lock broken, started to open, the lid lifting by some unseen mechanism. It moved very slowly and had opened perhaps an inch, but the light filling the car had become, impossibly, even more intense. The Skeleton and Ombra turned away, driven back, bent over like trees in a storm. At the back of the car the guards, covering their eyes, crawled toward the rear car.

The train hit another curve and leaned precariously to the left. A stream of golden brilliance spilled from the still-opening chest, spreading swiftly across the canvas-covered floor, seeping through into the metal beneath, the undercarriage, the wheels, and axles.

Then two things happened almost at once. One was that the train, leaving the curve, righted itself violently, sending Peter stumbling forward.

Watch out! chimed Tink.

Peter blindly raised his hands to catch himself. They struck the lid of the chest, slamming it shut. Instantly the brilliant light was gone. Peter's momentum carried him over the trunk. He fell sprawling in the center of the car.

The second thing that happened was that the train entered the Whitechapel station, which was in the open air. It was no longer underground.

And then a third thing happened.

⸺◆⸺

"We're flying!" said Neville, sticking his head out of the cab of the first car.

"*What?*" said Ted. He was with the others at the back of the car, trying to follow the action behind them. They had seen a blinding light fill the tunnel on both sides. Now, suddenly, it was gone.

"The train!" said Neville, scurrying back. "It's flying!"

"Good heavens," said Patrick, staring out the window. "He's right."

The train, all three cars of it, was ascending gracefully into the dark London sky.

Wendy ran to the passageway and peered into the next car. "Oh, no," she said.

⸺◆⸺

Peter, dazed by the fall, struggled to his feet. He no longer had the sword. And he was no longer next to the chest.

The Skeleton was.

Peter spun around, looking for an escape. The car door still stood open. Peter could see the lights of London, now hundreds of feet below. If he could get to the door . . .

But in front of the door stood Ombra.

Ombra started toward Peter, a walking corpse, eyes glowing, a charred hand reaching out. Peter took a step back. He heard a warning chime from Tink, and turned. The Skeleton, leaving the chest, was coming toward him from that direction.

He stepped on something. The sword. He reached down and picked it up. Ombra took another step closer. With all his strength, Peter lunged forward and thrust the sword into Ombra's body.

It went into his chest, all the way in to the handle. Peter, sickened, let go, stepping back.

Ombra kept coming. The sword impaling him had no effect.

Peter whirled around. The Skeleton was right behind him now, reaching out. The three of them had come together in the center of the car. Peter had nowhere to go. The Skeleton's claw hand brushed against him. Peter screamed in agony.

"It will be worse," groaned Ombra. "*Much* worse, before I let you die."

The Skeleton raised his hand again. Another horrible jolt of pain. Peter dropped to his knees, whimpering.

"Leave him alone!"

It was Wendy. She had come through the passageway.

She was standing by the chest. She put a hand on the lid.

"No," said Peter. "It'll kill you."

"The boy is right," groaned Ombra. "If you open it, you will die."

Wendy ignored him, her eyes boring into Peter's.

"Do you remember," she said, "how we got off the ship?"

Peter struggled to think.

"I trusted you then," she said. "I'm going to trust you now."

Peter frowned, desperately trying to grasp what she meant. Then, suddenly, he understood.

"No," he said. "You can't . . ."

Too late. With a fierce grunt Wendy shoved the chest forward hard, directly at the trio in the center of the car. As it slid across the canvas toward them, the Skeleton and Ombra both started toward her; but the moment they did, Wendy yanked up on the lid. Instantly the brilliant light again filled the car. Wendy, with a desperate lunge, pulled the lid all the way open as she dove sideways, hitting the floor and then hurtling out of the car and into the night, a thousand feet above London.

Peter was a half second behind her, but the starstuff had left him nearly blind. He spun around desperately in the sky, screaming "Wendy!" He heard nothing but the rushing wind around him, and a hideous howl coming from somewhere above.

And then he heard Tink, far below.

You'd better hurry, she chimed. *Because I can't carry her.*

Following the sound, Peter dove straight down, flying faster than he ever had despite his near-blindness.

"WHERE?" he shouted. "TELL ME WHERE!"

Over here! came the chimed response.

Peter veered toward the sound, then, at Tink's direction, veered again, and then again. His eyes were starting to adjust. He could see buildings rushing toward him.

Where was she? Where was . . .

"HERE!" shouted Wendy, and then he had her in his arms, holding tight, fighting with all his strength to slow their descent. He almost did; as it was, they came down clumsily, but not fatally, tumbling onto the roof of a butcher shop.

"Are you all right?" said Peter.

"I think so," said Wendy. "Next time, could you catch me a bit sooner?"

"Next time," said Peter, getting to his feet, "I might just stay on the island."

They looked up at the sky. The train was now about two thousand feet up, climbing rapidly and glowing brightly, like some strange comet.

"I'd better get up there," said Peter. "If I don't close the lid to that chest, they'll never get down."

"I suppose so," said Wendy.

"I'll be back," said Peter, launching himself into the sky, with Tink zooming behind.

"I hope so," said Wendy, to the night.

CHAPTER 74

CHE PROMISE

IT TOOK SOME TIME TO GET THE TRAIN BACK down.

Peter caught it quickly enough as it ascended gracefully over the vast city, now invisible beneath the cloud bank below. The brilliant light radiating from the open starstuff chest in the center car forced Peter to close his eyes as he drew near, although he could still tell where it was from the unearthly, yet somehow pleasantly musical, humming sound that filled the air.

With Tink's help, he was able to find the chest and shut the lid. Instantly the humming stopped and the car went dark, save for the dim moonlight coming through the windows. Peter, blinking as his eyes adjusted, looked warily around for any sign of Ombra or the Skeleton. But he was alone in the car.

"Hello?" called Peter.

"Hello?" answered a wary voice from the forward car. "Is that you, Peter?"

It was Ted, poking his head through the passageway. He was followed by Patrick and Neville, then Magill and Karl, all looking quite relieved to see him. Peter took a quick look into the rear car. Von Schatten's four guards were cowering back there, showing no interest in causing any problems for Peter, or getting anywhere near Karl.

"Is Wendy all right?" asked Ted.

"She's fine," said Peter. "When she opened the chest, she jumped out of the train, but I caught her . . ."

Thanks to me, chimed Tink.

". . . thanks to Tink," said Peter, "and we managed to land safely."

"I hope we can do the same," said Neville, casting an anxious glance out the door at the clouds below.

"I'll see what I can do," said Peter. He stepped out the door and flew over the train. Inverting himself, he put his hands on the roof and began to push downward. Slowly, the train responded, descending at a gentle angle. In a few minutes they reached the clouds; the wind picked up a bit. Then they poked through the other side, and below them, only a few hundred feet, were the lights of London.

"Does anybody know where we are?" shouted Peter.

Magill, apparently unconcerned about the height, stood in the doorway, peering down.

"Ealing," he said.

"Is there anybody right below us?" shouted Peter.

"No," said Magill. "You're all right."

The following morning a man walking his dog discovered a three-car London Underground train sitting on the grass in Walpole Park, Ealing. The man reported this to the police, who assumed he was drunk and were quite surprised to discover he wasn't. Over the coming weeks and months, many different explanations would be offered for the miraculous appearance of the train, including that it was some kind of prank by university students. But nobody really believed that even university students were capable of such a feat. And so it remained a mystery.

By the time the police arrived, the train's occupants had been gone for hours. Von Schatten's men simply fled into the night. Patrick, Neville, and Ted took possession of the sword, the tip, and the chest and managed, after a lot of walking, to get a cab, which took them back to the Scotland Landing Hotel. Magill and Karl made it back on foot.

Peter took off to look for Wendy, whom he found quickly with the unenthusiastic but effective help of Tink. He got her down from the roof of the butcher shop, and they walked to her parents' home. Peter offered to fly her, but she said she had been in the air quite enough for one night.

The next day everyone except Karl gathered at the Darlings'. George and Molly were looking and feeling much better after eating, bathing, and sleeping. When Mrs. Bumbrake arrived with John and Michael, there was a joyful family reunion, with much hugging and some crying. There was more crying when they paused a moment in memory of Leonard Aster. And then it was down to business as George, who had spent much of the morning telephoning various influential associates, summarized what he had learned.

"There's been quite a stir of activity at Buckingham Palace," he began. "The details are being kept secret, but apparently von Schatten has gone missing"—George arched his eyebrows at Wendy and Peter, who smiled—"and stands accused of engaging in a plot against the crown. The king, who seems suddenly to be a different person"—again, George arched his eyebrows—"has ordered a full investigation, starting with a thorough interrogation of von Schatten's assistant Simon Revile. Revile has been very cooperative, in hopes of saving his own skin. A Miss Scarlet Johns is also apparently cooperating willingly. The investigation has already produced some surprising results: Chief Superintendent Blake of Scotland Yard, who apparently was involved in a conspiracy with von Schatten, has been relieved of command and placed under arrest, along with several of his top subordinates. Meanwhile the men who went missing in the Underground have all turned up, telling strange tales of being held captive in a tunnel near the Westminster Bridge station. The tunnel has been located, as well as a mysterious vault under Westminster Abbey, but as of yet, nobody has a clue what any of it means."

"And the coronation?" said Patrick.

"It will proceed on schedule," said George. He looked around, beaming. "It seems things have gone rather well," he said.

"What about the Cache?" said Molly.

"What about it?" said George.

"What do we do with it?" said Molly. "What if they come after it again?"

"I hadn't thought of that," said George. "I suppose we need to hide it somewhere."

"I can hide it," growled Magill. All eyes turned to him. "In Wiltshire," he said. "There are caves there nobody knows of but me, Karl, and the wolves. I can hide it there, until you decide what to do with it."

George looked around the room. "All right, then," he said.

"I'll leave tonight," said Magill.

"What about the sword?" said Patrick.

"What about it?" said George.

"We've got the Sword of Mercy," said Patrick. "It was in the Underground car, with the chest. The tip was nearby; apparently von Schatten managed to weld it to the sword, but it must have broken off again when Peter used it to smash the lock on the chest."

Peter remembered the sound of the tip clattering on the floor.

"I heard nothing about any of the Crown Jewels being missing," said George.

"Perhaps they don't yet know it's missing," said Patrick.

"In any event," said Molly, "we've got to get it back."

"How?" said George. "We can't just walk into the Tower of London with a sword and . . ."

"I'll return it," said Peter. "I'll drop it off on my way back to the island."

"*What?*" said Wendy.

"Peter," said Molly, "you don't need to go back so soon. Surely you can stay a few days."

Peter shook his head. "Von Schatten told me they were going after the island, too," he said. "To get the starstuff there."

Molly frowned, remembering her brief encounter with von Schatten in the tunnel the night before. "He said the same thing to me," she said softly.

"So I have to go back there."

"We'll go with you!" said Wendy. "You helped us, now it's our turn to help you!"

How? chimed Tink, who'd been listening from her perch in Peter's hair. *You fly like a stone.*

"I appreciate it, Wendy," said Peter. "But Tink is right. You'd have to go by ship. There isn't time."

"But . . ." began Wendy.

"I'm sorry," said Peter. "I have to go. Patrick, if you'll get me that sword . . ." He rose, followed by the others, except for Wendy, who sat with her face buried in her hands.

"Good-bye, everyone," said Peter, his eyes on Wendy.

"Peter," George began formally, "I don't know how we can begin to . . ."

"Hush, George," said Molly.

George hushed.

Molly put her a hand on Peter's arm. "Peter," she said, "we can never thank you enough. Just know that we love you, and will do anything for you."

"I know," said Peter, looking down, his face red.

"And promise us you'll come back to visit."

Peter's eyes met hers, and they both remembered a moment long ago on the island, when Molly—then a girl Wendy's age—had asked him to make that same promise.

He nodded. "I promise," he said.

Wendy sobbed. Peter started toward her, then turned and went to the door.

CHAPTER 75

$\mathcal{T}$HE $\mathcal{S}$WORD FROM THE $\mathcal{S}$KY

"$\mathcal{H}$ERE IT IS," said Patrick, handing the sword to Peter. Peter shivered, remembering the last time he'd touched it—when he'd plunged it into the living corpse that Ombra had become.

"And here's the tip," said Patrick. Peter stuck it into his pocket.

"Do you know where the Tower is?" said Ted.

"I think I remember," said Peter. He and Molly had spent an unpleasant night there once, fleeing from Ombra. "Tink will get me there." Tink, thrilled that she was once again the lone female presence around Peter, beamed from her perch in his hair.

"And you're sure you don't want us to . . ." began Ted.

"Yes," said Peter. They'd been through this several times. "I'm sure."

"All right, then," said Ted. He wanted to hug his old

478

friend, but settled for a manly clap on the back. "Off you go," he said.

And off Peter went.

———✦———

The two bored Beefeaters stood guard outside the Jewel House. There was nobody to guard against; the tourists were gone for the day. But it was the Jewel House and their job was to guard it, so guard it they did.

The sword landed in between them. It fell with a hissing sound and plunged into the grass, its blade going more than a foot into the earth. For a moment the two Beefeaters stood still, stunned. Then one ran to the sword.

"Will you look at this," he said.

The other was staring at the sky.

"Did you see . . ." he said. "I mean, was that . . ."

The first Beefeater looked up; he saw only gray. "What?" he said. "Did you see something?"

"I don't know," said the other.

CHAPTER 76

STANDOFF

NEREZZA STARED OUT THE CAVE ENTRANCE. The rain had finally stopped, and dawn was breaking. For a moment his hopes rose, but then, by the gray light, he spotted the massive shape a few yards down the mountainside.

Nerezza spat out a curse. Mister Grin was still there, watching the cave, waiting.

Nerezza waded back to the place where he and the others had settled for the night, a relatively dry flat rock next to the underground creek. The last torch had sputtered out hours ago; the only illumination was the dim light filtering through from the cave mouth. The starstuff chest, locked tight shut, sat against the cave wall; the key was on a chain around Nerezza's neck. O'Neal and eight of the crewmen were sprawled around the rock, dozing. The ninth crewman was watching Shining Pearl, who sat with her knees drawn up to her chest and her head down.

O'Neal opened his eyes at Nerezza's approach. "Well?" he said.

"It's still there."

O'Neal nodded. "The Mollusks will be out there, too."

"I didn't see anyone."

"You wouldn't, unless they wanted you to," said O'Neal. "But they're there, believe me."

"A standoff," said Nerezza.

"Yes," agreed O'Neal. "So what do we do now?"

Nerezza's eyes went to Shining Pearl.

———⊷⊶———

Fighting Prawn's arms and legs ached. He had spent the night crouched in a tree overlooking the clearing; the rest of his men were in trees all around him. During the night, one of the younger warriors had dropped to the ground and tried to creep closer to the cave, but Mister Grin, whose sense of smell was extremely sensitive, had detected the intruder and gone after him. The warrior barely made it back to his tree.

At the moment the crocodile's attention was again focused on the cave mouth. So was Fighting Prawn's. His daughter was inside. He had to get her out. And he had to stop these men from taking the starstuff that had, for more than twenty years, made Mollusk Island a paradise on earth, where nobody ever got sick, or grew old. From the day this priceless gift had been bestowed on the island—literally falling from the sky—Fighting Prawn had worried that some-day, somebody would try to take it away. Now that day had come.

"PRAWN!"

The shout came from inside the cave. Fighting Prawn recognized the voice.

"I am here, O'Neal," he called down.

"We seem to have a problem," said O'Neal.

"We will not have a problem," said Fighting Prawn, "if you release my daughter, and leave the island. I will let you go unharmed. You have my word."

"With the starstuff?"

"No," said Fighting Prawn. "That is ours."

"Then we still have a problem," said O'Neal.

A pause, then a new, harsher voice came from the cave: "Prawn!"

"Who are you?" said Fighting Prawn.

"I am Captain Nerezza. And I believe I have something of value to you."

There was a whimper, and then Nerezza appeared just inside the cave entrance. His right hand held a knife; his left gripped Shining Pearl by the hair. His eyes were on Mister Grin, who watched from fifteen yards away, apparently judging Nerezza to be too close to the safety of the cave to be worth pursuing, at least at the moment.

Across the clearing, Fighting Prawn saw warriors fitting

arrows to their bows. Nerezza saw it, too. He pressed his knife blade against Shining Pearl's neck.

"If I die," he said, "she'll die first."

Fighting Prawn grunted a command. The warriors lowered their bows.

Fighting Prawn's eyes went back to his daughter. Speaking in the Mollusk language, he said, "Are you all right?"

She started to answer in Mollusk.

"Speak English!" snarled Nerezza, jerking her hair.

"I asked her if she was all right," said Fighting Prawn.

"Yes," she answered, tears spilling from her eyes. "Oh, Father, I'm so sorry, I just wanted to . . ."

She was silenced by another jerk from Nerezza.

"That's enough," he said. "Now, listen, Prawn. If you want her to stay alive, you will do two things. You will get that croc away from here, far away. And you will give me and my men—and the starstuff—free passage to our boat, and then back to the ship. I will have my knife at your daughter's throat the whole time."

There was a low growl. Mister Grin was apparently becoming more interested in the humans at the cave mouth. He moved forward a few feet.

"Get rid of him," said Nerezza, nodding toward the monster croc.

"How can I do that?" said Fighting Prawn.

"You'll think of something," said Nerezza. "You had better."

Still holding Shining Pearl's hair, he yanked her roughly back into the cave.

CHAPTER 77

THE EMPTY SEA

WAKE UP!

Tink's urgent chime aroused Peter from his stupor. He saw that this time he had descended to less than fifty feet above the wave tops.

He grunted, forcing himself to rise. His arms and legs felt like stone. He had never tried to fly the whole distance between England and Mollusk Island; he'd always had a ship to rest on.

He gained some altitude and glanced ahead, seeing nothing but the vast, empty sea.

"How far?" he asked Tink, as he had many times.

We're getting closer, she answered, as she always did.

"I don't know if I can make it," he said.

You have to make it, she said.

"Tink," he said. "I can't."

He felt himself drifting downward again. He fought to stop, but could not. He had nothing left.

"I just can't," he whispered. His eyes started to close.

I see a ship, said Tink.

CHAPTER 78

Safe Passage

*A*BOARD THE *Jolly Roger*, there was mutiny in the air.

The collision with the steamer had left the ship a barely floating wreck—her masts and spars smashed, her sails in tatters, her hull a sieve of leaks. They had made what repairs they could, and jury-rigged a sad pink sail. But she was hardly seaworthy, capable of making one or two knots at best. And the men had to work constantly at the pumps—twenty-four hours a day, day after exhausting day—to keep her from sinking.

The food was gone, and the water barrel was down to the last few putrid inches. The sun was blistering hot. Every man on board had one goal: to get back to Mollusk Island. That was their only hope; that was what kept them going.

And now they had come to a horrible realization.

Hook was lost.

He would not admit it, of course; he was *Captain Hook*, and Captain Hook did not make mistakes, especially not nautical ones. But the signs were unmistakable to everyone except the blindly loyal Smee. The ship had been going in circles—big, slow circles.

Clearly, Hook had no idea where the island was.

The question now was, what to do about it.

The sailors who were not on pump or lookout duty had gathered on the foredeck to discuss this matter. Hook, with Smee at this side, was at the helm, sitting slumped on a crate. Theoretically, he was steering; but as often was the case of late, he did not appear to be particularly concerned about what his course was.

The crew members had decided something needed to be done, and were now discussing what it would be. They were evenly divided: half wanted to throw Hook over the side; the other half wanted to slit his throat, *then* throw him over the side.

Either way, he was gone. The lone remaining question was who would become the new captain. This was a trickier issue, for Hook, despite his many flaws, was by far the most skilled navigator on the ship. If he was lost, the rest of them would be even more lost.

The crew was debating its next course of action when a hoarse cry came from one of the lookouts.

"It's him!" he shouted. "The flying boy!"

Hook was off the crate in an instant, whirling around, scanning the sky.

"Where?" he shouted.

And then he saw Peter, a few hundred yards off, flying toward the ship erratically and low to the water, clearly in trouble.

"Smee," said Hook.

"Aye, Cap'n."

"Fetch my pistol."

"Aye, Cap'n."

Smee disappeared below, returning moments later with the pistol, which he handed to Hook. Peter was now almost to the ship. Catching sight of Hook, he reacted with obvious surprise, and seemed about to veer away. But he had no strength left. With a last desperate lunge he swerved upward, landing precariously in the rigging above the ship's lone fluttering sail.

He looked down at Hook, who looked back up at him.

"Hello, boy," said Hook. Slowly, dramatically, he raised the pistol and pointed it at Peter.

"Good-bye, boy," he said.

He pulled the trigger.

The pistol went *click*. Hook stared at it disbelief.

"SMEE!" he bellowed.

"Aye, Cap'n."

"THERE ARE NO BULLETS IN THIS PISTOL!"

"No, Cap'n. There's none on board."

"THEN WHY DID YOU HAND ME THE PISTOL, SMEE? WHAT DID YOU THINK I PLANNED TO DO WITH IT?"

489

Smee frowned, thinking about it. Finally he came to a conclusion. "I don't know," he said.

Hook hurled the pistol to the deck and turned toward the sailors on the foredeck, who were watching these proceedings with interest.

"You and you!" Hook said, pointing to the two closest men. "Climb up there and *bring me that boy!*"

The two men looked at each other.

"No," said one, a big man named Crankins.

"No?" screamed Hook. "*NO?? I AM YOUR CAPTAIN, AND I GAVE YOU AN ORDER!*"

Crankins glared defiantly back at Hook. "You ain't the captain anymore," he said.

"WHAT??" screamed Hook.

"I said you ain't the captain."

"Says who?"

"Says all of us." The other sailors nodded, gathering behind their new spokesman.

Hook, always one to sense a shift in the wind, suddenly switched to a more reasonable tone.

"Listen, men," he said. "I know things haven't gone well for us lately. But all that will change soon, when we reach the island."

"You don't know where the island is!" shouted a sailor. "You're lost!" The others murmured agreement.

"Lost?" said Hook. "Of course I'm not lost!"

"Then which way is the island?" said Crankins.

"That way," said Hook, pointing confidently with his hook. "South by southwest."

"That's what you say now," shouted a voice. "Yesterday you were steering northeast!"

"But . . . but . . ." Hook sputtered. The men were advancing toward him, and he saw by the look in their eyes that they were done with talking.

"Wait!" called a voice from the rigging.

The sailors stopped and looked up at Peter.

"What?" said Crankins.

"I know where the island is," he said. "Actually, she does." He pointed to Tink, sitting in his hair.

"Which way?" shouted a sailor.

"We'll lead you there," said Peter. Tink chimed something in his ear. "We'll have you there in a day, if you'll give us safe passage."

The men spoke among themselves for a moment. Then Crankins looked up at Peter.

"All right," he said. "Safe passage."

Peter slumped against the rigging, relief filling his exhausted body.

"We're going to make it, Tink," he whispered.

Not if he can help it, said Tink, pointing down. Peter looked at Hook. The pirate captain was glaring back up at him, his dark eyes glittering with hate.

CHAPTER 79

THE SMILE

THE PLAN WAS SIMPLE. Very dangerous, but simple.

Bold Abalone and Fleet Snail would be the lures. Fleet Snail was the fastest warrior on the island, so he was a logical choice. Bold Abalone was not nearly as fast, but as the chief's son, he insisted on being one of the two.

To make themselves irresistible to Mister Grin, they went into the jungle and smeared their bodies with boar dung. When they were ready, they circled around so that they were downwind from the cave, to prevent the crocodile from picking up their scent too soon.

From his perch in the tree, Fighting Prawn watched as his son and Fleet Snail crept toward the clearing. When Bold Abalone signaled that they were ready, Fighting Prawn called out, "Nerezza!"

"What is it?" came the harsh voice from inside the cave.

"Look outside, and you will see," said Fighting Prawn.

"I'd better see the croc leaving," said Nerezza, "because I won't wait much longer."

Cautiously, Nerezza poked his wooden beak out of the cave mouth. In front of him, Mister Grin stirred.

"He's still there," said Nerezza.

"Wait," said Fighting Prawn. He nodded to Bold Abalone and Fleet Snail.

With high-pitched cries, the two warriors burst from the jungle and ran across the edge of the clearing, putting themselves upwind. Mister Grin raised his huge snout into the air. A second later, displaying amazing agility, he spun around and shot toward the spot where the warriors had just disappeared into the jungle. He plunged in right behind them, his massive body bowling over several trees.

Fighting Prawn worried that Bold Abalone and Fleet Snail had not gotten enough of a head start. Their plan was to lead Mister Grin away from the mountain trail, toward the steep slope that led down to the pirate lagoon. For several minutes, Fighting Prawn could follow their progress by the swaying of the trees as the croc brushed against them. From time to time, Mister Grin roared, but so far there had been no screams. As the snaking line of swaying trees disappeared down the mountainside, Fighting Prawn prayed that his two brave warriors would be quick enough to avoid the jaws of the beast pursuing them. For now, that was all he could do for them. It was time to concentrate on saving his daughter. He quickly climbed down from the tree and approached the cave mouth.

"Nerezza!" he said.

"I'm here."

"It is gone."

"It had better be, because if it comes back, I'll feed your daughter to it."

"It will not come back."

A moment later, Nerezza appeared in the cave mouth. As before, he had Shining Pearl by the hair, and a knife to her neck. He looked at Fighting Prawn, then at the other Mollusk warriors, who had also descended from their trees and now surrounded the clearing.

"Tell your men not to come any closer," he said.

"They will not," said Fighting Prawn, his eyes on his daughter's terrified face.

"Good," said Nerezza. "Now before we leave, my men are going to build a fire to signal the ship. They will need to gather wood. Tell your men to let them."

Fighting Prawn grunted a command. Four of Nerezza's men emerged from the cave and went into the jungle, walking warily past the Mollusk warriors glaring at them. They returned in a few minutes with armloads of wood, some of it green. The wood was wet from the storm, so it took them a while, as Nerezza grew increasingly impatient, to get a fire started. But eventually they did, and when it was blazing, they tossed the green wood on the flames, sending a billowing stream of black smoke high into the sky.

"All right," said Nerezza, "let's go."

Cheeky O'Neal emerged from the cave with the rest of the men. Two of them were holding the chest, which, being full of starstuff, weighed essentially nothing; the men were holding it down as much as carrying it. Fighting Prawn stared at it, wondering if he could really allow these men to take away the source of so much of the island's happiness. Then his eyes went back to Shining Pearl, and his heart sank.

They started down the mountain trail: O'Neal in front, the two men with the chest next, then Nerezza and Shining Pearl, with the rest of Nerezza's men behind. Ahead of them, behind them, and all around them were the Mollusk warriors, moving silently through the jungle alongside. Fighting Prawn stayed close to Nerezza, his eyes always on Shining Pearl.

The trail was still wet and muddy, so the going was slow. It took the group several tense hours to reach the beach. When they did, the *Nimbus*, having seen the signal and moved around from the village side of the island, was waiting for them, steaming back and forth just outside the reef.

Nerezza's men uncovered their launch and dragged it onto the beach and down to the surf. They loaded the chest aboard. The Mollusks watched helplessly, gathered in a semicircle around the launch. When Nerezza's men started to board the launch, Fighting Prawn stepped forward.

"Now let my daughter go," he said to Nerezza.

Nerezza shook his head. "Not here," he said.

"Leave her here, and we will not try to stop you from taking the starstuff," said Fighting Prawn. "You have my word."

"And you have *my* word," said Nerezza, "that when I am aboard the ship with the trunk, I'll send your daughter back on this launch."

Fighting Prawn's mind raced. If he had a canoe, he might be able to reach a bargain with Nerezza: two warriors in the canoe would accompany the launch to the ship and bring Shining Pearl back. But he had no canoe on this side of the island. The Mollusks had all come on foot.

With a quick, easy motion, Nerezza lifted Shining Pearl into the launch and climbed in after her.

"We're pushing off," he said. "Don't try to stop us."

Fighting Prawn looked at the warriors around him, poised to attack if he gave the word. He looked at his daughter, crying softly in the launch, the blade at her throat. Then he looked into Nerezza's cold, hard, eyes, the eyes of a man who was capable of any cruelty.

He stepped away from the launch.

"Send her back," he said to Nerezza, "or I will track you down."

For a moment the two men looked into each other's eyes.

Then Nerezza turned to his men and barked, "Shove off!"

Fighting Prawn turned and grunted some commands of his own. Three warriors took off running down the beach; they would go back to the village with orders to launch the war canoes immediately. But as he watched his men sprinting away, Fighting Prawn knew that no matter how fast they ran, the canoes probably would not get to this side of the island in time to do him any good.

He turned back to watch the launch, now past the breakers and heading toward the ship, Nerezza's men pulling hard on the oars. Nerezza, at the tiller with Shining Pearl beside him, was looking back at Fighting Prawn. He was smiling. Fighting Prawn didn't like the look of that smile.

——————

From the bow of the launch, Cheeky O'Neal watched the island recede. His eyes lingered on the tall figure of Fighting Prawn, standing rigidly on the beach, staring at the men taking his daughter away.

"I can't believe he let us go," he said.

"He had no choice," said Nerezza from the stern, also watching the beach.

"I suppose not," said O'Neal. He paused, then added, "Do you really plan to send her back?"

Nerezza turned to look at O'Neal.

"Don't be stupid," he said.

CHAPTER 80

ANOTHER BOAT

THE *Jolly Roger* WAS making good speed, considering her battered condition. Since the joyful moment when the island had been sighted, the crew had been busy rigging every possible square inch of pink sail. The men were giddy at the prospect of food—*fresh* food—and the pure, sweet island water. Even Hook was in a decent mood; with the improvement in the ship's fortunes, the crew had forgotten the recent unpleasantness, and he was captain again.

It was Tink, in the rigging with the still-weak Peter, who had spotted the island. And as they drew close, it was Tink who now spotted the steamship. She pointed it out to Peter, who pointed it out to the lookout, who pointed it out to Hook, who ordered Smee to fetch his spyglass. That had been two hours ago; now, as they drew close, Hook was still studying the ship, trying to make sense of its actions.

"It's going back and forth outside the reef," he muttered. "Why d'you suppose that is?"

"One thing I never understood," said Smee, "is why it's back and forth, and not forth and back. It seems to me it would go *forth* first, and then it would go . . ."

"Smee!" said Hook.

"Aye, Cap'n?"

"Shut up."

"Aye, Cap'n."

"There's another boat," Peter called down.

"What is he talking about?" Hook shouted to the lookout. Hook, refusing to acknowledge that the hated boy was a passenger aboard his ship, refused to address Peter directly.

"He's right," replied the lookout. "There's a launch coming through the reef, making for the steamer."

In a flash Hook had the spyglass to his eye. He found the launch. It was being buffeted by the surf around the reef, so it took him a few seconds to get a clear look. But then he saw it, between the bodies of two of the men rowing.

A chest.

A chest with gold fittings.

Hook knew instantly what was in the chest. He'd been aboard the flying ship that had brought it to the island in the first place. And he knew it took a special chest to hold it. It was a treasure more valuable than all the gold on earth.

And Captain Hook—*Pirate* Captain Hook—meant to have it.

With fire in his eye, he grabbed the wheel and began shouting orders.

—◆—

Peter and Tink also knew what was in the trunk.

They knew they had to get it away from the men taking it off the island.

They also knew they had to keep it from falling into the hands of Captain Hook.

Peter had not recovered from his long flight over the sea; he wasn't he sure how far he could fly, if he could fly at all. He and Tink conferred briefly in the rigging. Then, unseen by the busy pirates below, Tink took off, streaking toward the island.

CHAPTER 81

Out to Sea

$\mathcal{N}$EREZZA YANKED THE TILLER, turning the launch to
starboard as it pulled alongside the *Nimbus*.

Crewmen on the *Nimbus* deck dropped two steel cables
down from the boat hoist. Nerezza's men began securing
them to the bow and stern of the launch so it could be lifted
aboard the steamship. Nerezza glanced back toward the
island; no sign of pursuit. Apparently the chief had taken
him at his word.

Fool.

The cables were secure. Nerezza looked up, preparing to
shout the order to start the hoist. He saw two crewmen waving frantically at him, shouting and pointing aft. He turned
to look.

His mouth fell open.

Rounding the stern of the *Nimbus* was a craft unlike any
Nerezza had seen, looking more like a collapsed building

than a ship, with bright pink sails sprouting from it at all angles. It would have been funny, except for the look of the men on the ship, a look Nerezza had seen before, although not for many years.

Pirates.

"START THE HOIST!" he bellowed.

A second later the cables tensed and the launch came wobbling out of the water. It rose slowly, and with each second the pirates drew closer. Nerezza saw their leader now, a tall man with dark deep-set eyes and a huge black mustache.

And a hook.

Now Nerezza knew exactly whom he was up against.

"FASTER!" he yelled to the men on deck.

But the hoist had only one speed, and it was not quite fast enough. As the launch dangled on the side of the *Nimbus*, fifteen feet above the water, the pirate ship plowed into it. The launch spun and flew sideways, spinning out of control, then, with a sickening lurch, slammed into the steamer's steel hull.

Then the aft cable snapped.

The stern of the launch dropped like a rock, dumping everyone and everything into the sea.

Everything, that is, but the starstuff chest. For a few seconds, it hung in midair. Then it began to descend lazily, drifting in the breeze, until it settled gently on the foredeck of the pirate ship.

With a roar of triumph, Hook spun the wheel.

⋙⋘

Shining Pearl was a good swimmer, but she had the bad luck of being at the stern of the launch, which meant that the other occupants landed on top of her. An instant after she plunged into the water, a booted foot slammed into her head, stunning her; a second later another impact drove her deeper. Losing consciousness, she swallowed water and felt herself drifting down into the dark water below.

And then strong arms wrapped around her, and she was being lifted toward the light. She burst through the surface and turned to see her rescuer: it was Teacher, leader of the mermaids and an old friend of the Mollusks, who had been summoned by Tink. A moment later, Teacher's powerful tail was propelling Shining Pearl swiftly toward shore and her anxious father.

There were three other mermaids in the water, and they were not being so kind to the rest of the swimmers. They swarmed around the flailing men, nipping at their arms and legs with needle-sharp teeth. The terrified swimmers screamed for their crewmates on deck to throw down lines; they grabbed these and climbed them with desperate speed. When things finally got sorted out on deck, the crew realized that two men were missing: O'Neal and Nerezza. It was assumed that they had fallen victim to the savage mermaid creatures. Nobody wanted to go looking for them, not in these unwelcome waters. The remaining officers quickly made their decision. The *Nimbus* turned and, at full steam, headed out to sea.

Far astern, a pile of floating debris—some seat planks and canvas that had fallen out of the launch when the cable broke—moved slowly but steadily toward the island.

CHAPTER 82

So Close

*P*ETER, CLINGING TO THE RIGGING in the *Jolly Roger*, was trying to decide what to do.

Below him, Hook—who for the moment had apparently forgotten about his unwelcome passenger—was loudly celebrating his courageous defeat of the enemy ship—now steaming rapidly away—and his brilliant capture of the treasure. Hook stood on the foredeck, one foot on the chest, declaring to his crew that its contents would make them the most feared pirates on the sea, and even on the land, because now the ship could *fly*. Hook had seen it with his own eyes!

The pirates cheered. Hook beamed.

Looking down, Peter worried. Because Hook was right: with that much starstuff, he could do unimaginable damage, if he didn't kill himself and his crew first. Peter looked around for allies. The mermaids had departed, apparently satisfied that when the steamship left, their job was done.

There were Mollusks on the beach, but that was hundreds of yards away. Even Tink, at the moment, seemed to be missing. That left Peter, who wasn't sure he was strong enough to fly down to the deck, let alone take on a shipload of pirates.

But who else was there?

"Hook!" he shouted.

The pirate captain looked up, and the triumph on his face changed to fury.

"*You,*" he said. "Get off my ship!"

"The chest is dangerous," said Peter. "You'll all die if you open it. You can't keep it."

"Is that so?" said Hook. "And who's going to take it away from me?"

Peter stood up in the rigging. His knees felt weak; he hoped he had enough strength.

"I'm going to stop you," he said.

Hook smiled, revealing the row of irregular brown stumps that passed for his teeth. He drew his sword.

"All right, *boy,*" he said. "Come down and stop me."

Peter took a breath. His plan was to swoop down close to Hook, drawing him away from the chest. Then Peter would pull up and swerve around him, grab the chest, and carry it overboard. It was a good plan. The question was, did Peter have the strength?

He let out the breath and dove for the rigging.

The first part of the plan worked: as Peter swooped down, Hook came toward him, away from the chest. But as Peter tried to stop his descent and swerve around Hook, he found that he was far weaker than he'd feared. He slammed into the deck, barely breaking his fall with his arms, and rolled to a stop at Hook's feet, groaning.

The pirates started forward. Hook bellowed at them to stay back.

"This moment is *mine*," he said.

Peter, on his back, his body screaming in pain, opened his eyes to see Hook standing over him.

"This time," Hook said, "I'll make sure you're dead."

Slowly, enjoying the moment, he began to raise his sword. Peter tried to roll sideways to escape, but Hook's boot came down on him, shoving him back. The boot pressed against Peter's pocket. Peter felt something sharp.

The tip of the Sword of Mercy. He'd forgotten to drop it with the sword. Frantically, Peter reached for his pocket.

"Now, boy," said Hook. "*Die.*"

He brought the sword down. He was aiming for Peter's neck. His aim was true, but Peter's hand was just quick enough as he brought the sword tip up to meet Hook's downward thrust. There was a clash, and then a clattering sound, as the tip of Hook's sword tumbled across the deck and into the sea.

Hook held up his broken sword, staring at it in disbelief.

From the deck, Peter saw a brilliant light over the pirate's shoulder.

Tink. To Peter, she looked like an angel.

Stay down, she chimed.

For a moment, Peter wondered why. And then he saw the sleek silvery shape hurtling through the air.

Ammm.

The porpoise, having launched himself from the water on the starboard side, slammed into Hook's body, sending him sprawling on the deck. Ammm's momentum carried the porpoise over the port side. Before he reentered the water, two more airborne porpoises appeared on the starboard side, both aiming for the starstuff chest, their blunt noses hitting it at precisely the same moment.

"NO!!" screamed Hook as he watched the starstuff chest slide off the ship and into the sea. Realizing what was next, he shouted "GET THE BOY!!"

But it was too late. With a roar of fury, Hook watched as Peter, who had crawled to the edge of the deck, slipped over the side, landing gently on the starstuff chest, which bobbed in the water like a cork. Gathered around it were a dozen smiling porpoises, and a very self-satisfied Tinker Bell.

"LOWER THE BOATS!!" shouted Hook. "GET THE HARPOONS!! I WANT THAT BOY, AND I WANT THAT CHEST!!"

His crew, who knew that the *Jolly Roger* had no boats to

lower, and no harpoons, did nothing.

"Cap'n," said Smee, tugging Hook's sleeve.

"WHAT IS IT?" said Hook, whirling in fury.

Backing away nervously, Smee said, "I think we'd better be going."

"WHY??"

Smee pointed, and Hook looked. Coming around the point of the island were two dozen or more big canoes, each full of Mollusk warriors.

Hook looked down at the sea, where the chest—the chest that would have made him the most feared pirate on the sea or the land—bobbed gently in the waves, so close. . . .

Then he looked at the oncoming canoes.

Then his shoulders slumped, and he gave the order.

"Make for Pirate Cove," he said.

The battered ship made it that far, and no farther. When it reached the cove, its overburdened pumps finally gave out, and it settled to the bottom, in exactly the spot where it had sat for more than twenty years.

As if it had never left.

CHAPTER 83

CONCERNS

CTHE SUN WENT DOWN on a boisterous celebration in the
Mollusk village. There was much to celebrate, with the safe
return of the children and the recovery of the chest. There
was also much to talk about. Peter, with considerable prod-
ding from Tink, told of his harrowing adventures in the
strange place called London. Shining Pearl, Little Scallop,
and the Lost Boys told of their ordeal at the hands of Nerezza
and O'Neal. There was laughter, a lot of hugging, and some
crying, including a tearful promise by Shining Pearl to her
father that she would never, ever, *ever* again disobey the rule
about leaving the village at night. She also promised him she
would give him something for his birthday, although it definitely was not going to be a white starfish; Shining Pearl had
decided those weren't such good luck after all.

Fighting Prawn, though happy about the return of the
children, still had some concerns. One was dealing with the

starstuff chest, which sat now in the center of the village, guarded by warriors. Fighting Prawn had decided that the starstuff had to be returned to the underground pool it had been taken from. When Peter was strong again, the Mollusks would take the chest back up to the cave. There, Peter could open it and pour the starstuff into the pool. The Mollusks would then block the cave with rocks, so it could never be violated again.

But that was for another day. Fighting Prawn's greater concern at the moment was the fate of Bold Abalone and Fleet Snail. He had faith in them—they were both resourceful warriors, especially his son. He had every reason to hope that they had been able to avoid the crushing jaws of Mister Grin.

But he would not sleep until they returned.

CHAPTER 84

THE LAST SOUND

NEREZZA AND CHEEKY O'NEAL had decided to wait until dark before landing on the island. Hiding in the floating jumble of wood and canvas, they had managed to avoid the mermaids. They had seen the *Nimbus* steam away; seen the starstuff chest fall from the strange sailing ship; seen the Mollusk canoes pick it up and take it back to the island.

And then they, too, had paddled toward the island. They had hugged the coast, following it in the direction away from the Mollusk village, toward Pirate Cove. As they paddled, they talked in low voices, assessing their situation, forming a plan. Neither man was about to run from a treasure as valuable as the starstuff. If it was on the island, they would find a way to get it. They were both competent, ruthless men. They had no doubt that they would succeed against the primitive Mollusks. Especially since the Mollusks didn't know they were there.

512

Their first task was to find a place to hide. As night fell, they paddled toward shore, landing on a small curved beach. It felt good to have their weary legs on land again. They grabbed the planks and the canvas and started dragging them up the beach, planning to hide them in the dark jungle looming ahead.

They heard a crashing sound.

"What was *that?*" said Nerezza.

"I don't know," said O'Neal.

Another crashing sound, this one closer. They peered ahead, seeing only blackness.

Then a figure burst from the jungle, sprinting toward them. A man.

Right behind him was a second man.

The two men were running straight for them. As they came close, Nerezza and O'Neal saw that they were Mollusk warriors. Nerezza and O'Neal raised their hands, ready to fend off an attack.

The men ran right past them, one on each side. O'Neal and Nerezza turned and watched, stunned, as the men ran straight into the water and began swimming out to sea as fast as they could.

"What . . ." began Nerezza, but he was halted by the awful roar from the jungle behind them.

That was the last sound either man ever heard.

Three Months Later

"Tonight's story," said Wendy, "is why the moon changes its shape."

"You already told us that one," said John.

"Because the elephant eats it," said Michael.

"Which is stupid," said John.

"Well, if *that's* going to be your attitude," said Wendy, "perhaps there won't *be* a story tonight."

"Why are you so moody lately?" said John.

"I'm *not* moody," said Wendy.

"You are too," said John.

"I am not."

"Mum says she was moodly, too," said Michael.

"It's not *moodly*, you ninny," said John. "It's *moody*."

"That's what I said!" said Michael.

"*When* did Mum say she was moodly . . . I mean, moody?" Wendy asked Michael.

"When Peter left," said Michael.

"That's not why I'm moody!" said Wendy.

"So you *are* moody!" said John.

"Mum says he'll come back," said Michael. "She says he always does."

"Yes," said Wendy. "But not for *years*."

"How long is years?" said Michael.

"A long time," sighed Wendy. She was quiet for a few seconds, then said, "Well, do you want the story, or don't you?"

"Does it have to be the elephant one?" said John.

"Yes."

"Can it be a giraffe instead?" said Michael.

"Oh, I suppose so," said Wendy.

"All right, then," said Michael.

"All right," said John, a bit more reluctantly.

"Once upon a time," began Wendy, "there was a very hungry giraffe, who—"

"Wait!" said Michael.

"What now?" said Wendy, exasperated.

"Can't you hear it?" said Michael.

"Hear *what*?" said both Wendy and John.

"Listen!" said Michael.

So they listened, and this time they heard it.

Someone was tapping on the window.